Anonymous
SEX

Edited by
Hillary Jordan
and
Cheryl Lu-Lien Tan

SCRIBNER
New York London Toronto Sydney New Delhi

Scribner
An Imprint of Simon & Schuster, Inc.
1230 Avenue of the Americas
New York, NY 10020

First Scribner hardcover edition February 2022

For information about special discounts for bulk
purchases, please contact Simon & Schuster Special Sales at
1-866-506-1949 or business@simonandschuster.com.

The Simon & Schuster Speakers Bureau can bring authors to
your live event. For more information or to book an event, contact
the Simon & Schuster Speakers Bureau at 1-866-248-3049
or visit our website at www.simonspeakers.com.

Interior design by Lewelin Polanco

Manufactured in the United States of America

1 3 5 7 9 10 8 6 4 2

Library of Congress Cataloging-in-Publication Data

Names: Jordan, Hillary, 1963– editor. | Tan, Cheryl Lu-Lien, editor.
Title: Anonymous sex / edited by Hillary Jordan and Cheryl Lu-Lien Tan.
Description: First Scribner hardcover edition. | New York : Scribner, 2022.
Identifiers: LCCN 2021043182 (print) | LCCN 2021043183 (ebook) | ISBN 9781982177515
(paperback) | ISBN 9781982177522 (hardcover) | ISBN 9781982177539 (ebook)
Subjects: LCSH: Erotic stories. | Sex—Fiction.
Classification: LCC PN6071.E7 A56 2022 (print) | LCC PN6071.E7 (ebook) |
DDC 808.8/03538—dc23
LC record available at https://lccn.loc.gov/2021043182
LC ebook record available at https://lccn.loc.gov/2021043183

ISBN 978-1-9821-7752-2
ISBN 978-1-9821-7751-5 (pbk)
ISBN 978-1-9821-7753-9 (ebook)

If fields of autumn flowers
can shed their blossoms, shameless,
why can't I also frolic here—
as fearless, wild and blameless?

—Ono no Komachi

We fucked a flame into being.

—D. H. Lawrence,
Lady Chatterley's Lover

Allow me, in conclusion, to congratulate
you warmly upon your sexual intercourse,
as well as your singing.

—Muriel Spark,
The Prime of Miss Jean Brodie

Introduction

Some years ago, the two of us were sitting over dinner, talking about sex in literature—our mutual enjoyment of stories about desire and sexuality, and what a treasure it is when a work of erotic literature makes you see sex in a new way, as only great writing can. Stories by D. H. Lawrence or Anäis Nin can be more arousing than erotica that's just meant to turn you on—though as anyone with a pulse who's read those writers knows, it does that, too. Why wasn't there more writing like that?

By our second glass of wine, we'd hit upon an idea: an anthology of fictional erotic tales, penned by some of our finest writers, that would explore the diverse landscape of desire with stories as oblique or explicit, as earnest or playful, as strange or familiar, and as tender or fierce, as each author wished.

But we decided it wouldn't be enough just to have great writers. We wanted our contributors to be free to write openly about what fascinates and stirs them about sex. So we dreamed up a collection in which the authors' names would be listed in alphabetical order at the beginning of the book, but none of the stories would be attributed. Readers would have to guess which story was written by whom.

And the name of this anthology would be *Anonymous Sex*.

Years passed. We spoke about the project now and then but could never find a time when we were both free to turn our attention to it. Then came the pandemic: one of us in lockdown in Maine, the other in Singapore; both of us going out of our minds (along with pretty much every other writer we knew) from the isolation and fear and relentlessly grim news.

What better time, we thought, to commission a collection of brilliant, erotic short stories? We began by asking friends if they'd be interested in contributing. Julia Glass, who introduced us ten years ago at the Brooklyn Book Festival, was our first (and very enthusiastic) yes. From there we built our roster, prioritizing talent, renown, and inclusiveness in gender, age, ethnicity, sexuality, and nationality.

To our knowledge, no one has ever published an anthology quite like this. Our contributors include winners of the Pulitzer Prize, the National Book Award, PEN America Literary Awards, the Orange/Women's Prize, the Edgar Award, the Carnegie Medal, the Giller Prize, and more.

As we'd expected from such a gifted and disparate group of writers, the stories are all over the map. There's queer and straight sex, real and imagined sex, holographic and ghost sex. There's youthful sex, married sex, and senior sex (and one story that manages to cover all three). There are stories of sexual obsession and sexual love. Stories of domination and submission, power and surrender. There's revenge sex and sex with strangers; sex as rebellion and sex as holy. There's unrequited sex, funny sex, tortured sex, and tender sex. There's sex all over the world—Hong Kong, Nigeria, France, India, Australia, the U.S. There's past sex, present-day sex, future sex, and even sex in the afterlife.

There's a lot of sex in this book.

In thinking about how to describe the collection, we kept coming back to the last line of "Altitude Sickness," the fourth story in the anthology: "She grabbed the man's hand and kissed him without shame as the plane began to tilt." While the world has certainly been more atilt than usual recently, the truth is it's always tilting, in ways large and small, for each one of us. Sex can be a grounding force in that day-to-day pitch. It can also be part of the upheaval. Either way, it's a connection many of us both want and need, a way to reach across the divide and know that we aren't alone.

Which is what inspired us to take this leap together. We hope you enjoy every eloquent, provocative, delicious word.

Hillary Jordan and Cheryl Lu-Lien Tan
February 2022

Contributors

Robert Olen Butler

Catherine Chung

Trent Dalton

Heidi W. Durrow

Tony Eprile

Louise Erdrich

Jamie Ford

Julia Glass

Peter Godwin

Hillary Jordan

Rebecca Makkai

Valerie Martin

Dina Nayeri

Chigozie Obioma

Téa Obreht

Helen Oyeyemi

Mary-Louise Parker

Victoria Redel

Jason Reynolds

S. J. Rozan

Meredith Talusan

Cheryl Lu-Lien Tan

Souvankham Thammavongsa

Jeet Thayil

Paul Theroux

Luis Alberto Urrea

Edmund White

Stories

History Lesson

*Most of us get turned on at night by the very things
that we'll demonstrate against during the day.*

—ESTHER PEREL

T*he conference was always in April,* which meant that every
year around October, six whole months out, Denise
would start thinking about it: first just in flashes, and then in
prolonged obsessions, waves that would climb her legs. Every
email she got about panels and dinners, every stupid notice of
protocol, every scheduling reminder, would jolt her out of her
office and into her body.

Michael usually held off on texting until February or
March, but this year he emailed her personal account right before Christmas, with last April's video attached. He wrote, "I'm
going to want more from you this year. So I want to remind you
early what's at stake."

Late that night, she sneaked out of the bedroom where her
husband slept and took her laptop to the basement. The video
Michael had attached was forty minutes long, so she watched,
skipped forward, watched, skipped forward, watched. That
was her, her long torso, her wrists tied to the hotel headboard,
her ankles bound by the strap Michael had fastened under the

mattress. Her face, clearly visible. Michael's hand, smacking her labia, his fingers working their way inside her.

A simple deal had been in place for five years now. On the Saturday night of the conference, Denise would do whatever Michael wanted, absolutely whatever he wanted, and he would record her. If she was good, which entailed both pleasing him and having at least one orgasm, then that was it. The video was his to enjoy, and they'd go back the next day to meeting with colleagues, joking with friends in the hotel lobby, networking at open-bar receptions. If she failed to fulfill her end of the bargain, he would release the video, anonymously, to all three thousand historians on the conference mailing list, all of whom knew her or knew of her, all of whom knew her work. Denise did not actually believe that Michael would ever do this, not really, but the threat of it, the promise of it, allowed her to give herself over to him, to the things he wanted and she wanted, too. She did not relax easily, did not come easily, and she needed constraints—literal, physical ones, as well as constraints of time and threat—to get there.

In January, Denise was the outside reader for a thesis student at Michael's university, teleconferencing into the defense. Twenty minutes in, he texted her: *Take your underwear off.* She texted back: *Uh . . . no?* He wrote: *Do it, I don't care how.* He was lucky she was wearing a dress, lucky she was alone in her home office. She told him so. *Okay,* she wrote once they were off, but now he wanted proof. *You don't trust me?* she wrote. And onscreen, as the candidate rambled about Cecil Rhodes and the early correspondence regarding his diamond mines, Michael slowly, imperceptible to anyone who wasn't looking for it, shook his head, his bearded face. Denise used her foot to scoop her underwear off the floor, to get it to her hand. It was dark blue, mercifully not lacy. She took a sip of her coffee and then, as if the underwear were a napkin, dabbed the corner of her mouth with it. Michael wrote back: *Good girl.*

It was an arrangement she had not only entered willingly, but had been the one to propose. She and her husband had a work-trips-are-fair-play clause in their marriage, one she was sure Davis had taken more advantage of than her, at least in the years before he became too afraid of being #MeToo'd to approach anyone who wasn't literally throwing herself at him. He'd spent a good year stressed about ghosts from his past returning for vengeance. And meanwhile, Denise, who'd taken minimal advantage of the clause, was finding Michael. They'd known each other for a while, collaborated on a couple of articles, and been flirting for years when they finally fell into bed together at a conference in Denver. But both of them were drunk and tired, and it wasn't terribly satisfying. Later he texted her, *We need a do-over. Next year in Dallas?* Things had evolved from there.

Michael had suggested, the second time, when the subservience and videos came into play, that she needed a safe word in all of this, and she came up with one only to placate him. It was something unusual, something random she'd never say accidentally. But then, willfully, she'd forgotten it. Or almost had. In order to remember it, she'd need to follow her own mental bread crumbs back to the source, in the same way she had to do mental gymnastics to remember, say, the order of constitutional amendments twenty through twenty-seven.

She never told him this; he wanted her to have a safe word, and she did not want to have a safe word, and now they were both content.

After the thesis defense, Michael sent her a still from their last video, one in which her face was cropped out. He wrote, *I didn't like how you pushed back there. You questioned me. I think I'm going to post this on Twitter.*

Her neck pulsing hard, she wrote, *Okay.*

It helped their dynamic, certainly, that while Denise was a nationally recognized name in her field, Michael was just as happily tenured and well published; no one could help anyone's career here, but Denise was the one with significantly more clout. Which meant that Michael being the one in charge felt like a subversion—not the reification of some existing imbalance.

She couldn't imagine that he'd literally tweet this photo, which was from between her legs, looking up at her splayed vulva, her splayed body. But a minute later he sent a screen capture. Using a burner account, he'd posted the photo underneath a tweet from the conference itself. It would certainly get hidden, flagged, removed. But not for a while.

She couldn't stop staring at it. Her nude body, as far as she knew, had never been on the Internet before. She imagined colleagues, grad students, random historians clicking on "Show more replies" out of curiosity, finding her there, assuming they were looking at a cam girl rather than a thirty-seven-year-old scholar at the top of her field, someone whose work they'd cited.

In her office, Denise fingered herself until she came, and then she wrote back to Michael to tell him so. *I couldn't help myself,* she wrote.

He wrote back: *I like that, but listen. Between now and April, you ask my permission. Every time.*

Or what? she wrote.

Or I hit send. The whole video.

Right answer. She was aroused again, but this time she'd

sleep on it, fantasize about Michael, about the videos, and in the morning she'd text him and beg.

This was new, his control of her body from all the way in New York. She thought he'd get tired of it after a few days, but he didn't, and she didn't let herself cheat. There was no fun in that.

Often, in the following weeks, he'd tell her to go ahead, to describe it to him after she was done. Sometimes he said no. He told her she had to wait an hour, or two hours, or twenty-four hours. By the beginning of February, he was telling her when to do it, texting, *Make yourself come in the next half hour*. She'd text back, *I'm at school. I'm in my office*. And he'd write, *Lock your fucking door. Do it*. And she would, surprised at how easily she came. He wrote, *Go to the bathroom and take a picture of your tits for me. NOW*. She got that one in the middle of a faculty meeting. And she did it.

By April, she was a walking pile of sex. She felt like she'd electrically shock anything she touched. The airplane that took her to Miami was a machine designed to jostle her body, to vibrate her seat. Three times in the past week, Michael had directed her to get close to orgasm and stop. She wrote, *You're going to short-circuit me*.

The conference started on Thursday, and by the time Michael arrived at the hotel bar that night, she was already drunk, flirting more than usual, laughing too loud. She had worn a low-cut blouse for Michael's benefit, but had found herself bending over to pick up her purse in front of Keith and Franklin, a scholar of Caribbean history and a scholar of American Catholicism, respectively, whom she knew from a postdoc fellowship and Chautauqua, respectively. Both a little younger than her, both hairy in a way she liked. They seemed to come as a package deal at conferences, wingmanning for each other and playing off each other's jokes. The conference drew around nine hundred scholars each year, a lot of them revolving through only when a paper was accepted, other mainstays returning year after year. She looked forward to catching up with Keith and Franklin, to flirting with them both. Keith was always smiling; Franklin had sad, dark eyes.

But there was Michael, taller than she remembered, with brighter eyes and deeper laugh lines than she remembered, instantly surrounded by old friends. A blond woman who, in Denise's estimation, was prettier than her. An older lesbian couple that coauthored all their papers. The young professor of African diaspora studies who was halfway through his rocket launch to fame.

Although their groups eventually combined that first night, although Michael kissed her cheek and asked how she was doing, stayed close enough that she could smell the deep nutmeg-and-pipe scent of him, he acted as if they hadn't spoken in a year. No texts, no sly glances. For a brief, paranoid second, Denise wondered if everything for the past five years had been in her head, if the Michael in her phone and computer and memory was the product of extreme stress on her exhausted neurons.

But then on Friday, as Denise sat on her first panel, Michael showed up late and spread his long legs wide in the front row. While the man next to her droned on, Michael poked at his phone and then Denise's phone buzzed under her thigh. She was afraid to look at it, worried that he'd again demand her underwear off. And while there was a tablecloth hiding her from the audience, she couldn't do that next to her fellow panelists. Michael looked at her expectantly, and she eased the phone out from under her and into her lap. The message said, *Tell me you're a slut.*

To be clear: this was not a word Denise approved of in most contexts. But it was a word that, in this context, made her wet. She wrote back: *I'm a slut. I'm such a little slut and I'll do anything for you.*

He wrote: *You're going to have to prove that.*

Dinner that night was twenty of them at a tapas restaurant. Michael sat five seats from her, flirting with the woman on his left in a way that either bothered Denise or turned her on or both; she wasn't sure. Their date was for 5 p.m. the next night, twenty-three hours away. She knew this food was likely the last she'd eat before then. Maybe coffee in the morning. Some whiskey or champagne when he showed up in her room.

Keith and Franklin seemed content to mutually flirt with her, as if they were a single unit and the proximity of the other gave them license to joke, to tease her, to buy her one drink each. They were cute, both of them, especially together. She might have pursued something with either of them if she hadn't been laser-focused on Michael. On making him jealous, if nothing else.

The next day she was on another panel, and there was a round-table, and then out in the hallway Michael handed her the key card to his hotel room. A better hotel than hers, because his university was more generous. One downtown, with enormous windows and a sleek black lobby with neon accents. Cheesy for anywhere but Miami.

He answered his door in jeans and a white undershirt, a glass of red wine in his hand. He pulled her in by her collar. He said, "I have surprises for you."

Well, he always did. But specifically: he'd procured some kind of padded table. A massage table, it looked like, but wider, slightly sloped, and without the attachment for relaxing your head. She said, "Did you *rent* this?" but then his hand was over her mouth. He led her to an overstuffed chair by the window and handed her a glass of wine. The windows looked right out across the street to office windows, apartment windows, hotel windows. He hadn't closed the blinds. He wasn't going to.

She wanted to ask how his day had gone, wanted to know what he'd thought of the afternoon keynote, but there was time for that tomorrow. He said, "I'm going to ask a lot of you to-night."

"I'm ready."

Along with the table, he'd obtained a small tripod onto which he affixed his iPad. He set it up as she finished her wine. He messed with the lights until the overheads were off, the recessed ones around the room illuminating the table.

"Take everything off but your bra and panties," he said, "and lie down."

She did, with her head at the higher end, and from under the table he pulled four straps—two for her wrists, extended above her head, and one for each of her ankles, spread to the outer edges of the table. She tested each with a slight tug, and when she saw how tight they were, how genuinely tethered she was, she felt as if he'd turned up a dial somewhere inside her.

Her breasts ached, and her labia ached, and her breathing had grown shallow.

He told her to close her eyes, so she never saw what it was he put around her neck: some kind of wide collar—cold at first and then warm—that held her neck to the table. If she lifted up, just the tiniest bit, it choked her. If she lay completely still, she was fine. This was new to their repertoire. She'd left her necklace on, a gold chain with a bare golden oak tree pendant, and the chain pressed into her throat—the charm mercifully below the collar.

He said, "I want you to understand that as it gets dark out, people are going to see so clearly into this room." She nodded, and the collar cut into the soft part of her chin.

Michael was a year younger than Denise, married to a woman Denise didn't particularly like. His voice was a low rumble and his legs were muscled from the soccer he still played on weekends. She did not have romantic feelings for Michael—just a friendship built on intimacy as well as good conversation and mutual interests—but these yearly encounters, she'd come to realize, were foundational now to her sexuality. When she slept with her husband, when she watched porn, when she fantasized—it might go in a thousand different directions, but it was always now within the context of Michael, of what he'd think of this, or what she'd tell him she wanted, or what he'd tell her she wanted.

She had brought a vibrator with her, as Michael had instructed, and he began recording, then began rubbing the end of the vibrator around the cups of her thin bra, easing it closer to her nipples until she was already bucking against the collar.

He said, "You're gonna have to get yourself under control. I want an hour-long video, not five minutes."

A few seconds later—or a few hours later, it was unclear—Michael produced a pair of nail scissors and cut her bra, the small triangle of cloth between her breasts, so the cups fell to the sides. He cut her underwear at one leg and then the other. She wanted to object to this—what would she wear home, did he know how much those cost—but she didn't, and now he was praising her for waxing like a good girl. He was checking that she was wet. God, was she wet. He was rubbing the vibrator down the hood of her clit, telling her to breathe.

And then, to her delighted shame, she orgasmed, hard and fast, and loud, coming harder because she knew she shouldn't, shaking when it was over.

When she opened her eyes, Michael was grinning down at her, shaking his head. Still in his jeans and shirt. "Oh, honey," he said. "You messed up. That was very bad."

She was cold, and she wanted a blanket. She wanted a two-hour break.

He said, "Did I give you permission to come?"

"No."

"Why did you come without permission?"

"I couldn't help it."

He was biting his lip, still shaking his head. It dawned on her then, a feeling that crept down her sternum, that lifted her whole body even as it sank her down.

He said, "You know what we're going to have to do."

She nodded.

"Tell me," he said. "Tell me what we have to do."

And she couldn't imagine that he would, but she said, "Release . . . release the video?"

He thought a moment, or mimed thinking, his eyes on the ceiling. "Here's what's more interesting. We send *this* video out.

I'll blur your face, don't worry. And I'll blur mine. I'll change our voices. So this video right here—right now, the way you're spread on this table, the way your nipples are so hard, the way you're dripping. I want you to understand that this is what everyone will see. Do you understand that?"

"Yes," she said, and she was still cold, she was almost shaking, but she was electrified, she was ready for all of it.

Michael crossed the room and picked up the conference tote bag that Denise had carried there, the one with her vibrator and a toothbrush and phone. He put it on Denise's bare stomach and went to the iPad. She understood that he was zooming in, that he was making it clear to anyone watching this video that this woman was one of the five hundred–some women in Miami that weekend for the conference.

He said, "Do you understand that when you walk around tomorrow, everyone's going to have seen this?"

She nodded, collar and necklace cutting into her again, although she couldn't imagine he'd really get any eyes on the video.

He said, "I'm going to use the conference hashtag. I'm gonna post this under every other tweet that uses the conference hashtag. Everyone's going to be talking about it. Everyone's going to see it. By later tonight, dozens of lonely guys in their hotel rooms will be jacking off to it, wondering who you are."

He took his shirt off. He unzipped his jeans, but kept them on. He said, "And there aren't all that many possibilities. Not a lot of women here have this body. Not a lot of women have tits like that."

You'll get fired, she wanted to say. Somehow this will get us both fired. But the words didn't find her mouth. She was in a dream, she was in a world that didn't follow logic, she was on a distant moon.

Over the next hour, he put small clamps on her nipples, he brought her close to the edge with her vibrator and with his cock and with, improbably, the minibar whiskey he poured down her belly before pouring the rest in her mouth. He slapped her breasts with his open hand, and he slapped her breasts with a rolled-up magazine. He grabbed her tongue between his thumb and finger and told her to admit that she was a slut.

Denise was blindfolded for a while, and when he removed the blindfold it felt like waking up. The city sky had darkened around them. Lights were on in rooms across the street. The iPad was still there, recording. It might have felt, for a second, like a sobering, but it only sharpened her senses. She was still in a trance, but she was wired.

The thing was, she doubted she could come again. Partly because she already had, and partly because although the idea of being watched, the threat of being watched, was hugely arousing, the reality of it all was overwhelming. The reality meant she could feel each pore of her body. Letting herself come for the camera was a bridge she couldn't cross.

It wasn't that Michael read her mind so much as that he'd been at her with the vibrator, right on her clit, for a while now, and she was hyperventilating, but that was about all. He said, "I need you to let go. You're going to embarrass yourself, and that's okay. They're all going to see you. It's going to be humiliating. Are you ready to be humiliated?"

The clamps were still on her nipples; the collar was still on her neck. Her mouth was dry, and her fingers buzzed from her breathing too hard.

Michael said, "I think you need a finger up your ass. I think everyone needs to see that."

He slid something soft—a shirt, a small pillow—under her

so she was angled up more toward the camera. He licked his thumb and slid it inside her, where she felt herself pulse around him. He turned the vibrator off for a moment and it was a relief, until it was an absence, something she desperately needed back.

"They're watching," he said. "They're all watching. You need to come for them. You have to."

When he touched the vibrator back to her, gently, it was enough. She bucked against all her restraints, and maybe she needed to feel that they wouldn't give. She had no choice, they told her. She had jumped off the cliff and there was no way but down. She was screaming as she came, so loud that Michael put his hand over her mouth, and that was a release, too, knowing her voice was locked in.

Afterward, the iPad turned off, Michael carried her to the bed. Good, because she was a wrung-out rag. He rubbed her wrists and ankles and said, "You have a safe word."

"I do," she said.

He said, "You can still use it. At any moment."

Denise was wondering who had put a strobe light inside her body, why there was a strobe light somewhere inside her belly now turning her body to a pulse, turning the room to blue light.

Michael, who had not finished yet, had remarkably gentle sex with her, and she didn't do much more than wind her fingers through his hair.

She might have fallen asleep; Michael was emerging from the shower with a hotel towel around his waist.

He said, "Do you want to stay here? I'm going to edit this.

I'll be careful. Or you can go to your own place, and you can always text me to stop. I'll post it at eleven. You can tell me any-time before then."

Denise pulled the soft white bedspread up and closed her eyes.

Michael was gone when she woke up, but it was definitely morning. She used his shower, used the free toothbrush and toothpaste wrapped in plastic on the sink, and when she came out he was back, handing her a Starbucks. He raised his eye-brows, looked a bit nervous, and she understood: he'd done it, had done it hours ago, and was waiting for her to ask about it, waiting to see if she'd panic. Instead she took the coffee and kissed his cheek and told him she needed to go back and change. She didn't even have underwear.

Some years, the conference cleared out by Sunday. This year, though, Henry Benet, who rarely appeared anywhere these days, was giving a noon talk, and his former students and aco-lytes, plus the many younger historians who knew this was their only chance to see him speak, were sticking around. Denise's flight back to Minneapolis wasn't till Monday.

At 10:30 a.m., the main hotel bar was a sea of historians nursing hangovers over eggs and coffee or Bloody Marys. Den-ise rushed past them all, dashed up to her room to throw on new clothes.

And she checked Twitter. She couldn't help it. She typed in the conference hashtag, looked at the most recent tweets. It was hidden under "Show more replies" on some and "Show more replies, including those that may contain offensive" et cetera on others, but it was there, the thumbnail showing the tote bag on her stomach, nothing too far up or too far down. Above the video, Michael had written, "Fun and games at #hsoa5, NSFW."

It was— Oh God, it was her, her face blurred, but everything else shockingly clear. She sat on the bed to watch the whole thing, turned the sound up to verify that yes, Michael, bless his technical skills, had done something to both of their voices, too, so his sounded higher, hers sounded rougher and lower. Their whole conversation about the conference, about everyone watching, about everyone knowing. Until Michael started making these videos, until he started sending them to her, she hadn't fully believed she had a body that someone could see in this light. She hadn't, to be honest, been capable of objectifying herself. And now, yes. She could be both subject (most of the year) and object (a few days at a time).

She only noticed it on the second watching: her oak tree necklace, the one still around her neck, was visible. Here was the panic she'd been waiting to feel. She practically ripped it from her neck, shoved it into a pocket of her purse so she wouldn't lose it in the hotel room. Had anyone taken her photo yesterday with the necklace on? Not unless they'd photographed her panel without her knowing it.

In any case, she couldn't imagine the videos would stay up long. She couldn't imagine anyone had time, on this morning of hangovers, to click through the hidden replies.

But then, on her way back down in the elevator, two women with conference lanyards:

"It's a grad student. Has to be. I mean . . . It's someone who's in and out, who's never showing her face here again."

"Or," the other woman said, "most likely it's a sex worker, or

someone this guy found on Tinder. Right? Like, he's at the conference, he has the tote bag—" She suddenly glanced at Denise
and stopped talking, as if Denise would find the conversation
scandalous.

Down at the bar, there was an energy she hadn't noticed before. They weren't gathering around phones, nothing like that,
but there was more animated conversation than Sunday morning normally merited. People were leaning closer to talk. She
wasn't imagining it. They looked amused, not horrified. Everyone's eyes kept sweeping the room.

In the halls of the hotel, no one looked at her any differently.
But everyone she passed, or especially every vaguely attractive man she passed, she imagined having seen her body late
last night or already this morning, imagined them watching her
come, humiliated, imagined them zooming in.

She found a seat at the Henry Benet lecture behind Keith
and Franklin. They didn't see her; their heads were leaned together, talking.

"What I'm saying," Franklin said, "is that whatever your politics are, that's your politics. Your brain and your dick are far
apart on your body for a reason."

Keith said, laughing, "I want a panel on it next year. Everyone's personal take."

Franklin said, "My personal take is I took longer in the
shower this morning."

Keith said, "I feel like I'm looking at everyone with X-ray
goggles."

"Not everyone," Franklin said.

"Oh, God no. Not everyone. You know what I mean."

Denise was in a stupor the rest of the day. Back in her room that afternoon, she checked Twitter again. There was chatter about it now, people talking about "that video," debating what it meant, as if it had to mean something. No one admitting that maybe the reason they wanted to talk about it was that they wanted to think about it, wanted to watch it again.

She discovered that it had been retweeted beyond the conference, that a few people who seemed to have no connections at all to this bubble were talking about it. Not that it was the most exciting porn they'd ever seen, but they seemed fascinated by the circumstances of its creation and distribution. By the things Michael had said to her about posting it, about humiliation. "This would NEVER happen at a physics conference," someone wrote. "Who knew the historians were having all the fun?"

She watched the video again, touched herself, came hard— not over the video itself, but over knowing how many people had seen it, were seeing it right now, would remember it. If she and Michael did this again next year, there would be even more noise. There would be more speculation. People would calculate who'd been there two years in a row, make guesses. It occurred to her then, in the most reasonable part of her brain, that this wasn't fair to other women at the conference. That they didn't deserve that attention, the suspicion. She pushed it out of her mind.

That night, some stragglers went out for sushi: Michael, Keith-and-Franklin, the blond woman who'd been hanging on Michael the first night, the rock-star African diaspora scholar.

Denise felt punchy, adrenal. She drank too much white wine too fast. She found herself jealous of how Michael was laughing with the blond woman. She found herself impatient with all this polite, collegial chatter.

On her way to the restroom, she nearly ran into a waiter who, when he stepped back to let her pass, noticeably checked her out, scanned her body. She wondered if she was exuding something, if she reeked of pheromones. She wanted it to be true. She wanted to remain in this state, to carry it home with her like a collar she couldn't remove.

In the bathroom mirror, she looked flushed, wet eyed.

She knew what she wanted to do. Who was she kidding? She'd been hurtling toward it all along. And there were only a few people at that table.

She dug the oak tree necklace out of her purse, fastened it around her neck, made sure her collar was open enough to display it there against the tops of her breasts.

Back at the table, Michael was drawing something on a paper napkin for the blonde. Denise sat back down, turned to Keith and Franklin, and asked if they should order another bottle of wine.

He was only a second faster than Franklin, but Keith's eyes dipped down first. His eyes widened first.

Asphodel

1

In our world everything listens—the lamps, the chairs, our plush, ever-enduring pillows, and our counselors who are radiant geometric shapes. So we were listening when Evlin told her red cube that she'd had the conversation with her daughter.

"And how did she react?"

"As you would expect, as I expected, as I knew she would react. She ran away from me. She wept."

"You're a first generation."

"You're saying that I can bear it because I've done this thousands of times."

"Three thousand and thirty-six times."

"Is it always like this?"

"It is always exactly like this, Evlin."

"I can't bear it."

"But you have, three thousand and—"

"Shut up."

"Certainly. Shall we choose another subject?"

"Shut up. Shut the fuck up," said Evlin.

Evlin walked home, her footsteps hard on the path, tracing orange line distress. The sun was brilliant. Someone had put a pleasant chill in the air. Along the way, a spring apple tree with bees softly plundering the blossoms. We are known for such details. The scent was heavenly. Heavenly! This *is* heaven, the third of six corporately owned afterlives. Asphodel, Inc. Ours is the most perfect because of our standards in those we choose. Our admissions process has always been much like that of an exclusive early-twenty-first-century college. We choose colorful minds, visual minds, solid minds, thinkers, poets, artists, architects, scientists. We choose them for their ability to make our world from the stuff of consciousness. Ours is now the most sought-after model—a fascinatingly detailed piece of work. But we do have strict rules.

Adeline was lying facedown on the couch, under layers of fluffy throws, clutching her smooth compassion pets. When she heard her mother enter the room, she closed her eyes and pretended to be already dead. Evlin sat down beside her. Her hand hovered over her daughter's hair. From the times before, Evlin knew how confused her daughter was, how she longed for and also hated and feared, now, her mother's touch. Evlin sat a long time, waiting, until her daughter spoke.

"Were you lying? Mom? Please tell me you were lying. Because if you were lying about this, I would forgive you. It would be all right. I have read about fear. I have read about death. Maybe this is some kind of lesson . . ."

Evlin bent over and put her head in her hands. Why? Why not take them quickly in the night, as in that prayer, now I lay me down to sleep? But the answer of course was that Adeline had to be conscious in order to be forgotten. If Evlin had known, if she'd read the finest of the finely printed sixteen hundred pages in the legal agreement, but she had upped during a physical crisis. Her husband had chosen for her, and had died, later, under circumstances in which he could not be salvaged.

"So was it true when you told me that I'm not real?"

"I never said you're not real. You are real. You're real, my darling. A projection is real."

"I am your thoughts. You said I am your thoughts."

"But more, you're much more, you're everything that—"

"—the daughter you left behind hundreds or thousands of years ago or something. Which is why you got to make me up. I was in your contract."

"Yes, and not everyone has a contract that includes having a child."

"You didn't 'have' me."

"I know."

"Well, some kids knew already. I just didn't believe it."

"Where did you think you came from?"

"It's not that! I don't care where I came from! I thought I was permanent."

"Nobody is."

"Except the parents. Yeah, I get that. Now."

Adeline sobbed violently, thrusting Evlin's hand off. Suddenly she sat up. Her black curls sprang around her face. Her eyes were fierce.

"I'm scared, I'm scared, I'm scared."

Evlin knew it was best not to show her own emotion. Best to be consistent. Get to the point where Adeline would accept her embrace.

"Trust me," she said firmly. "You must trust me. I thought you up before. I'll think you up again."

"But why can't you just let me *grow* up? Because if I have to die . . ."

"It's not death, oh, honey, it's not."

"I have read about death and it *is* death," said Adeline. "I disappear. It is the end of me. I won't know who I am next time at all. I'll be a whole different Adeline. You will be with the new Adeline and she will go along loving you until she's ten years old. Then this. You'll tell her this. And she will have to stand this, all because you want a daughter. She'll be sentenced to die, too. You're cruel."

Evlin's heart emptied. Sentenced to die. Cruel. She felt sick. The others had wept. She'd held them. Eventually they'd given up and withered away like tender plants as she ceased to water them with her thoughts. Then she'd isolate herself with other thoughts, as she had been taught, and before long she would have a new baby in her arms. But never had any of them called her cruel.

There was something about this time, something different. Maybe there was something about this Adeline. She was stubborn. This conversation was far more difficult. And for the past thousand or so times, as far back as she could remember now, it had been increasingly difficult. She thought she would wait several lifetimes before she did this again. Essentially, when looked at from Adeline's point of view, the truth was on her daughter's side. The contract had been drawn up to make sure Evlin didn't use more than the portion of energy she'd paid for. Each thought has its basis in energy. Growing children require vast amounts of energy to change into adults.

Without a child, Evlin could travel. She could adventure.

She could take what still felt extraordinarily like risk. She could visit the new Arctic. Feel the piercing cold.

Adeline screamed and then began to sob in huge, shattering hiccups. Evlin put her arms around her daughter and Adeline clung to her like she was drowning.

"Please let me grow up."

Her hot breath filled Evlin's ear. She held her daughter tighter. She couldn't speak. Words wouldn't form, though she tried, cleared her throat, tried again. There was something wrong. It had almost happened last time. She now remembered that she had told the last Adeline the same things. Had she remembered? Or had Evlin somehow begun to project the memories of these conversations? At last, Adeline started down a familiar track. It was reassuring.

"Why didn't you tell me?"

"I did, but you didn't understand. You know I did. I tried."

"You're right," said Adeline at last. Sitting straight, her voice bitter, she spoke. Then she vomited over and over until she gagged and dry-heaved, exhausted.

I'm not thinking this, thought Evlin, what she's doing, this level of anguish. It is happening outside of my thoughts. I would never put her through this. I don't know what to do.

Evlin took Adeline into another room, washed her. She couldn't get the bad smell out of her mind. They fell asleep in exhausted despair. In the morning, when they looked at each other, it all flooded back. They said nothing. Adeline stared into her mother's eyes and her mother could not look away. She got up and went to the desk. Found a pen and a bit of paper.

"What happens if you don't stop thinking about me?"

"One of us has to be erased."

The other Adelines had taken that news very hard, but this

Adeline really was different. She looked at her mother with hope, with confidence, as if Evlin would of course make the choice to wither away and transfer her energy in order to give her daughter the allotment in her contract. Then Adeline wrote, *if you loved me how could you not take my place?*

Now they had gone past some boundary. None of the others had pushed this far. To actually ask, to assume, that Evlin would be persuaded, that she would allow her daughter to take over the contract. The room was robin's-egg blue because it was always their favorite color. Now the walls deepened to indigo.

"I've been trained to let you fade from my thoughts," said Evlin. "I report to my cube. It has to be this way. It's in the contract. Maybe you've seen other children, puckering up, turning watery, or wrinkling, or clumsy."

"Yes," said Adeline. Her eyes were steady on her mother.

"So you are going to make me die like them?"

Evlin tried to return her daughter's gaze with the compassionate regard she had practiced. This 3,037th Adeline had become so strong, she thought, and she smiled. She was so proud that she folded the bit of paper they had been writing on and fumbled it into her bra. That little bit of paper would be there when she began nursing the 3,038th Adeline, she thought. She held her hand out, surprised to see that she was trembling. Adeline took her hand.

"Shall we take a walk?" Adeline asked softly.

"Sartwinely," said Evlin.

"Hold on tight, let me steady you," said Adeline.

"Yassss," said Evlin. Her legs had gone wobbly. She stumbled down the steps and lay weakly in the glowing grass. She felt her energy leaking from her, soaking into the ground, which is a sort of living battery that always needs replenishing. Evlin tried to sit up, but it was a struggle. She tried to yell, but her voice was gone. She was made of cardboard. She was thinning to a cloudy paper. Soon she could see the color of the grass through patches on her legs and arms.

"Shhh, little mother, quiet now," said Adeline. "It won't take long."

2

It took longer than Adeline would have liked, as Evlin's consciousness was tricky, slipped inside the furniture, the blinds, clothing, anywhere it thought it could hide. But at last her mother turned to a floating watery substance that squeaked and popped for days before it fell silent. One morning there was a dry whitish powder scattered on the carpet. As Adeline vacuumed it up she heard her mother's scratchy-panicked whimpers. Once she emptied the tube into the trash and hauled it to the deletion bin, she didn't hear from her mother again.

Adeline occupied herself by growing up, choosing for her body intricate patterns that she meditated into being. For her skin, the blue she and her mother favored. Red for her hair, long and quiet down her back. Straight, silken, lethal. She made her hair into a weapon, trained it to form a tensile rope that she'd be able to sling around an attacker's neck. As for breasts, she wanted them small so as not to waste the space she needed for extra nipples. She doubled or tripled any place on her body that registered intense sensation. She dreamed another clitoris, an extra vagina, and decided to have a penis. She tried for two, but only one materialized no matter how hard she concentrated. She made it long, thick, and green. All of this took time, years if there was any reason to measure, but time was now her wealth. She had to hide her extras in her mother's shape before she went out to meet other bodies.

When Adeline had asked her mother where she was going, her mother had always smiled and answered, *Out to meet other bodies.* So she knew what her mother meant to do, but had no idea where she went. Her mother had kept a babysitter in the closet, a round orange cat that walked on its hind legs, popped up playfully when they had pillow fights, or curled around Adeline when she was sleepy. Adeline thought of taking the babysitter out of the closet and asking if it knew where her mother had gone on those evenings, but maybe there were places she could find for herself. For the sake of the contract she had to look something like her mother, but she didn't want to follow too closely in her footsteps.

Outside was cool, gray, and still. It was one of those days nobody had bothered to spruce up yet. Adeline liked it that way. She'd put a flowered black scarf over her hair, a trench coat over her business suit and yellow silk blouse. She could walk anywhere without showing much of her new body. Sometimes a tile jiggled loose from a wall or a piece of sidewalk gave like rubber, but most of this world was thoroughly imagined, until you got beyond the walls. Out there, the air was misty, the trees blurred, the birds not quite birdlike. Evlin had said that Asphodel should sign up more people who remembered birds and trees. Outside beyond the wall had always been their favorite place.

It was windier out there. In fact the wind . . . it seemed as though it wanted to play with Adeline. A volume of air slid along her skin, slipped inside her coat, warmed against her throat, raked down her nipples and hovered over the most exquisitely sensitive places on her body as she wandered along. Every so often, it seized her hips, pushed itself between her legs, so she had to stop, laughing, then gasping as it turned heavy, hot, solid, and sent a rush of sensation through some new central nerve she hadn't known about. She froze against a tree, waiting for the blinding, trancelike joy of it to pass. At last the little tendrils came out at her neckline as a rosy flush, a delicate whisper of air, and she lay down to sleep.

Her bed was yearning emerald-green moss. When she awakened, Adeline found that the moss had grown around her. Now it began rubbing her, vibrating lightly as it peeled away each piece of her clothing, making sure that without her coverings she was still warm and comfortable. It made a blanket of tiny, moving fingers that explored her all at once, then gave beneath her when she turned over and decided to see if the penis worked. A soft, thick-walled, narrow, deep aperture opened and she pushed inside. Once she did, she was lost in the plunging and bucking and hurting, yes it hurt, or she was hurting something she could also feel, and the confusion drove her out of her mind. She couldn't hold a thought, felt she might disintegrate, but there was no use trying to correct what was happening. What was correct here? Maybe she was doing the right thing. She kept on and kept on sliding in and in, nearly passing out when it gripped her, falling forward when it loosened and allowed her deeper, then so deep she felt she'd maybe slid entirely inside and would be lost.

But no, thankfully no, she must have been doing the right thing, because eventually there was a shudder of light and bolts of continuous glowing tension that consumed her, shook her like a rag, and dropped her, spent, in the tender moss.

Sitting up after she was back in her shape, stroking the pleasure-giving moss, she thought that now it would be perfect to rest and eat. She found her clothes, tied the scarf back on her head, hung the trench coat over her shoulders. But as she walked back toward her house a piece of wall stepped forward and resolved into a shape that was all holes and mouths and need. She fled home and hopped in, locked the door. There, she was safe. Everything was made to be stable and predictable.

It was us, us, prepared now to protect her.

Adeline hung up her coat and went into the kitchen. She sliced and grilled a tomato, then cracked two eggs into a sizzling pan of butter and toasted two pieces of rosemary bread. She popped the cap off a brown bottle of beer and drank it, glug, glug, we loved it. As she ate, we heard her wonder if we knew, but of course all is all, and we knew everything, felt everything, did everything, accomplished everything, were now desperately greedy for the next encounter and would continue to be so until at long last her contract expired. That sudden thought gave us a tremendous pang. There were centuries left, but her mother hadn't signed up for eternity. And she, like the others, had only merged with those bodies like her own. This Adeline, we hadn't expected her. None of them had ever considered us, their servant, their surrounding, so attentive to all they needed. None of them had ever desired everything. We were already thinking *more, more.* Some of us were already murmuring that we should cut her a deal. And the lucky chair that she was sitting on as she ate was growing a lump that she parted her legs to accept, eating placidly and slowly as with agonjoy we reached. When she finished her eggs, Adeline turned around, hugged the chair's backrest, and began to rock against ourself, faster, harder, shivering and pounding along the floor with mad, feral motions that hurled us over an edge in all of us that we had never known before and over which we kept falling, onto the floor, through the floor, through below the floor, into the random and meticulous creation we thought we knew until Adeline began to tamper with us, Asphodel, beloved field of the gods, where one small rare white flower grows.

En Suite

At the end of the block, they stopped and waited to see if he was following them. It was after ten now, and all the little shops and restaurants that usually lit up Ocean Street were dark. A distant traffic light blinked red, illuminating the overhanging Monterey cypresses and more of the same nothing.

"I think we're good," Anne said, and that finally prompted Linney to let go of her hand.

Still, they walked the last half block to the Ocean Suites in silence. Anne ushered Linney through the gate and across the lawn, which was splashed with yellow light from the hotel lobby. Only three hours ago, they'd stood in that same bay window, chortling through a complimentary port tasting and watching a pair of new arrivals inch a Nissan Leaf up the steep driveway toward check-in. The wife had eventually gotten out to stand on the curb and shout, "Frank?" in exasperation, while Frank stuck his hatted head out the window and roared, *"Hannah!"* back at her. This back-and-forth had proven infectious. By dinnertime, the girls were volleying *"Hannah!"* and *"Fraaank!"* at the slightest provocation, as though it had been a fixture of their friendship for the last fifteen years.

Outside their room, Anne looked back once more to make sure the street was empty before hustling Linney inside with a gruff "Come on, come on, come on," all business, naturally, now that the real danger was past. She cranked up the thermostat and sat down on her bed, relieved that the dim flush mount overhead, which had made getting ready all but impossible, helped hide her red cheeks.

Linney was on her own bed across the room, taking off her shoes. "Fuck that guy," she said.

"Really," Anne said. "Fucking mouth breather."

"Did you hear him?"

"He said something about your lipstick?"

"You're trying way too hard with that, honey." Linney sprawled obnoxiously for a moment across the imaginary bar top before her. *"Who's it even for?"*

"At least you gave it right back to him." It had all escalated too quickly for Anne's whiskey-fizzed brain. "I'm so sorry. I should've punched him."

Linney shook her head. "No," she said. "You were right to get us out of there. I should've spoken up the second he sat down. I should've been louder."

"Try it this way," Anne said. "He should've not been a piece of shit. The bartender should've told him to leave. None of this is your fault. You were just sitting there."

And what had Anne done while Linney was just sitting there? While Linney was just sitting there, halfway through her birthday-eve Boulevardier, nightcap to the lovely dinner and perfect day the two of them had shared, reunited after six dreary months on opposite coasts in this quaint and wildly expensive little seaside town Linney had always wanted to visit? Had Anne stepped in front of her best friend and said, *Hey, asshole, can't you see she wants to be left alone?* And, when that failed (as it was bound to with this guy, with his pink polo collar jerked up around his ears and the stench of some kind of teakwood spritz peeling off him), and he said, "You'd better be careful, bitch," had she said, at the top of her lungs, "Dude, are you serious, are you threatening a woman right now, in front of everyone here?"

No, real Anne hadn't done any of the things imaginary Anne felt certain she would do. And because of her caution or cowardice, Teakwood Spritz had felt free to lean in to Linney and say something more, something that finally made Linney turn to her and say, "Okay, you know what, let's go. Right now."

But what had Anne done? Grabbed Linney's fingers under the countertop and said: "No, finish your drink." And then waved down the bartender, who was, she realized, a bewildered kid of maybe twenty-three, and whispered: "Can we get the check?"

While the bartender closed them out, Linney had endured a further stretch of Teakwood Spritz's close-quarters muttering until his companion (a woman, to Anne's surprise) reappeared from the bathroom. Only when he turned back to her did Anne take Linney's hand. "Okay, *now* we go." And this illusion of taking charge, of delaying their escape until Teakwood Spritz was too distracted to notice, had restored some semblance of the courage and common sense Anne expected of herself. Here she was, protecting Linney. Just as she had done countless times before, when some drunk dipshit or another pulled up a barstool and started slobbering inanities into her ear.

"Well done, you," Linney had said once they were outside. "I wouldn't have thought to wait." Her appreciation only made Anne feel more like a fraud. That feeling worsened considerably when, halfway down the block, a male voice somewhere behind them yelled, "Hey, wait!" and she had grabbed Linney's hand and practically kited her best friend down the street and into the shadows.

"What did he say to you?" Anne asked now.

Linney was pulling on her pajama shorts. "He said if I was such hot shit, where was my boyfriend?"

"No, no. I heard that. After. When he whispered."

Linney shook her head. "Forget it."

"What? Tell me."

"No."

It must have been really bad. When had Linney ever refused to divulge the contents of some uncomfortable exchange? Once, when her college boyfriend broke up with her so viciously that she knew giving Anne a play-by-play would be prohibitive to a reconciliation when he inevitably came crawling back. And another time, when she had an awful fight with her stepfather the night her mom was hospitalized. And now, somehow, this oversaturated stranger had wormed his way into this legacy of meaningful secrets. He was going to sit there forever, like a bullet hole in the memory of this day, which had been perfect until the moment he'd swiveled to face Linney at the bar. Everything else (the beach walk, the trying on of ludicrous hats they couldn't afford, the ice cream guy serenading Linney as he handed her a free scoop of birthday gelato) had been eclipsed by this dark turn. When had she ever seen Linney shaking like this, with rage or anything else?

A blast of headlights drove through the half-open blinds, sending them both onto their respective beds.

"Oh my God," Linney said. "Is it him?"

"What? No."

It couldn't be. He would've had to follow them here, unseen, and then what? Wait for fifteen minutes while they got into their pj's? Anne stood up and went to the door.

A car rumbled up to the spot just outside their window and sat there, idling, blinding her. When the engine finally cut out, Linney edged farther up the bed, into darkness. The headlights died. Anne kept her ear against the wall. One car door slammed, and then another, and before she had time to process what that might mean, footsteps were hurrying up the walk toward her. She got ready to throw the door open, feeling stupid, vulnerable, reeling with disbelief. But at the last moment the footsteps veered, scraping past to stop outside 107 next door. She heard the slap of plastic against the door lock.

"God damn it," a male voice said, as clear and close as if he were standing right beside her. Nineteen sixties construction, Anne thought. You could refurbish these little roadside places with all the art deco brass hardware and charming Delft-inspired wallpaper you wanted, but if the place was sixty years old and the walls made of plywood, it was never, ever, ever going to be anything but the two-star shithole it had always been.

She was already composing the Yelp review when she heard a woman's encouraging murmur outside. "Come on, handsome. You got this."

"It'd be a lot easier if you weren't doing that."

"Doing what? This?"

Anne heard a click and the skirl of hinges, and then the door slammed shut.

Linney's head, ruffled and grinning, popped out from under the sheets. "Handsome!" she whispered, in that most-Linney way. "Dang!"

Two thumps from next door, and then a prolonged silence during which a whole lot of rustling unfolded. "Fuck, baby,"

Handsome's voice finally said. "You looked so good tonight. I was ready to just throw you over the table."

"What stopped you?" Baby wanted to know between kisses.

"Oh, I don't know. The screaming kids. The parents. That old couple who kept scowling at us."

"Mmm, I *love* that you're still talking about them."

Handsome laughed, and suddenly, Anne knew who he and Baby were. She'd seen them in the lobby earlier that evening: Handsome had stood in line for port right behind her. To be polite, she had poured his two snifters before her own. "How do we tell if it's any good?" he'd asked. She shrugged and he grinned and said, "Oh well, free booze, right?" and then carried the glasses back to the lobby chaise, where a woman (presumably Baby) sat adjusting a rumpled felt hat. Anne had admired her brazenness in pairing a blooming, glitter-shot, floor-length skirt with a pair of high-heeled booties. From the sound of things, those booties were probably tucked under the bronzed curvature of Baby's haunches right now, because somebody next door was gulping something with loud abandon, and it certainly wasn't Handsome. No, Handsome was hissing, "You like that?" and letting a moan rattle out of him every couple of seconds.

Across the room, Linney was mouthing, *Oh my God.* Her whole face was nothing but eyes. She jerked her thumb toward the door. *We go?*

Anne shrugged, *Where?* and Linney dropped her face into her hands.

"Stand up," Handsome rasped. "Turn around."

"Oh, it's like that, is it?"

"You bet your ass it is."

The ass in question now received one, two, three sharp slaps, each one punctuated by a yelp of delight.

"Lie back. Go ahead, baby, lie back."

Anne could imagine this interlude so clearly: Baby crawling backward across the starchy white sheets and drawing that incredible skirt up so she could spread her knees wide. For a moment, in her mind's eye, the strangers next door flickered into long-vanished apparitions: Baby's clit pierced with the silver drop Anne's ex-girlfriend had worn; Handsome sporting the blunt jaw of her college boyfriend while he stroked himself above her.

"You want this inside you?"

"Oh my God," Linney hissed. "What are these walls *made of*?"

"They should be charging us for this," Anne groaned. But she was inconveniently wet, and she wished Linney weren't there.

Out of nowhere, Baby said: "Wait, wait, wait."

"What? I'm sorry!"

"No—just. Leave them on, just pull them aside. Fuck. Yes. Like that." And then, the kicker: "Tongue fuck me."

Anne saw it about to happen. Linney's mouth dropped open, and then out of it came: *"Haaaaa—"*

Anne dove across the room and tackled her flat. She grabbed a pillow and mashed it into Linney's face and gator rolled her into the sheets, but by the time Linney's howls of laughter had subsided, the room next door was quiet.

"You girls okay in there?" Baby's voice.

Oh shit. Linney sat up.

Anne pulled her fist out from between her teeth. "Yes," she called. "Thank you!"

A beat, and then: "You sure?"

"Yes! Yep. Thank you. Sorry!"

"Okay." A beat, and then: "You're welcome to join!"

Linney's face twisted. *What the fuck is going on?*

"Thank you!" Anne clapped a hand over Linney's mouth. "We're good. You guys enjoy."

And they did, for another ten or fifteen minutes—a little more subdued now, maybe, but still decidedly on course. Baby came twice, at which point her moans became muffled by what Anne assumed was a reconfiguration that allowed her to sink her face into the pillows and scream freely while Handsome shook the adjoining wall with the rhythm of his efforts. Their bed obviously had a headboard, which Anne's did not—she and Linney were squashed against the wall, boiling to death under cheap sheets. Linney's eyeliner was all over the place, her hair a mess. She was smiling again, thank God, Teakwood Spritz forgotten. Maybe they could pull this birthday out of the fire after all. Obliterate the memory of Teakwood Spritz with laughter and the weird, hot turn the evening had taken.

Then Handsome finished up with one final, ardent thrust, followed by a series of diminishing ones. A few moments later, the radio crackled to life and there was Nina Simone, singing about the stars.

Linney sat up. "Wait," she whispered. Her eyes were glazed with drink and the breathless heat of being under the covers. "That's it?"

"I mean, he closed it out despite being laughed at. Ten out of ten, would recommend."

"Maybe we *should* have joined them."

"Can you imagine?" Anne said.

But she definitely could. And apparently so could Linney, because the next thing Anne knew, they were kissing, and her drink- and heat-addled brain couldn't quite untangle who had started it.

Did it matter? Of course it mattered. They weren't twenty anymore, making out at some house party and pretending (at least on Anne's side) that it was all for show, just a way to turn their boyfriends on. They were grown-ups. They owned cape blazers! They had both recently broken up with people because their schedules made dating more of a chore than a diversion. And each of them had, at some point in the past week of birthday festivities, started a sentence with: "My gastroenterologist says . . ." You couldn't have a gastroenterologist and make out with somebody and pretend one of you wasn't eventually going to reach for the other's buttons. Should it be her? She slid a hand down the small of Linney's back, past the waistband, and let it rest on the taut rise of Linney's glute— the very same one Linney had bared last year, telling Anne to *just do it already!* with her eyes already swelling shut and the EpiPen gripped so tightly in Anne's fist that she felt certain she would shatter it.

Linney began biting her lip insistently. She was still doing this when somebody pounded on the door.

Linney drew back. "It's him."

"Handsome?"

"Bar guy!"

"What? How?"

"It's him, I know it's him."

Anne leapt over her without thinking and looked through the peephole.

A hatted, middle-aged man was standing outside in the dim glow of their porch light, moths fluttering against his forehead. It wasn't Teakwood Spritz. It was Frank.

"Um," he said. "Yes—hi there."

"Yes?" Suddenly, imaginary Anne came roaring out of whatever recess in which she'd been hiding. She jerked the door open. "Can I help you?"

Frank was forced to catch his hat as he shrank back. "Sorry. Yes. My wife and I are upstairs? Trying to get some sleep?"

"And?"

He was peering into the room. "We were just wondering if you and your husband could . . . turn down your music?"

"You've got the wrong room," Anne said. She wanted to add, *Do you see a husband in here?* But Frank had a good six inches on her. She couldn't block his view entirely, and he had already taken stock of matters over her shoulder.

"Oh," he said. "Oh. I'm sorry, girls. My mistake."

She slammed the door behind him and tracked the racket of his heavy-heeled advance up the stairs. Before he reached the landing, he was already whisper-shouting, "*Hannah!*" And from somewhere above, oblivious to his blooming mortification, his wife answered his call: "*Fraaank?*"

Anne turned back to the bed. Linney was smothering a smile. "*Hannah!*" she said.

"*Fraaank,*" Anne whispered back.

It seemed possible, suddenly, that this whole situation wasn't just owed to being overheated and silly under the covers, or to the soundtrack of Baby and Handsome's Wild Ride ringing through the cardboard walls. Linney was still sitting there with the sheets around her, halfway out of her sleeve. Had Anne done that? Started undressing her? Perhaps she should finish. All she had to do was cross those maybe four feet of electric space and keep kissing Linney.

Linney, whom she had wanted to kiss on many occasions, for the longest time, a very long time ago.

"I'm just gonna," Anne said, and pointed to the bathroom. "One second."

It was strange to be the party needing a bathroom breather. Usually she was the one back in the bed, mouthing *hurry back* and keeping her nipples hard while some girl or guy took a few minutes to get it together in private. But here she was, turning on the water to drown out the tide in her ears, and the sound of Baby and Handsome's postcoital seventies sing-along.

Her hands were shaking. Linney's lipstick—the much-maligned Berry & Bright!—was smeared all over her chin. She scrubbed at it and brushed her teeth and tipped back the last of the mouthwash.

They should talk before they started up again. Even just a quick check-in to see if Linney was really on board. Linney who, to Anne's knowledge, had only ever slept with men. Though perhaps that had changed sometime in the intervening months. But if it had, wouldn't Anne have been the first to know? For years, every single one of Linney's sexual escapades had been instantly relayed to her in great detail. She knew about the ill-fated fuck on the roof of the Met. She knew about the time Linney had set a small fire trying to humor a boyfriend's predilection for candle play.

A bolt of panic sizzled through Anne's arms. She also knew the crucial fact that Linney had finally decided she could do without receiving head ever again, thank you very much. She hated the way men went for her panties without asking, as if they expected her to be amazed by this great benediction they were bestowing on her.

What a deadly mistake it would've been to somehow, suddenly, forget that.

Maybe it was a sign that Anne had no business taking this any further. Maybe they should just say good night.

Or maybe this was it. Maybe, after all this time, they were actually going to fuck. Or not fuck. Make love? And then what? She splashed her face. Would they try to spoon, crammed like freshmen against the wall? Or would Linney go back to her own little twin bed on the other side of the room to sleep? One way or another, morning would come, and with it the looming necessity of a conversation about where to go from here. When would this conversation take place? Before their respective showers? During a shared one, intended to stretch out the evening's fevered confusion? Eventually they would have to get dressed and leave this cocoon and head to breakfast. And not just any breakfast: Linney's birthday breakfast at La Baguette, where yesterday's cute waitress would bring the pastry basket and the butter while the two of them . . . what? Held hands? Now? After fifteen years of checking each other's teeth for spinach?

She ran the water again, this time until her hands were red.

Here was the thing. They'd laughed when Baby said, "Tongue fuck me," but it wasn't objectively funny. "Tongue fuck me" was the kind of thing you laughed about with your best friend but heard yourself say when you were becoming that other person, your bedroom self, whom your friend didn't actually know. The person you became when what you wanted was to get tongue fucked. And for the life of her, Anne couldn't think of any other way to say it. "Tongue fuck me" was just about it. And if she hadn't been staying in this room with Linney when things got going next door, there wouldn't have been anything to laugh about at all. If she'd been alone, in this preposterous little hotel, with its gold chevron bathroom tile and hollow walls, and had heard "Tongue fuck me" from the other room, she would've been lying with her head against the baseboard and her fingers between her legs, listening to Handsome fulfill Baby's directive in the next room, and thrilling from head to toe at the effort of having to keep quiet herself when she came. And furthermore, the next time she was grinding down on somebody's face (a week or six months from now), some remote file room of her brain might throw the memory of that moment right into the bright void behind her eyes where all her desires roiled, and she might actually find herself saying it. She might say, "Tongue fuck me," and mean it. And maybe the only way whoever was tongue fucking her wouldn't find that hilarious was if "Tongue fuck me" was where they started. Maybe you could know somebody too well, love somebody too much, to suddenly tongue fuck them—or ask them, in the plainest terms possible, to tongue fuck you. Maybe before you got to the sacred, you had to start with the profane. Maybe you couldn't reverse that order. Or at least, maybe Anne couldn't. The point was, she wanted to feel free to say, "Tongue fuck me," and know that the person hearing it would understand, and oblige, and store it away as part of the things she said in earnest, and then love her anyway.

Didn't this fucking hotel have any kind of insulation? Her cheeks were blazing red, but she couldn't get her hands warm at all.

And, Christ, how was she going to put this to Linney? It's too late for us—I'm pretty sure you're straight, but even if you're not, there's no tongue fucking to be had here, only making love, and I don't want to make love, to you or anyone, maybe ever. I want to pull hair and have my hair pulled, I want to grind down on tongues and cocks without any self-consciousness, and laugh, and have my ass slapped, and yes, sure, maybe find a bit of love somewhere in all that shameless fun—but only if the fucking stays fucking. And you and I, Linney, we already love each other. I don't think we can fuck. Maybe we could've, ages ago, when I was probably in love with you and not ready to admit it to anyone, including myself. But I was a different person, and I had to get over all that to reach this part of myself, not to mention this whole other love we have now, and I've been over you for, like, ten years, and you've *never* been into me, and I don't think there's any going back now.

That would go over well.

Of course, Linney would say. Then she would look around, frowning and saying um, as she always did at the beginning of a fight. Frowning. Umming. Hunting around for some fictitious misplaced item.

It's true, Anne would end up saying. You can't just fuck somebody when you *already* love them. It has to be making love or nothing. Doesn't it?

Wow, Linney would then definitely say. Happy birthday to me.

Don't be mad. Please. You don't really want to do this with me. You don't see me this way. This is just our real love accidentally spilling over into something neither of us actually wants.

Of course, of course, Linney would say. You're right. I'm sorry. It's fine. It's fine it's fine it's fine.

But it wouldn't be fine. It would be awful. And it would touch every corner of their friendship, possibly for a long time to come. She rested her forehead against the mirror and let the cool of it sink into her skull.

At least there would be something worse than Teakwood Spritz to remember when they looked back on this trip.

She opened the door. The swelter of the room rolled across her face. She was drunker than she'd thought. Her bed was empty. Linney was back in the other twin with the little bedside lamp switched on and *The God of Small Things* open on her knees.

Had Linney been out here, second-guessing herself and remembering that she was actually straight? Or, worse: had she grown restless, and then increasingly hurt as Anne's bathroom dilemma stretched into minutes, and finally decided to take the decision into her own hands? Anne felt sick.

"Are they done?" she finally asked. "Next door?"

"Um." Linney frowned. "Let's hope so."

"Do you want an Advil?"

"Hmm?"

"An Advil? Before you go to sleep? For that wine-and-whiskey nightcap combo?"

"No, thanks."

Anne couldn't seem to leave the doorway. "Some water?"

Without raising her eyes from the book, Linney felt around beside the bed for her Nalgene, held it up, and shook it to show that it was full.

"Oh," Anne said. "Okay."

"I'm just gonna read for a bit."

Anne smoothed out the sheets and got under them. The bed was still warm. Whatever had driven Linney to her decision must have solidified mere moments ago. Anne had missed her by seconds. While she had been hiding in the bathroom, wringing her cold hands about the array of theoretical fucks that a commitment to Linney would put out of her reach, her best friend had been out here sinking into pain. Realizing she had taken too long to catch up to the place where Anne had once waited for her. Realizing that she was alone, now, and way out on a limb. Until the whole thing became ugly and unbearable and she hurried back to her own bed.

Anne had a sudden, clear vision of Linney's face contorting with disdain at the intimation of these thoughts. "Um," Linney would say. "Wow. Don't be so fucking dramatic. You always think the worst of people, and you're always wrong."

Anne made herself lie still until the light across the room went out and Linney's breathing deepened. Well, that was the night over after all. Thank God she hadn't had to say what she feared might need saying. Thank God Linney had the sense or impatience to return to her own bed. In the morning, they'd be back to themselves, and soon enough they'd be laughing about this little flirtation with possibility. Ten to one they'd have a nickname for it by Christmas. And then it would pass into that jumble of in-jokes whose origins they could no longer remember.

Unless it didn't. Unless the next twenty-four hours elapsed in slow, crumbling agony, and it became clear that they should stop talking for a little while, and then that little while became six months, eight months, perhaps longer. What if this time next year, Anne found herself dreading calling Linney on her birthday? She'd make herself do it, and dial, and hear the cold, "Yes?" Linney reserved for the fundraisers calling from their alma mater. She'd say, "How have you been?" And Linney would say, "Fine. You? Shattered any friendships with your reckless lust lately?"

She was being ridiculous. Didn't it make all the sense in the world that Linney had simply retreated to her own bed because she was afraid of leading Anne on?

Anne went back and forth like this, half dreaming, half awake, until the gray haze of 6 a.m. brought her around. Handsome and Baby were back at it, more quietly this time: Baby's yeah-yeah-mmms a low rumble in the wall, broken up by the occasional thump of the headboard and some furtive tittering. Their single-mindedness was less admirable when you felt as infuriated with them as Anne did now. Something in this room still seemed broken, thanks in large part to their horn-ball antics. Much obliged, she wanted to say. I hope you enjoy your breakfast while we try to piece together the tatters of our friendship.

Across the room, Linney was on her stomach, one bare arm dangling off the edge of the bed, her head turned toward the wall. She shifted a little, and her breathing changed. She was awake. Any second now, she would roll over and sigh and say something, and whatever it was would set the tone for the rest of their day. Would it be a joke? Anne hoped so. But as the minutes wore on, and the silence persisted, she felt that possibility fade. Linney wasn't turning over. She wasn't turning over because she couldn't face Anne. Because she didn't know what to say. Because she was hurt. Because she was angry. Because she was—and that was when Anne's mind ran right up against the worst of thoughts, the one she'd been keeping at bay with all her might. Worse than the possibility that backing out had been a mistake. Worse even than the possibility of having wounded Linney by her hesitation.

What if, as Linney sat there, puzzling out her own participation in their little romp, she had begun to filter the entirety of their friendship through the lens of Anne's desire for the very first time? What if all their years of jokes and memories and little intimacies were now being poisoned by the baseless and basic misconception that Anne had somehow been pursuing her all this while?

Wasn't this Anne's greatest fear? That Linney would turn out to be so predictably straight in this one, heartbreaking way? That Linney would cease to believe Anne could love her platonically, with no ulterior motive, no secret design? Wasn't that why she had waited so long to come out to Linney in the first place?

But what exactly about Linney's reaction to that particular piece of news, when Anne finally shared it, had led her to believe this could possibly be the case? What had Linney done, when she heard? She had hugged her and said, "Why didn't you tell me sooner? Let's celebrate!"

And she had meant it. Anne's heart cleared. Yes, Linney had meant it.

And if she could hear Anne's thoughts now, wouldn't Linney be more wounded by Anne's lack of faith in her than by any of the thousand possibilities Anne had spent the night concocting?

She would. She really would.

Linney's arm disappeared under her pillow and she let out a soft cough. Linney. Thirty-one now. Pretending to be asleep, not because she didn't want to face her, but because she was giving Anne space to be the first to speak. To climb out of whatever hole of illogic Linney knew she'd backed herself into.

Just say happy birthday, Anne thought. Say happy birthday and get back to being yourselves. Your love is real. Have faith.

"*Hannah?*" she finally said.

Linney snorted and rolled over. "*Fraaank.*"

Altitude Sickness

The Making of Alice
Brisbane

Like a woman in a dream she boiled the eggs and burned the toast and laid out plates and cutlery. Washing up, she gazed out at the garden and saw a penny lizard emerge from the short grass near the water sprinklers. The flecks on its slender chocolate body seemed to expand and contract as it crossed the tiles leading to the arbor. She watched as its skin turned red as the stone. Lizards are the future, she said aloud. How she wished to be one. She showered, dressed, called a taxi, and said the usual words to her husband as she left the house, none of it real, not the words or the leave-taking or the setting forth, nothing real until she was in her seat for the twelve-hour flight to a city where the sun set at 2:30 in the afternoon. It was only then, in the air, that her senses returned and she knew her own appetites. She ordered a drink and sipped it slowly and examined the menu as the heat from the liquor mounted in her face. The taste of bourbon on her tongue, this was real to her, and her own scent that rose in brief, distinct wafts, the jasmine roll-on she had placed on her inner wrists when she climbed into the taxi's smell of cigarettes and air freshener. When she asked for another drink, the man at the window seat told the attendant he wanted one, too. Then, to Alice: here we are, defying gravity and waiting for whiskey, I think it's dismaying and marvelous at the same time. She didn't reply, only glanced at him and looked away. He wore old-fashioned horn rims and his stubble was white at the chin and near the ears. As if continuing a conversation with himself he said he always wondered if air travel brought him closer to God or further away. The drinks trolley returned and they were served in identical glasses with bowls of roasted peanuts and wasabi peas. She took a sip and felt the liquor burn its way past her chest into her belly, and how infinitely tolerable it was now to be alive, how pleasurable, how real at last. She said: closer, perhaps the only thing that brings us closer to God is when we're unmoored from the world. Unmoored, he said, that's the correct word for when you're thirty-five thousand feet above the ocean. What a relief it is for me to be unmoored. His accent was Middle European, or Belgian possibly, or Dutch, she wasn't to know. He kept twisting the band on his ring finger, as if to draw attention to it. And later, after the meal and the dimming of the lights, when he placed his hand on hers she did not pull away but leaned into his scent of Old Spice, the cologne her father had used his whole life. She took the man by the jaw and kissed him hungrily, as if she had not been kissed for a long time. She covered his mouth with hers. He grabbed the hand rests in fright and pulled away. Unmoored is another name for freedom, she said. What I want to know is, how free are you? Can you show me?

Ting's Element
George Town

All the way to the airport, for some thirteen or fourteen kilo-meters, she swore at the other drivers. No, no, no! You cracked in head, or what? Stupid brunettes, all learning to drive in same stupid school! They stopped at a red light and she leaned over to bang on the bonnet of a blue SUV. He felt her shaking with rage and worried she would crash the scooter. They passed a car with unknown plates and she said, country tourists worst. Then they were flying over the speed bumps, skirting a red ex-cavation in the middle of the road and the workers who stood around it doing absolutely nothing. An exhausted black dog crossed, its long tongue hanging. Construction dust filled their mouths. He held tight to the back struts of the scooter. The backpack bounced on his shoulders and his lucky boots kicked him lightly in the spine. At Sunshine Bar and Restaurant they passed a motorbike carrying a family of four, a small child in front of each parent. Only the father wore a helmet. She had stopped swearing but she was still angry and he knew it would take a long time to pass. Her anger was quick to descend and slow to lift. The scooter picked up speed. She said: When you come back? He said he did not know. She said: Why you not like sex anymore? Or you not like sex with me? Of course I like sex with you, he said. Why do you talk like that? I talk like that be-cause I not happy, she said. But why not, why aren't you happy? Behind them a truck horn sounded a long blast of cascading notes. What, he said, say again. She said: It's not like that, happy one time, sad next time. I happy and sad at same damn time. It was late evening now and the sun set rapidly through the sooty gray sky. Soon, darkness would leak over the buildings and the birds would announce the end of their daytime life. The scooter slowed to take the turn into the terminal and he smelled burning rubber mixed with diesel. The crowd at the airport was the usual mix of drunk and sober tourists in plastic visors and dirty shorts. A man without eyebrows carried a musical instrument on his shoulder, a gambus or rebab wrapped in newspaper and tied with string, the bottom resting on his backpack. She braked to a stop and he stood at the littered curb in front of the terminal, forgetting why he was there. Migrant father, she said, always told me men not good to marry. Better be single. Migrant father was clever man. He stared blankly and then he understood that she was talking about her grandfather not migrant fathers. Ting, she said, I not your wife, okay? You don't forget this. Her last words to him before she sped off on her scooter, *don't forget this*. He bought a bottle of water and took a deep, grateful sip, and remembered his friend, the Russian poet who ordered two meals on flights, one after the other, to stock up. He thought he might do the same. On the airplane he stowed his single piece of luggage and settled into his seat. The woman beside him was flying to Bangkok and then to Phnom Penh, because her divorce had finally come through. She had married in Cambodia and moved to Penang six years earlier. She ran a beer shack on Monkey Beach, rented by the month. Her husband had refused to give her a divorce when they separated, but now he wished to marry again and he was pressing her. Their daughters were twenty and twenty-two. She wanted to formalize the divorce and see her children again. She positioned the overhead lamp and her gold tooth gleamed yellow in the slim cone of light. The plane got in line for takeoff and lifted creakily into the sky. When the woman put her arm on the rest, her skin touched his and he was quickly aroused. The seat belt sign was turned off and he went in search of the lavatory. When was the last time? It was so long ago he could not remember. Now he thought of the woman's gold tooth and ejaculated into the bowl.

Tony Supersonic
Somerset

It was well known among a certain class of person that Tony only wrote poetry while flying. Correction: he only wrote poetry while flying Concorde. He'd tried other airlines but it didn't work, not in economy and not in first class. The lines he ended up with were stroppy rather than bold, helium rather than liquid hydrogen, no liftoff, no payload, no *sex*. It was equally well known among a certain class that only while flying Concorde was Tony able to achieve an erection. As the plane reached the speed of sound, surpassed and doubled it, the lines would flow from his pen and his old man's penis would swell with a young man's blood. At the peak of his sexual life he flew from London to New York and back twice a month. When he heard they were retiring the aircraft, he was filled with such dread that he paused his business, canceled long-standing plans, and hastily made new ones. He booked two seats from JFK to Heathrow and invited an old friend to join him, the actress who had first come to prominence when he was a young man, her famous cleavage and bee-stung pout on the cover and centerfold of the best men's magazines. It was October and the leaves were aflame, immolating themselves in the early sunshine, curling into yellow ash on the windshield of the BMW that took him to the airport. The driver sat impassive in his black suit and hat. Tony rode in the back as in a hearse, a dedicated passenger and scholar of the Concorde, the golden creation of the golden age of flight; and

now here he was, in attendance at the death. It was the passing
of the age of aspiration and nothing would be the same again.
As he left the limousine and approached the counter at the airport, the sense of mourning that had gathered around him lifted
slightly, and when Joan arrived, breathless, tottering, smelling
of vodka and bergamot, he was unaccountably cheered by her
tired eyes and expensive, outdated makeup. He saw her as she
had once been, the starlet with the vertiginous eyebrows and
unsmiling allure. When the great bird lifted into the sky it came
to him in waves, the thrill of velocity, the fiction of gravity, the
infinite lift, the *sex* (EXHILARATION = ACCELERATION, he wrote
in his teal Concorde-only notebook), and he loved her as he
had always loved her, without haste or understanding.

Kalita and Ming
Berlin

Her name was Kalita Sinha and they called her the Sinner, because sin was never far from her mind. The great sin is to lie
to yourself, she'd say. God wants you to do what you want to
do. Unhappiness is the true crime against nature. She was the
Sinner and they called her girlfriend the saint. Saint Ming and
Kalita Sinner, found most evenings at the Bunker, a cavernous
space where the music was drenched in reverb but bounced
off the tiles like tiny rubber pellets. Who designed this place?
Kalita said once to the barman. He smiled behind the oval
black holes of his wraparounds and said: Aliens? In the neighborhood Turkish women and children wandered from street to
avenue looking for something, while the club kids hurried to
mysterious rendezvous with dealers or parents. Everything was
true in the city of the dead. In the morning Kalita went to the

bank nearest their apartment on Muskauer Strasse, extracted a five-hundred-euro note from the small bundle of various denominations she had been given for her last performance, and presented it to the bank teller. The man looked at the note with genuine suspicion. He would not change it and he would not say why. They went to another bank, and another, and another, but no one would change the note. It's too big, said the teller at the last one, waving her fingers in the air. Too much money! So they went to Alexanderplatz, in Mitte, a neighborhood they disliked and tried to avoid, and at the first bank they changed two five-hundred-euro notes without any questions being asked. They understood that the problem was Kreutzberg, the hipster-punk-Turkish neighborhood where money was the enemy. Of course, said Kalita, recalling a friend who had started a nouvelle cuisine restaurant, and found, on the morning after the opening, that someone had defecated on the newly tiled porch. The euros, successfully changed at last, came from the most recent of Kalita's "Tie Me" series of performances. She appeared onstage in a white sari, the color of bereavement, while around her various lengths of red hemp lay pleasingly coiled. Audience members were invited to tie her up using any single length. Some tied her roughly, using the rope to blindfold and gag her. Others tied meticulous knots that were difficult to undo. Some used basic scout's knots or sailor's knots and one man resorted to the elaborate ritual of shibari, a slow process that took upward of an hour while she stood impassive, her sneaker-encased feet set apart for balance. Ming in the audience felt a thrill, because at those moments the woman she slept with and loved was unknown to her, a charismatic stranger she, too, wanted to bind. In the subterranean club that night they danced, alone, with each other, with others, until dawn trickled like milk into the room. They emerged sweaty and went to the corner park in which an airplane—a Dornier Do 17, sleekly maintained outside and in—stood on a metal stand among slate-trunked trees and deserted benches. Under the shadow of the plane's ungainly wings, Ming spread her army greatcoat, knelt, and offered her clasped hands. Kalita felt the give of the old rope as she tied neat rings from wrist to elbow and looped the ends around her fist.

Aquila
Nairobi

In the yellow building on the opposite side of the road lived the families who shouted if she and her friends got too close to their cars, which were parked all over the street. It was impossible to walk without edging past the vehicles, and then would come the shouts from the windows, stop, what you doing, get away. She thought they were mean because they were rich, until the young social worker, Mercy, said she was wrong. They were not rich; they were simply mean. She said: They struggle, too, but they don't want you to know, they want you to think they better than you. Of course they were better. Her family lived in one room. Because they were only three they were considered lucky. Some of the other hutments housed families of six and eight and ten. Her family was lucky because the tin roof had been repaired and the drain outside the front door clogged only rarely. Anyway, what was luck and who was lucky? Her family had been there longer than the families who lived in the yellow buildings. She knew this because her father told her. He had come to the city as a young man, intending to work there for a year, save money, return to the village, and marry. He had lived in the city for nineteen years, he had married and divorced, and his wife, her mother, was now wife and mother to people she had never met. When she played with her friends outside the buildings of the acting-rich, she heard the same advertisements for toothpaste and soft drinks that she and her friends heard in the hutments, because the television sets all blared the same shows and jingles. *Vicks Kingo lozenges clear the nose and clear the throat.* They had this in common with the yellow building people, Vicks advertisements. That much she knew. What else? They lived in the same city, so close they were neighbors, but the only way she or her family came into contact with them was when they went to work in their buildings as security guards and maids. Her first kiss was with a boy who worked as a driver for one of the yellow-building families. She was fourteen. In three years she would be married, a year after that she would be a mother. The night Longo kissed her for the first time they rode on his motorcycle to the airport where they parked by a fence and she allowed him to touch inside her dress. He placed her facing him on the motorcycle seat, the engine running in case they were spotted by police, and she took his penis in her hands as the planes screamed overhead. After their second child was born, another boy, she lost interest in her husband's penis; it was the source of her troubles, the daily unpaid labor, the chores she performed without help from Longo, who disappeared, sometimes for days, into his job as a driver for the tourist hotel at the center. When he reached for her she slapped his hand away. He came home one day with a look on his wide, flat face and without saying a word he took her by the hand to his motorcycle. As they neared the airport she held tight to her husband. In the dark, looking out for police, she took him deep and bit his ear. She bit hard so he would not climax first.

Ruby's Emma
Goa

Flight is happiness, the woman said, but I can't fly no more. She
patted her swollen belly. So I find happiness in other places, for
example in Emma. She held up a blue bottle of mineral water
filled with a sparkly white substance. And even if I wasn't pregnant I still wouldn't be able to fly because nobody's flying now.
The age of flight is over. You know why? Because of the so-called
sickness they all referencing. What I want to know is, what sickness? Don't believe them, honey. Do you know a single person
who's actually sick and not just talking about it? Where are the
carts trundling through the streets carrying the dead busting out
of their pustules? You know anybody like that? I don't, I mean
it. If it's so serious and so many people are dead, where are they?
Who owns the media anyway? The same people who own the
pharmaceutical companies. It's just a way of getting you to take
the vaccine and then they track you the rest of your life, that
GPS embedded in your skin. The rich get richer and the poor
stay high. You see it? Take a sip. Don't be worrying about the
Emma, it's only bad for you if you drink slow, it's only bad if you
snort it, but if you put it in a drink and sip? Like champagne,
baby. Go on, try some, you're in Goa, you owe it to yourself. He
tried some: flavorless and potent and in twenty minutes he was
chewing his teeth, watching sparks devour the air, wishing his
heart would stop beating so fast. She said: no, not enough, no
way, take some more. He took some more. When I was gainfully
employed I flew so much I carried my toys with me, and if the
customs guys saw they smiled because they'd seen so many, I
could tell, and I'd think of the hundreds of thousands of people in the sky at the same time, on hundreds of thousands of

airplanes, all those people carrying their naughty personal toys of liberation. I tried them all, but I settled down with the magic eggs. You insert them and control them with a remote and if you keep your face impassive nobody has a clue what you're up to. I always tried for a window seat. If I didn't get it, I didn't get it, wasn't going to stop me. I'd sit there vibrating. Takeoff is when I like it best, the plane revving, I'm revving, me and the machine matching beat for beat. Even now, I see one taking off? I get the old nasties. Have some more Emma, honey. She's your friend, best. Don't stop now, you're in Goa, everything simple is also complicated. There's too much at stake. Take that street-light and that one, you see? We cut down trees to make coal. Between the cut and the blood is the string. What's happening now, my hand is going, my veins taking wing, I'm going back to being numb. Her name was Ruby and these are the things she said and I'm saying them now to you.

The Making of Alice
Kuala Lumpur

She signed up for frequent-flier miles and used them immediately. She flew too often for the free miles to make a difference. In between flying for work she flew for pleasure, without telling her family or colleagues, sometimes taking a return flight within hours. Some weeks she spent more time in the air than on the ground. One morning in Lucerne she typed "best flight booking sites with metasearch" into the search window and found a message board and a community of people who flew all the time, purely for the pleasure of flight, who found the cheapest options from a seemingly limitless range and chose whichever destination took them farthest from their lives. And so she flew, for work, for pleasure, and for no reason at all, meeting others like her, men and women, in cities strange and familiar. In and out of Changi a few times a year, she came to know its butterfly park, a high forest bubble hidden among the endless walkways of the airport, and she learned the habits of the koi in the display ponds on the upper level. She took a seat on a curved bench and stared at the fish as they traversed the small space, the gorgeous blotches of orange and black, the speed at which they moved, submarining through the supreme element, breathing through their wide-open mouths, dreaming, she knew, of water; and she marveled at the easy synchronicity with which they paralleled and crisscrossed each other. On a beach in Vietnam she made the mistake of getting into the water, where she found garbage from all over the world, massed plastic detritus roiling in the foam, snaking against her feet. The water was brownish, with the rough solidity of oil, and she felt its strange and far-flung components break against her skin. What was there in those brownish or greenish wavelets that could harm her? This is what your body asks your brain when you feel no fear. From Singapore she flew to Kuala Lumpur, stayed one night in a backpackers' hostel, and booked a flight to Beijing because she found a heavily discounted ticket and had never been to China. At three in the morning she woke, thinking of the man she had met on the flight from Brisbane to Berlin, the flight that would determine the trajectory of her life. In the morning she walked to the central station and took an express train to the airport. The woman across from her held a small girl on her lap to whom she fed segments of an orange. The child stared at Alice, at her white-blond hair, and began to cry. It wasn't until Alice smiled and took her small hands in hers that she stopped, though it seemed as if the tears might return at any moment. She rested her head

against the seat and fell asleep and woke as the train came to a
halt. Outside, the night was humid and reeked of intimacy in
enclosed spaces. There was a little over an hour until her flight.
She rushed through check-in and security and was one of the
last people to board. From her seat she saw the luggage van, the
busy tarmac lit up like a small city. And then the Boeing 777
shuddered into the sky. She was sipping her second whiskey
when she felt the plane swerve in the air, dizzyingly swerve and
brake, and she thought it would stall and drop out of the sky, but
it righted itself somehow, though the sea was no longer where it
had been and then there was no land, only sea. What happened,
a man said, his voice high with fear. This is normal, right? Is this
normal? An attendant rushed down the aisle toward the cockpit, followed by another, and then the pandemonium began,
the shouting and the cries. The man beside her calmly opened
a pillbox and swallowed two white pills without water. He gave
her the box when she asked. To steady the nerves, he said. The
plane began to climb and gained altitude at a sickening speed.
The curtain at the front was pushed to the side. A family ran in
from business class clutching at each other. She felt anxiety rise
like bile to her throat. A mass of passengers joined the attend-
ants at the door to the cockpit, knocking with their fists, then
kicking. But the door was firmly shut and no answer came from
inside. Someone started to pray or moan, a low, keening noise
that rose to a shriek and abruptly died. The navigation map on
her screen buffered and went dark, then put them on a route to
Antarctica. She grabbed the man's hand and kissed him without
shame as the plane began to tilt.

Woman Eaten by Shark Drawn to Her Gold Byzantine Ring

S o I'm out way past the breakers, floating on my back, and it's a calm day, a very calm day out here with me lifting and falling in the swell of the Atlantic, and my man, bless his ravenous heart, is sunning himself somewhere on the beach and if he's opening one eye now and then when a shadow passes over his face to see if it's some bimbolette in a thong, well that's the way he is, and my sister would roll her eyes if she knew that here I am once more accepting his sometimes actionable impulse just because he pounded me good in our second-floor balcony room with the door open to the ocean and the morning sun streaming in and voices outside, he pounded me good, and when he started, he said to me *Don't make a fucking noise* and I can't help a little whimper and he says *Put a sock in it* and without missing a thump he jams a sock in my mouth, one of his socks from yesterday, still a little damp and gritty from the beach—he had it at hand for this very purpose—but I know he doesn't even get the joke—my man has no sense of irony at all—but that's okay, too, because he works me over good and all I can do is feel the way I want to feel, the way I deserve to but never know why, just that it must happen, and as I'm floating on the sea my sister is there, too, telling me I'm a disgrace to feel the way I want to feel, and she tells me that when I ask for a man simply to put me on my back or on my knees and take away my power and my will and turn it all into an act of violence against me—only enough violence that he can have me again the next time—when she tells me all this I never quite have a sufficient response, which I admit I should, I am an attorney, after all, I am a woman of the mind and of words, after all, and if my sister wants to do it delicate and with her on top and murmuring softly, then I'm not about to try to talk her out of that, but being who I am, I'm never satisfied with the words I find to answer her about what I want, and so I'm floating on the Atlantic Ocean and my legs are spread and bent a little at the knees and my arms are straight out and on the ring finger of my right hand is the gold Byzantine ring my father gave my mother long ago, long long ago, just before he ran off with his therapist, and I wear it always, and the first hit doesn't quite hurt—because of the shock of it, the abrupt thought of it, like rough sex, like a man who wants you that bad—my hand feels the grip and a letting go and then a sudden emptiness at the edge of me, at the far edge, an old emptiness, a going away, and I turn my face a little in that direction, toward my right hand, and I realize it's always been this way, I knew from the very first touch that it will mean the end of me, however long it will take I already have begun to die, have long been dying. And I know I am sad for that. Sad for me. And now I am gripped vast and tight around the hips. In the very center of me I am seized and held tight. And I am taken away with him. I am wanted so bad that it hurts. He is there with me and I am with him and we will never part.

LVIII Times a Year

The average married couple, he has read, fucks fifty-eight times a year. It is early December and, by his count, they have barely broken a baker's dozen. He knows this because every time they have sex, he enters a little corncob emoji in his laptop journal. It is less obvious than the contused eggplant.

The last corncob was more than a month ago.

He is clattering home on the A train, on the way back from a quick after-work drink with the guys. Sitting at the bar, they teased him about his wife. They read bits of her recent op-ed aloud to him. Called it the vagina monologue. Vagina diatribe. Asked him if he needed his dick valet parked. If he'd remembered to leave his balls at the coat check on the way in. Just good-natured bar banter.

It means nothing. No harm, no foul.

He will endeavor to end the drought tonight. Add another corncob to his fuselage.

He's forgotten about her book group. Eight women, mostly in their forties, armed with copies of Germaine Greer's *The Female Eunuch*.

"Evenin', ladies," he hears himself saying in a cheery bartender way as he walks through.

Some of them nod. Most ignore him.

In the kitchen he finds a platter of mini vol-au-vents. He scarfs a couple of them. She must have ordered them in. She doesn't bake. He cocks an ear to check they are still fully engaged, then pours himself a generous tumbler of Maker's Mark, throws it down in one gulp.

Thinking to curry marital favor, he places a white Williams-Sonoma dishcloth over his forearm, brings the platter into the sitting room, and processes among them offering vol-au-vents, bowing stiffly from the waist like a silver service waiter.

In his absence their conversation has turned to orgasms.

"Why is it called the G-spot anyway? What does the 'G' stand for?" a woman in cowboy boots and an embroidered Afghan waistcoat is asking.

No one can think of anything anatomical down there that begins with G.

He knows he should keep his own counsel. But as a regular *New York Times* crossword filler, he is triggered by the way the question is phrased like a clue.

"I know what it stands for," he says to an irritated silence.

"Go on, then, mansplain to us, I know you're dying to," sighs his wife.

At times like this he realizes why "marital" is an anagram of "martial."

"It stands for Gräfenberg," he says over his platter.

"Gräfenberg? What the hell is that?" she asks crossly.

"Wasn't he the guy who invented that static electricity gizmo with those little bolts of lightning?" says a woman with hennaed hair, a tiny tattoo of a female glyph—circle with attendant cross—on her left wrist, and a vermillion bindi on her forehead.

"No," he says. "You're thinking of Van de Graaff, who invented the eponymous Van de Graaff generator."

"That's an English rock band," says a woman with a blond bob and dream catcher earrings shaped like small snowshoes.

"They named their band as an homage to the generator," he insists. "And they misspelled it."

He awaits further invitation.

"Well, then," says his wife. "Dazzle us with your pub trivia."

"It's the surname of the German gynecologist who first discovered it."

"That's just *typical*," says the woman with hennaed hair. "Even our G-spot is named after a man."

"He must have been about the last male to locate it," says the woman with cowboy boots.

"Like Columbus 'finding' America in the wrong place," says the hennaed woman.

"Male hegemony, even in our vaginas," says Cowboy Boots.

"We didn't need men to 'find' our G-spots. We never 'lost' them in the first place," concludes his wife, and shoos him from the room.

When the conclave has dispersed, his wife finds him in the kitchen. From the purse of her mouth, he anticipates the approaching lash.

"You know, sometimes you can be such a . . ." She pauses, searching for the right word. "Such a . . . *dick*."

"I'm curious," he says. "How would you feel if . . ." He interrupts his own question to start the garbage disposal, knowing it will madden her. She waits for the whine of asparagus stalks and carrot tops, chicken cartilage, pear cores, avocado peel being diced and digested.

"If what?" she says.

"If I were to refer to you as a 'cunt'?"

"I meant it affectionately," she insists, leaving the room to conduct her evening ablutions. As she passes him, she pats him on the ass like a man would a woman.

The auguries are not good, but he feels he must press on tonight; it will only get more difficult as the gap grows. He must remount the horse, replant the corn. He tries to remember the last corncob. It went okay, didn't it?

He recalls her pale brown breasts above him, swelling improbably from her slim torso.

"You look magnificent," he remembers saying. "Like one of those carved wooden mermaids on the prow of a medieval sailing ship." She laughs, and her breasts tremble. She swoops down and plants a kiss on his mouth, and her stiffening nipples brush against his chest hair, making him shiver.

Quickly, before she changes her mind, he rolls onto her, slips into her, into the liquid tourniquet of her. She smiles, and in the low light her incisors, which he's never really noticed before, gleam dully like antique ivory.

It is always a race for him, the first twinges of postcoital tristesse—*la petite mort*—are already breaking through, overtaking his own orgasm. His lunges quicken and he comes. It is a race for her, too. She claws his buttocks more deeply into the clenched slop of her sex, seeking her own release before he fades.

He can't quite tell if she's come yet, so he persists, but with less energy now. He feels her hand snaking down between their sweaty bodies, her ring finger impatiently seeking the elf's hat of her clitoris. She begins thrumming herself, her eyes squinched tightly shut in the rictus of some private fantasy. He feels entirely incidental, a small boat tossed randomly on a choppy sea, a novice rider bouncing on an unbroken bronco. As she arches her back his penis plops out. He tries to reinsert himself, but his erection lacks conviction. He rolls off her and watches, deflating, as she expertly manipulates herself. Her toes splay, her face flushes, her breath comes in great ragged gulps as an orgasm pulses through her.

She lets out a sigh of contentment.

"Mmm, that was lovely. Thank you." She pats him absently on the shoulder, choosing to give him credit for her own culmination. Turning on her side she falls instantly asleep, her hands still squeezed between her smooth white thighs.

He watches her sleeping. Snuffling like a rodent softly foraging through the undergrowth of the goose-down duvet. It is the only time she seems to lower her guard. When she awakes, a wave of recognition will break over her face and fix it in the familiar mask of anxiety. Sometimes he wishes he could hang out with this carefree, sleeping, unmasked version.

He looks at her feet poking out of the duvet. Her varnished toes stacked upon one another, overlapping like piglets snuggling together. The rippled pads of her upholstered soles, the pink valleys between. So vulnerable, like the keels of two boats upturned on a beach.

———

He tries again, flicking through his erotic image bank for a time when it was good between them. The time before that, in the late summer, that went well, no? He tries to remember.

She is briskly swishing off her panties, a spray of static sparks in the gloom. Arranging herself on all fours, arching her back, and presenting herself to him like a mare.

"Coitus more ferarum?" he is murmuring. Like wild beasts, doggy-style.

He suspects that her preference for this position is so she doesn't have to look at him, can fantasize he is someone else. She waggles her buttocks impatiently. He peers through the chestnut fringe that frames her vagina. From this angle, it resembles a bearded mussel. And just like its marine version, he thinks, you should never eat one if it's closed. This one is not. It is curled open, coral lips glistening, ready. He leans forward, and she gives a start of surprise at the touch of his tongue.

When she is ready, he rears up. In the gloom he misjudges the angle, his bell end nudges her petite anal asterisk, a previously prohibited portal. Before he can punctuate it, the asterisk puckers into a period.

"Uh-oh! Wrong hole, big boy," she says firmly, and swats him away.

He remembers Stephen Fry eulogizing Christopher Hitchens at St. John the Divine. Hitchens had once said that the four most overrated things in life were, not necessarily in this order: champagne, lobster, picnics, and anal sex. Three out of four ain't bad, said Fry.

He moves down a notch and slides into her mussel. Her preference tonight is for the perfunctory and she comes quickly, efficiently. He, not so much. He feels she isn't present, just tolerating him. After a few minutes of desultory thrusting, he fakes his orgasm and disengages. She switches off her bedside light.

He sighs a ragged sigh.

"What's the matter?" she indulges.

"Oh, nothing, really," he says. "Just, you know . . ."

"Just, you know, what?" Her voice has risen, a danger sign.

"Post coitum omne animal triste est, sive gallus et mulier."

"What does it say about you," she asks, "that the only foreign language you can speak is a dead one?"

She rolls away from him. Then, grudgingly, because it is annoying her, "Oh, go on, then, tell me what it means."

"After sex, every animal is sad, except the rooster and the woman," he says.

When he gets to bed tonight, she is already there. She has sensed that sex is the salve necessary for them to reset, for them to survive. She is lying on her back, her opaque Aubade negligee already pulled to her upper thighs. She pats the mattress. He quickly sheds his clothes, kneel-walks over to her.

She cups his balls. Her palms are cold.

"Why do men's testicles hang at different heights?" she wonders aloud.

"So they don't collide with one another," he says.

"Why not be internal, like ovaries? They make much more sense. How odd to hang outside, so vulnerable." As she speaks she squeezes his balls, tighter and tighter, until he skitters past pleasure into pain. He gasps. She looks at him, unblinking, enjoying her power, enjoying his fear.

She unhands him and he quickly assumes the missionary

position, face-to-face. She must have been touching herself or used lubricant, as he easily penetrates her, a sword sheathing smoothly into a scabbard. Her eyes squinch shut in concentration. He thrusts slowly at first, bearing his weight on his arms, and she makes an appreciative little yipping sound each time he bottoms out in her. He imagines he can feel the mouth of her womb, pouting, sucking, bestowing little kisses, willing him to spurt his seed into her.

He speeds up, until he is jackhammering away. His face reddens, his panting quickens. She is frowning now. He has lost her, it has become somehow mechanical, metronomic, they are no longer in sync. His mind wanders. Her eyes flicker open just as he rotates one wrist slightly, casts a surreptitious look at his Apple watch. But not quite surreptitious enough.

"Why . . . are you . . . looking at . . . your watch?" she asks, between his thrusts. "Are you . . . late for an . . . appoint . . . ment?"

"No," he says, out of breath.

"Are you timing us?"

He shakes his head, continues thrusting.

"Well, what, then?"

He stops his thrusting, lets his body down upon hers.

She exhales at the burden of him.

He knows she will not be deflected now, implacable in her pursuit of radical transparency. So he falls back on Orwell's martial advice, that the quickest way to end a war is to lose it.

"I'm . . . I'm just seeing if my pulse rate is over 140 bpm," he admits.

A look of concern crosses her face, she half rises, onto her elbows. "Are you scared of having a heart attack?"

"God no," he scoffs, hurt at the idea that she would think him a carnal coronary risk. "I was just seeing if I could get up to aerobic level, you know, for interval training, I need to stay above 140 bpm for five minutes."

There is a pause, the burning of a fuse, as she absorbs the full implication of what he's saying.

She arches her back to unsheathe him. Bringing her knees up in one fluid movement, she places her red-toenailed feet against his chest and, without warning, pushes with all the strength of her SoulCycled, barre-classed haunches, launching him clear off the bed. Overshooting the area rug, he lands heavily on the parquet floor.

"I'm not your fucking gym!" she yells.

He lies there, braided in a twist of sweaty sheet, looking up at her. She is standing on the bed now, looming over him, her mermaid prow breasts heaving in anger. He gives her a lopsided, embarrassed half grin.

"Per angusta ad augusta," he says, just too low for her to hear.

Hard at Play

On foot
I had to cross the solar system
before I found the first thread of my red dress.
—EDITH SÖDERGRAN

Seduction is a high-cortisol process for someone like you: a person to whom nobody has ever really said yes. You presume that somebody must have at some point, probably when you were a dear little boy with harmless requests, but if they did, you don't remember. You don't have any memories of being a dear little boy with harmless requests either.

Let's not mope. Think whose son you are. You may have been loved and trained and raised from afar, but you still know how to strip information of emotion before filing it all away. Facts torn from other facts fester if their skins are left on; microorganisms flock to feed at the ripped edges, and after that it's not long before these things you've half learned hold power over you. None of that here. You'd better put your thinking cap on, blackmailer's son, and work out how this happened.

Betty's packing for her flight. Tomorrow she'll be going to her love. But that's tomorrow. There's still time to find out what you mean to her; with any luck it might not be necessary to ask her.

So, a glossary. Of signs, influencing factors, events. For future reference. You loathe the thought of anything like this happening with anyone else ever again. Which is a bad sign, of course. A sign that the limit of this coupling is beyond you.

Awkward landlord. On paper your status is comfortable. You've got the best understanding of social etiquette that money can buy. You rarely forget a name or face, always remember admirable or endearing facts about your interlocutors and never mention the rest. You have a dancer's poise and posture and a pleasant singing and speaking voice.

And yet everything you've acquired, everything you've been offered, has come to you reluctantly, at times even coated with disgust. Nobody knows you are the son of blackmailers. You were their most unassailably concealed weakness—nobody who knew anything about your people ever learned anything about you, and vice versa. But this is how the world has received you all the same, as someone reared on nasty secrets. You'd grown accustomed to avoiding physical touch and the other person's split-second recoil.

You curated your living situation so you were surrounded by (mostly) respectful strangers as soon as you had the means to do so. Your townhouse amid the throbbing lanes of Lan Kwai Fong is probably the only nonparty house for miles. Every one of your handpicked tenants is male. All of them consistently solvent, all moderate in their intoxications, and all of them respect your ban on female overnight guests. In exchange, they pay about 25 percent less rent than the going neighborhood rate.

So it's you, twenty- and thirty-something bachelors, forty-something hopeless cases like you, couples saving up to buy a place in the New Territories, and so on. The tenants mostly deal with the live-in caretaker when they have practical concerns. They don't need to talk with you; the only necessity is pushing their rent payment envelopes through the letter flap in your front door, and keeping that action timely.

You like living with your tenants. You smell the outcomes of their food preparation, hear their music sometimes, hear them talking and singing and laughing and squabbling (sometimes crying) in the halls and on the balconies.

Ball. The Qixi Festival ball you attended one night . . . with what hopes? Well, the theme was à la Versailles, which guaranteed opulent expanses of cleavage. Also, this being a charity ball, you fancied your chances of running into a goody-goody on the lookout for a man-shaped pet cause. Or a 100 percent baddie who'd blithely command you to join her harem. Your own desire was not enough for you to live on; you were half starved for the taste of another's.

Do you remember—could you ever forget that at first it seemed the evening would go well? The corridors and staircases of that grand hotel rustled with mulberry paper garlands; magpie bridges as far as the eye could see. Tuxedoed guests strolled around with cowboy hats on, and begowned guests flashed bracelets composed of weaving shuttles. Everybody you talked to was a banker, just like you. Smiles and approving nods followed you around the room, and each time you looked at someone they smiled first. One smiled brighter than most: a woman with rich russet skin, her soft and succulent figure clad in apricot-colored silk. She showed you her empty wineglass and made a gesture of appeal, you set down your own empty glass, picked up two full ones, and made your way toward her, nodding benignly and murmuring "excuse me" as you went, and she watched you come to her rescue, you, only you (she waved away other glass-bearing hands, gave no ear to solicitous murmurs from the group around her).

Yet something changed. No matter how carefully you sift your impressions, you can't pinpoint the moment your court-ship became unwelcome. All you know is that by the time you were about five paces away from this Vision in Apricot, her smile had grown fixed. Just a smidgeon too wide to be genu-ine. That was no catastrophe; maybe she was shortsighted and had mistaken you for someone she knew. Maybe she'd liked the look of you until you came into focus. People are allowed to change their minds. Still, you allowed malice to lead you a little, and you brushed your hand against hers as you passed her the wineglass she'd been waiting for. She didn't quite shudder—it was more as if every vivid shade in her dulled—and she gamely pursued conversation, drinking deeply from the wineglass as she welded scraps of small talk together, drinking more and more, absentmindedly wiping her mouth with the back of her hand each time you glanced at her lips. After a while you stopped answering her, only gazed and gazed. Eventually her voice died away to a hoarse whisper, the music started, and you asked her to dance. She closed her eyes. For a moment you thought she would finally refuse you, but she only put her hand in yours, with a meekness that confounded you. You led her away, to learn what it's like to drag a taut form around a ballroom floor in triple time. She was so scared. You couldn't understand it. It would have been the easiest thing in the world for her to get rid of you—she had only to *say so*—but she would not or could not. Her face crumpled up as you leaned even closer to whisper compliments and pleasantries to her. Tears flowed from her tightly closed eyes. When the spectacle of this began to appall you and you told her you were going home, she asked, through clenched teeth: "Do I have to—do you want me to go with you?"

Under narrow observation from all directions, what could you do but make profuse apologies, assure her that you'd do your best never to appear before her again, and then make yourself scarce?

Crossing. You were waiting for the green man, friend of careful pedestrians at Queen's Road Central, nonentity to the mass of jaywalkers streaming past. Your hooded jacket wasn't doing much for you. Raindrops tickled your eyelids, mouth, and nose. Because of this you didn't really see what happened, it was so fast. A lanky form in a padded jacket stood a few feet away, pointing at you—no, pointing something at you. Your fellow pedestrians saw more clearly than you did, and scrambled to get away. The pointing person seemed to briefly wag their chin at you—*Oh, it's you—hi*—before shooting the nearest person to the right and to the left of you, whirling around, and running in the other direction. You learned a little later that a few blocks away this person stopped running in order to shoot and kill himself.

No note, no shouting of a motto or creed, apparently the shooter was a junior petroleum executive. Unmarried, no romantic attachments, childless. He'd been feeling unsafe for some months. He'd mentioned that to a few friends and colleagues, that he didn't feel safe, but wouldn't go into detail: "It's okay. The less you know, the better. Trust me, I'm protecting you."

Other eyewitnesses mentioned the nod the pedestrian-crossing shooter gave you. Some of them saw you nod back, a few of them saw you shake your head at him as if refusing his fellowship, one heard you say something they didn't catch. Why did the shooter nod at you? Why did you return his nod? (*If*

that's what you did . . . the trouble with the conflicting eyewit-
ness accounts of your behavior is that every version strikes you
as equally plausible.) Why had the other man and woman been
shot and not you? You didn't know what to say. You only asked
how they were doing, the man who'd been directly to the left
of you and the woman who'd been directly to the right. The in-
vestigator told you they were in the hospital, but were both expected to recover. After a few moments she remarked that you
seemed unhappy about that. But that wasn't it at all. You were
nauseous with relief . . .

. . . and you weren't allowed to make any hospital visits or
send gifts there.

You were questioned extensively. Attempts were made to
examine your (nonexistent) political affiliations. Every aspect
of your background was combed over, as was every available
episode of your online history. Complaint was pointless. If you
hadn't been yourself, you'd be suspicious of you, too.

By the way: *C* is also for chapped lips. Betty's are perenni-
ally dry. The texture turns her kisses gourmet; you've savored
their raw, tender heat.

D doesn't signify.

Escalator. The worst of the shock lasted for about a year.
You stopped going to work after the shooting. You collected
rent and lived as if paralyzed in a kneeling position, your heart
rate crawling. Afraid to go out and afraid to stay at home, you
rode the Mid-Levels Escalator tens of times daily, riding uphill,
shuffling downhill, and starting all over again. You tried to sleep
standing up, shakily adjusting your hold on the handrail as you
wondered who put it into your head that you were ever a match
for this place, the nonchalance, the agility of this city as it scram-
bles up the heights of Hong Kong Island before bobsledding

back down to its depths, leapfrogging concrete spirals, turreted outcrops, and the tops of great, spreading trees so grand and old that cuckoo doves still trust them even though their branches snake out along ring roads and steel facades. This city is too much for some—too much for any who hesitate on the way across that steely tightrope between thought and incarnation. Perhaps Hong Kong was now making an example of you, dealing with you exactly as it had dealt with the pedestrian-crossing shooter. Doubtful persons both.

You fell into conversation with a monk who joined you on the escalator one morning. He was on his way back from a three-day interfaith conference.

"An interfaith conference?"

He'd conducted roundtable conversations with priests, rabbis, imams, pastors, nuns, pujaris, other monks . . .

"Ah, okay. And are you glad you went?"

The monk paused, then said yes. He'd encountered Buddha nature in abundance, and had learned many names for it. He also appeared to have some reservations he wasn't inclined to share; instead, he invited you to join him and his brothers in Tsz Shan. Just to walk on the earth and be where the mountains are. "Let's go right now," he said. Soothed by his sense of urgency, you followed him.

For the first three days out there you felt that something beautiful was happening. The life of the monastery was like a hushed beehive, each cell wholly given over to the practice of peace. When you walked the grounds, you were clothed in mist and a profusion of light where sun struck land. You saw a black kite swinging toward a mountain peak with something streaming from its beak—pork intestines from the barbecue site a few miles away? This is the only lift you know, each gratification stolen, laden with risk. Before you took sick leave from the office it was like that for you and your tenants alike—working around the clock for so many things, so many reasons. The time and space in which to play is hacked from cliff faces and sifted from seawater. You had four more days left at the monastery, but after that you could still have one more try at enjoying the life you'd grown afraid to live. You made a resolution that when you got home you were going to knock on tenants' doors at random and invite them over for dinner. You'd cook, and they'd bring the booze, stories, jokes, tips, party tricks, schemes that would either change the world or keep the neighborhood going strong.

You forgot where you were. On your fifth day at the monastery you stood behind a pillar for a while, observing a fellow guest. He was slight of frame, sharp about the shoulder blades, and his eyes were red rimmed with exhaustion. You'd seen that he didn't eat at mealtimes, and it didn't seem likely that he slept much. There was no determining the nature of the struggle this pilgrim was having with his body, whether it began in the mind or in the flesh, whether his physical destruction even had anything to do with the situation that was consuming him.

You stood behind the temple pillar and your fellow guest, apparently meditating, knelt on the courtyard floor with face upturned. As you watched, you began to see . . . something like hinges. All the lumpen, knotted places where the body had no strength at all, only the strength of separation, really. All of a sudden you became desperately afraid that this striver would be defeated right in front of you. A restless vista of green, gray, and brown swept all around the courtyard; life cried out from it, yet the very air stood aloof. You tried to keep track of this man's breaths. For what felt like a full second or two, he didn't seem to breathe at all. Then he did. And you spoke to him. Not as a fellow man: this was what the monk who overheard probably could not accept. You spoke to the man as if he had been praying, not meditating. You told him that you'd heard him, that he would have what he had asked for, but that it was time to eat now, and sleep now, so he didn't miss his answer when it came.

You were offered time to reflect, and later that day you apologized. You did so a number of times. To the monks who had offered you shelter, to the puzzled supplicant himself (who said, "But you do see, sir, that such thoughts I may have been having at that moment were not addressed . . . to you . . . ?"). You'd been watching someone die, you said, or watching their faith die. And you couldn't bear it. Even if that was what was supposed to happen, you couldn't . . .

Your apologies were accepted, but it was time to go home.

Foodpanda. That was the food delivery company your next-door-neighbor-tenant worked for. He's a long-haired white man in his early thirties. His name's Stanislav, his passport was Polish, and he told you the Foodpanda job was helping him to learn Cantonese faster than he normally would have. That and the local girls, you were sure. He emitted what you could only describe as hetero boyfriend vibes. A born boyfriend. Quite different from a born husband, since the born boyfriend doesn't tend to have the same girlfriend every day. You'd kept an eye on Stan for a year and a half, but there was no funny business with him when it came to the house rules. You saw the women—a white woman, a Japanese-looking woman, a possibly Turkish woman, a black woman, a woman of miraculously mixed ethnicities—you saw woman after woman kiss Stan good night outside your house or meet him in the morning, but aside from that you'd only see him sailing in and out of the building with his pink and silver uniform on. He didn't even bring friends back to his flat. When exactly did you last see Foodpanda guy—what date, what time? Did he hint at what he was planning? He might have. But you were miles away. He must have seen that and taken advantage; CCTV footage reveals that he moved out and helped Betty move in a full two weeks before your five-day temple visit; it was all done while you were riding the Mid-Levels Escalator on a muggy Monday morning. And going by the fact that Betty didn't make her presence known during those two weeks, both she and Stan were very much aware that you wouldn't like this little replacement game.

The camera footage shows the couple wheeling a quartet of bar carts into your building's lift, then out of the lift and along the sixth-floor corridor. There are Betty's possessions, crammed into canvas totes and tumbled along the cart shelves.

Stan's was the first door you knocked on when you got home from the monastery: *Let's find out what Foodpanda guy thinks I should put on my dinner party menu.* You hadn't yet seen the footage, so you blinked like a fool when Betty answered the door. (She only did so after a long time, and probably only because her phone started ringing shortly after you'd begun the third round of knocking.)

She was a Han woman in her midthirties. You're five feet eleven inches tall, and the top of this woman's head reached your shoulders. Her hair was smoothed up into a ponytail and her gaze was both irresistible and deeply uninviting; looking into her eyes was like getting boiled alive in a cauldron of dark chocolate fondue. She knew she probably wouldn't like what you had to say to her, but she intended to make you weigh your words first. This preemptive strike of hers was stirring, but there was more. She was in girlfriend attire: a red and white FC Slavia

T-shirt that clung and billowed its way to the exact midpoint of her bare and shapely thighs.

She folded her arms and didn't introduce herself, so you lit a cigarette and asked who she was while taking a close and ostentatious look at her ungroomed eyebrows.

She scratched her knee. "I'm Elizabeth. Never Liz or Lizzie— usually Betty. As in, *she's a total Betty.*"

"Surname?"

She told you, and you wrote it down.

"Occupation?"

"I work at an auction house. Of sorts."

You wrote that down, then underlined *Of sorts.*

"Stan's my boyfriend," she told you. "But he had to . . . go."

"Where?"

"I'm not sure."

"He's left the country?"

"That's right."

"Will he be back?"

"About that . . . I'm going to go where he is. He needs to get settled first, and I need to save up, so I'll just take over his lease for a couple of months. Three at the most—"

"I'm afraid that won't do at all. You can't live here. I personally vet all tenant applications, for the safety of everyone in this building. Your boyfriend must have told you that."

"He did. But—"

But what? *But I'm pretty?* Behind her, the ceiling fan hiccupped. You'd been meaning to have it fixed for months. You'd send the caretaker in once this Betty was gone.

"No exceptions," you said. "You're moving out tomorrow."

She gave you a dirty look, said, "Okay," and closed the door.

At the end of your journey around your building issuing

dinner party invitations to whoever answered their door, you
returned to your own flat, opened your laptop, and tried to find
out a bit about Betty. You didn't discover much. You found a
social media page she didn't seem to have posted on for about
five years. She was a bartender back then. Many of the flirta-
tious posts from male admirers support your twin theories that
alpha males completely ignore their competition and don't
give a shit about originality: *all I want is a drink that tastes just
like you. When are you going to give me that?* In response, Betty
had posted emojis of clocks and bundles of cash flying away on
angel wings.

Under your breath, you told yourself you really didn't like
that Betty. You didn't like the ominously uncoquettish tilt of
her head when she looked up at someone taller than her, the
way she seemed to stare across widths and breadths, taking precise measure of what she saw. Doubtless Betty would stare at a
naked man like that. Unless it was her Foodpanda, of course.
You can always tell when she's talking to Stan on the phone. It's
not a change in the tone or the pitch of her voice; it's her un-
guardedness, a delighted casting off of composure. Betty's composure, a cloak she wears with such grace that you rarely think
how heavy it must be.

(You've observed and accepted that this glossary of yours
has now come entirely undone.)

Three days after you told her to move out, Betty joined the
guests at your dinner party.

"I brought egg tarts," she announced, holding the paper box
aloft. "And wine." Your guests gaped, and so did you.

"So you didn't move out?" It was the closest you'd come to
shouting in years.

She shrugged. "Move out . . . ?"

"I told you it's not possible for you to live here."

"You did, but you were smiling a little bit. This part lifted up, you see"—she put the box down and lightly placed a fingertip at the corner of your mouth, to remind you how you smiled—"so I thought you were joking."

A couple of your other tenants began murmuring that they thought eviction notices had to be put in writing. They were not taking sides, they said, but surely you could understand their taking an interest in their rights.

"Mr. Landlord," she said. "I'm not asking a lot. Stan was a good tenant, right? Never caused any trouble? Just think of me as Stan. I can provide references as good as his . . . just wait until tomorrow."

She took a harmonica out of her pocket and started playing "Alouette, Gentille Alouette," slapping her knee each time she reached the chorus. You set about freezing her to the marrow with your stare. To no avail.

"Stanislav can't play the harmonica!" said Ground Floor Tim. Betty was a hit. And the thing is . . . she's on the level. Her glowing references are genuine, she manages her personal debt sensibly. She has a bit of a civil disobedience record; not untypical among thinking types. Your other tenants didn't need background checks before accepting Betty; she was immediately made part of the core squad whose doors were perpetually knocked on when they were at home. *Betty, do you reckon this is a deal or a scam? Betty, can you value this jewelry? Betty, you practiced our TikTok dance, right? I mean, you really really did this time? Or am I a fool for trusting you again?*

By the time a month had passed, you'd taken to spending a sliver of each evening—an hour, forty-five minutes—drinking a beer at Betty's (well, Stan's) kitchen table.

Betty swept rings and earrings with the searching eye behind her jeweler's loupe as you told her all about the Qixi ball
you attended, the pedestrian-crossing shooter, and your great
error at the monastery. Betty's a chin-in-hand listener, but a
couple of times, keeping her eyes on the pieces she was valuing,
she'd put out a hand and—she'd almost touch you. Her fingers
gliding just above yours, Betty told you that she, too, was somehow unable to move simply and gently among people. She'd
been a class clown. Not necessarily a cruel one, but certainly the
kind who made it clear that nobody was exempt from her jibes.
From there she'd moved on to making a living by prevailing on
people to buy things they didn't actually want. Anything from
watches to houses. When she ran out of nerve for that, she made
a blunt instrument of her libido for a while, hoping to stun her
acquisitiveness into silence. She knew that there were things she
wanted. She never dared to ask for any of them; something told
her that they were impossibilities. Unspeakable things. Or (far
worse) unimaginable things . . . ? Never mind—at least she had
a hobby to dedicate herself to: passport fucking. There was no
hint of suggestiveness in the way Betty described this hobby to
you; the impulse that sparked it is dead and buried. But not so
long ago, when she was still The Total Betty whose milkshake
brought all the boys to the yard, she would've made use of that
status to ask for your ID before serving you a drink. And if you'd
had the passport Betty was looking for that night, she'd have left
the bar with you once her shift was over.

Betty had set herself a challenge, and made meticulous
record of her progress. The plan was to bed three citizens of
each of the world's nations, thereby giving each passport a fair
chance of redeeming or otherwise amending the carnal charac-
teristics she'd go on to associate it with. Each night the bar Betty

worked at became a global blizzard of good-time girls and boys, so without this system of hers she could've ended up caught in all manner of traps set by conscious and unconscious biases. And then, halfway through her passport challenge, along came Stanislav.

"Really . . . so . . . Polish passport for the definitive win?"

"No. Stan for the definitive win. Body and soul."

"Of course. But if the win had been based on overall performance data?"

Betty laughed. "You seriously want to know?"

"I'm dying to know."

"You won't throw a tantrum?"

"No way."

"Taiwan."

"Taiwan . . ." So that's what a jealous rage felt like; aggressive tickling about the ribs, intensified by her response: "Yeah, no question."

"And Hong Kong? Where does your home territory rank, Betty?"

She waved that one off, saying that the whole thing was so subjective you'd need to conduct your own inquiries.

You didn't listen to Betty anywhere near as well as you could have. You heard her through a tingling curtain of static, the line drawn between your body and hers. (She may have felt this before you did; that would explain her caution when the two of you were alone together.) You looked at the framed photo of Stan she's put on one of the sitting room bookshelves. It looks like a full-length photo that's been cropped into a head-to-shoulder-length portrait. Stan appears to be wearing a white lab coat. There are glimmerings of grassy meadow behind him, he's twirling a daisy between his teeth, and the wind is busy styling his hair after its own devices. You can tell it was Betty who took the photo; his crinkle-nosed smile is shy (what is she seeing right now?) and proud (she thinks I'm worth taking a photo of!).

As you eyed the photo, your thoughts kept going along the lines of *If this woman's affections, attentions, melting, yelping, shuddering pleasures can't be mine outright, can't I at least borrow . . . ? Just for a few weeks. She'll only be here for a few more weeks. Days, even.*

Not content with background checks, wanting to learn something about Betty that would in some way repulse you, you've tracked her movements, from home to work (not an "auction house," as she'd claimed, but more of a five-star hostess bar situation) to various Western Union counters. She sends money to her Foodpanda every week. You haven't bothered making inquiries into Stan's issues. Betty's been treating Stan's odyssey as a sensitive matter, and it's all too easy to ask the wrong people about those, thereby turning someone else's problems into your own.

After about a month and a half as Betty's awkward landlord, talking became too much of a strain. You and Betty began kissing. You couldn't keep from passing your hand around her waist and drawing her to you. She couldn't keep her lips from yours. But you stopped. Even as she was kissing you she pressed her fists into your chest and you stopped. Both of you. You left her flat. A minute later you lost your head all over again and tried to go back to her. She wouldn't let you in.

Four long days passed before she'd speak to you again, then another three days until she'd see you. You . . . touched yourself differently. You'd never say this aloud, or write this anywhere but here, but this is what's happened: the woman in love has entered you, and is in your fingers. Lingering strokes and whirl-wind tugs—this is how Betty takes you, with eagerness and greed. You pant, cry out, and come like a fountain spurt.

When you were with her again she was in your arms again, the kisses deeper than before. You both laughed at this torment you'd invented together. You laughed mouth to mouth. Well, Betty chuckled. You sniggered. Your tongues touched. You drew back, held her face in your hands. There was still no end to the need; nipping at your fingers, Betty straddled you and stirred her hips so that you breathed her name. But there was the framed photograph of Stan, good old Stan, looking on. You couldn't have cared less, but she stopped.

You should probably have asked her to meet you at your flat. But perhaps she wouldn't have agreed to that.

Betty made you both some coffee.

"You never asked me about my work at the auction house," she said.

Hostess bar, you thought, but aloud you said: "Let's see . . . what script is this? *Good Girlfriend, Guilty Conscience*? Are you about to suggest introducing me to a nice colleague of yours?"

She wasn't. Instead, she told you what the auction house was, and how it worked. Her clients began to arrive at around 7 p.m., usually the soonest they could get away from work. She mixed them their favorite cocktails, offered hand and foot massages, talked about anything and everything they felt like talking about, helped them unwind so they'd open with generous bids once the bidding began. There were eight auctions per night; the winning bidders retired to one of the auction house guest rooms with the man of their choice and usually didn't reappear until breakfast time. According to Betty, there are really no words for the morning radiance of the winning bidders. Betty was sure that orgasms contributed to that glow. But so did the very act of making yourself a present of a single night, wrapping hours of darkness in starry gauze . . . Could an assault on time get any more sumptuous than that?

You picture Betty stomping her way to the MTR to start her work commute, the shoe bag that holds her high heels bulging the leather of her backpack. How is she dressed? Lots of gray, punctuated with pink. An inverse of the Foodpanda uniform, in a way, though the shades of gray and pink differ in brightness and depth.

What about the men, the ones you'd seen leaving and entering her place of work, smoking cigarettes outside? Once you even saw one of these male colleagues of Betty's (a tall, lean bespectacled black guy) juggling five Rolex boxes as if they were rubber balls, laughing his head off all the while. If only you had access to before-and-after profiles for each of these men. Now it's not possible to know whether it was that rugged ease of these men that attracted bids for a night with them, or whether they became like that after the bids proved how much they were wanted. For some reason you feel . . . required to ask Betty if Stan is someone she knows from her auction house, if hers was the winning bid for him. But you don't actually want to ask that, and manage to dismiss the question. *So you two are reincarnations of Roxelana and Suleiman the Magnificent, turning one night into a lifetime of love? Good for you; now fuck off.*

Betty seemed to be making you a job offer, and you weren't sure if you felt flattered or dejected. But that wasn't her point. She wasn't inviting you to soothe your soul by putting yourself up for auction for the night. She was telling you that you would be wanted now, that the sky was really the limit for you in terms of female interest . . . you could quite effortlessly surpass Stan's standards. One of the first things Betty had learned from her auction house work was that the first bid was usually a hesitant one. It wasn't that the bidder was ashamed of his or her desire; it was the self-exposure that was nerve-racking. *I want*, while the desired and desirable *you* emerge as that which a palate exists for. After the first bid opened the arena, however, the others followed, thick, fast, and increasingly ardent. You didn't need to go to the auction house to experience this effect—you only had to go across the street to a bar and let nature take its course. What Betty was telling you was that now that one woman wanted, very badly, to fuck you, other women would quite naturally put in their bids, too.

It was three in the morning. You went back to your flat and texted a few tenants to see who was awake, willing and able to go for a drink without jeopardizing their work the next day. Awkward but responsible landlord. Forty-five minutes later, you, Ground Floor Tim, and Third Floor Tim were sat at the bar of a speakeasy, staring at each other openmouthed as three graduate students of the would-normally-never-look-at-you-twice variety frisked around your barstool and repeatedly offered to buy you a drink before taking turns to declare *I saw you first*.

You've slept with Betty, yet you haven't slept with Betty. She can truthfully tell her fucking Foodpanda that you and she were never lovers. But these weeks and weeks of escapades and idylls have all been with proxies of Betty. A callous mode of interaction with real, live people, but no less callous, perhaps, than the terms of each woman's willingness. Each time it's only for the night, and only for one night. And each time it begins with, "Let me buy you . . ."

Meals, concert tickets, a Central Star Ferry ride (such thoroughly indecent fun on the top deck), a bespoke suit you

warned its buyer not to tear . . . What's offered is less important than the crystal clarity of being bought for the night. Every
full-throated ripple, every sweat-slicked meeting and parting of
skin, each dab of the tongue and thundering of the heart—all
these were things you wanted (want? have?) not with these
proxies, but with Betty herself, who comes again with you later
when you tell her, step by step, how the latest bids were placed,
and how were they fulfilled.

First Lust

*A*lthough *I have a small penis* and entered puberty at the ordinary time, nevertheless I was stung from a very young age by sexual desire—a constant, nagging lust or "hankering" as nineteenth-century translations of Buddhist texts call the general source of our attachment to the world, the longing that ties us to the wheel of endless rebirth, which Buddhists fear and the rest of us want.

I must have been in fifth grade and hence ten or eleven when I developed a maniacal attachment to Cam. He lived with his mother in a big wooden house in Evanston, Illinois. When you look at old movies of the late 1940s and early 1950s, the houses were dowdy—warrens of many underfurnished rooms and their rugs of dusty, pale blue wool, not fitting wall to wall (that came later), but stranded with a wide border of parquet on all four sides. Easy chairs with tilted lamps beside them. Everything in witless shades of brown. A huge and inefficient kitchen with shiny counters under narrow windows. Nothing remarkable, nothing stylish, a freestanding radio like an upended child's coffin.

Cam's mother was never around in the afternoons and mine

didn't get home from work till 6:30. From 3:30 to 6 we were alone in that big, boxy house, always overheated. Cam would go to the icebox and pour himself a glass of orange juice made from frozen concentrate, just as we made it in my house. I was intensely aware of him as he moved about and peeled off his sweater and threw it on the couch, covered with scratchy wool faded by the sunlight to a ghostly teal. He was small and very pale, his face as pretty as a girl's but too big for his body and made bigger by his carefully oiled and combed hair, a gleaming, immobile structure weighing him down like Hungary's hereditary crown. He had a small black mole on his neck and another one on his right cheek, which gave him the look of an eighteenth-century woman. His eyes should've been sapphire blue, but they were small and black. His lips should've been rosy but they were bloodless, almost blue, but wet.

We would wrestle for hours, not out of hostility or competitiveness, but because it felt good, to rub our crotches into each other or to have my biceps pinned down by his knees and to inhale the odor of his piss-stained denim jeans. I didn't think Cam's mother washed his jeans more than once a month, and after weeks of wear they had a lovely history, a funk, that you would have noticed only if you had your nose buried in his crotch, as I did. We were young, clueless boys; we didn't wear deodorant or shower very often, and we wiped only in the morning in the most cursory way, but we didn't smell. Sometimes our breath smelled of tuna or peanut butter or Tootsie Rolls.

But Cam's glands were pine knots waiting to be lit, and even now quietly dripping oil. His arms and legs were small and round and compact like greaves; if you cut them in half, they would be round at every point. His face was as charged with

color as the heart of the peony, as florid as his lips were pale.
Even in the strongest sunlight his face betrayed no fuzz no matter how soft or pale. It was as smooth and matte as talc. His voice
hadn't changed from its high, silver, Magnificat clarity. He was
strong and fearless, and though much smaller than I, he usually
won in wrestling. I should say "wrestling," since I was obviously
playing another sort of sport, a zero-sum game that meant we
were always in each other's arms, breathing hard, turning and
twisting. It was a game I aimed to lose and that I contested only
to keep it going, pinned down, a denim crotch in my face. We
long for something, a cock, and then fetishize what guards and
disguises that thing, blue jeans and their metal grommets.

Maybe a year later—or could it have been six months?
Youth has only two dates, the beginning of school and the
end—I invited Cam to spend the night. I suspect such an invitation itself seemed pretty weird. As casual sounding as I could
be, I said, "Come over for a pajama party. My mom will make us
dinner, we'll watch some TV (still a novelty then), and you can
stay over and we'll drive you back in the morning."

I wonder now how it was all arranged. My mother was always filled with inchoate longings—for my father to remarry
her; for the bruiser on the next barstool to buy her another high-
ball; for Mr. Preston, the rich guy she'd met on the plane and
who'd invited her to his mansion in Santa Barbara, to ask her
back for another "romantic" (i.e., sexual) weekend—so maybe
she recognized in me my equally insistent and incoherent desires. She didn't approve of homosexuality—who could have in
1951?—but desire, if it remained undiagnosed, unnamed, pure
desire, all-consuming desire was something that spoke to her, to
her innermost heart. She went along with my desire, especially
since I'd known Cam since second grade, four whole years ago.

Our friendship was consecrated by time. Besides, I didn't seem to have many friends, or any! My mother didn't want to discourage my burgeoning amicability. Even at that age I agreed with William Blake that it was better to strangle an infant in its crib than nurse an unacted desire.

Once Cam and I had eaten the bland pork cutlets and brussels sprouts my mother prepared, along with tall glasses of milk and Oreos for dessert, we watched *Your Hit Parade* on TV, in which nearly the same hit songs recycled week after week, each time produced with a new theme, new sets, and new dances, so one week Rosemary Clooney's "If I Knew You Were Comin', I'd've Baked a Cake" was a solo dancer in a house-dress and an apron bending before an oven, and the next was a mustache-twirling French chef in a white toque unboxing a tiered wedding cake to the surprise of a cavorting couple. Cam and I watched that with dulled fascination as I kept stealing sidelong glances at his childlike body. Soon it would be unwrapped like a mysterious Christmas present.

In my room I had twin beds that formed an L in one corner and wooden chairs and a knotty pine desk and burlap curtains and brown corduroy bedspreads, the oblong of the upper mattress outlined in brown piping.

We each stripped down to our underpants (I studied his crotch—no tenting) and climbed into bed. I said, "Good night," and he mumbled something and I turned off the bedside lamp. The room was electric with the sort of suspense the family feels before a verdict.

I couldn't sleep. As my eyes became adjusted to the dark, I could make out the outlines of Cam's pale face, orchid white, crowned by black hair. Was he awake? Was that the sound of his eyelids batting against the pillow?

Finally I couldn't stand it anymore. I leapt out of bed without a plan, approached his bed, retreated, said hoarsely, "You awake?"

And he peeped, "Yes."

"Can I sit on your bed and talk a minute?"

"Sure." He sounded dubious and drew the word out experimentally.

I sat down and could feel the presence of his leg through the covers, but he wasn't moving it; it was a stone. But I was at the age (and would be for many years) when all my desires felt, necessarily, reciprocated, as though the high wattage of my longing sparked an equal interest in the object of that desire.

Was he lying there with a hard-on as rigid as mine? Was he frustrated by his own shyness and wondering why it was taking me so long to make the first move? Was he aching to be jacked off?

Propelled by my fantasy of reciprocal desire, I reached under the covers and felt his penis. He turned on the light, threw off the covers, wriggled out of his underwear. He hadn't gone through puberty yet! I felt as if I'd dipped into the chalice and there was no blood turning into wine.

Find Me

O n the platform at Union Station, snow embellished the encroaching dark with shifting skeins of swirling white. Eloise could feel the chill through the silk stockings on her calves, but her ankles were protected by sheepskin-lined boots and the rest of her by a thick wool coat with a black fox shawl collar and cuffs. A matching fur hat pressed down over her loose black curls, so her pale face and light eyes appeared suspended in a mantle of darkness.

She was twenty-five years old, already a widow after four years of marriage to a man who had never given her cause to feel strongly one way or another about anything. Twice during this marriage, her husband's cousin, a successful rancher "out west," had visited the couple. Henry Pickles was a plainspoken, plain-featured, socially awkward, largely humorless fellow, but he had won Eloise with his frank admiration of her and envy of her husband. Henry had waited exactly one year from the day his unfortunate cousin succumbed to a virulent influenza before penning a short, sincere, and persuasive message, asking Eloise to be his wife.

She had no other prospects and was eager to leave the

claustrophobic, frigid world of the upstate New York town where she had passed a quiet and unremarkable life. Henry had included a photograph of her new home, an ocher stucco ranch house with a deep porch, a tiled roof flanked by two large mystery trees, and a truck parked to one side. *A rancher's wife*, she thought. She might learn to ride a horse.

Henry Pickles, her family agreed, had done well for himself, and Eloise's hope that her new husband might be more attentive to her feelings than his cousin was strengthened when he sent her a first-class ticket to Reno. She would have a room and bath to herself for three long days and nights, while the train steamed steadily through the Northeast, along the Great Lakes, across the Central Plains, and into the western states, arriving at last in an unknown land called Nevada. Even the word felt like a warm breeze to her.

As she bustled along the platform, she spotted the porter who had taken her bags earlier waving her to a carriage with the word "First" stenciled in gold on the door. She climbed the three steps to the vestibule and stepped into a narrow, carpeted hall lined with tall windows on one side and shiny wine-red door panels on the other, each marked discreetly with a gold leaf number. Hers was number 3.

Hesitantly, she opened the door. It was like entering a charming, luxurious parlor. The walls were paneled mahogany. Above the dentil molding, the vaulted ceiling, lacquered a creamy viridian green, gave an unexpected impression of height. The thick carpet, in the Aubusson style with a pattern of blousy roses on a background of pale blue and cream, softened the color scheme. Two dark green, tufted leather couches faced each other on either side of a tall window shadowed by heavy damask drapes and a half-pulled shade of gray brocaded silk. A table had been deployed beneath the window and Eloise's vanity case placed upon it. On the opposite wall, her large case and hatbox were stowed alongside a low built-in desk with a chair drawn up beneath it and a framed mirror above. Beyond this, a smoked-glass door opened into another space. Eloise peeked past it to find a bright bathroom with every convenience: a porcelain basin with a handheld shower attached and a brass drain in the floor, a toilet discreetly hidden beneath a mahogany seat, and a brass rack stacked with neatly folded towels. "They've thought of everything," she said.

After a solitary meal in the half-empty dining car, Eloise returned to her compartment to find it transformed into a spacious boudoir. The couches had become a comfortable bed with a leather headboard, made up neatly with starched linen sheets, and piled with pillows in matching cases. A mauve velvet duvet lay folded at the foot. A matching chenille throw hung over the back of the desk chair. On the desk, an artfully arranged wooden tray held two glasses, a carafe of water, and a square lacquered box of chocolate truffles. Eloise had drunk half a bottle of wine with her trout dinner, and the effects of the alcohol combined with the constant rocking of the train as it hurtled through the night caused her to stagger slightly when she pulled the compartment door closed behind her. She turned the latch and sat down hard on the mattress. The room was warm, perhaps too warm. She tugged off her boots, leaving them where they fell. Then she pulled at her collar and opened the front of her travel suit. She felt deliciously free. The shade had been drawn. She leaned back, raising it halfway, but all she could see was her own reflection in the glass. This filled her with a secretive and sensuous pleasure. She pulled her jacket off, unbuttoned the blouse underneath, and without thinking, stood up, took two steps across the carpet, and helped herself to one of the chocolates. It collapsed against the roof of her mouth, releasing a rich, sweet cream that spread evenly across her tongue. "So good," she said softly. She took her dressing gown from the closet and laid it on the bed. It was a simple garment of yellow silk, the color of the wine she had drunk at dinner. Languidly she undressed, hanging her skirt and blouse next to her coat, folding her slip, bra, underpants, and stockings, and stowing them away.

Then she was naked and alone, a condition that made her feel both vulnerable and daring. As she turned to take up the gown, she caught her reflection in the mirror above the desk.

She was not particularly vain, but over the years of her marriage, the occasional long look at herself in the cheval glass had provoked in her the same wistful thought: what a waste! She was young and strong; her body glowed with health, yet if she chanced to appear even without her bra before her husband, he was quick to avert his eyes. On her marriage night, dressed in a soft crepe gown, she had slid modestly beneath the sheets, and her husband, after turning off the lights, had joined her, pushing down his pajama bottoms and raising the gown carefully to her waist. Cautiously his hands moved over her, as if he feared to encounter a sharp object, settling at the base of her spine.

Later he would discover the delights of waking to find her back pressed against him. Slipping his erect penis into her, he could arrive at his strangled orgasm before she was even fully awake. Satisfied, leaving her sticky and drowsy, he left the bed, went downstairs to the kitchen, and returned a few minutes later with a tray bearing a pot of fresh-brewed tea and a flowered cup. This he set on the nightstand, offering her a peck on the cheek and a cheery "Good morning" before going off to his own ablutions. Married lovemaking, she concluded, was a routine like any other. It wasn't unpleasant, and occasionally she waked enough to experience some mild pleasure in it. Like a dog who takes a reward where she can find it, Eloise began each morning looking forward to that delicious cup of tea.

Now she pulled the dressing gown over her shoulders, leaving it open at the front, still tantalized by the sensation of being alone in a luxurious chamber, hurtling through the night to a future she could scarcely imagine. Taking up the Willa Cather novel she had chosen for this journey, she plumped the pillows in a stack against the leather headboard and stretched out across the sheets. She read only a few pages before drowsiness overtook her, and she closed the book, turned off the light, and lay dreamily contemplating the black night pressed up against the window.

When the porter tapped at the door to announce breakfast the next morning, she woke to find herself spread out flat on the mattress with the sun streaming over her bare breasts as the train slowed to a crawl on the outskirts of Chicago.

Daylight was sobering, and the hours dragged on: breakfast, reading, lunch, reading. Through the window the frozen fields of Iowa drifted by. At each stop more passengers departed than got on. When at last the call for dinner came, Eloise felt jaded and headachy. She looked forward to the wine and the transformation of her sitting room into a boudoir. This time, she ordered the roast beef and drank a full carafe of red.

Again, tipsy and strangely excited, she returned to her compartment and stripped off her clothes. She stood at the sink, soaping her armpits and breasts, her stomach and crotch, then rubbing herself everywhere she could reach with a cool, wet washcloth, and finally rinsing herself down with the handheld shower. She pulled on her gown, unpinned her hair, and sat on the desk chair brushing it while the miles slipped away beneath her feet. A flash of light on the wall made her turn to the window. The train was passing through a town; a few cars were lined up at a crossing. Eloise crawled across the bed and knelt before the window, switching on the reading light. She opened her gown and shrugged it from her shoulders. It made her feel reckless and oddly powerful to know that some stranger waiting listlessly in his car at a crossing might look up at the bright window of the train streaking past and see her kneeling there, her bare flesh golden in the lamplight—then gone in a flash, like a dream. She sat back on her heels, carefully brushing and brushing her hair, rocking slightly with the insistent rhythm of the train, while a sensuous lethargy swarmed up from inside.

The reading light was still on when she awoke to a screech of brakes and a jolt that sent the hairbrush flying across the carpet. The train screamed and clattered to a halt. Raised voices filled the air. Through the window she could see two men with flashlights running toward the front of the train. There were popping sounds—two, then one more. Gunshots? She heard the heavy carriage door clanging open, the sound of running footsteps down the corridor, then the door at the other end, opening and whooshing closed.

She sat up, groggy and confused, hastily pulling on her dressing gown, tying the sash at her waist. Again the whoosh and whine of the carriage door, this time from the front. Foot-steps approached, not hurried. Almost hesitant. It must be the porter, she thought. She could ask him what was happening. She went to the door to open the latch, but just as her fingers turned the steel deadbolt, the panel jerked abruptly from her hand, slid halfway open, and a bear burst into the compartment, knocking her to the floor. The creature yanked the door closed and lurched across the bed. As it surged past her, she felt the cold rising from the luxuriant fur and heard more running and shouting outside the train. The bear flicked off the light, and the moonlight flooded the bed with a pearly glow. She lay flat on her back on the carpet, utterly confused. Was this a dream?

The bear turned its head, looking back at her. "I really have to thank you for not screaming," it said.

Of course, it was a man. The bear was a coat. The man had black eyes, long, straight black hair. How improved relations be-tween the sexes might be, Eloise thought, if every man began his acquaintance by thanking the woman for not screaming.

He moved to the edge of the bed, looking down at her, his brow furrowed with anxiety. "Are you hurt?" he asked. "I didn't mean to be rough, but I needed to turn out the light. They can see in if it's on."

Eloise raised herself to her elbows, panting lightly. The gown had come open; she was utterly exposed, her legs splayed apart, her breasts lifted. She made no effort to adjust her gar-ment. "I'm okay," she said. "Just shocked."

"You look like an angel thrown down from heaven," he ob-served cheerfully. He unwrapped a gray silk scarf from around his neck. "My partners got the gold, but it looks like I found the real treasure." He began unfastening the coat. "It's warm in here," he said. He shrugged off the coat and spread it out, fur side up. Outside they heard shouting and a thunderous rumbling. "They're pulling the wagon off the tracks. We'll be rolling soon."

"Did you stop the train?"

"We did. The plan went fine, but I got caught between the cars, and they came after me."

"What will you do now?"

He looked around the little room, then back at Eloise. She hadn't moved. "I know what I'd like to do."

"And what is that?"

"Pick you up off the floor and lay you down on my coat here."

"And then what?"

He smiled, a toothy, lupine grin. He was clean-shaven and square jawed, with high cheekbones and a smooth complexion. His black hair had fallen across his face and he pushed it back with one hand. "Start slow," he said. "With a kiss."

Eloise was caught between the sense that she should be terrified, and the certainty that she wasn't frightened at all; that, in fact, this man enlivened her in a way she didn't recognize. She sat up and held her arms out to him. He leaned forward, catching her across her back and beneath her knees, and lifted her in one quick movement, settling her down smoothly on the chilly fur. "Just lie still," he said, leaning over her. He took up a pillow, lifted her head, and fanned her hair out over the linen. His lips touched her forehead, then he sat back and began unbuttoning his soft chamois vest. Two voices shouted, one answering the other, then with a shudder, a huff, and a jolt, the train began to move. "What's your name, my dear?" he asked.

"Eloise," she said. "What's yours?"

"It's probably best you don't know that. You can make up

a name for me if you like." He stripped off the vest and then the flannel shirt underneath. There was yet another shirt under that. She repressed a little surge of impatience.

"I'll think of something," she said.

Off came the undershirt, revealing a strong, furless chest. "And where are you bound, all alone in this fancy accommodation?"

"I'm going to Reno to be married," she said simply.

"Ah," he said. "Not yet a bride."

"He will be my second husband. My first one died."

He stood up, sliding his trousers down, turning toward her as he processed this information. "So," he said, with undisguised relief, "not a virgin."

No underwear, she observed, glancing quickly at his cock, which stood at half-mast. It moved lightly, as if waving at her.

She laughed. "No."

He sat down again, struggling with his boots. Eloise noticed a turquoise ring on the little finger of his right hand. She turned her gaze to the moon, which seemed to be tethered to the train, bobbing along helplessly as the engine accelerated. When she looked back, he was naked, leaning toward her with one arm braced against the mattress. Their eyes met and held. Eloise caught her breath. So much in that look—so much curiosity, so much excitement, so much trust. He laid his palm along her cheek, while his eyes traveled down to her feet and, slowly, appraisingly, back again. "You're lovely, Eloise," he said.

Eloise felt a rush of blood to her cheeks, but she wasn't blushing from modesty. She was thinking that she *felt* lovely. His hair brushed across her face as he closed the space between them, until his lips were pressing hers. It was a slow, exploratory kiss, his tongue lightly seeking hers, quickly withdrawing. She put her arms around his neck and clung to him as he shifted his body alongside her. Then he did with his hands what he'd done with his eyes, moving from her neck to her breasts, circling her waist, down her back to her buttocks, exploring her, pulling her in closer, while her hands played across his shoulders and she brought her mouth to his sternum, pressing little kisses there. She was conscious of the dense, surprisingly soft fur beneath her back and a pleasant odor of outdoors, of pine and juniper, crisp and fresh. He lifted his torso, readjusting her against him so he could press his mouth against her breasts. He circled the nipples delicately with his tongue, then took one in his mouth, sucking gently. She felt this first as a surprise and then as a plunging sensation, like a fishing line weighed by a lead sinker, down through her center to her womb. As if to follow it, his hand moved to her groin, and with the flat of three fingers massaged the flesh over the pubic bone, slowly and circularly, gradually sliding down and inside, while the insistent sucking at her nipple kept her motionless and rapt. She opened her eyes and gazed blankly at the coffered ceiling while sensations of ease and sensual pleasure washed over her, and from somewhere deep in her throat a vibration started that issued from her parted lips as a deep, guttural sigh. Her lover covered her mouth with his own, then slipped down her torso, leaving a trail of kisses until his mouth found her sex and he replaced his fingers with his tongue. This tongue was like a living creature, now pointed and forceful as a finger, now flat, warm, and wet, lapping lazily at her until she sighed from deep within her chest. Holding her hips between his hands, he pulled her down until her head slipped from the pillow. She turned her face to the side, pressing her cheek to the fur, and looked out, without knowing what she was seeing. Her hands drifted down and clutched his hair, her fingers riffling through it tenderly. He rose up over her, his eyes clouded with desire. Smoothly, he fitted his cock inside her and she lifted her legs around his back, holding on tight. It seemed to her that her whole body was drawing him in ever deeper, while the rocking motion of the carriage, the dull roar of the engine, the racket of the pistons, and steady churning of the wheels combined to drive all thoughts but one from her mind, and that one a single word: *Yes.*

They rested and shared their wonder at finding each other. "When that latch flipped to open, I couldn't believe my eyes," he said.

"I was calling you," she said.

He nuzzled her neck, whispering into her hair, "You were calling me." They lay still, side by side, nestled deep in the fur.

"What kind of fur is this?" she asked.

"Black bear," he said. "I won it from a rich man in a card game."

"I'll call you Ursus," she said.

He growled, pulling her in tightly. "Ursus major," he said.

More caresses, more kisses. Ursus led Eloise on a tour of her own body, eliciting sensations that were entirely new to her. Her skin felt electric beneath his touch, as if his fingers drew a current through her veins. He gripped her buttocks. "Hold on," he said. "We're turning over." And over she went, coming out on top. She sat up, stretching her back, her neck, still joined to him, yet free. She rested her hands on his chest and pushed her hips down hard. "Oh," she said, touching her flesh below her navel. "It feels like you're up to here."

"I'm heading for your heart," he replied.

She squirmed, raising her arms over her head while he

began thrusting up and up beneath her. She held on tightly with her thighs, laughing at the wildness rising in them both. She felt her eyes roll back in her head. Her hands, fluttering frantically about for anything to hold, found his shoulders and gripped with all their strength. Her orgasm was not the pleasant shivering she had experienced earlier, but a powerful, convulsive clenching and unclenching that wrenched a cry of joy from her throat. For a moment, the world went red.

When her vision cleared, she looked down to see his brow knit as in concentration. He gasped for air, his eyes closed tightly. Then, as his back stiffened beneath her, he opened his eyes and a deep, throaty groan answered her cry. She folded over him, burrowing her face in his chest as his arms came across her back, holding her firmly in place.

They rested again. They were sweating, and wet from sex. Eloise got up and fetched a cool cloth from the bathroom. They wiped each other down, ate all the chocolates. They talked, giddy with their secret pleasure.

He would have to leave the train after they crossed into Nebraska. The first stop was Cheyenne, but that wasn't until midmorning. How to keep the porter out of the room until then? "I'll tell him I'm feeling ill and ask him to bring a breakfast tray," she said. "You can hide in the bathroom." He nodded. His hand strayed across her thigh. Somewhere in the midst of a caress, they fell asleep in each other's arms.

In the morning, Eloise's plan proceeded perfectly. The porter was sympathetic, the tray sufficient for two: boiled eggs, a silver rack of toast, sliced melon, a large urn of coffee. She and Ursus sat on the bed and ate.

"What's the name of this fellow you're marrying?" he asked.

Eloise slathered her toast with butter. "Henry Pickles," she said.

"Oh lord," he said.

"He's a nice man. I think. I don't know him well."

"And he lives in Reno."

"He has a ranch, somewhere north of that. Near a lake."

"Mrs. Pickles," he said.

She nodded, refilled her coffee cup. An enormous sadness descended upon her. She couldn't call Henry Pickles to mind. Would she even recognize him when she saw him?

"I'd better get dressed," Ursus said. He glanced at the clock built into the dresser. "We'll be in Cheyenne in fifteen minutes."

The train slowed, coming into the station. Eloise, neatly attired, her hair gathered in a braid, stepped out into the passage and looked up and down. She could see the porter between carriages at the front end of the car. A well-dressed couple emerged from the compartment nearest that exit. The man struggled with a large suitcase he was pushing toward the door. Eloise stepped back inside and informed her lover that the coast was clear. She would go out and chat up the porter while Ursus made a quick exit from the other end of the carriage. There would be a good deal of coming and going in the second-class cars. He could slip out without being noticed.

They faced each other, dressed and presentable, like an ordinary couple. Tears filled her eyes as he drew her to him for a final embrace, a kiss so hungry and deep her knees buckled and she clung to his neck. The train had slowed to a crawl. "Cheyenne," the conductor shouted.

He released her, stepping back as she opened the door into the hall. The couple with the luggage was struggling, blocking the passageway. The porter couldn't open the door. "Now," she said over her shoulder. Without looking back, she walked briskly down the corridor. "May I help you?" she said to the wife.

"Why did we bring this ridiculous bag?" the husband complained.

By the time Eloise returned to her compartment, the train was pulling out of the station. Her startled eyes fell upon the coat, arranged like a living creature with its arms stretched out wide across the bed. The collar was open and a folded sheet of paper stood propped against it. She picked it up, read the three words printed there: *I'll find you.*

She thought of his hands, his tapered fingers, neatly trimmed nails, that small ring on the pinky finger; the well-cared-for hands of a thief. Then, unbidden, came an image of the large, bruised, work-worn hands of Henry Pickles.

As the train picked up speed, churning and surging ever westward on the last leg of her journey, Eloise pressed the page to her lips and fell back into the warm embrace of the coat. "Find me," she whispered to the empty room. "Please, please, find me."

The Next Eleven Minutes

I *tell him I got upset last* night and kicked a wall. I say I was wearing boots, so the wall lost.

"Don't take it out on the poor wall," he says. "I'll be there in twenty. Less."

I hang up and go upstairs to look at my new bedroom. It's empty except for a mattress on the floor. One suitcase. I drag the suitcase into the closet so I can see the room almost totally bare, then fight the urge to move the mattress into the hall and the suitcase to the office closet so the room is one hundred percent empty. I wonder how the walls would look painted matte navy. I wonder how much weight a human torso can take before collapsing and cracking in half.

"For starters, I'll need you to lock that door," he says, ambling in. He opens his arms. "Come here, bird. I'm starving for you."

I fall on him and ride his long exhale. I feel his stubble and his warm neck.

He looks around at the state of things. There are boxes everywhere. He laughs softly and shakes his head.

"Welcome to hell," I say.

He says wow.

I tell him how much I resent the person who packed the boxes. He asks why and I say I'm about to explain, if he'd only listen. He says Christ you're adorable and I say I'm aware, thanks, and he says it may help matters if you'd suck my cock for ten seconds.

"We'll get to that if you stop interrupting." I begin, "The problem isn't—" and he cuts me off with, "Don't you want your surprise first?" and I say LET ME FINISH.

I tell him that the packer underpacked each box and filled the empty spaces with packing peanuts that are now completely everywhere. They feel alive. If you hold them up to the light, some have faces. They wiggle and fly around and won't be controlled, and every opened box means a new swarm freed. Another corps of white worms doing their fucking air ballet.

"They make everything take twenty times as long. For three days I've barely slept and eaten only coffee."

"Coffee's not food," he says. "Please let me give you one tiny something."

His eyes do this thing where one shuts when he gets excited. They're light brown, like amber. He's good at bringing things to help me relax. He's actually an animal at it.

I hold out my hands. "Ready," I say.

"Close your eyes," he says. "Guess."

I say, "Hmm. I smell a big, fat cock?"

"That kind of language will get you in trouble," he says. His hand slides up my nightgown and nudges my legs apart. "Seeing you with your eyes closed gets me all riled up." His finger circles around down there and he whispers, "What's your final guess?"

I tell him I can't focus when he's fingering me, and he says fine, open your eyes. On his palm is a fat sugar doughnut oozing yellow custard.

I tip my head back. "Put it in my mouth," I say, licking my lips and opening wide. "I'm ready."

He bites off a hunk and slides the gritty sugar and cream into my mouth with his tongue. He rubs against me and says I get him so hard he could break a car window with his dick. I say I'm looking forward to climbing aboard it if he'll help a little with the boxes first. He says what's wrong with now and I say nothing, depending when now starts.

I do want him now, but more than that I want everything put away. Or I want me put away.

He asks if I can let it go until morning.

"I really can't," I say. I try to look balanced when I tell him I'm not doing great. He asks if I got in touch with my doctor, but I ignore that and say how I hate the peanuts.

"Jesus, they're everywhere." He picks a peanut off his pant leg.

"They are stronger together," I say.

I grab a fistful and say watch. I try throwing them down, but most stay stuck to me, despite me shaking my hand like crazy, like it's on fire.

I see what you mean, he says. Like little leeches.

I feel a brush of something at my ankle and shake it. "I know it's the peanuts, but each time I feel one on me I'm convinced it's a spider or a ghost."

"Wait, that *is* a spider," he says.

"Fucking hell!" I scream. "Get it off!"

"Hold still." He plucks it off me and flings it into the sink. He peers at it for a second and runs the sprayer on it. "It's out."

"But I can still feel it."

"It's gone," he says, "down the drain and gone." I ask if it looked poisonous. He says, "Um."

"I won't live to see forty," I say.

I tell him that I need to pee and I wish the bathroom had a Narnia closet. "I'd just come after you," he says. I put my hand on his back as I slip by and tell him I'm not entering any other realms without him. It feels like I mean it.

When he cranes his head around the bathroom door, I bark GET OUT but I'm laughing as I sit on the toilet. I laugh until I gasp, loudly, I guess, because I hear "Everything okay in there?" from the other side of the door.

Curled up like a turd-shaped cloud on my panty's center strip is a peanut.

He knocks softly. "Baby girl, are you crying?"

"I don't know," I say.

I come out and lean against the door to catch my breath.

I tell him I want to set off a bomb in my house and watch my future burn. I say I also sort of want to be inside my house when it burns and film the whole thing so all the people who ruined my life can watch me die and celebrate.

He asks, "But then how—"

"They won," I say, my voice cracking. I hold it up. "Look. There was a packing maggot in my fucking underwear. If I'd sat down with enough force, it would have fucked me."

He tries not to smile but I say, please go ahead and laugh, I am. He says, "Look, let's get you dressed and go for a drive."

"I'd love to," I say, handing him the peanut. "But first, take this piece of shit and shove it up my ass." I bend over a box. "Do it! I want it to suffocate inside me."

My eyes feel hot and I only know I'm shouting when he says, babe, you're shouting.

He kneels beside me and my middle convulses with every sob I'm struggling to suppress.

"Let go of the box, honey," he says. I'm gripping it with my nails. He hands me his handkerchief and I blow my nose. I whisper that there's too much noise in my head and it's only gotten louder.

"Don't you think I know that?" he asks. He pets the top of my head and I say please don't. I tell him I don't need tenderness now. I say I need the other.

His head falls on his hand. "I really . . . don't think that's good."

"Just a little," I say.

"I told you not to go without sleep and food." His voice is tight. He unlaces his boots and kicks them off. I don't know if he's into it, or mad that I asked for something I said I wouldn't ask for anymore. I did promise I wouldn't.

"I've been so bad," I offer gently.

"Okay," he murmurs. "You have."

I give him a moment, and then what seems like half of another moment. When I'm just about to ask for it again, his hand slaps my ass hard enough that my teeth clatter. I moan and poke my ass in the air. His hand whips down again and the smack numbs my legs, my back. I'm shivering but starting to get warm, the good warm. I want more. I want ten smacks in a row, fast and hard, until everything shuts down and I'm numb. I want it harsh and just mean enough and I don't want him to speak when he does it unless it's to call me an awful name.

He could be anyone doing it. I hope he doesn't know that, but I suspect he does.

I sit up to wipe my mouth because I'm drooling but he shoves me back down onto the box and asks if he gave me permission to move and I say no. Hold still, he says.

I say no. He asks if I said no, and I say yes. Yes, I say, I said no. I hear him unbuckle his belt and unzip his pants. I close my eyes and say please whip me with it. He says no. I look up and he's staring at the ground. I hold my breath and hear it slice through the air before it strikes the floor next to me. My ass gets warm and I tremble from the sound, the threat.

My eyes are closed but I hear him walk to the back door and pull the blinds down. I say please use that belt on me. Just once, really hard. He says don't ask me that again, but I don't know if it's part of the game or what.

He crouches next to me and moves my hair off my back.

"What would you do with the girl right now?" he asks. I say which one and he says the one I brought you.

"Oh," I say, "the girl."

I tell him she's right here. I say I pulled her in the shower with me and I'm soaping her tits. He starts rubbing my back. "I'm playing with her tits and they're so heavy," I say. He takes my finger and puts it between my legs. "I'm rubbing her nipples and she loves it. She wants me to suck them. I flick my tongue around one nipple while I pinch the other one. She says it hurts. She says it's too hard, but I don't stop."

His voice is sharp. "Stop when she says it hurts," he says.

I say okay. I tell him I'm kissing her with my eyes open so I can watch him watching us. I tell him to take out his cock so I can look at it while I pour oil on my hand and lube her up, while I get her ready for him, and she says don't stop but I'm spreading her ass open. I'm holding it open for him. I want to watch him do it to her.

He says put her face on you, make her taste you. I tell him she's doing it. She's licking and using her fingers, too, and one is in my ass, and it's so good. I'm pulling her hair. "What color is it?" I ask. "What does she look like?"

"She, uh—" He stops and laughs like he's thrown. "I don't—Christ," he stammers.

"What?" I ask.

"I don't fucking know, all right?" he says. "I mean . . . you. Honestly, they all look like you."

"God, are you mad?"

"No, it's just . . . Sorry, that's all I got." He throws up his hands. I don't know where to look.

He says I'm going to bruise, and he'll have to see it. I remind him that I asked for it so he's off the hook. I say this is a really bad time to make me feel guilty.

He blows out his cheeks and stands.

My mouth tastes all bitter. I get a searing wave of dread, with no idea what's coming.

He starts to pace. "Listen," he says, "I might not have—" He stops and punches a box. He shouts FUCK. He sighs and starts again with his head down. Then he looks up suddenly and says, "I don't like to look at you when you're like this. I'd rather be alone."

He asks if he's understood. I nod once to show I get it. I'm too ashamed to swallow. My legs throb and not in a good way.

I imagine burying myself alive to rot. My nose and mouth are filled with dirt. No one goes looking for me and everyone forgets my name.

I picture the spider crawling out of the drain covered in brown muck and I watch myself eating it. I see myself running over a small dog and I hear the sound. I see that three times in a row before I watch myself set fire to an old woman.

"You're flinching," he says.

He puts his hand on my shoulder and I don't move. He puts his mouth on my ear and whispers to stay put. I hear him opening all the windows in the room. It takes a while.

He asks if I can feel the cross breeze and I don't respond because I can feel it and it's nice. I don't want to speak and then jinx it.

He says he missed my voice in the dark this week. "And I missed this part of your shoulder," he says, voice halting. "This wee angel bone"—he traces it—"and these crazy baby hairs on the back of your neck, curling. And your weird . . . theories."

He puts his hand between my legs and holds it there like it's my hand. I'm never doing that stuff again, he says.

He scratches the back of my knees and up my legs. He kisses the bottom of my ass where it becomes the top of my leg and says he wants to taste me. He says he wants me on his tongue and is that okay?

I barely nod. He gently splits my legs open and hoists one thigh on each of his shoulders and slides me back into his face. He makes me wait, breathing heat there for so long I wonder if he changed his mind.

I'm drifting off when I hear, "Just fall asleep if you want," and he starts so lightly that I'm not sure if it's happening. It goes on until he stops to tell me to relax and then I do. I give in. I feel myself pushing back into his mouth, his tongue, my hips let go entirely and one leg slides off his shoulder.

Abruptly he stops and pushes back. He sits up and says, baby, you're falling off the box. He takes my hands and brings me to my feet. Pushing my hair out of my face, he says I'm the most unpredictable weather he's ever encountered. He strokes my hair back over and over.

He unbuttons the top of my nightgown, and taking hold of each side, rips it all the way down and open with two yanks until I'm naked in front. He slides it off each of my arms and lays first his flannel shirt on the floor, and then spreads the nightgown on top of that.

"Hold on to my neck," he says.

When he lifts me up, I look in his eyes without shrinking away. I ask why he's this good to me, and as he lays me down on the clothes he says, "You're not at all ready for the answer to that."

He asks is my back okay. I run my hand down his hip and tell him I'm sorry I'm a broken machine, always spilling so much bullshit everywhere.

"Don't," he says. "I understand all your . . . battles, but please drop them for the next eleven minutes."

He opens my legs with his knee and pushes inside me all the way. A drop of sweat from his brow falls on my nose, and when I reach up, he thinks I'm wiping it away and apologizes, and I say no, your hand. I just wanted you to hold my hand.

He thrusts into me so deeply that I gasp. I wrap my legs around his waist and try to look in his eyes without imagining what he sees. "Keep doing that," I say, and watch his face contort. When he lets go entirely, it goes on so long that I wish I could have memorized it. I wish I could rewind it.

When I wake it's barely light out and he's behind me.

"Your arms could wrap me around twice," I say.

"*Envelop*? Isn't that a word?" he asks. I tell him yeah, it's like he could mail me.

I ask where he'd send me, and he says definitely not to the future, not for any amount of money. He says he wants us to last.

I tell him forever is for songs and he says bull. He says all you need is a starting mark and the balls to hang on.

He goes to the window and lights a cigarette.

"I sometimes imagine your expressions when you have your back to me," I say, "and I bet I know what you're thinking."

I ask if he's ready for me to predict his thoughts and he says no. Some other time for mind reading.

"I bet the light will be nice in this room," he says. "But altitude is going to make nights chilly."

I ask him why it would be colder at the top of a hill when isn't it true that heat rises?

I'm not listening when he answers.

I've never lived anywhere this high up. Last night to keep from yelling I went out and lay on the hammock. The air was thin, and the stars felt close enough to peel off the sky. For a moment I understood the temptation to fire at an easy target. I'm sure people aim at things all the time only because they're near enough to hit. They pull the trigger for the satisfaction of ending something with barely any effort, just to watch another light go out.

Rapunzel, Rapunzel

Her hair, her hair: for as long as she could remember, it had been all about her hair. When her father tucked her in at night, he kissed her head and said, "A woman's hair is her crowning glory, and yours will make you a queen." When her mother brushed it, gliding the boar bristles through it with exquisite gentleness, so as not to break a single strand, she said, "Your hair is a precious gift, more valuable than gold or jewels, and you must never, ever cut it." Adults cooed over it, and other children yearned to touch it. Rapunzel endured their unsettling attentions, standing politely while their grubby fingers stroked it like they would some shy, fey creature they feared to startle. They never imagined that she herself was such a creature, and that all she wanted to do was flee.

In fairness to them all, Rapunzel's hair was glorious: as soft and lustrous as mulberry silk and wondrously variegated, shifting with the light and the seasons from the palest ash to champagne to honey gold. By her teens, it fell in luxuriant ripples to the tops of her thighs, and boys felt the urge to grab it in their fists and yank on it, laughing at her shrieks of outrage. A few years later, the young noblemen they became begged for locks of it and wrote odes to it, penned in feverish script on curled sheets of vellum bound in red satin ribbons, comparing it to the wings of various birds and fields of ripening grains, rivers of molten pewter, and other equally ridiculous substances.

In time, she allowed a chosen few of them to bury their faces in it and wrap its length around their stiff cocks. She watched them take their pleasure with equal parts wonder and exhilaration that it was she who made them fling their heads back, exposing the tender columns of their throats; she who wrung the helpless gasps and groans from their lips; she who made their strong limbs tremble and their faces contort, emptied of all sense. When they spent into the tangled silk of her hair, Rapunzel felt a rush of power and an answering pulse between her legs, like the beating of a tiny, secret heart.

She invited her favorite, the one who cried out her name instead of God's, to walk with her down to the river, where she drew him into the bower of a willow whose trailing branches sheltered them from curious eyes. In the past, she had stopped his hands (and indeed, all their hands) from roaming below her waist, but today she let them go where they wished. When he found her at last, stroking her heat through the light muslin of her gown, she leaned into his touch with a soft moan of pleasure.

He knelt before her, his hands inching her skirt up her calf. "Now," he said with a sly smile, "let's see whether the petticoat matches the bonnet."

It took her a moment, but when she grasped his meaning she shoved him away, sending him sprawling onto his back. "That is something *you* will never know," she said.

She left him there and strode back to the keep, visualizing how splendid his handsome head would look on a pike.

By that point Rapunzel's hair brushed the ground, and when people weren't rhapsodizing about its beauty, they were stepping on it and tripping over it. Twigs and pine cones became ensnared in it, and mice tried to nest in it. It twined around her limbs as she slept, leaving her damp and sticky in the mornings, and weighed down her head, dragging behind her like a lame, useless appendage. Even with the help of her maid, a chatty peasant girl named Elke, keeping it clean and tamed was an onerous chore. No wonder, then, that Rapunzel began to resent her hair, along with all of its overzealous admirers.

The next time a new suitor came calling, she instructed Elke to plait her hair and coil it tightly to her head. Elke said that would take at least an hour, and what if the young sir left? To which Rapunzel replied, "The young sir can wait or not, as he pleases."

"But it's so beautiful," Elke protested. "Why would you want to hide your greatest treasure from him?"

Rapunzel gritted her teeth and told Elke to do as she asked, in the icy, imperious tone her father used with merchants who tried to overcharge him. Tears rolled down the maid's cheeks as she obeyed, but Rapunzel was unmoved.

The young sir waited, and when she joined him an hour later, showed no signs of disappointment that her renowned locks weren't on display. He was charming and clever besides, so after she'd played the pianoforte for him in the music room, she let him steal a kiss. He tasted luscious, like salted almonds, and his tongue flirted more skillfully with hers than those of her previous suitors; nor did he paw at her breasts as so many of them had. Instead, he grazed her nipples delicately through her dress with his knuckles, back and forth until they were swollen and aching.

"Please," Rapunzel said.

"Please what?" Pinching them, he insinuated one leg between her thighs, rocking the hard meat of his cock against her sex. "Please this?" His tongue pushed her lips apart, thrusting in and in and in, matching the rhythm of his hips, the insistent tugging of his fingers on her nipples. "Is this what you want, Rapunzel?"

"Yes," she moaned.

"Then I will give it to you . . . if you will let down your hair for me."

He reached behind her head, fingers plucking at the jeweled netting that bound her braid. She stepped back and slapped the offending hand away, then yanked so violently on the bell cord that she ripped it from the ceiling.

When a footman hurried in, she said, "Escort this gentleman out, and see that he never returns."

Except he did return; all of them did. Rapunzel sent most of them away and received the others with undisguised indifference, always with Elke present and never for longer than the quarter hour politeness dictated. The more aloof she became, the more desperate they were to see her, and the harsher her rejections, the more ardent their supplications. Their poems and bouquets piled up in the hall, the former unread, the latter left to wilt and molder.

Disgusted with the daft, tress-obsessed lot of them, she withdrew with Elke to the tower of the keep. The maid came and went, bringing food and bathwater and emptying the chamber pot, but Rapunzel locked herself away, ignoring her father's commands to rejoin the family. At night she closed her eyes, lifted her gown, and touched herself, envisioning a different kind of man. She could never make out his features, but she could picture his hands cupping her face, her breasts, her mound; his fingers threading through her hair—her mousy-brown, shoulder-length hair—as he kissed her, and somehow this was the most erotic image of all. Her own fingers grew slick as her excitement built, but the release she craved remained elusive.

A week went by, then a month. Rapunzel's father threatened to hack open the door and haul her down the stairs like a sack of flour, but in the end, his wife persuaded him that their daughter's retreat was a brilliant piece of strategy. After all, while Rapunzel had had many noble suitors, no prince had yet come.

Nightly, the young men stood at the foot of her tower, calling, "Rapunzel, Rapunzel, let down your hair!" Nightly, she answered them with contemptuous silence.

When they'd given up and gone home, and Elke was snoring on her pallet at the foot of Rapunzel's bed, she unbolted the door and crept down the winding stairs to the gardens. There, she meandered into the small hours, her fingertips skimming the lush petals of the flowers, her hair trailing behind her like a bridal veil, carving dark swaths in the dewy, moonlit grass.

One night she was so restless she walked until light stained the eastern horizon. As she hurried back to the tower, she was startled by the sight of a man among the rosebushes—one of her suitors stealing a bloom for her, she assumed, until she registered his rough clothing, the wheelbarrow of cuttings beside him, the pruning shears in his hand. A gardener, getting an early start on the day's work.

He doffed his cap to her. "Morning, milady," he greeted her, in the informal dialect of the country folk.

"Good morning. I didn't realize it was so late— Well, early." She couldn't see his face clearly, but he didn't seem familiar. Still, her father employed many gardeners and other servants; she couldn't be expected to know them all.

"Do you often walk here alone at night?" he asked.

The question, coming from a stranger, ought to have made her wary, but oddly, she had no fear of him. "Yes," she said. "I find it calms me when I'm feeling—" She broke off. How to encapsulate the snarl of her emotions?

"Pent?" he suggested quietly.

"Exactly," she said, surprised that a simple gardener would so easily comprehend what others couldn't. "How did you know?"

"It's how I would feel if I were in your place. It's how I often do feel."

His words held a gruff edge of truth and an echo of her own frustration. A little ashamed of the assumptions she'd made about this not-so-simple gardener, she peered at him in the dim light, wanting to see his face.

"Sun'll be up soon," he said. "I'd best get back to work." He turned away and bent to his pruning, the rasp of the shears slicing the peace of the morning.

"Please don't tell anyone you saw me," she said to his back. It was broad, and it strained the seams of his homespun shirt. "I'm supposed to be in seclusion."

His hands stilled, and the world was quiet once again. "If it's not impertinent of me to ask, why have you shut yourself up in the tower and turned away all your suitors?"

"None of them want *me*," she said. "None of them even see me, just my hair."

A silence, then the gardener said, "I'll keep your secrets, Rapunzel."

She wished him a good day and ran back to the tower, slipping into bed mere minutes before Elke woke with a sigh and a yawn. Rapunzel lay feigning sleep for some time, her heart thudding as she reflected on his last words. He'd used her name, not *milady*. And said *secrets*, plural.

He wasn't in the gardens the next night, though she lingered until just before sunrise, hoping to see him again. Then came three days of thunder and rain. Rapunzel paced her tower room—pent, indeed—and sent Elke off on one invented errand after another to escape her nattering.

The fourth day dawned clear. Rapunzel wore one of her most fetching gowns and had the maid braid her hair, then waited impatiently for nightfall. When the last of her disappointed suitors had slunk away and Elke had finally nodded off, Rapunzel made her way down to the gardens. She walked the familiar paths with impatience and, when the gardener didn't appear, a growing disappointment of her own.

"Evening, milady. I hoped I'd see you tonight." His voice came from close behind her. As she turned to him, the fat gibbous moon slipped out from behind a cloud, revealing his face.

"Oh," she said, dumbstruck, not so much by his looks (though he was quite handsome), but by the directness and intimacy of his gaze. It felt like the time she'd taken an illicit gulp of her father's whiskey: an initial burn, followed by a lovely warmth that seeped through her entire body, leaving her skin flushed and prickly.

"May I walk with you?" he asked.

They wandered the grounds together, talking with surprising ease. He asked her question after question, listening to her answers without interrupting or, even more astonishingly, steering the subject to his own manly accomplishments and opinions. Not once did he mention her hair.

As they walked, their bodies drifted closer by degrees until they were almost touching, and Rapunzel's thoughts turned sensual. She wanted to put her nose where his neck met his shoulder and discover his scent, wanted to feel his work-roughened hands on her smooth skin.

As if he'd read her thoughts, he stopped and took her hand, his thumb stroking the sensitive center of her palm. "Rapunzel, Rapunzel," he said, in mocking imitation of all the others. But instead of the words she dreaded, what came was, "Let down your dress."

His gaze was so warm, so steady. Before she even thought about it, her fingers were rising to her bodice, untying the ribbon that held it closed, and pulling down the neckline to bare her breasts. His eyes never left hers, but his hands took the offered gifts, making lazy circles around her nipples until she squirmed and then rolling them between his thumbs and forefingers. He didn't kiss her, as she expected. Instead he watched her face as he caressed her, taking in every little shudder and moan. Rapunzel had never felt so exposed, nor so intensely aroused. She closed her eyes and felt him kissing her throat, her collarbone, and finally her breasts, his tongue bathing and suckling her tender nipples. Dizzy from the pleasure of it, she twined her fingers in his hair, gripping it like she would a horse's mane to keep herself from falling.

The raucous crowing of the rooster jolted them apart. He

swore under his breath, and Rapunzel fumbled to right her clothes. "Let me," he said. As his fingers nimbly tied the ribbon of her bodice, she saw the dirt beneath his nails and felt a sudden flare of shame. What was she thinking, letting this workman fondle her, and where anyone might see them? In panic, she looked back at the keep. The servants rose early. Someone could come upon them at any moment.

He took her face in his hand and leaned in to kiss her goodbye. "I have to go," she said, and ran—from him, from the coming dawn, and most of all, from herself.

Rapunzel didn't go down the following two nights, but on the third, she decided to seek him out. Not, she told herself, for more of his attentions, but to inform him she couldn't meet him again, and to be sure of his discretion.

The moon had set, so she went carefully in the starry darkness. When she made out his silhouette, her pulse leapt. He was pacing, waiting for her. Wanting to observe him unawares, she took off her slippers and crept toward him, her bare feet and skirts a mere whisper on the grass. She was still some distance away when he chuckled and said, "Good evening, milady."

"How did you know I was there?"

"Soldier's instincts."

Before Rapunzel could ask him how a gardener came to possess such, he said, "I'm glad to see you. I feared you wouldn't come again."

"I can't stay. I just came to tell you . . ." She faltered. The words were there, right behind her teeth. Why couldn't she make herself speak them?

He moved toward her, closing the distance between them.

She knew she should go, but her feet were so rooted they may as well have been tree trunks.

"Rapunzel, Rapunzel," he said softly. "Lift up your skirts and show me your sweet cunt."

If he'd tried to touch her she would have fled, but he stood very still, waiting for her once again, and there was something powerful and seductive in that. Though his face was shadowed, it wasn't hard to picture his taut, yearning expression, nor to imagine the sensual curve of his lips when he heard her skirts rustle as her clenched hands drew them up past her calves, to her thighs, to her waist.

He dropped to his knees and embraced her, pressing his face against her, murmuring muffled endearments into the bare skin of her belly. He slid her drawers down her legs, lifted her feet one at a time to remove them, and nudged her knees wider apart. Rapunzel grasped his shoulders to steady herself, and as she did her skirts fell over his head, swallowing him up like a delicious secret. She heard him take a long, deep inhalation and flushed, knowing he was smelling her intimate scent. Then his warm finger stroked her, unerringly finding the place she most wanted to be touched, and in the joy of it her embarrassment fell away as easily as her drawers had done.

She must have cried out, because he said, "Shhh," his humid breath sighing against her sex. She shivered as she realized it hadn't been his finger touching her, but his tongue. It found her again, and she felt a hot rush—she was turning to liquid, her flesh was dissolving, and there was nothing solid but him and his mouth moving against her, winding her like flax on a spindle, tighter and tighter until it was too much, she would break, she would be broken. She tried to pull away from him, but his hand gripped her buttocks, holding her against his unrelenting mouth. "Let go, Rapunzel," he said. One of his fingers grazed her lips and slipped inside her, and she came apart.

He caught her as she crumpled, easing her to the ground and emerging from beneath her skirts to cradle her in his arms. "How do you feel? Less pent, I hope?" His voice was low and amused.

"Much," she said.

His chest was warm against her back, and her limbs felt loose and heavy. Her eyes were starting to droop when he said, "The sun will be up soon, milady. You should get back to your tower." She let out a little groan of protest as he stood, drawing her up with him. "Until the morrow?" he said.

"Until the morrow," she said. He kissed her then, and she tasted herself on his mouth. The morrow, she thought, could not come soon enough.

But he was not there the following night, nor the one after that, nor the ten or twenty after that. If Rapunzel's emotions had been a snarl before, they were now a thicket of cruel thorns that pierced her from the moment she awoke in midafternoon until dawn, when she trudged up the tower stairs after another solitary night in the gardens. Fury, despair, longing, worry— she felt it all, sometimes within the same quarter hour. She ate little, snapped at Elke, and wore the soles of her slippers thin from pacing. How could he have just vanished without a word? Was he married? Ill? Dead? There were times when all of those possibilities seemed preferable to the one she suspected, which was that he'd simply lost interest in her.

She burned when she recalled their intimacies, with shame and desire both. Once, she conjured him and fingered herself until she spasmed, but when she opened her eyes and found herself alone, she felt so wretched she never attempted it again.

A month after his disappearance and two months into her self-imposed exile, Elke brought a note from Rapunzel's father: either she would end her tantrum at once, or the next thing she heard would be the sound of his ax splintering the tower door. It was time for her to marry, to choose one of the suitors who were hangdogging about the keep, driving everyone mad. Besides, he said, he and her mother missed her.

Rapunzel sighed. She'd missed them, too, and she'd known all her life that she was destined to marry and make an alliance with another noble family. Still, she'd dared to hope it might be a union of love and not just duty. The moonlit face of the gardener entered her mind, and she bid him a silent farewell. Even if he returned and asked for her hand, she could never wed a workman.

She went down to her parents, hiding the heaviness in her heart behind a smile as she embraced them. She had a footman gather up the piles of letters and poems in the hall and bring them to her rooms, promising her parents she would read them and make her choice within the month. And if she cried herself to sleep that night, no one was there to hear it but the mice.

A fortnight later, despondent and still undecided, Rapunzel went out to the gardens for the first time since she'd quit the tower. There was a nip of autumn in the air, and the roses were blowsy and faded, drooping on their stems. Soon, she thought, they would all be dead, and she would be wed to a man she didn't want, which was its own kind of death. The roses would bloom again next year, but she would be interred in a loveless marriage forever.

As she bent down to smell their perfume, she heard the crunch of footsteps on gravel. "Good evening, my lady."

It was unmistakably his voice, but the country dialect was gone, as was the rough garb of a gardener. A nobleman in court dress stood before her. He wore a sword on his hip, and gemstones glinted on his fingers. The leather thong that had tied back his hair had been replaced with a black satin ribbon, and his scruffy boots with gleaming Hessians. He was beautiful, Rapunzel thought. And a vile, deceitful, lecherous cur.

She wanted to hurl herself at him, to hurt him as he had hurt her, but she held herself still and silent, her hands clenched at her sides.

"I know you're angry, Rapunzel, but please, listen to me," he said. "I'd planned to tell you the truth about who I was the next time I saw you, but that morning I received a message that my mother had taken ill. I didn't dare wait another day. I rode out at once for Saxony. She had a grave fever, but by the grace of God it passed. As soon as she was out of danger, I came back to you."

"That doesn't explain why you lied to me in the first place and pretended to be someone you weren't," she said, unmollified.

"I should think you of all people would understand that," he said quietly. "Every lady dreams of marrying a prince. I wanted to find a mate who desired me for myself."

Rapunzel heard the words *prince* and *marry*, but it was the word *mate* that triggered the fluttering in her belly and the hot pulse somewhat lower.

She ignored both. This man had betrayed her trust once; she would not give him a second opportunity. "The others may only want me for my hair, but at least they're honest about it," she said.

"The others are fools. I want *you*, Rapunzel. I want to spend my life with you."

"Have a safe journey back to Saxony, Your Royal Highness." Rapunzel gave him a stiff curtsy and left him, adding his head to the long, bloody row of pikes in her mind.

The next day, her mother announced excitedly that Prince Stefan of Saxony had heard of her beauty and was coming to court her. He would be here in three days' time.

Fine, Rapunzel thought, let him come. She would be stone.

A frenzy of unwelcome beautification ensued. The seamstress came to fit her for new gowns. Her nails were oiled and buffed, her skin bathed nightly in milk. Her Aunt Remilda in Freiburg, who had the second-best hair in the family (a distant second, it must be said), thoughtfully dispatched the afterbirth of a sow to ensure that her niece's locks would shine as brightly as possible for the prince. Rapunzel brooded while Elke worked the nasty stuff into her hair, prattling all the while about Prince Stefan, who was reputed to be as handsome as sin, a beloved ruler with the most splendid castle in Saxony.

When he arrived, Rapunzel's parents held a lavish feast in his honor, seating him across from her, at her father's right hand. Rapunzel's hair, the guests agreed, had never been more dazzlingly resplendent, and she herself looked quite pretty. From the number of smiles and admiring looks the prince bestowed on her, he was plainly smitten. By the time dessert was served, there was no doubt in anyone's but Rapunzel's mind that she would soon become a princess.

With the flagrant approval of her parents, Stefan proceeded to court her. There was no escaping him. He sat with her at meals and rode beside her on the hunt. If she went to the library or the gardens, he would soon turn up, needing a book or a stroll. Rapunzel had expected him to have haughty manners, but she found Prince Stefan much like the nameless gardener: warm, attentive, gracious—and maddeningly persistent.

Every evening, before they said good night, Stefan asked, "Will you not forgive me, Rapunzel, and be my lady wife?" Every evening, her refusal came a little slower and sounded less convincing.

He began touching her in small ways—his thigh brushing against hers when they rode alongside each other, his hand grazing hers as he passed her the bread. Over time, these seemingly innocent touches became less so. As he boosted her onto her palfrey, his fingers caressed the hollow behind her knee. When he kissed her hand, his tongue probed the delicate webbing between her fingers. Through it all, his gray-blue gaze constantly sought hers, promising pleasure and more if she would only relent. Rapunzel began to feel once again the sensation of being wound ever more tightly, only this time at an excruciatingly slow pace. She was not stone, she was flesh, and every inch of it ached for him.

There came an evening when she answered his question not with a no, but with a question of her own. "If I agree to marry you, Your Royal Highness, will you promise never to lie to me again?"

"I will, my lady," Stefan said with a smile so sweet and yearning it made her breath hitch.

"Then I might be persuaded to say yes."

He took her in his arms and kissed her, drawing her tongue into his mouth and sucking on it until she was panting with need. "And now," he said, stepping back from her, "I will bid you good night."

"But—I'm not fully persuaded," Rapunzel said.

He kissed her on the forehead, the corners of his lips quirking with amusement. "I'm afraid you'll have to live with your misgivings until we're wed."

He asked Rapunzel's overjoyed father for her hand the very next day. The banns were read and the wedding planned for a month hence in Saxony. In the meantime, Stefan would return home to make preparations and see to his lands and people.

That night, he refused to do more than kiss her, despite her unsubtle efforts to tempt him further. When she said good-bye to him the next morning, he gave her a long, narrow box tied with ribbon, whispering in her ear that she was to open it later, once she was alone. Inside she found an opulent peacock's feather and a note: *Let this feather do as my lips and hands will once we are married. Yours, Stefan.*

Rapunzel dismissed Elke and locked her door, then eagerly stripped off her nightgown and lay naked on the bed. She closed her eyes and ran the tip of the feather across her lips, imagining his kiss. It tickled, though, and made her giggle. She trailed it down her throat and across her breasts. Her nipples stiffened, and she tried to picture him squeezing them with his deft fingers, but the pressure was too light. Even as she dragged the plume down her stomach and parted her legs, a dark suspicion was forming in her mind, one that was confirmed when the feather brushed across her intimate flesh with that same infuriating lack of pressure. This gift of his was not meant to assuage her need while they were apart; it was meant to torture her. "Beast," she muttered, tossing it aside. She touched herself then, frantic for release, and spent so fast and hard she yelped.

Elke's concerned voice came through the door. "Is everything all right, milady?"

"All is well, thank you, I just singed my finger on the candle."

The next morning, Rapunzel chose her prettiest silk drawers and wore them for several days in a row, then sent them to her intended with a note of her own: *I hope, in my absence, that these are of as much comfort to you as your gift was to me. Yours, Rapunzel.*

Between the feather and Stefan's increasingly explicit letters, Rapunzel spent the next month in a constant state of arousal. The waiting, the journey to Saxony, the wedding, the feast— none of it was over soon enough for her.

But at long last, she was settled in her sumptuous new bedroom in her husband's splendid castle, preparing for their wedding night. Elke had laid a fire and lit candles all over the room. She had just started to take down Rapunzel's hair when Stefan knocked and entered.

"I'll tend to that," he said. The maid bobbed a curtsy and left.

Rapunzel sat before the looking glass while Stefan stood behind her, removing the pins one by one from the coronet formed by her braid. Finally, it fell free, coiling on the floor at his feet. He drew her up and began to unhook the buttons on the back of her gown, his eyes seeking hers in the mirror as he removed her clothing, pausing to kiss and caress every newly bared spot. When she was naked, he stared at her for a long while.

"My magnificent, fearless wife," he said. He placed a long, slender box on the dressing table. "I have a wedding gift for you."

"If there's a feather in that box, this will be the shortest marriage in the history of Saxony," Rapunzel said.

Stefan smiled. "No, it's something I think you'll find much more satisfying."

She picked up the box and opened it. Inside was a gleaming pair of pruning shears. "I don't understand," she said.

"You will." He took them from the box and led her to the bed, setting them between the pillows. He swept back the eiderdown coverlet, then he picked her up, laid her on the sheets, and began to undress himself.

Rapunzel watched, mesmerized, as Stefan revealed his body to her. He was V-shaped: wide shoulders tapering to a narrow waist, where a tantalizing line of hair funneled into his breeches. When he stripped them off at last, she stared in wonder. The other men's cocks she'd seen had stuck up out of their rumpled pants like some sort of outlandish growth. This was the first time she'd ever seen one attached to a naked man, and it all made exquisite sense now. She stretched her arms out to him, desperate to feel his body against hers.

He took her wrists in one hand, pulling them over her head and binding them round and round with her braid. "What are you doing?" she asked.

"Patience, my love." Stefan kissed his way down her body, nibbling her ear and her neck, teasing her nipples, spreading her thighs wide, and licking her folds. Wild to touch him, she tried to free her hands, but they were too tightly bound.

He rubbed his cock against her wet opening, letting only the tip enter her before pulling out again, stoking the nagging emptiness at the core of her. She thrust her hips up against him, moaning in frustration when he moved out of reach.

"Rapunzel, Rapunzel. Tell me what you want."

She turned her head and saw the shears by the pillow. She understood, then, what he was offering her. She'd sworn never to cut her hair, but he had made no such vow. "Release me, Stefan," she said.

He entered her in one long, deliberate thrust, and she hissed from the pain. He held still, moving his hand between their bodies to stroke her. When she was undulating beneath him, her nails digging into his back, he began to move, slowly at first, then more urgently. Rapunzel felt her pleasure gathering, coiling within her like the braid around her pinioned wrists. Stefan reached for the shears, watching her face. Waiting for her, as he had always done.

"Now!" she cried. The shears rasped, slicing through her braid, and her body heaved, her cunt clenching around him as he spilled himself into her with a hoarse shout of joy.

Later, while her husband watched from the bed, Rapunzel marveled at her reflection in the mirror. Her hair was just past shoulder length now, and her head felt remarkably light. She shook it, laughing aloud, then returned to him, molding herself against his warm body. The braid lay on the sheet like a headless snake. She picked it up and considered it: this thing that had once been a part of her, had once defined her.

"We'll burn it, if you like," Stefan said.

Rapunzel kissed him, then took his hands and began to wind it around his wrists. "Oh," she murmured, "I don't think we need to get rid of it just yet."

Pearl River

In *the languid late sun, Cao* Ming leaned against the railing of the Maiden's Bridge. The wooden planks beneath his feet, though smoothed by time, were thick and unyielding, and the balustrade at his hand glowed gold and crimson. The officials of White Swan Village, Cao's hometown, took care to keep the bridge in good repair. Not many travelers came to the village who had no business to transact; the few who did came to view this spot. They came to stand where Cao now stood, to see what he now saw: beads of foam, round and white as the finest pearls, breaking free of the rushing water, rising and falling back. Over and over, pearls rising and falling, a never-ending cascade. Today the sunlight coaxed a rainbow from the water for the pearls to dance through. On gray days, the pearls shone white through the mist. At night their radiance echoed the glint of the stars. Even in the pounding rain, the droplets emerged, pale, separate, and eternal.

These were the Maiden's Tears, wept in a time beyond history by the gooseherd's daughter, Lin Meimei, abandoned by her lover. He was a young scholar, poor but clever, who, having done well in the imperial examinations, had left White Swan

Village to take up a post in the provincial capital. The scholar and the maiden had pledged their hearts to one another, and after he left she went about her daily tasks singing, smiling at those she met, playing games with the village children, patiently awaiting the day he would return to marry her.

Then word reached White Swan Village that the young scholar had taken a wife.

The maiden ceased smiling; she sang no more. One day, it is said, she left her flock and walked to the peaceful stream that flowed gently through the village. After standing for a long time weeping on the bridge, Lin Meimei, the gooseherd's daughter, threw herself into the water.

Immediately the quiet stream roiled, swirled, crashed as it wrapped itself around her and carried her downstream. From that day on, the water at the bridge was never still, and the churning foam blossomed perpetually with the maiden's tears.

It was said the ghost of Lin Meimei dwelt on in this world, smiling on devoted lovers, bringing doom to faithless ones.

Cao Ming did not believe in ghosts. Nevertheless he had come here to gather his courage. If a gooseherd's daughter could find the mettle to drown herself for love, he, once just a farmer's son from White Swan Village, now a prosperous young merchant in Beijing, could do what he needed to do also.

Cao Ming pulled his city coat tighter at his throat. He no longer wore the quilted jacket of a villager, though it might have kept him warmer in the countryside. Especially in this spot. Even in midsummer the air on the Maiden's Bridge stung the skin with cold. It was said that in the time before history, when the stream flowed gently through the village, the bridge on a summer's day was the most pleasant place in the valley: it held the water's soft murmur, the ripples sparkling in the sun, and the caress of a warm, mild breeze always rich with the scent of wildflowers.

Until a lover's betrayal and a maiden's death had set the water raging and frozen the very air.

Nonsense. Atmospheric conditions had changed, as they do. Still, the maiden's courage must be acknowledged, and as she had found hers, Cao Ming would find his. Straightening up, squaring his shoulders, he left the bridge and returned to his parents' home. He bid them farewell, walked once more through the familiar, dusty lanes of the village, and boarded the train.

He would write the letter once he was back in Beijing, and send it from there. Some might say a man of true honor would have delivered this news in person, but though he had found his courage, Cao Ming was a practical man. He was aware of his own limitations. Before he'd gone to stand on the bridge, he'd spent the afternoon with Li Ying.

He'd arrived at White Swan Village planning to tell her, but those hours, lying on a soft quilt in the sweet-smelling grass of a hidden hollow, had shaken his resolve. Li Ying, to him, was warmth, was welcome, was home. Her soft skin, soft breath, soft hands, had always set him moaning. She had seemed from the first to know where her warm touch was welcome, where it was needed, where and when it would render him blind and dumb with craving until his final release of roaring, shouted joy. Her plump seamstress's fingers were capable of an excruciating precision that caused his own hands to grasp and knead the soft, thick flesh of her buttocks, caused his legs to writhe and his mouth to travel the curves of her face and throat as if to devour her.

Knowing the afternoon would be the last time he would lie with Li Ying on the quilt in the sweet grass had heightened Cao Ming's every sense. The breeze swaying the many-colored wildflowers, the dappled sunlight glinting through the trees, the scent of Li Ying as she moved to lie beside him in the moment before her warm flesh touched his, were nearly too much to bear. Even now, on the Beijing train, he felt himself responding to all this in memory.

Uncomfortably, he shifted in his seat. No, he was right to take this step by letter. The idea of having to look into Li Ying's eyes as he delivered this news was more than he could bear.

Cao Ming decided to spend the night of his return to Beijing alone. Certain of his decision though he was, he found himself not yet ready to return to the bed of Lan Shu.

Oh, Lan Shu: lithe and graceful, slim and elegant, her skin cool, her touch quick and commanding. Her eyes ceaselessly assessing him, she took his measure; her slender body demanded from Cao Ming devotions he could not always deliver, though when he satisfied her his pride in himself as a man knew no bounds. The attentions she gave him she often protracted to such lengths that he could not tell desire from agony and didn't know, hearing his own voice, whether he was begging her to stop or pleading with her to continue forever.

An afternoon in the glade on the quilt with Li Ying had always left him feeling quietly filled, renewed. An evening on Lan Shu's broad bed in the stark, wide-windowed flat would leave him shaken and spent.

Plump, sunny Li Ying, her warm skin browned by days spent in the open air—Cao Ming had known her since before his memory began.

Lan Shu, pale and slender to the point of gauntness, was a

woman of the city, a woman of the future. Cao Ming's future. She was sharpness, severity, speed.

Li Ying offered the sigh of safety; Lan Shu was the gasp of peril. The knife's edge, the danger of every moment of city life, the dance on the verge: this was Lan Shu and this was what Cao Ming wanted. He was leaving behind the comfort and peace of the countryside to become a city man, to share his life with a city woman. He had pledged to Lan Shu his future, his body, and his heart, and she would have them; but for one last night he wanted to rest in his memories of Li Ying, memories of welcome, of warmth, and of home.

Arriving at the station, Cao Ming made his way on foot through the loud and hurried city to the laundry-hung lane and his small room. He considered making a cup of tea, a bowl of noodles, but he did not wish to encounter any of the other tenants with whom he shared the kitchen. They'd ask, with friendly envy, about his trip to his hometown, about the health of his parents and the situations of his friends.

Nor did he write his letter that night. Tomorrow was time enough.

Instead he went to bed, falling almost immediately into a deep sleep. Through his dreams rushed a river, whose cold tossing water he was now above, now below, pulled and pushed, thrown like a tumbling twig, while he flailed and shouted soundlessly for help. His limbs grew increasingly heavy and, unable to move or draw breath, he sank into a frigid, suffocating darkness.

The panic in his pounding heart shuddered him awake. He fought off his tangled covers and lay on his back gasping. No wild river, only his bed; no choking water, only his jumbled blankets; no inky blackness, only his room where the thin light of morning leaked around the blinds.

His lungs filled and his limbs lightened. The thumping of his heart reduced to where he could no longer feel it smashing against his chest. The cold didn't leave him, though, so he arose, dressed, and left the lane to walk to his shop. He stopped for a bowl of noodles, and at the shop he prepared tea, but still he felt a chill. Autumn must be coming early to Beijing.

He wrote his letter in the quiet of the afternoon; the afternoon hours had been Li Ying's, and it seemed right. He chose his words with care, thinking that, with the pain he felt as he put them on paper, he must surely be paying his penance. At day's end he closed up the shop, posted the letter, and took the subway across the city to the tall glass tower where Lan Shu lived.

Lan Shu greeted him at the door of her fourteenth-floor flat. Her pale skin and crimson lipstick were set to glowing by the white folds of her long gauzy dressing gown. Cao Ming smiled and reached out a hand, touching his fingertips to the cool of her cheek.

Lan Shu smiled but did not move from the doorway. "Did you visit with your country girl?" she asked, her voice mocking.

He told her he had.

"And have you had a change of heart, and you've come to bid me farewell?"

Not that.

"So you have written your letter?"

Yes.

"And posted it?"

That also.

"Then you are mine!"

Oh, but he always had been, from the lonely night under the boulevard's lights when he'd first seen her lithe form slipping through the doorway of a bar. The triumph in her tone now mystified Cao Ming; surely she'd known that?

Lan Shu stepped aside. He entered the flat and she shut the door behind him. Without a pause she laid her long, cool fingers on the sides of his neck, and pressed her lips to his. Her tongue searched for his, caressed it, while with one hand still at his throat she unfastened his trousers. Cao Ming, aching with anticipation, knew better than to aid her. When he was able he stepped out of his trousers and his underwear also. Disregarding his rapidly growing rigidity—except for one slow, cool, almost unbearable stroke of a single finger along it—Lan Shu relieved him of his shirt. She regarded his nakedness and laughed. Placing her hands on his hips, she applied her tongue first to this nipple, then to that, then, while he ran his hands through her glossy hair, shut his eyes, and arched his back, she let her lips and tongue drift down his torso until, kneeling, she took him in her mouth.

He stood gasping and shaking while she brought him to the brink, then opened his eyes in disbelief when she withdrew. He started to speak as she stood, but she pressed a finger to his lips. With his eyes he begged her to continue. She smiled, and, wrapping her fingers around his wrist, bade him follow her across the room. She slid the terrace door wide and they were standing in the chill of the open air, she with her white gown billowing, he shivering from cold and desire.

Her fingers tightened around his wrist to the point of pain. He looked and saw, not flesh and red-painted nail, but bone;

and whipping his head up to her face he saw the same: the grin of a fleshless skull. As he watched she rose into the air. She yanked his hand with wild strength and he flew up and over the railing, his wrist still in her grip as she tumbled beside him into the sky. They started to fall, but not, he saw in his terror, to the street below. That had been replaced by a roiling stream shining white in the pale night. He gasped as he felt her touch revive his fading rigidity. Her hands still on him, they splashed together deep, deep into frigid water and just as he was at the point of reaching a glory he'd never yet known, she left him. *No*, he tried to cry, tumbling and spinning, but he couldn't make a sound, couldn't stop rolling, and could feel himself neither finishing nor failing. Her wild laughter echoed for a long time until it, too, disappeared.

Cao Ming knew then that he had not yet paid the penance for his faithlessness, and that this would be his punishment: to be tossed perpetually in icy water, not permitted to fulfill desire nor allowed to let it fade, until his suffering no longer amused the Lord of the Underworld. With this knowledge, Cao Ming began to weep, and he understood a final truth: that not all the pearl tears rising and falling at the Maiden's Bridge had been shed by the gooseherd's daughter.

One Day in the Life of Josephine Bellanotte Munro

*T*hanks *to yet another Hand of* God cloudsplitter over the weekend—the kind of storm, once exclusive to August, that flings sailboats against the seawall surrounding our harbor—rain breached the ceiling of my third-floor classroom, which means that I arrive Monday morning to find the books I left on my desk thoroughly drenched and my A-block section of freshman honors exiled to a ground-floor rehearsal space. Not a desk in sight: for the students, chairs at music stands; for the teacher's command post, an upright piano displaying the songbook for *Sweeney Todd: High School Version.* Cannibalism, murder, and lust! You go, Barb, I think. Except that the musical's on ice and Barb is conducting her stage-starved singers on Zoom.

"Distance, everybody, distance. Do not skip the sanitizer. Mask *up*, Gordon; it's not a codpiece for your beard."

Laughter. Not that I fall for it. To my face, I'm Mrs. Munro or Mrs. M; out of earshot, the Meat Grinder. I'm the teacher that every ambitious parent prays will appear on a child's schedule

and just about every child would kill to avoid. ("You've got
Meat Grinder, dude? Sucks, man. My heart goes out." And yes,
dude, you, too, will memorize and perform entire speeches
from *ohmygod fucking Shakespeare*. Even if you're captain of the
ohmygod fucking football team.)

So in they file, snorting at the layout, no doubt hoping that
the ten-minute delay means we won't start with recitations;
maybe I won't even ask them to talk about *Things Fall Apart*,
which tends to startle and tongue-tie my almost-entirely-white-
and-well-off wards. Not that I don't share their good fortune,
though I, bookish girl from a big Irish Italian Catholic family,
married into this seaside haven of college professors and finan-
ciers, skim-milk Unitarians who wouldn't know original sin
from artisanal gin.

Lindy, one of the rare students who treats me with foolhardy
reverence, is mid-Juliet when, through the picture window at
the back of the room, I see a truck pull into view, a certain green
Ford pickup with an arboreal logo on its flank. Leaning over
the tailgate, three young trees toss blossoms in its wake, as if the
truck might be carrying newlyweds off to the Russian roulette
of marriage. It parks at the edge of the grassy swath separating
the wall of this room from the paved entrance to the school.

I cannot take my eyes off the truck until I see the driver get
out. Yes, him: José, known around town as the Tree Genius;
known to me, in the deepest of private places, as the man with
whom I would eagerly spend a long, sleepless weekend at a
Motel 6.

Father, I have sinned. Though is it really a sin just to imagine?
Really?

Lindy, who is no doubt bereft at the loss of school plays, has
successfully erected the actor's fourth wall as, bending over a

virtual balcony the required six feet to my left, she faces her in-adequately caffeinated peers and declares, through two surgical masks, "Or if thou think'st I am too quickly won, I'll frown and be perverse and say thee nay." It's like Shakespeare condomized, but I'll be damned if I let a virus lower my pedagogical stand-ards.

Cam Barlow is texting behind his music stand. Normally I'd call him out (Emily Dickinson by heart is the penalty for phone use), but I'm fixated on José, beyond our actual fourth wall, as he unloads the trees and stands them up on their bur-lapped root balls next to the window. As he does, he glances through the wide pane, sees me, raises his glossy eyebrows, and waves. My heart jumps. I wave back. Poor Lindy is just finishing her soliloquy as the entire class twists around to see why I'm waving—and, though half my face is hidden behind my mask, probably blushing like a maniac.

I have achieved countless solo orgasms with this man. I've conjured scenes starring the two of us in my bed, in my garage, in my deserted classroom, even on my husband's sailboat: José is above me, beneath me, on his knees, or standing while I fall on mine. I've imagined gymnastic trysts high in the tree house that he built in his yard, just down the street from mine. How vividly I have surmised what his compact hardworking body would feel and look like unclothed, though I've seen close up his sun-crinkled dark brown eyes and his thick hair, black streaked with just enough silver to make him—never mind that he's married and so am I—reasonably age appropriate. (Yester-day, as I compared pandemic grading standards over the phone with Erin, who teaches math, she told me that what she dislikes most about masks is that she can't see her students' mouths. I said, "You miss flashes of Melissa's pierced tongue? You miss slutty black lip gloss and ballooning wads of gum?" No, she agreed, but some of the boys' mouths . . . didn't I ever sometimes wonder . . . ? "Fuck no!" I exclaimed. She assured me her speculations are pure hypothesis. Still, I was shocked.)

I haven't laid eyes on José, not even on his truck, in months, and in all the schizoid ups and downs, all the torque and pivot of teaching in a plague, I haven't had much mental space for him, not even in my baroque, parapsychotic dreams. For a year now, my three teenage daughters have been pacing our less than palatial house like nubile panthers while their large father, with his large voice and large professional ego, takes depositions and goes to court in the home office once considered mine. I don't know what's worse: being ignored by my two older girls in the halls of the high school or listening to them trash-talk my colleagues every day over lunch in our kitchen.

So the latest return to actual school—all the slings and arrows (the sounds and smells; my God the *smells*) of teenage togetherness—feels almost idyllic. The school committee swears we'll stick it out till summer break.

José is, of course, planting those trees, directly outside the window. Which means that he begins by digging three holes. Following that storm, the weather is hot for late April; before long he discards his shirt (though not his mask), and my attention to the discussion about Okonkwo's killing of Ikemefuna is not much sharper than that of Cole Winters, a back-row guy who reeks of weed and made honors only because his mother likes to intimidate guidance counselors.

When the bell rings, I have ten minutes to shift gears for my advanced senior seminar, Reading the Russians. We've bushwhacked through Tolstoy, Dostoevsky, Turgenev, and Chekhov; Solzhenitsyn and Akhmatova remain. Outside the window,

José's smooth, hairless skin shines in the sunlight. He's removed his mask and wrapped a white kerchief around his unruly hair.

As I watch, he pauses at his task, thrusts the shovel into the rising mound of soil, and pulls a canteen from his back pocket. As he leans back to drink, the sun spills down his flexed torso, sparking the thin gold chain against his neck and illuminating his nipples: the precise color of eggplant. I have no idea how I'll be able to concentrate now.

Though I have never deployed them in an emergency remotely like this one, I have an arsenal of pop quizzes cocked and ready for all classes, one of them asking students to compose an imaginary interview with an assigned character from their reading. Ivan Denisovich, you're on deck.

Once the students have adjusted to the odd layout—and I persuade William that much as the piano probably needs playing (and yes I love Sondheim, too), we do not have time for a song—I break the news, to predictable groans, tell them they'll find the quiz on their student portal, stay long enough to see them open their laptops, then promise to return within twenty minutes.

The book closet is, according to my dubious privilege as department chair and the tragic fact that most of my colleagues issue readings online these days, my private domain. As if it contains the nuclear codes or a copy of the Gutenberg Bible, only the vice principal and I have keys. It's on the third floor, near my flooded classroom, so I hurry up the two flights— empty, since we're midblock—and am there within three precious minutes. It's a long, narrow, windowless space lined with cupboards and shelves, all jammed top to bottom with multiple copies of everything from *The Canterbury Tales* to *Beloved*, and it functions as both mortuary and trading post. George and Lennie, Holden Caulfield, and Dorian Gray all await the hearse to book oblivion (a women's shelter in a town less prosperous than ours), while cartons containing *Another Brooklyn*, a postqueer edition of *Moby-Dick*, and an anthology of neofeminist poetry are stacked at the butt end of the closet, waiting to take their place. *Lord of the Flies* had a recent stay of execution, but Sherman Alexie's been given the boot and Junot Díaz is on probation. I can remember when cultural politics had nothing to do with any of it and I didn't have to live in fear of students disdainfully informing me that such and such an author had been canceled or #MeToo'd. (Chaucer, dude, I'd watch your back.) I almost long for the era when all these kids ever read beyond class was Harry Potter (whose fans seem oddly unfazed by those transphobic tweets).

I lock the door, strip off my favorite yellow cardigan, and toss it on the hook that holds the inventory clipboard. This place could double as a sauna. I turn off the overhead fluorescents, remove my mask, and tuck it into a pocket of my skirt. For only the briefest beat, I wonder what the fuck I am doing, but in a moment of do or die, burning woman with no time to waste, I lean forward in the pitch black—my left forearm braced against a row of books I cannot see yet know are the Signet Shakespeare paperbacks with the fanciful Milton Glaser cover designs, my pelvis level against the counter below—unzip my skirt, and plunge my right hand beneath the front waistband, fingers curling into the damp velvet cavity between my thighs and finding my labia.

"Christ," I whisper. And, out of pleasure even deeper than I'd imagined, "Oh *fuck*." I don't even need to take my fantasies far; the thought of my teeth grazing those violet nipples is more than enough.

I lean my forehead against my raised arm, panting. I am forty-seven years old and I have just masturbated in a supply closet at a public high school while my students, two floors below, struggle to write a make-believe interview with poor, unjustly imprisoned Ivan D.—and somewhere else in this building, two of my daughters are, or had better be, doing something similarly diligent.

From an early age, I was easily aroused (by certain novels and "marriage guides" sampled in the library stacks; by movie stars ranging, over time, from Christopher Plummer and George Peppard to Ken Watanabe and Christian Bale; by the sight of my older brothers' friends in their silky basketball jerseys, sitting in our kitchen playing cards) and mastered the art of tending my desire even in a house overrun by a family of eight. I was effervescently orgasmic—not without a catechismal shame, but I reasoned that God took into account my being a helpful daughter and an excellent student. Fortunately, my father won out on choosing Italian nuns for our education, over the dour Irish scolds our mother might have preferred. (Her consolation was having us baptized with Irish first names.) Italian nuns leaven the guilt with humor, the self-flagellation with celebration. The glimmer in Sister Paola's eyes when she addressed the sanctity of marriage told us she knew more about the ins and outs of sanctity than she let on.

I became so efficient at satisfying myself that I did not yield to sex as a shared experience—who needed the complications of mortal sin or mitosis?—until Richard, whom I met in a college seminar on Romantic poetry. Starting on our third date, we fucked like rabbits—and bears and giraffes and whales and raccoons; like the entire animal kingdom. Richard, who'd been around the block a few times, told me he'd never met a girl with such "stamina." We needed no toys or potions, mood music or lighting; limbs, tongues, fingers, voices, and the slick of our own youthful sweat kept us happy.

Richard is, as I mentioned, a large man in every respect: in personality, in ambition, in voice (he sings sea shanties in a local chorus). And then there's Richard's dick. But if, at twenty-five, I thought my husband's sexual gusto the best male dowry a bride could hope for, two decades later I find it exhausting. Having him at home all day has made it more so. Yes, all three daughters are omnipresent, but sometimes that only gives him a welcome challenge (persuasion the make-or-break of any decent litigator). He has ambushed me in the basement, on my visits to our extra freezer; behind the garden shed, when I pruned back the garden for winter; and even in the attic, when I went up to fetch the Christmas tree stand.

I make it back to the music room within the promised twenty minutes and tell the quiz takers they have five minutes to wrap up. Looking out the window, I'm disappointed to see the truck gone, though the trees have yet to be planted. Perhaps he's gone home for lunch, and at least I'm able to reclaim my teacherly decorum. I can still feel the subsiding waves of a not-so-literary climax as I instruct Pamela to collect the quizzes of those (my favorites) who've chosen to write them out rather than send them blithely through the ether. I tell her to drop them on the piano bench, then sanitize her hands. As she listens to me, I see her eyebrows tense in disapproval or concern.

"Mrs. M, what's with your arm?"

I look down to discover that the Signet Shakespeares left a ladder of rosy indentations along the soft underside of my left arm—and realize that I forgot my sweater. "Oh!" I rub my arm and say, "I have no idea, how odd!"

Pamela's classmates are too busy checking the time or packing up their gear to notice how flustered I am. I call them to order and review the next round of assignments. Just as the bell rings, José drives back into view, parks, and (shirt back on) leans against the hood of the truck talking on his phone.

Would it be suspicious if I offered to get him a soft drink from the vending machine? But just as the last student leaves the room, Gerald, our principal, looms in the doorway.

"Josie, I'm sorry," he says. "Will you be able to tolerate this relocation for the rest of the week? Getting a roofer these days is impossible. Toilet paper one day, shingles the next! Hey, did you hear about the national shortage of Grape Nuts?" He's well accustomed to providing the laugh track to his own jokes and does so now.

"Gerald, I'm nothing if not adaptable." And oh, how true. I am apparently capable of making myself come twice within five minutes, even in the company of such ecstasy assassins as Joseph Conrad and Henry James.

"Don't forget the AP meeting. Field house." He taps his watch and pushes off from the doorjamb.

I had indeed nearly forgotten. I look longingly out at José, now sitting on his front bumper eating a sandwich. I'm hoping he'll turn and wave at me again, but he doesn't. I'm suddenly chilly, but I don't have time to retrieve my sweater.

In order to have socially distanced faculty gatherings, we meet in the gym, which, like the music room, has lost its sense of purpose in these contagious times. Not that the gym doesn't continue to reek from competitions past. The padding and mats that protect our children's bones from fracture are repositories of every athletic odor under the sun.

A dozen of us sit at different levels on the bleachers while

Gerald strides back and forth along the edge of the court, as if he's coaching the Celtics, and talks to us about just how the College Board, in true merciless fashion, plans to make sure our most hyperachieving students do not miss out on taking their advanced placement exams this spring—and how, despite the return to actual school, we're to hold our review sessions via Zoom. Oh joy, I think, envisioning yet another sheet of animated postage stamps, this one comprising my smartest, most terrified-of-anything-less-than-Princeton students.

Who could have guessed how cynical teaching in this era would make us? I think of José again, hoping that he won't (or will) have finished his task outside the music room before I return for E-block sophomore honors.

I met José several years ago, when he moved into a house down our street, renting it with another man. It's a kind of half house, charming but tiny, that was a horse barn two hundred years ago. But it boasts a long, narrow yard and a massive ancient tree that stands twice as tall as the house. Almost immediately, the new tenants began to construct a fanciful structure in that tree—for whom or why, no one knew. It was summer, so I was often at home (when not ferrying the girls to camps and lessons). One day the hammering started, and when I stepped out my front door, I saw the two men carrying what looked like old barn boards into the yard. Since the house is on a corner, the stretch of yard along the side street is flanked by a stockade fence.

I had to stand on tiptoe to see over the fence, and I devised errands to take me that way on foot as often as I could for about two weeks. At first, I was just generically nosy. I'd glimpse one or both of the men weaving and buttressing those boards through the boughs and branches of the tree, along with driftwood hauled from nearby beaches, salvaged windows, sections of ladder, lengths of sturdy rope. One day, having grown to think of myself as invisible (the superpower of middle-aged women), I was stunned to hear someone call out from inside the dense foliage, "Come have a closer look." I froze until he repeated, laughing, "Yes, you. The gate in the fence is open."

I did as I was told, approached the tree, and looked up from the base of its thick brindled trunk. The man whom I'd noticed doing most of the work was climbing down a series of cleverly constructed ladders, one platform to another. When he stood beside me, he smiled, said, "José," and held out his hand.

"Oh." I took it. "Josie."

He laughed. "We share our name!"

In theory I'm a word person, but it took me a long moment to grasp the connection. "Oh," I said, startled again. "I'm actually Josephine, but nobody calls me that."

"Then I will not call you that either," he said. "Did you wish for a tour?" Why say no? At least I was dressed to climb a tree, in jeans and tennis shoes. He directed me to go first, guiding me now and then with a glancing touch at the base of my spine. We passed through the inner sanctum formed by hundreds of reaching, twining limbs, and as I glanced around, I could see how few of the larger branches had been severed. On the highest platform, I gasped. Through the lacework of leaves, I could see clear over dozens of rooftops to the harbor, to the fishing and sailing boats moored, large and small, opulent and modest, from one shore to the next. I could even spot Richard's boat.

"What do you think?" asked José.

We stood next to each other at the rail, and I said, "My God."

"If you have one," said José, "then here he is closer."

This made me laugh with genuine joy. "When I was little, one of my teachers said it's silly to pray upward. She told us that God sees it all, including us, from every angle." Channeling Sister Carlotta, I said, "And don't you ever forget it!" That's when I noticed the surprisingly delicate gold cross around his neck. Christ, what if I'd offended him?

But he just smiled, José, almost as if admiring me. I noticed as well both how short he was and how fascinating his face: a face intimate with all-day, every-day sun; nothing like the faces of my husband and his friends, tanned through seasonal cultivation (nautical summers, ski-slope winters), slathered with lotions and goggled in designer shades. José's T-shirt was damp with exertion, and he smelled like sawdust and cider. Our arms were adjacent, the brown of our skin nearly identical; every August, my coloring broadcasts my father's Calabrian roots.

I made myself return to the view, and we stood there for about ten minutes, during which I asked rote questions about the tree house. When I asked why they were building it, he said, "To advertise for building others." This seemed both strange and logical. And then, glancing down, I saw my oldest daughter, three blocks away, walking toward home.

Descending before me, he reached the bottom first. I stumbled slightly on one of the tree's serpentine roots, but righted myself before he could check my fall.

"Well," I said when I'd regained my balance. "I needed that."

"Come anytime," he said. "Bring your daughters."

It shocked me that he knew I had daughters—but how silly. He could observe my life on the street, the comings and goings at my house, as easily as I could spy on him. That night, making his debut in my dream life, he knocked on my kitchen door and, when I answered, came in, wrapped his arms around me, and whispered, "You are the most remarkable woman I've ever met." Knowing it was what he expected, I bent to kiss the cross at his throat and had just begun to unbutton his shirt when I woke to a crescendo in Richard's snoring and a gust of cool air from the window. I turned onto my belly, yanked up my flimsy nightgown, and spread my legs wide enough to make room for my hand but not to rouse my husband.

Over the years since, I've hired the Tree Genius twice: once to diagnose an ailing lilac hedge, another to repair a severe split in a maple tree caught and mangled by a large truck driving too close to our yard. At some point, the roommate moved out of the little house down the street, and a wife moved in.

My F-block juniors are a blessedly studious group, and unless my intuition is off, there's no history of entanglements, sparing me hormonal drama. As Heska, an exchange student from Rotterdam, puts her American classmates to shame with her astute presentation on *Death Comes for the Archbishop*, I'm able to steal lengthy glances at the planting-in-progress of those pink-petaled trees, which call to mind A. E. Housman's classic poem. Those fifty springs remaining to him? They're nearly behind me now.

As class ends, I watch José use his shovel to enunciate the edges of the circular bed surrounding each tree. I see the bags of mulch still stacked by the truck, which I calculate leaves me time enough, in my next open block, to retrieve my cardigan from the book closet, eat a protein bar from my shoulder bag, and head outside to say hello.

This time as I make my way upstairs, I am forced to perform the awkward distancing dance at which we've all become more or less expert by now. The sound of adolescent flirtation and quippery through face masks is, if you stop to listen, pretty

funny. I've decided it's what centaurs would sound like if they
went to high school.

I have unlocked the door to the closet and am reaching for
the light switch when I realize it's already on. I experience that
sitcom suspension of time in which you know exactly what
you're seeing (and, alas, hearing) yet refuse to admit it. Most
glaringly prominent are the rivetingly muscular moon-pale buttocks of a tall young man, his waist firmly encircled by a pair
of slender legs, and, tucked into the cleft of his right shoulder,
the flushed in flagrante face of (this part I disavow for possibly
five seconds) my eldest daughter, Dana, who is seated on—or
held midair just above—the stack of boxes containing Herman
Melville, Jacqueline Woodson, and those feminist poets. Avert-
ing my eyes toward the floor, I see a puddled floral fantasia that
I recognize as the dress I took a chance on ordering from An-
thropologie for Dana's birthday and was so delighted to see that
she actually loved. (How often does one hear from the lips of
a seventeen-year-old daughter, "Oh my God, Mom, like, how
fantastically awesome!")

Dana is the first one to realize they've been caught. "Oh
fuck!" she gasps, pushing the boy backward. Jeans around
his ankles, he nearly falls into me as, reaching out to clutch at
a bookcase, he drops from his right fist a pair of fuchsia lace
panties that I recognize from numerous rounds of laundry. It's
almost impossible not to admire how deftly, once he catches
himself in space, the boy simultaneously pulls up his pants and
pivots to face me. One of Dana's hands still rests on his shoulder
as he groans loudly and says, "Oh my God, Mrs. Munro, like, oh
my God, I'm so sorry, like, we—"

"Stop," I say in a voice I seem to have borrowed from *The
Exorcist.*

Dana starts to speak, but I say, "Not one word from you, young lady."

She remains cowering on the boxes, behind Tim Bullard Jr. (Can this possibly be the same little T.J. whose goaltending I cheered at Soccer Tykes—wasn't that just a few years ago?)

I'm grateful for Tim's long shirttails as he clutches the fabric around his groin, so mortified that he hasn't yet managed to zip his fly, let alone buckle his belt (patterned with the burgee of our yacht club). His facial expression tells me that I resemble a one-woman firing squad.

I step aside from the door and say, "Tim, put yourself together and get out."

He casts a woeful glance at my daughter before he leaves us alone. Except for a bra that she is scrambling to fasten, Dana is naked. I tell her to get dressed. Crying softly, she obeys, and my anger wobbles. Once she has the dress on, she sits back on the boxes, face in her hands, fingernails painted in ten shades of blue.

"Well," I say. "I wouldn't call that social distancing."

Through her hands, unable to meet my eyes, she says, "We use condoms!"

I lean down, pick up Dana's underpants, and hand them to her. "We're going to have to talk, and when your father—"

Her face rises from her hands. "God no, Mom, please, no!"

I say quietly, "Give me your keys."

She pulls her purse off the counter and fishes inside. "*Please* not Dad."

I take her key ring. Yes: the shiny one. Clever girl, she copied my key to the closet. "How long?"

"Like, not— Just since—"

"You weren't exactly a virgin this morning, were you?"

Speechless, she looks stunned and mournful.

She's seventeen and using condoms. The man enclosed by her strong young thighs wasn't a sleazy thirty-five-year-old stalker or even Handsy Hal, who teaches American History in a style some suspect is a bit too Clintonian. No, he's the guy who would be taking her to the junior prom if it were not, for the second year, being canceled. What can I objectively object to, other than her fornicating on school property?

I tell her to get back to study hall or wherever she's supposed to be in G block. "Go straight home afterward. I won't tell your father till later. But then we'll talk."

I reach into my bag and hold out a tissue. "Put your mask on," I remind her. She retrieves her sandals and passes me without a word. After she's gone, I wonder if I should have hugged her. How much trouble is she in? That's up to me, isn't it?

I look around my tiny kingdom, which now smells of whatever aftershave grown-up little T.J. is wearing. It smells expensive. Probably mooched from Tim Sr. I am tempted to phone Richard right now, though my phone won't get a signal from in here. And I promised I'd hold off.

Three daughters, and here we are: the first evidence that one of them is having sex. I picture Sister Paola's face as she tells us that God forbids certain kinds of communion outside marriage. I picture Richard, in Father Cecil's office at the church where I was baptized and confirmed, agreeing to raise our future children in the Catholic faith (a job we've essentially phoned in). I also picture myself taking the host onto my tongue during Thanksgiving break of my junior year in college, for the first time since going to bed with Richard—wondering if lightning would pierce the roof above the nave and fry me to a crisp before I even got my visa for eternity in hell.

I generally use Monday G block for grading, but I can hardly grade papers at a piano, so I will sign out early and head home. I walk out the front door into an afternoon of balm and breeze and trees that seem to have just this minute burst into a song of phosphorescent green. Between the music room and the parking lot stand those three saplings, each a bit taller than I, each wearing a hoop skirt of coffee-colored mulch. Three maidens: metaphors abound! José's truck and equipment are gone, broom strokes of dirt on the sidewalk the only evidence that he was here.

I text Dana to drive herself home; I'll walk. That key chain of hers includes a key to my VW (a privilege I suppose we'll take away, after The Talk we'll have tonight).

In this half hour of rare solitude, I find myself thinking of Sister Paola, everyone's favorite among the nuns who taught us in junior high. She taught math, but also music. Where we might have expected some tepid early Beatles slipped in with Handel and Bach, she gave us U2 and the Talking Heads. She also taught a course she called Your Health and Your Faith. No one made fun of it. She seemed to be someone who *relished* her life, which we pubescent girls found astonishing to contemplate. We argued about how old she was—maybe a bit older than our mothers?—and some of us fantasized that she had come to her vocation after a wild, fulfilling life of carefree sex and fancy cocktails, rejecting the yoke of marriage under which we saw our mothers bowed (and to which we swore we'd never surrender). I think of the cross around José's neck. Is that a clue to my wayward cravings?

I reach home before the end of the school day. Tricia, who's in seventh grade, will be taking the day's last class in her room; our cramped middle school must operate on a do-si-do of two days there, three days at home. When I enter the kitchen, Richard is prowling through the refrigerator. He's startled to see me so early and turns around with a hunk of cheddar in one hand and a grin on his broad, clean-shaven face. (No pandemic beard for him!) The words *Our daughter is having sex* almost cross my lips.

"You missed me!" he says, putting the cheese on the counter.

"I always miss you, darling," I say in my dime-store Dietrich.

He takes my shoulder bag and sets it on a chair. He kisses my neck.

"Oh, Richard. I have grading."

"Josie. Johhhhhsie," he whispers into my hair. He knows how to spin my name into a feathered plea. "You delay grading, I make dinner."

"Honey, Dana and Lucy come home in fifteen minutes."

"Plenty of time! Tricia's buried in some science project and the Wi-Fi's shaky." He takes me by the hand and leads me to the den, where boxes of legal documents now cover most of the rug hooked by my mother in her last lucid years. His massive monitor has sidelined a row of my favorite photos, including one of me with my five siblings when half of us wore braces.

Richard's khakis are off in a trice and he's attending to my zipper, peeling off my skirt. He leans back on the couch and I kneel over his lap and pause, the customary tease before lowering myself, me and my counterpart to his reliable erection, and he groans as he slides his big freckled hands up the front of my blouse to cover my breasts. He doesn't bother with buttons or hooks. "Josie, you were lying," he whispers. "You were ready for anything but grading." And then we are at it, a practice we know like a liturgy. Both of us come, our cries subdued, and I try, mostly succeeding, to shut out the image of Dana and that boy-man trespassing in that closet.

We're resting from our labors when I hear Tricia pounding down the stairs. But she'll be aiming for the fridge. I know my daughters' habits; or do I?

When Richard and I have reassembled our clothing (though I'm headed for the shower), I am about to tell him what I know—how can I not?—when he opens the door to the hall and bellows, "No finishing my favorite crackers!" And while I'm in the shower, I hear the rise of female voices from below; the other girls are back now, too.

Good as his word, Richard makes dinner. "Puttanesca! Puttanesca!" he sings as he stirs the sauce. "Don't you love that word?"

The girls are all upstairs in their rooms. Dana made it there before I was out of the shower and dressed. Now I'm at the kitchen table grading the Ivan Denisovich interviews. I say, "Richard, you do know what it means."

"Whore!" he says gleefully, brandishing a wooden spoon. "Which is not a fun word. That's why I married a mezzo-Italiana. I married into the fun words."

I tell him the pandemic is making him lose his mind. He tells me there are worse things to lose.

Dana comes down later than her sisters to the meal; as the one dealing with precollege stress, she's excused from dinner-time chores. At the table, she cannot meet my eyes, and I avoid making that happen. She glances occasionally at her father, no doubt trying to figure out if he knows. I wonder if she heard him extolling the Italian word for "prostitute."

Conversation is about the start of the sailing season. Richard races, and Tricia crews for him. They muse and speculate about whether last summer's restrictions will be lifted; come June, surely the oldest sailors will have had their shots. And when will we put the boat back in the water? Dana asks to skip dessert, muttering something about a Spanish exam.

It's Lucy's night to load the dishwasher; Richard retires to work on a brief; and to my surprise, I look out the window to see that it's still light. The clocks sprang forward a month ago, yet I'm still adjusting to the longer days. The sky is a liminal pink, the sun is below the houses across the street, but here we are at the cusp of the season for which we all live. Summer feels like a fish that's just tugged at the line; we have only to reel it in. I leave the house and start up the street without a destination. Two masked children on bikes pass me, and I notice how many windows are open, conversations audible; television, music. My neighbor Patsy is cutting dead canes from her roses.

The late light fooled me into confusing it with warmth; again, again, I realize that my daffodil-colored cardigan still hangs on the hook with the inventory list in that closet. Closet of iniquity, I think. Cabinet of libidinal curiosities.

I honestly hadn't meant to steer myself past José's house, but there it is—and there he is, sitting on his front stoop, with his wife, the two of them eating ice cream cones. Before I can turn around, he sees me and waves.

I stop and greet them; I have met the wife only a few times in literal passing and cannot remember her name.

"Twice in one day," says José.

"Pretty trees," I say. "The ones you planted."

"Yes." He nods solemnly. "A memorial."

I frown. "Someone died?"

"Oh, many people have died," he says. He's suspended the

eating of his ice cream, and it begins to drip toward his callused hand. He is smiling sadly now, while I pretend to understand, and then I do.

"Of the virus, yes. So the trees . . ."

"I am told there will be a stone with a brass plate."

"A plaque," his wife says. She has finished her cone, and she takes her husband's, licks the margins efficiently, and hands it back. "Eat it before it melts," she tells him.

José licks the ice cream enthusiastically—so now I've seen his tongue!—and I say, "Enjoy your evening." The wife wishes me the same, and I turn the corner. I walk slowly around the block, looking shamelessly into all the uncurtained windows of a busy, beautiful Monday evening as it leans toward a beautiful night. *Bella notte.* But for Richard's overbearing mother, I would have kept my maiden name. Ms. Bellanotte, my students would call me. Would I have been breezier, an easier grader, the teacher you don't mind running into at the Fourth of July parade?

By the time I arrive back at home, darkness has fallen and it looks as if lights are on in every single room. (Cue my wearisome role as conservation heavy.) I focus on a second-story window, my daughter Dana's. She is up there now, probably texting furiously with Tim Jr.

I stand beneath the maple tree whose split trunk José bolted together three years ago, saving its life. Watching him mend the damage, I thought of broken hearts; what if you could just call in an expert who knew how to bolt them together again? That was another theory about Sister Paola: that she'd surrendered herself to Jesus after a near-fatal heartbreak. A man had promised her the moon and left her for another woman; she had come close to ending her life. How we despised this man to whom she had given herself, whose existence seemed briefly as real to us as that of the Holy Ghost.

Something suddenly occurs to me: What if the day had been differently scheduled and my daughter had been the one to walk in on me? I feel a hot surge of relief, and I laugh out loud. What kind of a talk would we be having then?

I see Dana's shadow cross her lacy curtain. I need to end the misery of her suspense, and I'll do it now, without telling Richard. I'll talk to her about desire and joy and risk and faith (the no-name brand); oh, and trespassing. For good measure, I'll take away car privileges—even though we're all still basically grounded. She'll be horribly embarrassed, wanting nothing more than for her chatterbox mother to leave her room. But before I do, I'll hug her, hug her tight.

I'll climb into bed with Richard, who will be surrounded by his various digital connections to a world of crime and punishment, and I'll read some poetry, then turn out my light, then go right to sleep. Who will enter my crazy dreams is anybody's guess.

How I Learned Prayer

W hen *I was a kid* I went to church and Sunday school and Bible study every week. Had to memorize Scripture, learn every song, and know the steps necessary to dance on the head of the devil if the organ demanded. How to lift my hands and cry out for a savior I'm not sure I've ever actually believed in. And though the hallelujahs often felt a bit hollow to me, my mother, now gone on, would've been so proud to know I've finally learned to pray.

The first time was overwhelming, perhaps because I never knew prayer to feel like anything other than performance. But on a Sunday evening, Misha Ferndale, a theology student and tea drinker, taught me to pray some kind of truth.

I met her at work. Served her Lapsang, which came at my recommendation because she wanted a jolt but not too much. I've worked in a tea shop for a long time. Took the place over after my mother passed. I grew up there, a child peeking over the counter watching my mom steep pot after pot, listening to her preach about how with tea the flavor is often based on restraint and timing. Sermons on how much tea is the right amount, how to watch it change the color of water, how to time it to ward off its bitterness. I've also learned over the years that the people who come into tea shops aren't the same as those who frequent coffee shops. Teahouses seem to be—and I don't know this for a fact—but they seem to be more intimate. There's no growling grinder, or gurgling milk frother. No slamming espresso cups, or nasty attitudes with complicated orders. It's just about time. The people who hole up in teahouses typically come for the peace of it. There's something, I don't know, holy about it. They come with the intention of calmly waiting for water to be transformed coupled with the eagerness of that first sip. That, and studying. People serious about studying do so in tea joints.

"You believe in heaven?" I asked Misha one day, setting a single-serve teapot, cup, and saucer in front of her. She'd been coming in consistently for weeks, and I'd always pick her brain about what she was reading. Some days she'd go on about the history of matriarchal religions. Other times it was comparing and contrasting different prophets. Once we even spoke about what got her interested in theology in the first place, and her response was that it felt ungodly that her father never spared the rod. On this day, though, it was about the creation of the afterlife.

"Like, as a destination?"

"Yeah, I guess." I desperately wanted to believe there was such a place as heaven and that my mother was there sipping Assam with milk. But I had my doubts.

"That depends," Misha said, sliding her pencil into the gutter of her theology book, closing it.

"On what?"

She poured herself a cup, held it up to her face, and closed her eyes. She smelled it before slurping.

"On whether or not one believes in prayer."

"You mean God?"

"I mean prayer. God is too big. Too . . . everywhere. Prayer feels more graspable. More immediate, you know? And if prayer is real, we could all probably build heaven with it as long as you know heaven, according to what I've read, isn't permanent."

"It's not?"

"From what I'm studying, it's basically a teahouse where we're the teapots. We're the water being changed and prepared to comfort a new world." She picked up her book, flipped through the pages, then set it back down on the table. "But I don't know anything. I mean, do any of us? I guess that's why I'm saying prayer is an easier concept to give oneself over to."

"I'm telling you right now, if I get to whatever this new world is and I'm still making tea . . ."

"I'd become religious, because it would then be confirmed that God don't make mistakes." Misha hid her chuckle behind the lip of the cup, took another sip—on this day, rooibos—then let out an overexaggerated *ahhh* of satisfaction.

"Okay, so . . . you believe in prayer?" I asked, trying to hide the fact I was just as intrigued by Misha as I was the topic.

She smirked but didn't answer. And she didn't have to, because a week later she taught me that prayer could happen in all sorts of ways. Showed me that it could taste like decent Shiraz, branzino, or sumptuous chatter about oolong and hojicha, or unanswerable questions about whether or not sin is a thing, or if there is a praise that hasn't been named. Questions that attached themselves to us, that were now part of this prayer that I was learning could walk back to her apartment. This prayer that could climb steps, leave shoes at the door. That could sound like the shish of a silk dress being pulled overhead after a second date I had to beg for because Misha was so busy with the business of earning a master's. This prayer, like no prayer I've ever known, could sound like a woman telling me to genuflect.

"Get on your knees," she said, almost as if she'd stolen language from my mouth. Her voice oscillated between whine and whisper. She'd already stripped me, already unbuckled and unbuttoned everything, my varnish vanishing in the dark. She'd pressed her lips to my chest, scraped her teeth across each of my shoulders, kissed my forehead, and finally my mouth.

"Get on your knees," she repeated. "Please."

The light from outside cut through the open blinds pulling stripes of brown from her silhouette, and I followed them down like rungs on a ladder.

When I was a kid, whenever it was time to pray my mother told me to close my eyes and press my palms together, but never said why. I figured maybe it was a symbol for those who were to be counted by the Lord in case he returned during eleven o'clock service. I also figured it was so I could imagine God, tiny and trapped between my hands. This way I could hold him close enough to hear me. Sometimes it made me feel like I was doing something. Most times it made me feel silly. But at this altar—the altar of Misha Ferndale—though my body was folded, nothing about me was meant to be closed in such a moment of reverence. There was nothing small to be captured in this hallowed space. Prayer was happening to me. Happening in me, around me. Prayer was standing in front of me, in panties.

Misha put her fingers in my hair, let them tangle in the thick of it, the perfume from earlier still on her wrists, wafting rose all around us. My hands on the backs of her knees, on the backs of her thighs, on her ass. My face resting on her stomach.

"Salvation?" I murmured while brushing my bottom lip across the skin just below her navel. It seemed like a random utterance, but it was an answer to a question she'd asked on the walk home. A question I was sure she'd forgotten.

To my surprise, she replied. "Maybe."

Misha gently pressed on the crown of my head, asking me without asking me to lower myself.

I ran my nose along the lace elastic, dipping it down into the cotton, the only partition left dividing us. It was then and there I felt overcome with confession. Where I wanted to admit how I've never believed. How perhaps there is a penance for this. Atonement. I pulled her closer and pushed my face into the fabric, breathing into the soft tuft protecting the small space the same size my hands used to make when I tried praying as a child. I was now certain God was there. Certain God was close enough to hear me.

"Sanctuary?" I asked, trying again.

"Maybe." She gasped, squirmed in her skin, slipped her thumbs into the waistband of her panties, and tried to push them down. But I stopped her. Moved her hands because it wasn't time. Not yet. I glanced up and was stunned by the streak of light across her breasts, another across her clavicle, another across her mouth. I wondered if I looked as beautiful to her. I wondered what it was like to see me halved and still whole.

"How about ceremony?" I asked between kissing her creases and corners, stroking the hinges of her.

She couldn't get the answer out before it became air. She tried to say it again but it caught in her throat. Her hands returned to my head, as did her weight. She wanted me to submerge, knowing our prayer contained baptism, patient steeping. She knew there was an anointing to come. A blessing she had for me, and I for her. We were to be sacrament, Communion, both ready to sip and be sipped from.

Then I did what she wanted to do—what she'd tried—and slipped my fingers between waist and waistband, began to slide them down. A shiver worked its way through her body, a spirit caught, a dance trapped, and she now raised her arms in a praise that hadn't been named.

"Ceremony?" I repeated, steeping my fingers deeper into the holy water.

And after a moment, she managed in what seemed like a final breath to say twice more, "Maybe. Maybe."

And as I prepared to meet my maker, to be introduced to a fleeting heaven, to sing a new hymn and whisper amen to a savior I'm now convinced is real, I replied, "Oh, God, tell me, then, what *is* another name for rapture?"

Love Doll

ike most night school classrooms, it smelled of anxiety and misfortune, and in the Honolulu heat it was saturated with the industrial odor of floor polish, the tang of mildewed ceiling tiles, the stale whiff of chalk dust, and the hum of noodles in grease-stained take-out oyster pails. Throughout the class, the yawns of the students, the creak of their desks, the clank of their chairs as they shifted to get comfortable. All of them had done a day's work, and were glassy-eyed with fatigue.

But, new to Hawaii, and now sleep-deprived himself with a small baby and a weary wife—accidental baby, accidental wife—Stan Blanton had asked to teach this extra subject, Business English, because he needed the money. He realized how resentful he was when the students, all of them immigrants—working at menial jobs, wishing for better—in the course of a lesson, jeered at the people in Hawaii, and he smiled. Their contempt diverted him and relieved the tedium of the hated ninety minutes.

It had started with Balsamo, the Brazilian in the front row, patches of his wild hair tinted blond, who said, "I am go to the *museo—*"

"I went to the Honolulu museum," Blanton corrected, gesturing for him to continue.

"I waynt to the Honolulu museum and I see all the feengs they are robbed from odder countries, even my country. These people are feefs!"

The students laughed—all but one, Miss Van, the Vietnamese woman at the back, who sat with her hands folded on her notebook, her silence like a reproach, as though she were sitting in judgment. Her straight-backed upright posture made Blanton self-conscious, and among all those drudges, her singular beauty gave her an aura of power, the hauteur of a priestess. He desired her, and though he hated teaching night school, he went gladly to the class, eager to impress her, his hunger for her keeping him wistful.

"And the *museo* not clean," Balsamo was saying. "I know, because I am clean the airport."

"And we cleaning, too," said Wesley Hauk, tapping the shoulder of the man next to him, John Wia, who nodded yes. They described themselves as "Micros"—from Chuuk. "Hawaii people they no want this work."

"Too much lazy these people," Marivick Fargas said. She was the one Filipina, an older woman, who washed dishes in a nursing home. "Too much they throw paper and stuffs in the street."

The Thai boy, Sah, chipped in with, "They play music all the day"; the severe Chinese man, Mr. Bai, "Dey makes nothing here. Dis bad paradise."

Speaking slowly, Blanton wrote the words on the blackboard. "These people are very lazy. They tend to leave rubbish by the roadside. This is a bad paradise."

And they chanted this, while he led them, even Miss Van,

who had not volunteered to speak. She silently moved her pretty lips.

"What do you think, Miss Van?"

"Some people good, some not good. It is the world."

"Very wise," Blanton said, and then enunciating slowly in his correcting voice, he said, "Many people are good. Some are not. That's the way things are."

As Miss Van repeated this, Blanton gazed at her with a longing that pinched his throat as he asked her to say it again.

"Time up!" Balsamo called out, tapping his wristwatch.

"Okay, see you next week," Blanton said. "Leave your essays on the table."

Irritable and sleepless, because the baby was so wakeful, Blanton took a reckless pleasure in hearing the students complain. They were new Americans struggling for a foothold, anxious to learn, and as though to justify their presence, disapproving of Hawaiian work habits. Blanton was disapproving, too—feeling he'd made a mistake coming to teach on this expensive island, where he lived in a small apartment, and still had not paid off his student loan. Faye, who'd been a librarian in Seattle, was fully occupied with the baby.

When Blanton returned home after work and saw her cradling Lily, he was struck by how contained, how remote, she seemed, staring at the baby, preoccupied, like a Madonna. She often held a small doll in front of the baby's face. It was a hula girl in a grass skirt, a lei of red flowers covering her breasts, arms behind her head in a provocative pose, a big bloom tucked at her ear—a piece of island kitsch that was also a bank. A coin pressed into its base activated a spring inside, and the hula girl shimmied mechanically, her grass skirt twitched, and Lily gurgled. Faye had discovered it in a souvenir shop and seemed to find it weirdly

satisfying, its shimmying on command, with the insertion of a
coin. The baby on her lap, Faye herself was like a girl with a doll.

An accidental doll. A year ago, when they were living together in Seattle, Faye said she wanted to move out, and Stan
had been relieved that she'd at last understood what he had seen
for months, that they had no future. She was practical, but her
need for order made her impatient, and sometimes repetitious.
His unfinished dissertation was always on his mind—he carried its incompleteness around with him, and he was in debt,
the student loan growing more burdensome. He became like
her negligent son, and so when she said, "This is not working,"
he said, "I think you're right. We need to reboot—with someone else, somewhere else."

They had what they called their breakup dinner, and drank,
and made love one last time, and separated. They were briefly
happy apart, they still talked. But two months after the dinner,
Faye came to him and said, "Guess what?"

They became partners again, for convenience. Faye was
granted maternity leave, and said she would not be a burden to
him, but that they needed this arrangement for now, in the way
accidents always forced obligations on you. And in another ac-
cident, Stan casually applied for a job in Hawaii and was hired,
and disliked it at once, the sprawl of the city, the sprawl of the
provisional. Lily was born, and Faye was fully occupied. His
misery was always, How will this end?

He was overworked, he felt old, he felt poor. The mockery
of the night class helped his mood: he was among other mal-
contents, but they were worse off than he. His daytime classes
were routine, monologues on literature; but teaching English
language required dialogue, a tiring back-and-forth, and constant correction. Yet these night class students were motivated.

They had paid for these weekly sessions. They did their home-work; the stack of essays before him was proof of that. He al-ways read Miss Van's essay first, wishing for—what? Perhaps a clue to what was in her heart.

To provoke her, the previous week he had chalked the words LOVE and LIKE and ADMIRE on the blackboard and explained the distinctions, and tried to initiate a conversation.

"Love—you know what love is," he said, and they had nod-ded. "A great feeling, like a dream." He faced the weary students, their eyes glazed with fatigue, but Miss Van was unreadable. "I love you. I love my children. I love my mother. Balsamo?"

"I love my mudda."

"Good. Do I love to drink beer? No, I *like* to drink beer. I *like* my friends. The word is less powerful. What do you like, Mr. Hauk?"

"I am like drink beer." And the others laughed.

"What do you like, Miss Van?"

She stiffened, she did not smile. She shrugged, she said un-helpfully, "I like some things. Other things not like."

"Then there is 'admire.'" Blanton tapped the word, whiten-ing his fingertip with chalk dust, and took a step back. "You look up to this person. You might love them, but really the person is bigger than you—maybe better, someone special."

Now they were apprehensive—he recognized the vibra-tion, the fear that he was going to pick on one with a question. He smiled at Balsamo, who smiled back and said, "I am admire Pelé. Footballer. *Grande homem.*"

At the end of class he had assigned an essay, just a para-graph, he said, slashing at the blackboard with his stick of chalk, so they could copy: "A person I love, or like, or admire."

It had been a hard week, not just teaching his usual courses

(Stevenson, Twain, Jack London, Somerset Maugham, and others who'd visited and written about Hawaii), but dealing with Faye and the baby, the night feedings, the shopping. He thought, *If I sit down I will go to sleep.*

Now he was reading *I admire Auntie Ong. She is a mother to me, because my mother died from the Agent Orange cancer. Auntie Ong had a hard life, first absconding from the country by a small vessel. In the ocean water for more than a month period, she saw the weak ones expire. But she making good business in America and know how to manipulate the inebriation ones who do not admire her.*

Miss Van, with a dictionary. The following week, handing her the paper with *Good job* written at the top, and the grammatical mistakes corrected, he said, "Aunt Ong sounds amazing."

Miss Van folded the paper without reading it, and slipped it into her notebook. She seemed to hesitate; she had a habit he'd noticed of saying, "What?" She mouthed that word now.

"Which country did Aunt Ong escape from?"

"My country, Vietnam, but long time ago."

"I've read about that. She watched people die. What does she do in Hawaii?"

But Miss Van bowed her head and clasped her notebook, and for a moment looked fragile, her skin feverish seeming in its pallor, her hair in a bun, wisps of it and ringlets trailing on her skinny neck. She was the size of a schoolgirl, in her mid- or late twenties, but her aura was majestic.

"Business," Miss Van said, expelling the word like a breath.

Blanton said, "You're very pretty."

As Miss Van stiffened and backed away and averted her eyes—lowering them Blanton saw her lovely lashes—he thought, *I'm a fool.*

He'd promised Faye he'd bring some food home. And so he

bought two cartons of wonton saimin and fought the traffic to the small apartment, and the laughter of his neighbor's TV, the odor of teriyaki sauce wafting from upstairs, a fugitive salty hint of seawater in the air. And Faye with the baby on her lap, tapping a coin into the hula doll to make it twitch.

He'd accepted the job, to prop himself up in the period of "We'll figure something out"—the accidental pregnancy, the accidental marriage—and they'd come to Hawaii promptly, knowing there'd be a time when Faye would be too far along to fly. The small apartment and the new job had been a strain, but the weather was better than Seattle. Hawaii sunshine made his life bearable.

Faye reminded him to look for a baby carriage, and he kept saying, "I'm on it," by which he meant to ask if any of his colleagues had one to spare. The problem was money—paying off his student loan, making ends meet here, car payments, rent and food, the extra cost of the baby. Thus, night school, the language class.

Teaching language involved hectoring students to open up and talk. But they were tired, too. Balsamo the Brazilian was the only animated one, Mr. Bai was tense, the Micronesians smiled in ways that suggested they did not understand much. Miss Van at the back was watchful, but did her silence mean she was confident? She replied when spoken to, but volunteered nothing. He loved the contours of her angelic face, her pretty lips, her thin, bird-bone fingers.

"Language learning is an activity, like play," he said. They did not react. Perhaps they knew little of play. He taught the expressions "This is mine" and "This belongs to me" and "I would like this for myself." These statements made them smile. All they knew was deprivation.

He placed a banana on a table, and invited each student to grasp it, repeating "This is mine" and "This belongs to me." Balsamo clowned with it. Mr. Bai merely tapped it, Miss Van plucked it in her pretty fingers, saying with seriousness, "This belong to me. I would like this for myself."

"Let's go through some responses," he said, writing on the blackboard, *Would you like to join me?* and under it a list of choices, *Yes, I would,* and *I'm not comfortable,* and *Perhaps later,* and *That's what I want—I'd enjoy that.*

They recited in turn, choosing from the list, stammering at times, while he corrected their pronunciation; and then, "Miss Van? 'Yes, I'd enjoy that.'"

"Yes," she said—and Blanton held his breath—"I'd enjoy that."

"Homework," he said. "One paragraph. 'What I Enjoy.'"

And he was out of the room while they were still gathering their papers. He had parked near the library, so by the time he found his car it was ten to nine. Passing the bus stop on University Avenue, he saw Miss Van, standing on the curb, and, peering anxiously at the oncoming traffic, she was looking straight at him.

She stepped back when he drew next to her and called through the window, "Need a lift?"

Miss Van crossed her arms against her upper body, as though in defense, but the gesture also made her seem demure.

"It's okay. Come on, get in." Leaning across the seat, he pushed the door open.

Only then did she seem to recognize him. She slipped in and was silent.

"I can take you as far as Kalakaua. I'm picking up something at Holiday Mart."

"Yes," she said.

"You're going near there?"

"Yes," she said, the same hiss.

"Would you like to join me?" he said, and laughed. When he saw that she did not react, he said, with emphasis, "The lesson."

Miss Van exhaled softly in recognition.

He could think of nothing else to say, and remembered that she was the one student who did not offer any criticism of Hawaii, but sat and stared, and reminded him that he was wrong to encourage the others in their banter. Her silence gave him a greater awareness of her physical presence, and for the first time her perfume, an aroma of flowers that seemed like an entreaty to him, more eloquent than words.

As they turned the corner onto Kalakaua, approaching Holiday Mart, she stirred and said, "Here."

"You live here?"

"Thank you."

He could see only shops, a grocery, a computer store, a bar, a pawn shop. Once out of the car she had darted away. He looked to see where she had gone, but she had vanished. After he'd bought the diapers at Holiday Mart and was driving back, past the spot where he'd dropped Miss Van, he looked again. It was not a residential area. A short distance away he saw a looming new structure, steel and glass, Pacific Park Tower lettered over its entrance, clearly an office building.

Was she trying to fool him by asking him to drop her at this empty soulless junction so he would not know where she lived? He could not rid his mind of the pale, slim woman, so serious in class, in a jacket and blue jeans, disappearing into the shadows, slipping away from him.

In the succeeding days, after classes, his routine trips to

Holiday Mart for groceries, for diapers, allowed him to size up the area. It seemed even less inhabited in daylight—the dry cleaners, the liquor store, the shop selling curtains; and that large commercial building, Pacific Park Tower.

"You're a darling," Faye said each time he returned from Holiday Mart. And though the acknowledgment he knew was unspoken, she was grateful he was not pestering her for sex. It had been months, but she was fatigued with the baby. The presence of the baby in the bedroom killed his ardor, and her breastfeeding the baby, so sweet, was another form of exclusion. The baby had taken possession of her body, of the vitality of their marriage, filled the apartment that had become a dollhouse.

And there was something about Faye's ignoring him to amuse Lily with the hula doll that annoyed him, her fiddling with the coin, the whisper and scratch of the spring, the doll's predictable shimmy, the twitching of the grass skirt.

"Got a nickel?" Faye asked one night.

Blanton slapped his pockets and smiled. "Sorry."

He looked for Miss Van at the bus stop the following week, and again saw her facing the traffic, awaiting a bus, but she stepped back when he slowed down next to her. She shrank, and said, "I rather not," as in the lesson.

"'I'd rather not,'" he corrected.

The insistence of her refusal made him reflective. The blunt rebuff stung him. He saw that he had hoped to make her a friend, perhaps more than a friend, and the grim thought that he was lonely for her made him angry. He was mulling this the next day when Ray Kellogg, his office mate (Blanton was too junior to have his own office), walked in and said, "Union meeting."

"I hate those things."

Kellogg said, "Your absence will be duly noted."

"So you think I should go?"

"We're voting for a salary increase—cost-of-living supplement."

"I'm in," Blanton said, and then, "By the way, you know this big building on Kalakaua, Pacific Park Tower?"

"Six floors of whores," Kellogg said.

Hearing this, Blanton sensed a glow rise up the back of his neck and settle on his scalp, and a warmth around his eyes that made him blink as, tasting the dryness on his tongue, he steadied himself for a breath, grateful that Kellogg was still talking.

Another week, another class, and at the end of this one Blanton parked near the bus stop and, when Miss Van boarded, he followed the bus to Kalakaua and the Pacific Park Tower. Seeing Miss Van crossing the street, he double-parked, leaving his warning blinkers on, and watched her enter the lobby. He did not follow her until the elevator doors closed, but then he hurried in, to watch the illuminated numbers in the panel over the door stop at four. The elevator was empty when it descended, its doors grinding open.

A board in the lobby listed the businesses on the fourth floor. There were three—an insurance agency, Aloha Pest Solutions, and Love Doll Spa.

That night, although he was exhausted, he lay in bed, awake. Faye slumbered beside him, the baby in the crib emitted a soft bubbling snore, the hula girl on the bedside table. He smiled at his sleuthing, and he considered the bewitching words "Love Doll."

In the week leading up to the night class, a period he had once dreaded, he became impatient, eager to see Miss Van again. And when she took her usual seat apart from the others, at the back of the room, and the class began, he spoke directly to her and studied her features, the words "Love Doll" revolving in his mind.

That was his name for her now. He saw that her pallor was strange and waxen on an island that was bathed in sunlight, her thin face made her seem tense, she wore her jet-black hair straight now and it fell to her shoulders. Her lips were set, pursed in doubt, and her stare, her distinct cheekbones, her stillness, gave her a mask of concentration. She kept her hands clasped, holding a pen, and now and then she disentangled her fingers and made a note, then clasped them again. Her smock-like jacket was loose and revealed her body as slight. Her face was angelic.

Blanton devoted the class to questions asking for help, variations of "Would you mind telling me," and "May I ask the way to," and "I wonder if you could help me find the way to," and other similar expressions of helplessness. As always he encouraged the students to address each other.

"Would you mind telling me the way to the post office?" Mr. Bai asked.

"May I ask the way to the beach?" Mr. Hauk asked.

"Miss Van?" Blanton said. "Ask me a question."

"Please," she said, straightening, fixing him with her gaze. "Help me find my way home."

Blanton tried to reply but only stammered, staring at her. The plaintive appeal, almost anguished, touched his heart, and in that moment, in the simplicity of her appeal, he desired her more. This was something greater than lust—a glimpse of a future, the recognition that he would never tire of her. This reverie eased the tedium of the night class, the burden of fretful fatigue and Faye, remote, purposeful, head bowed, amusing the baby in the small apartment with the cheap hula doll, his disenchantment with Hawaii and the debt that had nagged at him. It seemed childish, but he saw Miss Van as a potential ally, someone to dally with, to lighten the monotony of his routine, to lift his spirits.

The trouble was that a whole week separated the night school sessions, the times when he could see her.

One evening, crouching by the crib with the twitching doll, Faye said, "Things must be improving."

"Why do you say that?"

"I heard you whistling." She seemed hopeful, as though his whistling meant they had a future.

Had he whistled, and if so what was the tune? He laughed, and said, "Actually I'm more hard pressed than ever. I need to spend some time at the library tonight."

Her new habit was not to turn away from the baby, but to maintain her maternal watchfulness, staring fixedly at the child, the shimmying hula girl in her hand as she spoke to Blanton.

"Don't wake me when you get back. I need to sleep."

All he wanted was to visit Pacific Park Tower, find Love Doll Spa, and see whether Miss Van worked there.

"You need anything at Holiday Mart? I could swing by."

"Diapers," she said, gazing at the child.

Buying diapers at Holiday Mart made him feel less furtive, gave him a reason to be in that neighborhood, and allowed him a place to park. He threw the bag into the back seat, and walked to Pacific Park Tower. He entered the lobby and took the elevator to the fourth floor, where he saw a Love Doll Spa sign on the wall with an arrow pointing right. At the far end of the corridor, a door was slightly ajar. Using the back of his hand he pushed the door open, and recognized the odor—the sugary perfume and mild disinfectant from Miss Van's homework paper, and an aroma he had not been able to identify until now, the clotted smell of incense. A taper burned before a small gilt shrine on the floor against one wall, a fierce deity, a gleaming orange in a dish with some coins, and the stick of smoldering incense, upright in a jar of sand.

"Yes?" A woman approached through a parted curtain. She was elderly, and though she was shapeless and calm, her mouth was crooked, tugged down, her lower lip torn, disfigured by an old scar, which gave her a slushy way of speaking as she said, "I can help you?"

"Just looking for someone," Blanton said. He glanced around, glad that no other man was there. But it was early.

"You want massage?" the old woman said with the same slushiness, and this time the words seemed vicious.

Blanton could not suppress a giggle. He said, "Maybe," and then, "Miss Van."

"No Miss Van," the woman said, pronouncing it *Vang*. She picked up what looked like a restaurant menu from a table—it was an oversized folder, plastic covered, sticky to the touch—and she opened it to a page of photographs. "But these girls working tonight." The women wore bathing suits, their names below their picture: Leilani and Sukumi and Minh. "More girls coming later."

She was Leilani, in a red bikini, but wearing makeup, her mouth reddened and full lipped, the lank hair upswept, a large blossom tucked over her ear, one of her slender fingers pressed to her cheek, smiling. Blanton had never seen her smile.

"This one," he said, dry mouthed again. "Leilani."

"Cash or credit card?"

"How much for the, um . . . " he began, but could not finish.

"Fifty dollar for house. You pay girl separate. One hour, very nice." And seeing him slapping his pockets, she added, "We have ATM machine."

He knew because he had just been to Holiday Mart that he had two twenties and some ones in his wallet. Faye would see the credit card statement, so that was out of the question. The ATM would generate a line item on his bank statement. He took out his wallet and, pinching it, weighed it before the old woman as though casting a spell.

"Thirty dollars—cash," he said. "Half hour."

"You trying to cheat me," the old woman said, chewing her damaged lip. Blanton was mortified by the directness of her accusation. "Leilani very good. She worth more."

"Okay, forty. Can I just see her—talk to her?"

"Sorry, mister."

As she was moving toward Blanton, to evict him, the door opened. A stout older man began to enter, then hesitated, straightened, and cleared his throat. When he saw Blanton he crept to the shrine, smiled at it, and fled to an armchair. As he lowered himself he snatched up a tattered magazine and held it before his face, humming softly, plucking at the pages, avoiding eye contact, like a man in a doctor's waiting room. He wore a baseball cap, an aloha shirt that was tightened by his paunch, and flip-flops on his dirty feet.

"Thanks," Blanton murmured, turning away from the man and keeping his head down. In his car it occurred to him that the piggy man might have chosen Miss Van—Leilani—from the album, and the thought disgusted and angered him.

"You're early," Faye said when he arrived home. "Did you find what you wanted at the library?"

In the house all day, attending to the baby, she was buffered in her bliss by her motherly warmth from all the wrongs of Honolulu, existing in a glow of innocence that radiated from her child.

"I'll have to make another visit tomorrow," Blanton said with a shallow cough.

"Doesn't anyone in your department have a baby carriage they don't need? The cheapest one I've seen cost two hundred bucks."

And when, the following evening, he punched two hundred dollars into the keypad of the ATM machine at Holiday Mart, he became grim, thinking of the baby carriage; then excited, thinking of Miss Van. He tried to imagine a plausible lie for Faye when she saw the credit card statement and questioned the withdrawal.

The old woman with the torn lip greeted him at the door, and this time she seemed like a sorceress.

"Auntie Ong," he said, to dispel her aura of power.

"How you know my name?" she said accusingly, drawing away from him.

"Everyone knows you," he said. "I want to see Leilani."

"Fifty dollar for the house."

"Here you are."

"Pay girl separate," she said, palming the money, scuffing out of the lobby, gesturing for him to follow.

In the dim pinkish light of the corridor, he passed doors opened to small empty rooms with beds, like a dollhouse, he thought, until he saw that each room had an oversized wall mirror, each mirror reflecting a fretful, hurrying man.

At the last room, Auntie Ong said, "You wait inside," and when Blanton slipped in she pulled the door shut.

He turned away from the mirror. A double bed filled the room, and on it a big beach towel—lettered Aloha—had been spread over the sheet. Apart from the chair on which he was sitting there was no other furniture. No window, a mirror above the headboard, a clock.

When the door opened, he stood abruptly and swayed, dizzy from the suddenness of being upright. Miss Van in the doorway, half in, half out, leaning and then partly withdrawing. Her expression did not change, yet Blanton thought he heard a subtle ticktock, as faint as the click of a ballpoint; but he knew, her little tongue.

"Cannot," she finally said.

"I paid," Blanton said.

"I not comfortable," she said, and stepped away, closing the door.

He sat, then got up, scowled at the mirror, then went to the door, which was vibrant with murmurs. He snatched it open and saw Auntie Ong holding Miss Van by the wrist.

"What's going on?"

"You wait," the old woman said.

"I paid," Blanton said.

"Go inside. She coming now."

He stepped back and shut the door and, facing it—and the murmurs—he considered leaving. Yet he had come so far. He thought: *If she joins me—fine. If she refuses, I will go home to my wife and baby. But I need to wait and see. I will accept whatever happens,* and remembered to add, *As my fate.*

The door opened in his face. Miss Van stepped in. She was paler than he'd ever seen her, but maybe this was the effect of reddened lips and her black dress, which was loose and short, and perhaps not a dress at all but a sort of gauzy lingerie. She stared at him in a way he could not read, though he noticed (her hair was upswept and lovely) an almost imperceptible shake of the ringlets beside her face, as though in disbelief.

"What now?" he said.

"Hundred dollar." With this a beckoning, a twitching of her fingers.

"For what?"

"Special."

"God," he said, and reaching to claw his head realized that he was still wearing a baseball cap. He pulled it off and sat on the edge of the bed, sighing.

"Okay, I go. I rather not."

"Miss Van," he said.

But she interrupted, "I not Miss Van. I Leilani."

"All I have is a hundred."

"That what I want."

He counted the money into her hand, wishing that he could see her expression. But she was facing down, counting, too. Then he slipped off his clothes and lay back on the bed, centering himself on the towel, while Miss Van pushed the money into a purse.

Seeing her approaching, Blanton said, "Aren't you going to take your clothes off?"

"Twenty dollar extra."

He extracted the bill from his pocket saying, "Take them off slowly."

She did so, stroking them against herself, teasing him. When she was naked he leaned toward her, propping himself on one elbow. What he took to be a green belt at her waist was a speckled snake tattooed on her body, encircling her, rising up her spine, the wedgelike head of the snake resting between her shoulder blades, its forked tongue extended toward the nape of her neck.

"No kiss," Miss Van said, framing her lips in disgust.

Fumbling beside the bed for his wallet Blanton found a twenty-dollar bill and pressed it into her palm. As Miss Van folded her fingers over it she lowered her head and kissed him, her soft lips tremulous against his, as though imploring him.

And then he lay back on the bed, and glancing past the pale spidery form of Miss Van, got a glimpse in the mirror, and was appalled by what he saw, the pudding of his white misshapen body, his pinkish face and crazy hair, and had to look away, keeping his face averted, as he did when a doctor was drawing blood from his stinging arm.

"This is mine," she said, her voice an insistent whisper, taking hold of him, and began to chant it. Breathing hard, she was transformed, working herself into amorous panting that was something like frenzied prayer, as she straddled him, facing away, her buttocks chafing against his face, still massaging him. Then she turned aside, facing him, and leered and tugged, murmuring, "Mine."

"Yes" burned in his throat.

"Watch Leilani," she said eagerly, working her tongue against her lips. "This belong to me."

As he began to whimper, "Yes, yes," he became breathless himself, and her whispering, as of someone starved, stopped with a gasp, as she took him into her mouth. It was ecstasy, for seconds.

"You like it?" he asked in a groan as she slid off him, shimmying to the edge of the bed, reaching for her clothes.

"It work."

"Don't go, baby," he said, because she was dressing.

"Finish," she said, and was out of the room before he could think of anything to say.

To his surprise and pleasure Miss Van was in her usual seat at the next night class. He was encouraged by the sight of her, he smiled at her, though she did not smile back.

"This product is interesting," he said, and wrote the words on the blackboard. "This product is more interesting," he said, still writing. "This product is the most interesting of all." And when he finished, got the students to recite these phrases.

"Football is interesting," he said, speaking to Balsamo. "Is baseball more interesting?"

"Football is more interesting product forever," Balsamo said.

"What do you think, Miss Van?"

"Football is interesting," she said.

"What is more interesting than football?"

"Business is most interesting of all," she said.

"What business?"

"Noodle shop," she said, and hesitating, added, "I want to make."

"Excellent," he said, and turned to the others, using the last half hour to explain the Department of Human Relations—its meaning, its purpose, and at eight thirty, said, "Until next week." He beckoned to Miss Van as she was leaving.

She approached him, hugging her backpack to her chest, shielding herself.

"Nice to see you," he said. "I thought you might not come to class."

"I pay for class." She tossed her head, flinging a lock of hair to the side. "I come to class."

Blanton considered this. He said, "Are you hungry? We could go for noodles?"

Miss Van frowned, that sneer of disgust, a slight convulsion in her body that was more emphatic than no.

"A date?"

A slight twitch of her head, the lock of hair falling across her face, a sniff, another no.

"I could give you a ride," he said, and heard a flutelike beseeching in the words.

"I go now," she said.

Blanton struggled to say, "Work?" and only managed it with a catch in his throat, for never had such a simple word held so much anguish for him.

When she was gone he felt abandoned—worse, that she was leaving him for an assignation with another man; and then he remembered, *other men*. In this mood, he stopped at Holiday Mart to use the ATM and saw on the screen: *We are unable to process your request at this time*, and he knew his account was overdrawn.

I am possessed, he told himself, and there is no remedy for it except to see her. He hungered for her, and having no money until his next paycheck, he longed for the night class to see her. That was something, but it was not enough. He taught his literature classes to the reluctant readers, and sulked in his office with Kellogg.

"Union meeting," Kellogg said a few days later. "We're looking for someone to collect dues in the department."

In the past, Blanton had sometimes reflected on friends who were drunks or stoners, who lamented the wastefulness of their addiction but said they couldn't help it. He'd told them, *Just stop doing it, it'll make life easier*, and he had been surprised that they had continued drinking or drugging, bringing more misery upon themselves.

Now he understood: they were in the grip of a force and could not break free. Perhaps it was not misery, but triumph, an act of rebellion, objecting to the servitude of the everyday. The force was not sinister, not grim, it invited him on a quest—not reckless, but taking control of pleasure, like churning the cosmic ocean to be washed in the nectar of immortality. He was possessed that way now, and it excited him, and promised euphoria.

In the office, with the tin box of union dues, he thought of Miss Van. Sitting at home, across from Faye holding the hula doll at the baby's face, he was happy, Miss Van on his lap. In Holiday Mart, at the beach, in traffic, Miss Van was with him, a comforting wisp, easing his mind.

So Blanton returned to Love Doll Spa, to Auntie Ong, the payment of the fifty-dollar entry, and the bedroom with Miss Van.

"I want to be your lover," he said.

She stared, she sniffed a little. She said, "Hundred dollar."

When he leaned to kiss her, she ducked and twisted away. Then he gave her another twenty. "For your noodle shop."

She softened and smiled beautifully, and sighing with longing, she raised her arms to welcome him, then led him to the bed. He sprawled like a chieftain as, naked, she hovered over him, stroking him. "This belong to me." He groaned with pleasure, aroused most of all by the words he had taught her—her talk made her sexier. And drawing close to her, in the heat of his lust, he whispered his desires to her, and she repeated the wicked words exactly as he'd spoken them, with the same crazed emphasis, her hot mouth against his ear. The act was one thing, but it was a blur; her reckless words, those mad perversities, breathed back at him, thrilled him like nothing he had ever known.

When it was over and he was alone on the bed, Miss Van stepped into her clothes. She scowled, smoothed her skirt, and was gone.

In the sour-smelling heat on the nighttime sidewalk, Blanton stood across the street from Pacific Park Tower. He hesitated. The facts were pitiless—his obsession was like a criminal instinct. If he continued this way, he risked losing everything— Faye, discovering the huge overdraft, would scream, backing away, clutching the baby in one hand, the ridiculous hula doll in the other, and would leave him. Disgraced for the theft of the union dues, he would become a pariah in the department and would be fired, and probably prosecuted for embezzlement. He would never pay off his student loan. Miss Van, with all his money, would start the noodle shop, at which he'd be a customer, perhaps ignored, possibly refused service for pestering her. They were not possibilities—they were certainties, the wild froth of an insane wave about to break over his head and destroy him. Everything pointed to disaster.

He walked quickly, turning his back on the rising darkness, and—excited, eager, hungry, certain—hurried toward Miss Van and the light, the thickness of bills in his pocket like flesh between his fingers.

I Don't Miss You

So . . . *this thing* is anonymous, right? I confess, I tried to squirm out of it a few times. I wrote a few lines, then different lines. I figured, better play it safe. Get in and get out: a good story, a few juicy similes (*cock glistening like a glazed cudgel . . . a salted caramel thigh, buttocks like a plum tomato . . . no a Carolina peach . . . no a plum tomato*). But then the contract looked pretty airtight on secrecy, and I thought, is this really the way to use this opportunity? A few tired titillations? The chance to say "cock" on the playground? Here I am, with an anonymous platform, and nobody is ever going to guess my name.

And . . . look . . . here you are on the same list. *You* will know who I am, no matter what I write. So I might as well tell you some secrets.

Once at seventeen, I stood with one foot on a toilet rim, scissors aimed at my hymen, thinking I'd break it myself. I didn't do it—but I've been *that* stupid before.

Once a gyno told me I have a beautiful clit, like the plump dewdrop tongue of a baby cat. I always wanted to tell someone that, and to ask if it was okay for her to say it.

And that was me fucking in the bathroom at the Brooklyn

Book Fest. That whimper you heard as you washed your hands and shook them dry—that was me, as a much-too-young beard scraped against the soft flesh just past my thigh . . .

. . . but you already know that, though you didn't at first. You ignored us, because it was a unisex bathroom in a far-flung part of the festival, and you smirked at the thought of some horny young couple about to get caught. But then you heard me say a word, a syllable, and you stiffened. And in that beat when you could have left, you teetered on your leather-soled shoes (you still wear those) and stayed, holding your breath. Why didn't you go away? You must have felt the mood shift inside the stall. Through the crack in the door, I watched you stretch your wrists. Do they still ache?

"I love the connecting parts," you used to say. And then you'd kiss me in all those curious, unloved places: wrists and ankles, the web of veins bursting away from toes, the place where the pale skin of an underarm softens into torso, the pencil-thin lines where buttocks break from thighs and breasts sprout from a chest. The smudged corners of mouths.

"Is this asshole just gonna keep standing there?" he whispered against my cheek. You shifted from foot to foot, turned on the water again, rinsed your hands the way you do, fingers laced. He mouthed, "Oh Christ," and started performing for you. "Like that? How about a blurb, then?" he breathed loudly. And I snorted, and he said, "Say it's stunning . . . say it's groundbreaking."

We both laughed (not him and I; you and I). I heard you, across that metal door. *Some accidental wit*, you might say, *good for him*. He slapped a hand across my mouth. I saw the sleeve of that olive Barbour jacket you wear. He grabbed my chin, turned my face toward him . . .

God, it's weird to see your name beside mine again. How've you been? What will you write about? Not that I plan to go looking . . .

Then his fingers slipped under my skirt, and I forgot you—pretty completely, I swear—and I groaned into his chest. And he pressed himself against me and bit my ear, and one of my earrings—remember the gold ones?—fell into his mouth. He spit it out.

I pulled away, scrambled to catch it. I heard it clink across the tiles.

"What are you doing?" he muttered.

"I want my earring," I said, squirming away from his fingers. "Stop that."

Do you remember how I used to watch you eat? You ate in a way that made everybody hungry, in that sumptuous but elegant way—scraping chocolate with your teeth, licking oil off your lips and nodding, and wiping the plate clean with a morsel of bread, rapturous over braised short ribs. You used to growl at your meat and tell it not to be scared, it'll be over soon.

Our first meal together, we argued about economics and politics. I didn't tell you that I had studied all that. I called them soft sciences and dared you to give me any term and I'd divine its meaning. You laughed, took another bite, and you said, "Giffen good." And I said, in a mock-girlish voice, "Sounds like . . . maybe, um, the kind of good where if the price goes up people want it more?" And you moved to my side of the table and kissed my cheek and whispered against the corner of my mouth, "You little hustler." Then you noticed my gold earrings and said, "Those are lovely."

The gold stud skipped toward a drain. He pushed my skirt up around my waist. "I said stop."

He sighed, found the earring, and worked it back into my earlobe, a tight smile asking if this bullshit was finished now. "Try to relax," he said.

Do you remember (maybe you'll write about it) that month we lost? It just vanished off the calendar. It's strange the details that have stayed and gone. I don't remember what we ate or the color of your sheets. I don't remember how many chairs you have in your bedroom or if we left the lights on. I remember the sweaty, musty smell of the bed in the morning, after we'd spent the whole night wrecking it, the scrape of your dry knees against my thighs as you parted my legs. The way you bit my collarbone, bit my lip and the tips of all ten fingers. I remember your enormous hands sliding down my back, thinking, *Does my back curve like that? How nice to feel so much of me, so much forgotten skin, at once.* The way you threw me into fits of laughter by growling at my flesh like the meat. When we fucked, the sweaty hairs between us rustled and merged, our mismatched colors, and I thought you might crack my pelvic bone.

Afterward, a coarse black hair drying on my hip, curled like a question mark. I told you about your hands, how they set alight vast spaces I've forgotten. You inspected my fingers and quoted a line from E. E. Cummings: *nobody, not even the rain, has such small hands.*

"Get off, I can't breathe," I told the hipster in the stall. And he did.

Do you know he's vegetarian? I wondered at the start of this if vegetarian lovers ever do that kind of play . . . pretending they'll eat you. It wouldn't be convincing, would it? Well, he does other things.

I took a nervous breath. You were still there, waiting without reason, defiant now. Why didn't you just leave?

"I think that creep's listening," I whispered, the betrayal landing like a bad swallow in my chest.

"Good, let him listen," he said, and bit my earlobe until it stung.

"I don't want to anymore. It's gross in here."

"Fine." He zipped up, straightened my skirt, and shouted, "Hey, buddy, some privacy, please?"

You cleared your throat and left. When we emerged, you weren't outside.

I came to your panel. I saw you in the back row of mine.

What are you doing in this anthology? Did you know I'd be here? Maybe somebody told you, and you started thinking about the old days. I won't go looking for your story. I don't miss you at all. And it's pretty pathetic, you following me into that bathroom, and then here. Because you know that what we had wasn't love. Love is newness. Love is hipsters in bathroom stalls begging for blurbs. Love is success and fun and never fighting about the sheets, the dishes, the bills. Love is fascination, discovering each other's forgotten corners—and we can't do that again for the first time, can we? Love is a series of small erasures, until that final unimaginable one.

But . . . I just wanted to say thanks for staying, for keeping your ear to that door. That guy wasn't bad, you know. He was great, actually—and so was his book. It was groundbreaking, astonishing, stunning . . . and the prose. The prose was like a glazed cudgel . . . like a Carolina peach.

Don't laugh—that's the actual blurb I gave him. He didn't use it. And I don't think he's coming around again. Funny the snatches that survive the years, after every other detail has been erased. Your scratchy knees. Your playful growl. Your teeth scraping my collar, your hands, your salted caramel laugh.

Odi et Amo

Odi et amo. Quare id faciam, fortasse requiris?
Nescio, sed fieri sentio et excrucior.
I hate and I love. Why, you might ask?
I know not, but I feel it so and I am tormented.

—CATULLUS

I*t was hate at first sight.* And she felt it, too, if the message her body conveyed was to be believed, the way she came fiercely down the stairs with every muscle taut, her hands clenched into fists, elbows pumping, face strained, her jaw held tight, her small, firm breasts leading the way like the prow of a miniature steel warship. She reminded Leonard of the windup tin drummer boy he had owned as a child, its drumsticks long lost so just the fists pumped up and down as the tension of its unfurling spring marched it mechanically along. She barely glanced at Spitz, who looked briefly chagrined, but gazed ferociously into Leonard's eyes and demanded: "And just who the hell are you?"

This was supposed to be Leonard's time to paint, after months of working nonstop at the newspaper during the week, and teaching the basics of perspective, color charts, and simple sketching to amateurs on the weekends. It was Labor Day weekend 1941, and after months of writing about the looming specter of war, Leonard had asked for an extra day off from the *Chronicle*. Now he had four glorious days to be on his own, to reimmerse himself in his art. And then Spitz had come along, had insisted Leonard join him on this trip up north into the redwoods, saying that he needed someone to help with the driving and to make sure he did not fall asleep at the wheel. "Imagine if I doze off and drive off a cliff into the Pacific and my mother knows you could have been there to prevent it," Spitz said. "Just think what kind of hell she'll make of your life." It was a persuasive argument, knowing Spitz's mother. A bronze statue of a woman at least Leonard's own height of five feet eleven inches, she had taken a long time to unthaw to her patrician son's Jewish friend, her primary redeeming feature being her unedited adoration of her only child. She would, no doubt, be an implacable enemy.

Spitz was meeting his girlfriend, Marie, at the Inn of the Golden Ray—Leonard and Spitz would be sharing one room ("Don't worry, old son," Spitz told him. "There are two separate beds.") while Marie occupied another. Leonard thought of how he loved the light of Northern California, clear and bright as white Burgundy as it filtered through the tall evergreens. This would be Spitz's last free week before he shipped out, having volunteered his piloting skills to the Eagle Squadron to help defend Britain against the German onslaught, an act that endeared him to Leonard.

They left on Thursday evening after Leonard finished work, first grabbing a dinner of steak and roasted marrow bone for Spitz, cioppino for Leonard, at Sam's Grill. Spitz insisted on being the first to drive, despite his two large glasses of wine at dinner, and as they headed north on the dark ribbon of the 101, Leonard understood why Spitz's mother might have insisted on his having a companion. But Spitz showed no sign of sleepiness or impairment, chatting away about his affection for Marie, his tennis playing, and his paying an aircraft collector and former WWI fighter pilot for extra lessons in maneuvering an aircraft in a dogfight. It was still illegal for Americans to fight abroad and difficult to get training ahead of time, but they knew it would not be long before the U.S. joined the war.

"I intend to survive this adventure, you see," Spitz said, beating time on the white leather-bound steering wheel of his Cord 812 Phaeton. (Although Leonard cared little about cars, even he could see this was a rare and expensive vehicle.)

"Perhaps that would be more likely if you drove a little slower," Leonard suggested, noticing the red line of the speed-ometer creeping steadily higher as the highway curved and zig-zagged.

"Don't be such an old woman, Len." Spitz laughed. "You're only a couple of years my senior, not fifty!"

It was a pleasant enough drive once Leonard relaxed, and it wasn't long before they reached the entrance to the inn. It was close to eleven and the building was mostly dark. Spitz turned off the engine, and before rolling up his windows, said, "Smell that fresh pine air. It's glorious here—I know you'll be glad you decided to join me." The warm engine ticked in the dark, and Leonard, too, sat quietly for a moment, taking in the air, the dark shadows of trees around him, and the looming Victorian building's ocher silhouette against a pitch sky studded with brilliant stars. He felt the stress of the city shuffle off him.

"By the way," Spitz said as he opened his door and stepped out, reaching for his suitcase. "Marie has a friend with her . . .

Zelda. She's damned fine looking, but kind of a *bee eye tea cee aitch*, if you know what I mean. Parents made Marie bring her along as some sort of chaperone, but you're good with the ladies. You'll figure out how to handle her."

Leonard let out a slow breath. If Spitz weren't a good four inches taller than him and with biceps as round and large as softballs, Leonard would have punched him on the nose. So this was the secret purpose of the invitation: Leonard was supposed to play amanuensis to Marie's chaperone.

"I'll be taking the car out into the countryside tomorrow to get some painting done," Leonard declared.

"Sounds fine to me," Spitz said, grabbing Leonard's suitcase as well. "I'm sure Zelda will enjoy seeing the countryside."

After they'd dropped their bags in their shared room on the third floor, they met the girls on the front porch. Marie had persuaded the owner of the inn to let her check them in so he could go to bed and had also gotten a plate of sandwiches from the kitchen. Spitz had thought to bring along a wicker basket of several excellent wines, and now they shared a Loire red that he uncorked with a pop loud enough for Marie to shush him.

"I promised we wouldn't disturb the other guests," she said.

They sat on two parallel porch swings, Zelda having quickly claimed a seat next to Marie. She sat with one leg crossed over the other, her foot swinging; a tenebrous profile of womanly curves. Leonard was surprised by how hungry he was—the sea-and-mountain air was already working on him. The sandwiches were hearty and delicious; a local cheese, Marie had said, and bread baked by the owner. ("Likes to put things in the oven, does he?" Spitz had remarked, cocking an eyebrow.) They spoke in hushed murmurs, listening to the soughing of the wind in the tall trees and the distant, plaintive call of a night bird.

Zelda revealed that she was in a nursing program, and that she planned to use her skills when America joined the war effort. She had a faint German accent—a buzzing Z just evident in the S, so she almost said "*nurzing*"—and an overlay of an English accent, too. Leonard asked politely about this, and she shared that she had spent a few years in the Midlands of England, and had had an English governess as a child in Germany.

"My father is a chemist and we were quite well off," she said unselfconsciously. "But, of course, all of that has changed."

"Zelda is your coreligionist," Spitz remarked to Leonard.

"I never much cared for religion," she said, "but there were those eager to remind me of my religion and their dislike for it."

"Leonard is a famous painter," Spitz said. "Well, an almost famous painter. He had a solo exhibition in the Stern Gallery last year."

"*Sterner*," Leonard corrected.

"I have not heard of it," Zelda continued. "But I have little time for such things these days. My favorite painter is Paula Modersohn-Becker. Do you know her work?"

Leonard thought for a moment. "Rilke's friend? The one who died young?"

"Ach, you men! You only think of a woman in relation to the famous men she knows. She was one of the great Modernist painters of Germany. *Bahnbrechender* . . . what is that in English? A pioneer."

"I've seen reproductions of her self-portrait . . ." Leonard murmured.

"Of course that is what you would remember!" Zelda said. Turning to Marie, she added, "It's a nude portrait. *All* is revealed."

"I'm sorry if I'm not an expert on German painters," Leonard said with growing irritation.

"We've been waiting for you to arrive to go into Eureka," Marie interrupted. "I've heard it's a lovely town, with old buildings." She went on to say that there was no rush to sightsee, as she'd arranged a late breakfast so they could sleep in. Leonard had always found Spitz's girlfriend a little too bland and wholesome, but now he admired her competence and attempts to keep everyone cheerful. Her friend was going to be a problem; he wondered how he might avoid her over the next few days.

As they started up the stairs, Spitz attempted to linger with Marie for a good-night cuddle, but Zelda quickly interrupted, saying, "Come on, Marie. I need your help with that clasp that has gotten stuck." With an apologetic glance, Marie followed her, the two men walking behind.

"Bee eye . . ." Spitz whispered, not so quietly.

"What's that?" Zelda demanded.

"Leonard has a fabulous painting of a bee's eye," Spitz said cheerfully. "Quite *wunderbar.* Ask him to show it to you sometime."

After a late breakfast, the four of them decided to go on a tour in Spitz's Phaeton. So much for Leonard's plans to get work done. Breakfast had not been without its tensions. The innkeeper, Robert, had stopped by to see if everything was all right. Robert, a neatly put together middle-aged man with streaks of silver in his brushed-down hair and an effeminate manner, was barely out of the room when Spitz prissily pursed his lips and let his wrist flop. Leonard shook his head. When he looked over to Zelda, she was glaring at both of them. When Leonard was young, he once borrowed the leather-enclosed magnifying glass that belonged to his grandfather and went outside into their yard. Finding a large black carpenter ant marching across the bare ground, he narrowed the circle of light from the magnifying glass until it was a blinding pinpoint, the ant smoldering and writhing in its compass. Finding himself caught in the narrow cone of Zelda's blazing stare, he could almost smell the acrid scent of scorched formic acid. Leonard sighed. He found Spitz's prejudices tedious, but there was no point battling over each one; the fellow was not going to change.

In the car, Marie had contrived to sit in the front, so Leonard found himself seated in the back with Zelda. It was a sunny day with no sign of rain, and Spitz had lowered the roof of the car. Marie offered Zelda a scarf to tie down her hair. The drive through the redwoods down to Eureka was glorious, lifting Leonard's mood. He might have spent the day stuck in the office otherwise, smelling printer's ink, instead of being out in the fresh air with these handsome young people. Marie, conventionally pretty with smooth, pale skin, blond hair, and almost invisible pale eyelashes framing her topaz eyes, looked different out here from the social gatherings in San Francisco, her squarish jaw not so tightly set, her features softer. Spitz, too, was fair-haired, his big square head set on an athlete's thick neck.

"Brunettes in the back, blondes in the front," Leonard murmured to Zelda.

"And I thought you were an artist with an eye for color," she responded. "My hair is more red to auburn, yours . . . well, a sort of mouse brown."

He almost snapped back at her, but then saw a twinkle in her eye. (So, the martinet is capable of humor!) Yes, her hair was red when the sun's rays caught it, and her eyes were quite a lovely shade of hazel flecked with green. Aesthetically, he could appreciate her quiet beauty; but still, he didn't want to be stuck with the damn woman for the next four days.

After touring the old lumber town with its wooden Victorian houses, they drove along the bay. When they stopped at a pullout to look at the water, Zelda took off her shoes and wandered down to the bay's edge.

"There's a dock here," she called out. "Marie, would you bring me a towel from the bag in the car? I'm going to swim. And any of you are welcome to join me."

"You won't catch me in that frigid water," Marie said, laughing. Leonard watched from a distance as Zelda quickly stripped to her underwear, lingering for a moment in a tableau worthy of Berthe Morisot, the tranquil late-summer light framing her as she undressed with spontaneous nonchalance. Then she dove off the dock into the water and began to swim a fast, efficient crawl out into the bay. He seized a towel and walked over to the shoreline to take off his own clothes. He laid them neatly on a slab of rock, then waded into the water. It really was cold, and he had to force himself to keep going in. He swam out from shore, trying to keep his body in the warmer upper layer of the water, his breaststroke effective but inelegant compared to Zelda's effortless freestyle. The woman seemed to glide through water like a fish, transparent white bubbles forming in the aquamarine wake behind her.

"Come on, slow coach," Zelda said, turning over on her back to splash him with her feet. "See if you can catch me."

Leonard tried to dart forward, but she was already gone, a

dolphin in the blue-green water. He swam a little farther out, glad now that he had entered the water. He lay on his back and watched a seagull and some terns pass overhead. By the time he did swim back to his clothes, he was cold. This made him walk more swiftly on the sharp rocks close to the water's edge, and the side of his foot hit a barnacle-covered rock. A thin carmine ribbon of blood drifted into the water, attracting a bottom fish that had until that moment resembled a stone.

Leonard quickly toweled himself dry and got dressed, pulling his sock on carefully over a torn flap of skin on his foot. He wrung out his underwear and wrapped it in the towel, then stumbled over to the car. Spitz and Marie were behind the car in a tight embrace, Spitz's arm hidden inside Marie's blouse. They hastily separated when Leonard coughed. Zelda showed up at the car a few minutes later, her towel also rolled and indicating that she had removed her wet underwear. He noticed the dimple of a nipple pressing against her shirt, feeling an arousal that disturbed him. Zelda looked at him with concern.

"You're limping," she said.

"Scraped my foot getting out," Leonard replied. "It's no big deal."

"You should have used the dock like I did," Zelda responded. "It's the easiest way to get in and out of the water."

"I thought you would want your privacy."

"In my youth group in Germany, men and women would swim naked together all the time. It didn't bother anyone," she replied with a smile.

So now I'm a prude for respecting your privacy? Leonard thought. There was no pleasing this woman.

———

The following morning, as they were going downstairs for breakfast, Spitz's foot slipped and he landed on the stairs with a heavy thud. Marie hurried to him and asked if he was all right. He slowly got back to his feet, wincing.

"I think I've pulled my back," he said.

"Shall I look at it for you?" Zelda asked.

"No need," Spitz said curtly. "I know what it is. It's happened before. Marie, help me back upstairs."

"I'll take you to my room," Marie said. "There's a larger bed up there and you'll be more comfortable. You two go on down to breakfast." As they hesitated, she waved at them in a shooing motion. "Go on, now. I'll take care of him."

Leonard was none too pleased. He had hoped to take the car out early, so he could start painting while the light was not so harsh.

At breakfast, Zelda asked, "How's your foot today?"

"It's fine," he said. He did not tell her it had throbbed during the night, keeping him awake.

"I hope you cleaned it well," she said. "Shellfish cuts get infected easily. I didn't think to bring some Mercurochrome with me on this trip, but I should have."

"I've put a plaster on it," Leonard said.

"You men. You can't go a day without hurting yourselves somehow," Zelda said. The faint laugh in her voice did not remove the words' sting for Leonard, who, as the son of older, protective parents, had been unathletic in his childhood and mocked for it.

About fifteen minutes later, Marie came into the breakfast room and told them that Spitz had injured a disk, something he'd done before, and that he would need to rest for the whole day. She would stay and take care of him. Leonard noticed she was a little flushed. Marie avoided looking at him while putting together a plate of food, then she announced, "Zelda should go with you today and see something of the countryside. I'm sure she'll be no bother."

"I'll get myself ready," Zelda said, buttering her berry muffin. "I'll arrange for a basket lunch with the kitchen. I'm sure Leonard hasn't thought of that."

Leonard was about to object when Marie put her hand on his arm.

"Please," she said. "For us."

Leonard did not say a word as they drove away from the inn. Zelda was beside him, her eyes half shut, holding a book in one hand. Leonard glanced at the cover, which featured a curly-haired woman in the act of unbuttoning her blouse. He noted the title, *The Age of Innocence*, and almost said he was sure that's what was being lost at this very moment, but thought better of it.

Zelda lay back on her seat, her head slightly turned to look out the side window. Leonard could not help observing the fine contour from her chin to her waist and the long, slim legs and muscular calves that her thin cotton dress barely covered. Judging by her swimming the day before, she was extremely fit . . . a beauty, someone he would normally have been attracted to.

Leonard began to relax with the drive, taking in the tall, thick redwoods on either side of the road. Each tree seemed to contain a soul of its own, and he loved how they fractured the light, glimpses of an impossibly blue sky showing through. As they drove north, he could see a rugged landscape leading

down to blue water. One of his colleagues at the *Chronicle*, Rex
Mattison, had spent his childhood in Orick and he had recom-
mended Leonard try painting the vistas around the old Pat-
rick's Ranch area near Trinidad. After almost an hour, Leonard
turned off onto a narrow dusty road leading toward the ocean,
following his friend's written directions. He stopped the car and
grabbed the bag filled with his paints, canvas, and easel, along
with a large canteen of water. He would have to be a gentleman
and carry the lunch basket as well.

"You won't be able to hike very well in those," he said, pointing at Zelda's sandals.

"I have walking shoes," she replied, reaching into the back,
"and I wouldn't recommend *you* hike far with that bad foot."

"I'm fine," he snapped. But he was glad that they didn't
have to trudge for more than twenty minutes before he found
a vista that pleased him, a natural cleft in the rocks that opened
out to a view of an inlet at the edge of the ocean, with chimney
stacks of rock jutting out of the water. A mix of coastal plants—
Sitka spruce, red alder, coastal pines, and even ferns—fringed
the sandy path, their bright green leaves creating a symphony
of color against the sand, the rocks, and the distant blue water.
Leonard found some flat rocks, undid the straps on his portable
French easel, and lowered its three legs to form a tripod that just
fit the space he'd picked out.

"I'm going to be busy for a while," he muttered, his head
down as he sorted his paints and adjusted the easel's position
for the best viewpoint. "I'm sure you can find something to oc-
cupy yourself," he said, as Zelda was still just standing there.

"Of course I can," she said, walking away with a toss of her
head that almost caused her wide-brimmed hat to fly off had
she not grabbed it swiftly.

Once she was no longer in sight, Leonard gazed out at the vista before him, trying to let the ever-shifting light, the harmony of land, plants, and water enter into him so it would be the emotions of this particular stretch of coast that informed his paint choices.

A couple of hours passed and, after making several quick sketches, Leonard had just stepped back to allow his finished watercolor to dry, when Zelda called him over to join her for lunch. She had created a pretty collage of her own, with plates and a wicker basket, along with a bottle of Spitz's wine resting on a white cloth she'd set down on a bare patch of ground.

"What the hell are you doing?" Leonard shouted.

Zelda looked up, nonplussed.

Leonard had realized that the "tablecloth" was a pristine sheet of canvas from his artist's bag. This was an expensive finely woven linen from Belgium, almost impossible to get hold of during wartime, and here it was on the dirty ground! He hastily began shoving the plates and cups off the canvas, yelling, "Get this damn rubbish off my canvas!"

He snatched up the cloth, brushing and blowing off the dirt. He was relieved it had not been torn and could, with some tender ministrations, still be usable. Zelda grabbed a sandwich and a bottle of wine, poured herself a cup without looking at Leonard or offering him any, then walked off to sit beneath the far side of a tree.

After painting for several more hours, Leonard found Zelda under a Douglas fir, her body relaxed as she read, the soft shade from the tree bringing out her high cheekbones and her long eyelashes. He would have liked to make a quick sketch of her, but he knew that even though she hadn't looked up, she had noticed his approach.

"I'm sorry," he said. "But you have no idea how hard it is to get quality canvas today. I was worried that it would be completely ruined."

"You were *so* angry," she said.

"Sorry."

She nodded.

Well, he thought, *I did try.*

That night they drove to a fish restaurant near Eureka. Spitz told the story of his first meeting with his flying mentor, how the man had come out of his ranch's front door with a wine bottle in one hand and a shotgun in the other.

"'What's that about?' I asked him," Spitz said. "'Wellll, if I didn't like the looks of ye, I was gonna send you packing with a little rock salt to help along the way.'"

Marie laughed loudly at this tale, though Leonard knew she'd heard it a few times before. She had kept her hand on Spitz's leg throughout the drive. Zelda had sat as far from Leonard as possible, leaning into the car door.

"Had a nice time with Miss Zelda today, did you?" Spitz said, elbowing Leonard in the ribs as they walked behind the two women toward the entrance of the restaurant.

"Not as nice a time as you two did. Your back seems better. I guess you got a massage."

"Several . . . in different places. The ache kept moving around . . . but leave the insinuations out here, will you?"

In the restaurant, Spitz pulled aside the waiter and, in an audible whisper, said: "It's a celebration. We'll start with a bottle of your best champagne." When the waiter said they did not carry champagne, Spitz demanded, "Your best white wine, and make damn sure it's cold."

When the wine arrived, Spitz held his glass aloft. "I wish to announce the engagement between Mr. Charles 'Spitz' Radcliffe and Miss Marie Shaw!" he declared.

"Congratulations," Leonard said, clinking glasses with his friend.

Zelda held her glass up and gave Marie a tight smile. "That's lovely," she said. "A wartime romance."

Spitz laughed. "Yes. If I get all shot up, then I'll have someone to look after me when I come home."

"Don't make jokes like that," Marie snapped.

Spitz kissed her on the cheek. "Can't think of a better reason to come back in one piece."

They began with cracked spider crab legs, fresh from that morning's boats, washed down with white Burgundy. The only thing wrong, Leonard thought, was how stuffy and hot the room was.

"It's warm in here," he remarked, unbuttoning the top of his shirt.

Marie looked at him, one thin, artificially shaded eyebrow raised.

"I'm actually cold. I was just about to slip on my cardigan, but I didn't want it smelling like crab."

The main courses arrived. When the waiter set down a flounder cooked with beurre noir and almonds, Leonard asked for another glass of water. Zelda had barely glanced at him all evening, but now she looked concerned.

"You're very flushed," she said. "Are you well?"

"Just a little warm . . . and a bit of a headache." He didn't have much of an appetite either, and the fish tasted like sand.

As they were ordering dessert, Zelda leaned over and touched the inside of her wrist against his forehead.

"You're burning up," she said. "And you were limping on the way to the car. You must have an infection."

They skipped dessert and drove back to the inn. Robert told them there was only one doctor in the area. He tried to call him but came back saying, "He's kind of a"—he made a drinking motion with his hand—"which is normally no problem, but every few months he goes cold turkey. I'm sure that's why he's not answering his phone."

"Give me his address," Spitz demanded. "I'm going over to pick him up, DTs or no DTs."

The doctor came, complaining that Spitz had threatened to assault him. His hands trembled furiously, but he was able to give Leonard a shot of penicillin by holding his wrist with the other hand.

"Your nurse friend was right," he said. "You're on the edge of developing a blood infection, but this should stop it in its tracks."

"The doctor said someone will need to keep an eye on Leonard," Marie said to Zelda. "It's best you do that. Spitz can sleep in your bed, you can have his. That really would be best."

"The two of you are engaged, Marie, and I honestly don't care where Spitz sleeps," Zelda replied.

Leonard fell asleep, then woke up shaking. Zelda sponged off his face with a damp washcloth. "Thank you," Leonard said. "I was so damn hot before, and now I'm freezing. Could you get me more blankets?"

"I don't know where they keep extra blankets, but I can warm you up."

Zelda climbed into the bed and held him close, feeling his whole body shake. Gradually, Leonard's fever subsided as he drifted off. He woke to find Zelda dozing. Her face was clear and calm, her long eyelashes leaving shadows on her smooth cheeks in the half-light. Such an awful woman, and yet so beautiful. And here she was, lying in his arms.

Her eyes fluttered open.

"Oh, you're better," she said.

She searched his face for what seemed a long time, though it couldn't have been more than half a minute. Leonard's own eyes softened; he didn't know what to expect. Then she leaned forward and kissed him, at first softly on the lips, but soon with insistence, her mouth open to his, her tongue delicately exploring. Leonard wrapped his arms around her body, noticing its warmth and strength and how smooth her skin felt beneath her thin nightshirt. He kissed her back, hard, as if he were seeking to devour her, his hands traveling up her nightshirt to touch her everywhere he could, all at once. The flesh of her behind was so absurdly soft and smooth, with the play of muscle beneath it. His hand went to her vulva; she was already wet, and he caressed her gently at first, then with more determination. He found himself clutching her tighter with his arms and legs, while his fingers circled above her clitoris more vigorously, touching it occasionally with the finest of brushstrokes. He thought of all her harsh looks, her using his fine European canvas as a ground covering, her intrusion on his peaceful weekend, and he kissed her even harder, biting at her lip, his hand clasping her firm, high breast roughly. She struggled against him, and for a moment he wondered if he should stop, when, with a twist of her muscular body, she flipped him onto his back and straddled him.

Zelda pulled her nightshirt off with one quick movement, then leaned down to seize Leonard's lip gently in her teeth before kissing him, her auburn hair a curtain over his face, her nipples brushing his chest. She seized his rigid penis and slipped it inside her and then began moving rapidly up and down on him. Leonard heard his own rough gasps mingling with her high, fluting cries as he slipped back into the delirium of his fever and saw in his mind the beating waves of the Pacific that afternoon, crashing down onto the rocks. And then one enormous wave lifted him high in its warm, wet embrace and crashed him onto the sand, everything in him spilling forth with an enormous groan.

Zelda lay spent on Leonard's chest. After a while, she lifted her head and kissed him in the hollow between jaw and ear.

"I hope I wasn't too loud," she murmured.

"No, you were lovely," he said. "Though I'm still mad as hell at you."

"And me at you," she replied, her head on his chest, breathing softly.

They made love again shortly after dawn, then both dozed off. Leonard rose before Zelda, who slept on with the covers down, the morning light rising behind the small, round hills of her breasts, exposed to any who might enter the room. Leonard pulled out his pastels—he wanted to draw her, his imagination calling forth the style of painting she so admired and, like Modersohn-Becker, he added an amber necklace and two pink California poppies to highlight the rosy hue of her nipples. He slipped the sketchbook away to give to her later.

At breakfast, Marie was alone. "Spitz overdid it yesterday, I think," she said. "He needs to rest." She handed Leonard the car keys. Zelda said she would ask Robert's advice on where to swim and left the dining room. Putting her hand on Leonard's wrist, Marie leaned forward and said: "I appreciate you giving us this time. And I'm glad you're better . . . and getting on better with my friend. She can be a little stern, but she's a wonderful person."

"She was nice enough to me when I was ill," Leonard said.

Zelda returned, saying she'd gotten directions to a great place where she could swim and there would be views for Leonard to paint.

"Zelda used to be a champion swimmer in Germany, you know," Marie said.

"Ach, not a champion. Just competitive . . . until I was told I was undesirable, *unerwünscht.*"

"Well, you're not undesirable now," Marie said.

"No," Zelda replied, a faint smile playing across her lips.

They drove east through forests of redwoods, some with trunks wider than the car. The giant ancient trees stood tall and still like soldiers on parade, saluting their passing. Ferns of several varieties created daubs of bright green against the red tree bark. Eventually, they turned down a narrow dirt road, jouncing along on rocks and potholes.

"Robert must hate Spitz, if he sent us along this way in his fancy Phaeton," Leonard said. "I hope we can turn around somewhere."

They did find a turnaround, and Zelda said, "Now we hike. I'll carry the food, you can carry your painting gear and try not to hobble too much."

She had carefully bandaged his foot that morning, Leonard thinking *German efficiency* as he watched her swift, economical movements. He felt no pain on the lengthy hike following the Mad River, not even when they traversed a path fit for mountain goats along a granite cliff, guided by a ragged piece of rope tied to wooden stakes. Finally, they came upon a sheltered pool, the water a startling turquoise. Leonard set up his easel while Zelda stretched in the sun. Zelda had brought a bathing suit, but Leonard watched as she stripped and boldly walked down to the water, her lithe muscles rippling, her gait balanced and elegant. After a while, she came over to him, dripping wet, and took his hand.

"Enough working. Come in with me."

The pool sparkled in the crystalline sunlight and was noticeably warmer than the bay had been. Leonard swam over to Zelda, who at first dived past him, darting here and there to elude him, making him pursue her. Then she swam over and embraced him, the water creating a silky second skin between their two bodies. Zelda bit Leonard's ear and said hoarsely, "Fuck me now."

It was strange having sex in the water. The sensations were muted, and finding a comfortable position in which no one drowned was tricky. Zelda did not make it easier by throwing her body around, sometimes playfully dipping him under as he slipped in and out of her, until at last they found their rhythm, culminating in a joined, rapturous cry.

After, Zelda stood with the water up to her thighs while Leonard kissed her neck and then her clavicle, then each breast, circling the nipples with his tongue and then down to her navel. Her gleaming, unblemished skin reminded him of Rutelli's marble statue of the Naiad of the Rivers, a symbol of physical delight and jealous destruction. All she needed was to be clutching a water snake.

"You have the most gorgeous anatomy," he told her.

"Stop, or I'm going to jump on you again," she smiled. "But we should eat first."

As they waded out of the limpid water, Zelda laughed. "I saw you take your fancy canvas out of the bag this morning," she said. "You don't think I'd make the same mistake twice, do you?"

"I have some expensive Winsor & Newton watercolor paper you could use for napkins," Leonard replied. "Or you could make paper airplanes."

He reached for her again after lunch, and they tangled and tussled in the warm sand between two large rocks, biting and grasping each other, then swam again, and afterward made their way slowly back to the car. Zelda told Leonard about her life as an Olympic hopeful, "in a team of BDM girls, until I was no longer allowed."

"My aunt married an American and she sponsored me," she continued. "I hoped to finish my education, but I had to work to get my parents out of Germany. Even now, I owe money to my aunt." She threw up her hands.

In bed that night, Zelda said: "Tell me again about my gorgeous anatomy."

"I need some visual aids," Leonard replied, unclasping her bra and pulling away the sheet. He kissed her navel and said, "You have the most delightful iliac crest and a glorious acetabulum. A man could get lost contemplating it."

"You certainly know how to flatter a woman." She laughed.

His lips lingered on the delicate triangular bones forming the top of her pelvis; he saw it as a Charybdis from which he might never emerge. His face slid slowly downward. "I admire your tensor fasciae femoris," he murmured. "And you have a beautiful cunny."

"Is that the polite way of saying it?" she murmured, groaning as his tongue began to explore.

"Ever so polite." He raised his head, then returned to his exertions, enjoying her more rapid breathing and soft cries until she sat up, grabbed him under the arms, and pulled him up and over her with surprising strength. He thrust into her brusquely now as she murmured and groaned encouragement, then urgency, then sounds that were no words at all.

Morning came too soon, and Leonard followed Zelda with his eyes as she got dressed. He would be leaving with Spitz after lunch, and earlier that morning he and Zelda had talked about their lives in San Francisco. "I'm also studying anatomy," she said. "I was hoping for a cadaver, but that is just for medical students, not for lowly nurses."

"We get live models," Leonard said. "None as pretty as you."

Zelda mentioned that she had little free time, as she worked several nights a week at a café to earn her school fees and rent. Neither of them said anything about whether—and how—they would meet up again.

"I'd better get up and pack," Leonard said, belying his words by holding out his hand to Zelda. She came over to the bed and sat primly. Her eyes were flat and hard, and he could not tell what she was thinking.

"You didn't think to wear a johnny anytime, did you?" she said.

"Well, I . . ." he said, momentarily taken aback, then irate. "You didn't suggest it."

"You didn't ask."

He looked away.

"I'm sorry," he said.

"I'm okay. It's a safe time for me."

She glared at him, then said, "Oh, you stupid man," and flung herself at him, pushing him down on the bed and raising her skirt, then pulling down her underwear. Fury and love flooded through Leonard as he once again entered the warm waves and found himself borne high aloft, swimming, swimming with her, then crashing down together in unison.

As they drove away, the women waving from the porch, Spitz and Leonard were both silent. *I should have asked to stay one more night*, Leonard thought. He felt racked, relieved to be away from the fray, already missing her hazel-green, amorous eyes. As the car surged forward, the distance grew between him and the woman his body yearned for more with each passing mile.

Spitz, too, seemed deep in thought. Leonard looked at him, imagining his friend pondering the challenges that would soon confront him when he flew to England to fight.

As they headed south, trees no longer pressed in on either side of the road, sunlight flooded the car, and cliffs stretched down to the tumultuous waves below. Leonard realized he had forgotten to give his sleeping sketch to Zelda. It might be a good gambit to call and offer it to her, "a gift from the artist." Or should he just send it to her? Anonymously, or with a signed, affectionate note?

Spitz cast frequent glances at Leonard, as if trying to read him. Finally, Leonard asked, "What? What is it?"

"Just surprised," Spitz said. "I thought the two of you didn't like each other."

Leonard looked at his friend.

"We don't," he said.

This Kind

She *came to him when he* asked her to come to him. It was night. The security gate lowered halfway. She went under, her hair catching in the metal slats.

The shop looked different at night. The stacked, slatted racks that held boules and braided loaves were empty, the baskets for rolls and knots turned over. The dark room smelled warm, yeasty, with a lace of cinnamon and almond.

Forgive me, she said. I don't know why I've come.

I don't belong here, she said. I'm not this kind of woman.

He sat her in the chair and got on his knees. No, he said, you are this kind.

Let him try, she thought, and she closed her eyes. She could go on this way. He worked at her, his mouth moving against her; she found she'd get there, just there, to an edge, almost beyond that edge where she wouldn't be able to hold, but then, with the slightest shift, pulling a little back, she kept herself at the crest, not cresting; and the more insistent he became, the more she refused, could hold back, wanted to, the greater his resolve.

She opened her eyes and saw the shape of the two of them slurred against the metal wall of ovens.

Am I killing you? she said.

He looked up smiling. Are you trying to?

Or he took her down the narrow stairs. The walls were stone. A light hung from the low ceiling. Pipes crisscrossed overhead, the steady sound of water dripping somewhere farther back. There was nowhere simply to lie down as two people might. Boxes everywhere. Flour sacks. And broken furniture. She was always tilted, turned around, hooked. Above her head more boxes stacked on sagging shelves. Unwieldy, it could all topple down.

They both had wives.

I believe that makes us even, he said.

She loved to gather her wife's hair in her fingers, to hold it tight. Her wife's long dark hair, with its first surprise of gray, was always in their faces, strands in their mouths. In certain light, her wife's skin seemed furred. She kept her fingers nimble and hovering, until her wife called out and clamped her hands down hard.

Leaving the house, she said she was just going out for what they needed. Something was always needed. A thermometer, ACE bandages, milk for morning. And sometimes that was

enough. To park the car, walk the dark streets, stop in door-
ways, and imagine him waiting for her among the boxes in the
musty basement. To tuck into the night away from him and
away from her family's unwinding into the slow breath of bedtime stories.

Best were the hands. Baker's hands, he had. Kneading, releasing, letting her slowly rise back toward his fingers.

In my business, he said, it's all about the waiting.

Or she'd run from the car, arriving already winded, and he'd
rush close to her saying, Have I taken your breath away?

What? her wife said, rubbing thick cream on the bare heel of
her foot. What are you looking at?

What wasn't there to look at? Length and curve, the bronze
of leg, the faint stretch marks rounding her hip. That astonishing dark of nipple under the thin T-shirt.

My luscious wife, she said, and helped slip the cotton sock
over the oiled foot.

It was hardly about his cock. Though how would she explain
otherwise if it should ever come to that? He certainly acted as if
he were showing her a new invention, strutting through the narrow space, or standing back to display how it sprang up when
pushed down.

How to explain? It was being almost nowhere. The dank

basement, the metal clank of the pull-down gate, this is what took her breath away.

How to explain? He was not a child. Not a woman. She gave him a different name each night she drove toward him. Fred, Frédéric, Joaquin, Alexander the Great, Tom.

All day was the efficient hum of family plans. Quick kiss. Quick message. Pick up and drop off. Swift scold at a grabbed-away metal truck. Praise for feeding the cat. Praise for cleared dishes. Even sex was kind and efficient.

She came back with applesauce, jam, toilet paper, and three pints of ice cream.

And look what I nabbed for French toast. The bread shop was just closing, she said, pulling sourdough loaves from a paper sack.

But what took so long? came at her before her parka was off. Did you have to bake the damn bread yourself?

What took so long was her, rogue, outlaw, bent over a broken chair, no longer someone equipped to supervise math home-work, pack knapsacks; no longer someone to fix a healthy lunchbox or remember to include a weekly knock-knock joke written on a scrap of paper. What took so long was nowhere that belonged on a color-coded family calendar, him hoisting her leg over his shoulder, him no one she ever needed to think about.

Once, after, he started to complain about his wife.

Wives are perfect, Baker Man, she said, and grabbed him by the wrist.

So, say yours is, if you want us to stay even.

Her nose nestled in the amber musk of her wife's neck, one hand threaded in her wife's tangle of hair, the other slipped under the T-shirt holding the loosened belly—this is how she slept. She woke from her dream to a dream the wife was in the middle of telling her.

He kept a candle in the basement. It was already lit when he led her down the stairs.

There was a problem, he said, and lifted her over a running stream of water. He settled her on a high bed of boxes. Don't get me started on plumbers.

I won't, she said. Promise.

You know, problem solved; you actually make this mess look appealing, he said. Now what can I do for you?

After, she looked down and saw the date on the cardboard boxes. Whatever was in them had already expired.

The butcher, the baker, the candlestick maker. Wasn't that what they'd said when the inevitable person wouldn't stop with the invasive questions of the *how* of their daughters and son?

Even the butcher sounds sexier than turkey baster, her wife said.

Not when you're wielding one, she said.

No! she said when he said, I need to tell you what happened today.

No, to his need, no, to ancient grains, the chemistry of barley and rye. No, to funny shop stories about the lady who insisted on pushing her long nail into cinnamon buns.

Want to see what I'll be doing at four in the morning? he asked. And before she could say no, that she never wanted to think about his four in the morning or his ten at night, that she barely thought about him right here right now, he'd pulled open the refrigerator to show her trays of proofed baguettes ready for the dawn oven.

Driving home was never like driving there. Driving there was like airport waiting time, unhinged from a here or there. Almost anywhere. Always the temptation when passing boarding gates offering cities and countries she'd never landed in. Driving home was roads she took too fast, familiar moon shadow on snow, pine dark then the sharp curve, one hand off the wheel picking at the seams of her jeans for stray sesame or poppy seeds. She had three possible stories by the time she put the key in the front door.

Some nights it was the wife who grabbed the keys and went out for what was needed.

She lay on the bed with the kids' legs thrown over hers. Sometimes it was easier to be the only parent in the house deciding all the rules.

Not tonight, she said when the kids said, Momma, let us have extra cookies.

But when the kids fought over the bedtime book, she let them each choose a book. Three! they said. Are you sure? And hugged her before she changed her mind.

But it had taken her wife so long to return with the few things she'd gone out for.

Scrubbing the sink, then the stove, she imagined split trees, the burned cringe of rubber skidding across asphalt. But then she imagined the muscular clench of her wife's large thighs around a stranger's back. Her wife's throat arched, a final stuttery sharp cry.

She squeezed out the sponge and waited at the kitchen table.

No, she said, I need to go, and slipped off the table where, by day, he worked and shaped his dough. She started to pull on her jeans.

He lifted her back onto the table, leaned into her so that she had to brace herself. Let me, he said. He secured a hand at her hip.

She tried to sit forward.

Close your eyes, he said.

She tried to keep them open, to keep her focus; then couldn't. But she would keep herself as she needed, at that edge, never giving over, never fully lost. He worked slowly. She pressed, grabbed him to derail his steady tempo, but he kept to it, persistent, disciplined; her resolve shifted, narrowing, narrowing until there was nothing to back away from, no holding back, only sudden expansion, unlimited, trembling, complete.

She heard his yeah, his chuff of satisfaction.

She pushed from him, untangled the twist of denim on her leg, and hunched back into her jeans.

No more, she said.

Hey, he said.

But she was out, over with it, already bending under the security gate.

Now her wife is curled beside her on the couch. The room all picked up; tea candles glowing in jam jars, bowls, spoons, and two half-filled glasses on the table. The spin of music low and husky.

She straddles her wife's lap. Runs a finger slowly down the cord of her wife's neck; their gaze fixed, open, joined.

Her finger slides down between her wife's breasts.

That's some sneaky business you've gotten into, she says. Giving out extra cookies! That's just wrong.

Her wife, her head thrown back, is laughing, that thrilling, abandoned laugh.

She snugs down until she feels their fit and her wife's breath catch, hips pushing back.

A mom's gotta do what a mom's gotta do to survive, her wife says, all dare and jut of chin.

Tell me about it, sugar, she says and runs her tongue along the wet seam of her wife's full lips.

What the Hands Remember

And I lie here now, facing the end of my days. Thinking that surely this sweet breeze coming in the window, sliding itself across my chest and down between my legs like a soft tongue tasting the salt of me . . . is the breath of life itself. In these moments I believe I am still young. I wish to embrace all my memories and be clamped tightly inside her. But I am no longer young. I can touch my body, but I don't care to look. Perhaps, when my nurse comes, with her warm water and her soft sponge, something might stir. Would I be ashamed? Ah, this spring breeze, it is the tongue of Josephine.

I know time slides away like a cat burglar, and it tries to carry every piece it can fit of us in its bag. It has taken much from me. But time is death, and death is stupid—it has never understood that all of me—all my dreams, all my delights, all my love— might go, but the hands will be the last. My hands will still feel Josephine's dark nipples hardening against the palms, her flowing river when she came with my fingers inside her. Death has never understood all the things the hands remember.

Even in death, I will remember the astonishment of touching her body.

How many lovers? Many. But Josephine was the first. She asked me, on that fumbling shaking afternoon: "Am I your first lover?" Though she might not have said "lover." She might have said "time." It was the way she spoke, words of the country life, not the city. Words like "lover" were not yet in her vocabulary.

And of course, being a boy, a bit younger than she, I lied. I was ashamed of my youth, my inexperience. It seemed every other boy I knew already had much more swagger. They told tales I know now were false, for I told the same ridiculous legends. When Josephine asked, I was a little afraid.

"No," I lied. "Of course not."

I know now, too, that she saw through me and forgave me, and as I blundered atop her, she moved herself so I might find the sacred spot and whispered, "You are my first."

I had never experienced that sensation—of the perfect connection, two parts of two people who were cocreating this new thing that was the oldest thing on earth. I believe I have tried my entire life to relive that first vivid perfection, the ferocious tenderness of that first engulfment. It never occurred to me to find out what it was like for her. If I could see her now, I would be afraid to hear what I think to be true—it could have been better. We must learn to laugh just a bit at our young, fumbling selves, no?

I thought she would have experimented before me. But that was a different time, and a different place, and she did not have the freedom we took for granted in the city. It was her father's world, and her mother was like his sheriff. There would be no great adventures for Josephine, not even university. I was utterly unconscious of these things.

I wished at that moment that I had not lied. That I had not denied her a gift. No, that is the old man speaking. I wasn't that wise, I was simply ashamed. Especially after I exploded inside her as soon as I arrived. I tried to mop up the mess I had made, something that felt akin to Noah's flood as I burned and blushed and stared into her openness.

I did not realize until much later that she meant no insult when she asked, "Is that all there is?"

I resolved to show her there could be much more. I didn't know if that was true, but I did know how badly I wanted there to be. Josephine was already like a drug. I was too callow to admit that I was hoping she could teach me.

She was like a book of secrets, and her body was my own body's validation. I was unusually silent on our long drive back to the city. Her scent was on my hand, my fingers. I hid my hands in my jacket pockets and took furtive breaths of her when my parents were not looking. Much like I now suck at the oxygen tubes when the nights turn dire.

And that night, though I was sore, I smelled my left hand as my right stroked me into one of my socks.

Before we made love that first time, there were the awkward encounters one has. It started in her room. I was allowed to study there, for it was quiet, at the back of the house, and none of the adults could imagine such fires in its sanctity. Josephine had a large bed and a small closet with a hanging cloth for a door. A dressing table with a round mirror and her lipsticks and face powders on top. Her days were busy with chores—it did not occur to me that she spent the day cooking and baking and cleaning for our visits, which were seen by her parents as the arrival of royalty. As the mothers puttered in the garden, and the fathers strode about chopping wood and clearing brush and harvesting olives and grapes for the red wine they made together, Josephine swept and cooked and created cakes and tended our family's beds. I lay upon her own with my books and my notebooks.

It began with the scent of her hair, her perfume, on her pillow. My hands wanted to feel everything in the room, as badly as my eyes wanted to see her secrets. The clothesline was outside her bedroom window, and I watched her underwear moving in the breeze, yellow and blue and white. I held my breath as I slid open the drawers in her dresser and found her underthings, becoming aroused as I ran my hands over their softness. That was when I heard her come into the room. I had my back to her and froze. I couldn't say anything. My face burned.

"Do you like them?" she asked.

"I'm sorry."

"It's all right. You're curious."

She closed the door. We could hear our parents outside, laughing and drinking vino. I still could not turn to her. I was too ashamed.

She came up behind me and reached around me. She put her hand over mine and squeezed it upon her underthings. Hypnotized, I pulled the underwear out and held it to my face. It smelled of sky and soap.

She showed me the inside of her closet.

Her unwashed clothing was there.

"Don't play around in there, bad boy," she said, and left the room and shut the door.

She would stand before the mirror, preparing her face—cream, eyes, lips. I loved all her secrets. I loved the scents and the art of her preparations. I could look over her shoulder, pressed behind her, and watch her breasts in the reflection; lock eyes with her as I pushed against the firmness of her bottom, hard, painfully hard. I could watch my hands take hold of her breasts. Slide down her stomach and move between her legs. I was drunk on the mound there, hypnotized by the firm pliancy of that delta. I had not yet seen it, of course. As she had not yet seen me. I delighted in massaging her, holding that lovely thickness, and watching my fingers knead her. When I tried to bunch up her skirt so as to reveal her underwear, she would pull it back down like a falling curtain between acts at the opera. And I would begin again. Listening to her pant. Her dark eyes aflame in the mirror until they rolled and her lids clamped shut and she crouched down just a little.

I did not understand that she was coming.

And when she was sure the flush had faded from her cheeks, she went back out to do her chores, and then I flogged myself and exploded into her underwear.

I was alarmed that touching her would make my penis drool—did men suffer such things? There was no one to ask. I had wet stains down my left leg, as I always tucked myself to the left. I hid my underwear from my mother when it was time for the laundry.

Josephine called it "your little fountain."

She would push my hands aside and stare.

"Oh, you have wet yourself," she would say, putting her tongue to the fabric.

I thought we had both gone insane.

And then she asked me to show her. To take it out for her, which I had never done for anyone. I had only shown it to myself, in the bathroom mirror, in taboo fantasies of women seeing me, so eager.

She touched it.

"If I put it in my mouth, will I get pregnant?"

Oh, heaven! I became a professor, fast-talking with a shaking voice. "No, no. Impossible. We studied this in science! The mouth goes to a different place, you see, to the stomach. If you eat chicken, you don't lay an egg! Ha! I—"

She bent down and licked the salty flow off me. And then she took me in her mouth. My knees buckled, but she was strong—she held me up.

How she delighted in making me wet. And sighed when she made me come. My hands, when they went to my hardness in the night, were her lips, her palms.

If I could rise to her now, my hands would play her role.

Wait.

I might yet.

Oh . . . Josephine.

I feel full in my own hand, I feel as though I am healthy, just for a moment, hot and dense and full.

Josephine's father was my own father's oldest friend and my godfather. We were city people, and they had their lands in the country. You must understand the times we were in. I was intended to be the scholar, the man of substance. She was expected to be someone's wife and create the next round of important men. Our fathers had plans for her, as though she were one of my godfather's prize horses. I listened to music she did not understand. I read poems. I brought her strange notions from the city. We were somehow made of the same stuff, and I delighted in delighting her. One flesh. I knew her yearning and her despair. But I could never convince her to run away with me.

Every time my parents and I left for home it was agony. She'd give me her underwear and kiss me secretly and whisper, "I will be your flower with you in your bed. Smell me tonight."

You understand that Josephine is not her real name.

Who can explain such things? Who can define what love is? Lust? Lust with love is the most lulling and addictive power in the world. And she had taught me so much with her strong, delightful hands.

She showed me how to brush the horses, how to pry ticks off the barn cat's neck, how to pick the pea pods on the vines. And she showed me how to find what she called her "pomegranate seed." How to touch it, how to move around it in circles. "Dance with it," she whispered.

The day we first made love, the adults were drinking, or rushing off in my godfather's ancient Ford to enjoy feasts with old friends kilometers away. Josephine showed me how to apply lipstick and then asked me to do it for her. I was terrible, I confess. I made her look like a clown. But she wiped her mouth clean and had me do it again, lips slightly parted.

And then she did it to me. I didn't know what to think. I looked at myself in the mirror and was shocked how much I liked how I looked.

She wanted to kiss the lipstick off my mouth.

And later, she taught me how to dance and how to hold

hands with my lover. "You always lace your fingers together," she told me. "You show her that she is yours and you will never let her drift away. Never make us think you will part from us. Show the world you are proud of us."

"Can we kiss again?"

"No," she said. "I think the kiss, it will break my heart. We can give everything to each other. But"—she paused—"maybe that is the thing we must save for someone else. It will matter one day."

"I want to," she said.

"Want to what?"

"See you. Show me."

"Do what?"

"Do yourself. I want to watch."

"Will you show me?"

"Yes."

"You will do it, too?"

"I will."

I slid my pants down. My underwear. Hands shaking. No one had seen me like this. In this state, I lay back across her bed.

"Touch it for me," she said.

I did.

"Do it," she said. "Up and down."

I did.

"Now I will help you."

She reached up between my legs and went to the back and put her finger in me. Then her other hand pushed mine away and she did her magic and the eruption crossed the room and hit her lamp and we fell off the bed laughing.

"Now," she said, "I will show you."

One hand moved in circles and the other went in and out.

That was the only time she said she loved me.

This is not a confession. It is my prayer. Because heaven itself knows the depth of my emotion. My hope is clear. She'll be old now. She will feel unlovely and worn from the weight of the life she didn't know how to evade. She was always more adult than me. All I had to offer her were illusions. But I wish she had agreed to leap into my dream of a life. Touching each other, tasting each other, laughing, weeping, breakfasts and baths, walks and ocean swims and orgasms together. Forever.

It is Josephine who stays in me after all the others are gone and forgotten—Josephine, who opened the world for me, who introduced me to myself. Josephine, who trusted me with her secrets and who so tenderly opened my own. Josephine, who taught me that putting your hands upon a woman, reaching inside her body, is a sacred act. That while the foolish world calls it tawdry, it is the holiest of holies, deserving of awe and devotion.

I send out this prayer knowing, knowing to my bones, that she will feel it. My hand shakes now as I write. I know she will know, and when I die, she will find this room. She will push everyone out of the way, and she will close the door. Bolt it. She will undress my body. She will kiss me. She will touch me everywhere. She will kiss my sex. She will kiss my weary hands good night.

This, my hands remember.

Tomorrow Morning

For ten years she'd waited for this day, but it had seemed relentlessly distant—untenable. All that time she'd been living on the thin line of life like one condemned to a sentence, like Lekan himself was. But then, the days had begun to end more swiftly, bringing with them a sudden tide of change as if some god to whom she'd long prayed had finally heard her entreaty. Then when she last visited the prison the previous week, they gave her a date: "Twelfth July." She returned speechless, stunned and somewhat exhausted by the overwhelming sense of respite it gave her. She went home and began planning to set things straight, clean the house, cook, disentangle completely from the married man with whom she'd been having an intermittent affair, and prepare for his arrival.

And now that day had almost come, separated only by one stroke of nightfall. She could not concentrate at work, hanging on the clouds of her thoughts and mostly looking out the window into the noisy Lagos streets as if she could find him among the teeming crowd. At three, after the state's minister of education had concluded her visit to the school in triumph, she wanted out. With her face folded into small ridges of pain, she told her superior she was feeling sick—her painful period again. Soon she was out the gate, the noisy wave of children's voices behind her.

On the bus, she closed her eyes, unwilling this time to play her usual game of trying to find how many men would look at her lustfully. Today, through the howling and yelling of the conductors and street hawkers, she thought only of him; of the years past and all she had done to atone. Sometimes, when submerged in the noise of the world and she thought of all that happened, it felt recent, as if the decade were only a few days ago. She had just moved to Lagos, to the same compound as he, a quiet man, well composed. He owned an old Volvo in which he'd taken her on a ride to the university twice. As he drove the first time, he'd avoided eye contact with her and hesitated to speak, exuding a boyish shyness uncommon in men in 1990s Nigeria. She had gotten a fair exposure to being men's object of desire for some time. Being only nineteen, unmarried, and choosing not to live on campus or in shared housing with other girls, had merely served to worsen it. Even though she'd been busy rushing off to school from this place every morning and returning home in the evenings, sometimes spending the weekend in the hostels with her friends, she'd noticed the intensity of the eyes of men in the compound. If she came out to the backyard to fetch water from the well, suddenly the empty well would become crowded with other tenants, most of them married men, pretending to want to draw water at that exact time. Then she'd noticed the landlord's antics. It had been as though he were monitoring her, and anytime she was at home he'd knock and go in, saying he wanted to inspect the wall to see if there was water leakage or if the screed paint was starting to peel as the estate surveyor had predicted.

During their second and last ride together, Lekan had tried to impress her with his speed. When he nearly collided with a mammy wagon, she shot him a look and in apology, he'd slowed down, his right hand grazing over the wheel. He turned on the radio and a Christmas carol spilled out as if it'd been waiting. She lowered the window, threw her gaze outside, wanting to laugh. When she faced him again, he was turning the knob of the radio, dimming the voice singing "We Wish You a Merry Christmas." He cleared his throat with a small, croaky cough.

"Ehmm, Nneka—right?"

She nodded and looked at him. She could tell that he remembered her name but had added the question because he was unsure how to begin the conversation.

"Okay, okay." He nodded, his hands slipping up and down the steering wheel, which was wrapped in a synthetic yellow cover. "Lest I forget, then, have the landlord been disturbing you?"

"Disturbing me?"

He stared only with the side of his left eye. "Yes."

"Ehmm—ehmm, in fact, yes. Oh, God! How did you know?"

For the first time, it seemed, he laughed. A bright contour appeared on the side of his face.

"I know him," he said, his voice falling into a whisper as if the landlord, a man in his sixties, potbellied, bald, and with a slow, cautious gait, were within earshot.

Something, a fuse she did not know and a wire that had been concealed, met and gave spark. She told him of the many times the landlord had come into her flat the week before, and then, something stranger had happened. She'd returned from work to find one of her underpants, the purple one with butterfly patterns, on the bed. She had not recalled removing it from the closet, and she certainly wouldn't simply have dropped it on her bed. And in the house, there had been a smell, as of a man's body, like her former boyfriend in Aba used to smell. Now she'd put it all together and, in this summing up of things, there had been fear. The landlord, having entered her house in her absence, was stalking her.

When she came home that evening from campus and saw again, this time, her bed undone, the smell on her sheets, she'd been too afraid to stay there. She'd climbed the stairs, raced up to the third floor, and knocked on the door of room 6. She'd knocked before thinking she did not know anything about Lekan, if he lived alone or was married; she'd simply wanted to tell him what had happened and to see if, for her safety, she could sleep in his flat that night.

She climbed down from the bus now, the back of her blouse soaked in sweat. The sun had risen increasingly throughout the day and now, even if somewhat dimmed, she could feel its intensity. She walked quickly to her apartment now in Yaba, ways and years away from the apartment block she'd shared with Lekan and the other tenants. Now, as she walked past the stores, the mobile phone tents, it struck her how much had changed in those years. How would Lekan see it all, these things? As she entered the apartment, the sober thoughts fell out of her body. Something tightened down her stomach, as if it were being sewn with a taut thread. She felt then the damp of her vagina. She drew her breath and she placed her hand gently on the broad front of her underpants, pressed her two fingers against it until she could feel the fine end of her labia. She moaned again, slipping her tongue down her lips and back into her mouth again. She lifted her finger, then almost with a rush, put it back and gave in wholly now to the surge of pleasure she felt, as if with each gasp, she were swallowing pieces of her heart down her throat.

She lay in her bed afterward, her relaxed fingers still between her thighs, wondering what would happen in the coming days. She had shared this revulsion of desire that often seized her a few years before with her friend Sade, who had said it was because of lack of sex. She had only had sex four times before Lekan was arrested and jailed, and one of those times had been with him. And when he was arrested, before the corrupt judge sentenced him to ten years in prison for attempted murder, she'd vowed to share in this punishment he was undergoing for her sake by keeping herself and waiting for him. Why would she have sex with another man when he was being denied everything, even his basic freedom, because of her? So she'd kept herself as much as she could, for years, until that fifth year when, the sexual seizures now frequent and tormenting, Sade had warned her she was wasting her youth. A few weeks later, she let her colleague, who had been chasing her for a long time, make love to her almost daily—in an avalanche of pleasure, until her conscience striking at her during every iteration of it finally drew the spear through her soul.

She cut away from the colleague after the three weeks in which they'd had sex nearly forty times. After one of the most intense episodes, she had feared she would become tied to this man and break her vow to Lekan. The colleague had taken her to dinner at Victoria Island and they had been stuck in traffic for hours that night. The man had driven then onto a lone street, up into a path that seemed deserted, and stopped. He turned off the ignition, the lights, and they went to the back seat. At first he had kissed her, both of them sitting side by side, nudging at each other. Outside, the sound of night insects collected into a continuous din, deafening and persistent. He locked the doors, slowly edged her toward the right door, and opened her legs. She clawed slowly at her pants, surprised at the smell of herself. He knelt with one leg on the seat of the car and slid into her. She'd felt his every thrust, the car rattling, her purse sliding from the front seat to the floor. When he came, she felt an equivalent spasm in the lower region of her body. And later, between the throbbing in her vagina and the semen still sliding down her legs long after he'd dropped her at her apartment, she'd made the decision never to see him again.

She pledged herself, again, wholly to Lekan. And when, months later, she again began to feel the wasting urge, an idea came to her instead. That same day, she left the school, took as much as she thought she needed from the bank, and headed to the chief warden's office at the prison complex. Her request, it occurred to her, was not abnormal, only desperate. It could be done. And later, when the deal had been sealed, she waited for him to be brought into the room unchained, dark curtains draping the usually clear windows. The table and chairs had been moved to the side and instead, on the floor was a mat. He came in too shocked to speak. She drew slowly into his arms, whispered that all they had requested was that they not make any noise, and it was to be for only thirty minutes.

She soaked the clean hanky she'd brought in water and wiped the mouth and edges of his penis. Then, she unclasped his trousers. It was the first time she had seen it, having made love that night in the dark, she too shy to look at him. It had been a quick encounter, bearing the marks of its unexpectedness. Once he saw she had allowed him to kiss her, he'd swiftly entered her. In the years since, his penis had erected itself many times in her imagination, occurring in different shades of her dreams.

She saw his mouth fold up, stifling a quiet laughter. He pushed his hand down toward her waist, but stopped, staring at her breasts. He moved his mouth to them, licked her left nipple. He closed his mouth against it, slowly moving his lips against the hardening tip. She felt sharp pricks from the bottom of her feet. He seemed to detach now, his lips colored with saliva. He knelt, his eyes staring at the roof behind, the wall, and around the room. He seemed suddenly afraid, as if he were still not sure they had been permitted. She sat up, took his hand, and gently lifted it. "Lie down," she whispered. He looked at her, nodded, and moved toward the mat. Once he lay, she bent over him, took his penis, and like a fleshy pipe, put him into her mouth. He was raw, veiny, and the texture of cast iron. She grazed the tip with her tongue, raised it upward, and kissed its underside. There seemed in her a race of emotions, as of a body of water emptying into a fall. She closed her mouth on his penis and felt him quiver, as if in panic, his legs shaking, then steadying. Then, when she sucked, its tip grazing the roof of her mouth, he laughed.

They had only thirty minutes, so once she knew he was hard enough and hungry, she wiped her mouth with the back of her hand. He was still standing, his eyes closed, the wet penis glossy from her saliva. She stripped quickly, everything below her waist, down to the beads at her hips. She'd been wearing them since she was seventeen but had stopped in the years after his arrest and her vow to be celibate while he was incarcerated. She'd put them on this morning and turned her head back before the mirror to see them seated atop her waist above the indentations just above her twin buttocks. They'd shone in the mirror, and in the moment, she'd imagined him behind her, inserting himself, fingering the beads.

She took his hand, and in the faintest of whispers, said, "Touch me." He followed her down, hunger flashing in his eyes like fresh fire. She let her eyes remain focused on the rounded smile on his face. She could tell that he had been wanting her, too. That he had been waiting all these years to do this, and that this was one of the reasons he was here.

She felt him with a lateral shudder. He waited first, for a few afflictive seconds at the mouth of her vagina, looking down at it with steady, penetrative eyes. She felt, then, his full intent. Her body pulsed and her legs moved slightly as if to get her away from him.

"Are you all right?" he whispered.

She nodded, pushed herself up, then directly against him, and said, "Yes."

Again, he seemed to inhabit her fully, leaving no breadth of space in her. He began to thrust at first with measured hunger, then, with a force that hurt but pleasured her all the more. For the first time voices had appeared outside the room, guards hovering, their footfalls loud and clicking. She could tell that he was quickening, trying to meet the time. She let her hands play around his back, then lose their composure, racing up his back, falling to his knees, wherever she could touch or hold, squirming and trying to stifle her gasps and to muffle her moans till, with a sharp, hasty rush, he pulled out of her, flinging his semen so far it landed just beside her head. He fell against her, buried his head beside her neck, sobbing. As she raised her hand to pat his head, she looked at her wristwatch. They had beat the time and there were fifteen minutes more.

Yet she could not help the words that kept singing in her head—a name, it seemed, for what they had just done: *prison sex*.

"Tomorrow morning," she whispered to herself almost like a caution, a promise to herself to be patient. Her fingers were still between her thighs now, still wet. Outside, somewhere in the neighborhood, a party was in full swing, loud music and the buzz of the MC speaking into a squeaking microphone. She tried to hook her mind to this event to distract herself. But like smoke rising from the bottom of a smoldering heap, the images of that night that could not be repeated lifted themselves out from beneath the voice of the MC, who was at this point asking Oga Sylvester to rise from his seat and come to the podium. She saw herself passing her shaking hand over the tip of his penis as the MC shouted, "Come, come!" She had clasped her mouth over it, the hard flesh turning momentarily soft as if dead in her mouth, then stiffening—like a thing shot through again with life. She gasped and slowly moved her fingers to her crotch again until the middle finger was inside her vagina.

She was the only person he knew at the prison the following morning. Lekan had told her the last time she'd visited that he would not tell his family the precise day of his release so she could take him home. The prison visitor's lounge was crowded, some dozen people waiting, rowdy. She went in a taxi, an old yellow and blue–painted car with a loud, grating rattle that had squeaked for the twenty-minute journey here. She asked the man to wait outside for a return service, hoping to spare Lekan the hassle of hopping on a bus. From the counter, a long, dark hallway led to the visitor rooms. She sat on one of the benches, looking through the window every few minutes to see the driver still waiting outside the gate. She'd brought a James Hadley Chase novel, the cover torn and misplaced, but a fraction of the image of a woman with shapely fingers smoking still coating the edges. She would raise her head every time she heard footsteps across the hallway, her heart ejecting out of its place, then returning again.

He came out when she was not expecting him—at the point when she'd risen to go to the toilet. She stepped back into the hall to find him nodding at something the warden who had arranged the prison sex was saying, dressed in an old familiar shirt that hugged him so tightly he could barely button it. She flung herself at him, dissolving into tears.

Through the ride to her house, she could not look at him. His hands, between hers, were cold and hard. She had felt them more closely during that encounter in the room at the prison. Now, their texture made sense. The years had changed him, frozen things in his life, hardened him. As she watched him stare with ardent curiosity out the window—at the streets, the changes, the things that seemed unable to be remolded, she knew that although the morning she had been awaiting had arrived, it would not be as she had dreamed it.

He stood behind the door once it had been closed and wept. He would not sit down. She stood close by, careful not to touch him.

"You won't understand what my eyes have seen," he said. "You won't understand what they—they have done to me."

She sat down on the sofa, feeling the urge to weep. In the fridge, the pot of stew rice she'd made to welcome him remained unopened. In the bedroom, there were the new sheets and the room freshener spray. She had envisaged a celebratory reunion. It had not occurred to her that the pain he'd suffered would predominate, that all he would want to do would be to take stock of what had been stolen from him.

She knelt before him, took his hand.

"It is okay. It is okay," she said. "God will help you stand again."

He shook his head, shut his eyes with such violence it seemed the lids had folded into their balls.

"God?" he murmured. "Where was he?"

He sobbed until midnoon when he removed his shoes, dragged himself to the sofa, and fell asleep.

For five days, she woke to find him in the sitting room, awake, seated on the sofa or the floor, his head placed on his hand. He occupied the space around the sofa unmoving, as if it were a cell. There were signs that he left the spot—to eat, use the toilet, and wash himself. But immediately after, he was there again, his presence hedged around him like an animal protecting its space. Two evenings before, after work, she'd tried to make him watch the telly, but midway through the news he had begun shaking his head in bitterness again.

At work all day, she thought about what to do, how to help him heal, how to connect with him before he went home to Akure to see his parents for the first time in ten years. What if he did not return? He was not the man she'd expected. He was not, she feared with the ache of certainty, the same person she had thought he would be. She had fallen into despair, unable to frame a plan when, as the bus entered her street, the idea came to her like a thing promised now suddenly fulfilled.

At home, she passed him lying on the sofa and made straight for the bathroom. She washed herself, let the water flow down her crotch as she removed the last thistles of hair. Then she applied the baby oil she'd bought—gently over the bally plum of her breasts, around the brown patch around the nipples. She oiled both breasts up the scar until they shone in the mirror. Through the door, she could hear him talking to himself the way he often conversed with himself in the cell when alone. And with the exception of two years when he shared it with a robber with whom he fought and squabbled until the man was taken elsewhere, he had spent the time mostly alone.

She came out of the bathroom with only the evening light spread into a patch on the front wall of the sitting room from beneath the hitched curtain on the window. Lekan was seated on the floor, one leg raised, the other stretched flat, his head in the crook of his hand. He had been mumbling when, suddenly, he stopped. She saw him raise his head, moving his mouth but uttering nothing. A drop of oil dripped on his leg as she bent down, spreading her hands to enfold him. For the first time since his release, he smiled, he made her kneel, then, level with her, he fondled the breasts, the veins rising as if inflamed. He sucked at them, the oil in his mouth, smothering the curves around her nipples. She tilted herself backward and he followed with his tongue on her until her back rested on the carpet. He sucked on, stroking the nerves with the tip of his tongue as she poked at him with her legs, squirming. She shoved him slowly, then disentangling from her, he found himself kneeling—his penis hard and heavy. He understood, as she reached for it, her fingers stroking through its rough underside.

He laughed—*"Ololufemi,"* he said.

"My love!"

He raised his head. "Eh?"

"Welcome back."

He licked her, slid between the flaps with his fingers, and grazed the interior. Nneka felt the cry slide out of her mouth as if something had escaped captivity. He saw that her face had become shadowed, somewhat darkened.

"Is it paining?"

"No!" she said in haste. "No, darling. Come inside."

He hesitated.

"I want you—inside."

When he got in, the whole weight of him was on top of her, then it shifted as if a fraction of him had been sliced off. He was looking down at her, but now she could not look at him. She felt every bit of the thrill with her eyes closed, as if the light of the dying day were a nuisance. Her waist throbbed, the oil mixed with the rushed dampness of her insides. He felt full, heavy, and rich, as of a thing meant to be in her and remain forever there. This time, as if he'd suddenly discovered what he had and how much, he seemed to want it to last longer. He'd pull himself to the tip of her vagina, its fleshy doorway, and dip in a few times, as though afraid to probe deeper. She felt each dip, like a clutch pulling at her insides, flushing her blood full with anxious desire. When he pushed back in, the damp had doubled, swallowing him like a foot in a miry pool.

As he moaned and thrust, her mind veered past him, past the evening, beyond the next day into the future she hoped with all her heart would come: of him back to her healed, married to her and both of them looking at their child in the cot. She opened her eyes to see him shaking, her insides burning as if filled with warm pap. She lay there until he was firmly asleep on the floor, an arm over her belly, assured, knowing.

In the morning, after he'd left, taken the first bus to Akure, she stood gazing at her unwashed self in the mirror, at the traces of the oil on her breasts, the semen around her thighs, and the dry crust on her neck. She knew that something had changed last night and that it would be her new life and, if she was not unlucky, it would remain so.

Holo Boy, 2098

It is thirty-two minutes before her date with Lake Frost, and Inesz is breathing too fast. She rushes from the living room of her downtown NeoCity penthouse into her home lab and calms herself with the familiar rituals of taste creation: she picks out containers labeled Strawberry 4, Toasted Almond 5, and Boiled Egg 2a. Fills a small beaker with five milliliters of water. Transfers 0.3 to 0.5 milliliters of each flavor into the beaker with a pipette. Takes a mixing rod and stirs the solution for ten seconds. Brings the mixture to her nose to smell, then puts several drops on her tongue.

As Inesz suspects, this novel combination tastes enough like strawberry cheesecake that it can be used to flavor low-grade synthetic food. While she continues to adjust the flavor balance, her wristcom vibrates in a familiar short-long-short pattern. She taps on it twice as she sets her forearm down on the table, the metal surface making a faint ringing sound.

Inesz's older sister Rita's holographic head and shoulders project from the device. "You're still in your robe," she observes. Her face is dark and heart shaped like Inesz's own, except Rita's large eyes are a deep brown instead of hazel, and her cheek-bones are softer, like clay to Inesz's rosewood.

"He can't see me, so I can wear whatever I want." Inesz ima-gines her sister watering plants at her part-time nursery job, on the outskirts of San Francisco where the two of them grew up. "I'm not sure I can go through with it, though. It just seems so desperate."

"I know I said that. But I think you're right, it might be good for you." She asks Inesz to hold on while she assists a customer.

Rita sent her sister the link to the holo boy website as a joke after Inesz's most recent breakup, with a soccer star–turned-techrepreneur who accused her of loving her work as a flavor specialist more than him. The model-influencer before him said the same thing, as did the DJ-slash-physicist before that. The keen sense of smell that, along with her smarts, has driven Inesz to the top of her field also betrays her when it comes to choosing men. Her nose is hopelessly drawn to the athletic, ambitious ones with highly symmetrical features, who emit a specific scent that her body considers an ironclad prerequisite to physical attraction. She knows this is a primitive holdover from the days when women used smell to search for a mate who would sire the fittest children. The problem is, such men also expect her to configure her life to revolve around them—something she has never managed to do to their satisfaction.

"If you hire a holo boy, you won't have to smell him," Rita teased at the time. Inesz imagined her sending that message as she watched a video game tournament with her engineer hus-band of more than a decade, along with their two bright and affable children. Maybe Rita would have refrained if she weren't so convinced that Inesz's problems were of her own making.

A woman as attractive and successful as Inesz deserved a man who would put her needs before his—as though hordes of such men were just waiting to be chosen. NeoCity may have legislated equal representation and pay in the workplace, but Inesz has found that the male desire to come first in relationships remains beyond the law.

She replied to her sister's message with a "ha-ha" and a fire-breathing dragon emoticon, then never opened the link. But one sleepless night a few months later, after she'd bought this penthouse for herself, Inesz activated her holocomputer, found Rita's message, and clicked. She noted that the holo boy site catered to men, as did the half dozen other sites she found when she did a search—presumably because residential holorooms like hers were still new and enormously expensive, so a market for women didn't exist yet. She was about to shut down the computer when she spied someone who looked like he would smell really good.

She tapped on the image and pulled up the profile for Lake Frost, a man with arresting blue eyes like twin bodies of water, bisected by the elegant slope of his nose. Lake stood with hand on jutted hip, holding a polo mallet and crop while cradling his riding cap. His prominent temple gleamed with sweat, and the bottoms of his leather riding boots were caked with dirt, yet his polo shirt was only slightly rumpled. He looked on the verge of laughter, like someone free from any worries.

Inesz closed her eyes and imagined the smell of an early summer day, the cool pungency of fresh-cut grass, the faint aroma of earth and hay on a horse's skin. Then she imagined the smell of Lake Frost's sweat in his hair, under his arms, in the hidden recesses of him. It occurred to her that if she were to hire this holo boy, the entire encounter would only be about fulfilling her fantasies, not his. What would it be like to receive pleasure without concern for the man's desires? In a matter of minutes, Inesz found herself using an anonymous account to book Lake Frost for the following Saturday.

"Sorry, that took longer than I thought," Rita says when she gets back on. "You okay?"

Her sister must have noticed Inesz's image shaking as her wrist trembled. "Just scared."

"Take deep breaths," her sister replies. "Remember you can always turn off the program if you don't like it."

"I'm more worried I'll like it too much."

Once she disengages from Rita, Inesz takes her beaker and transfers its contents into a jar that she seals and labels Strawberry Cheesecake Draft. She activates her holonotebook and jots down the formula. She's tempted to send these notes to Rufus Lee, her partner on a UN-funded project to feed climate refugees, but she doesn't want to bother him on the weekend.

She wishes her nose liked Rufus, an Aussie transplant with bushy eyebrows who always defers to her judgments in flavor balance and is clearly attracted to her. They've bonded over being NeoCity immigrants, recruited to this progressive, technocratic city-state that declared independence from the American mainland a decade ago. Inesz finds his languid eyes adorable, but the one time she thought something might happen—when they'd gotten tipsy at an office party and ended up snuggled in a booth together—Inesz smelled the sluggishness in Rufus's musk and scooched away so he wouldn't get the wrong idea.

Realizing she can't dally any longer, Inesz shuffles out of her windowless lab space and walks to her bed. The world around her has shifted from dusk to evening. The undulating lights of NeoCity, particularly vibrant on a Saturday night, glow in an infinite array of colors on three sides of her spacious apartment. She takes off her robe, sets her wristcom on her nightstand, and lies naked in her magnetic floating bed with a platinum vibrator in her hand. Then she takes a deep breath and says, "Activate holo boy application." She hears the projector hum, and then Lake Frost shows up, indistinguishable from a man who's physically present, except Inesz knows that if she reaches for him, she will only grasp air.

"A pleasure to be here," he says. "I hope I meet your expectations."

"We'll see," Inesz finds herself saying. She's using the system's voice-masking capabilities to disguise herself as a man, so her airy voice comes out of the holoprojector's speakers in a low baritone.

Lake is, in fact, more than she expected. He wears a polo outfit exactly like the one in his picture, except his tight shirt is white instead of navy. His facial symmetry is even more remarkable in 3-D, his features so well aligned that if a bead of sweat were to fall from his forehead, it would trace a perfect line down his nose to his philtrum, and finally fall down the cleft of his chin with no alteration to its trajectory.

Lake gracefully swings his polo mallet over one of his shoulders, exuding the unmistakable air of wealth—an illusion Inesz did not expect him to maintain outside of two dimensions. "You look well practiced with that mallet," she says. Her newly low voice makes the observation sound like a come-on.

"My family owns a horse farm in Argentina," he replies. "I used to spend summers there."

"So you enjoy riding?"

"Very much."

"Maybe you'd enjoy riding me," Inesz says, then opens her mouth without making a sound, shocked at her brazenness.

"I might have to whip you first, just to make sure you're broken in," Lake says. Inesz replies with a low grunt and breaks into a grin. The holo boy takes this as his cue to get on the bed with his crop, which is well worn and made of a finely textured leather.

"I'm ready to gallop!" she announces. She shuffles around and gets on all fours. Lake seamlessly anticipates her need to watch him by moving to one side of her—impressive since what he sees on his end is just a cartoon male outline. She whinnies when she hears the crack of his whip, then finds herself slapping her own ass to simulate the feeling. He smiles, revealing predictably bright teeth.

"Ready for the ride of your life?" he asks. She tosses her head back in a gesture of equine assent, and he takes off his shirt, revealing sculpted abs that are almost paintinglike in their symmetry. His shoulders are precisely the same height, though one is pocked with a small round birthmark over which he has tattooed an image of the sun. He pulls his white jeans down to the top of his riding boots, leaving only his briefs to cover his groin. He cracks his whip a few more times and asks her if she's really ready. She neighs impatiently, eager for the ride to start. The cock Lake unveils reminds her of the new hyperspeed trains that take NeoCity's citizens to the mainland in under a minute: sleek and smooth, yet brimming with hidden power.

She plunges the vibe inside herself when Lake thrusts his hips, a simulation so accurate that Inesz momentarily forgets they're not really in her bedroom together. She closes her eyes, and what comes to her mind is not an image but the figment of his unnamable scent, of grass and wildness and musk. As she reaches her pinnacle, Inesz lets out a series of squeals that come out through the speakers as satisfied grunts. She turns around and lies down to watch him climax, his neck long and graceful as he tips his head back.

"What a finish," she says. Her breathing slows, and the tension flows out of her body. She can't remember the last time she was this relaxed.

"I'd say we won that match," he replies, receding from her bed. He gets dressed, grabs his crop, and slings the mallet back onto his shoulder. Inesz feels a sudden panic at the thought of his disappearance.

"I'd pay a lot of money to know what you smell like," she finds herself saying.

"That's something we can arrange," Lake replies.

Inesz knew that he couldn't be located too far away, since bandwidth limitations prevent live holostreaming between distances of more than a few hundred kilometers. But she didn't expect Lake to offer his used underwear for sale (which Inesz agreed to buy in the haze of her desire) or to propose leaving them in a public laundromat dryer so she can remain anonymous.

Now, with the appointed hour approaching, Inesz's finger circles around her wrist as she debates whether to message Lake and cancel, but she finds herself unable to.

She puts on a synthetic leather jacket over a casual button-down then walks to the nearest public laundry, a few kilometers downtown in the basement of a substandard-income building. NeoCity feels magical at this hour, when the evening lights have been turned on but the sky isn't completely dark.

One could gander at the sheer variety of architectural styles, a product of the city-state's enormous wealth and sophisticated projector technology that turns building facades into a hybrid of actual and augmented reality.

In contrast, substandard-income buildings like the one where the laundry is located are designed for maximal efficiency, with their block shapes and bare white exteriors. The room is crowded when Inesz enters, and she starts to back out. But then she sees Dryer 14, with Lake's briefs spinning behind the machine's circular glass. She looks to make sure he isn't in the room, then rushes over, opens the dryer door, and inhales.

Lake's odor is luxurious and wild, like fine cheese aging on a wooden plank. She slips the briefs into a plastic bag that she seals and throws into her canvas tote, then she rushes out of the building and hails a passing yellow Dryve to take her home.

But the driverless car hasn't gone three blocks before Inesz is panting in panic. The entire reason she hired Lake was so she could wean herself from her addiction to the scent of men, yet she has just paid an unreasonable amount of money for his used underwear and picked it up in the middle of the afternoon among dozens of people.

"Stop the car!" she yells as the Dryve reaches Founders Bay. She gets out and runs to the promenade, which is crowded with joggers and tourists waiting for sunset. She takes Lake's underwear out of her purse so she can throw it over the guardrail, but then she begins to panic again. She leans down, placing her hands on her knees, and senses someone close to her. She looks up to find herself staring at Lake's radiantly ideal face. The brief wonder she feels is immediately replaced by a sense of violation.

"Get away from me," she says.

"I can explain."

Inesz runs back in the direction she came from, but when she stops to hail a Dryve, Lake catches up with her.

"Look, there's a Synth right in the corner," he says. "We can just sit and talk." She sees the artificial food chain's green-and-white logo, then walks wordlessly across the street and inside. She orders synth-fries at the automated station, then walks toward a pink hexagonal table in the back corner of the half-empty restaurant, where she sets her tray down on the glossy surface.

"I'm not your customer, by the way," she says after they both sit down. "I'm just his messenger, and he'll be furious that you were following me."

"Hand me my underwear."

"Why?"

"Just give it to me." Inesz slides the briefs over to Lake. He extracts a chip the size of a sequin out of a hidden pouch, puts it in a pocket of his gray coveralls, then seals the bag and hands it back to Inesz.

"There. I took out the location tracker."

"You were going to blackmail him."

"No," Lake says firmly. "I'm a social sculptor. I use trackers to map what parts of NeoCity my customers live in."

"So you can out them?"

"I just show the general areas they're projecting from. My art challenges the structures of society." Lake looks down at her fries. "I wasn't sure if you'd want to eat synthetic food."

"It's what I have at home."

Lake nods in approval, and Inesz realizes he's distracting her.

"So why *did* you show yourself to me anyway?" she asks. "You were going to get away with it."

"I don't know . . . I don't usually follow customers, but I had a feeling about you. Then when you left the cab I got worried. It looked like you needed help."

"And I'm just supposed to believe you?"

Lake sighs. "My gallery's close by if you want to walk over. I have a big opening next Thursday."

Inesz appraises him while they finish their food. "Okay," she says after she swallows her last fry.

They don't have to walk far before they reach an unlit storefront with tall windows. Lake stands in front of the biometric reader at the entrance, and the door slides open. Spotlights turn on to reveal an industrial space with concrete floors, exposed wires, and finely rendered schematic drawings. The largest of these is a map of the city as seen from above that takes up a whole wall. A hand-lettered sign over the drawing says LAKE FORESTER: HOLO BOY, 2098.

"Forester's your real name? As in one of the NeoCity founders?"

"Gordon Forester is my grandfather. Sorry about the mess," he says as they walk around the wires. "I've been installing all day, but we still have a ways to go before the opening." He taps a button at the end of one of the wires with his foot, and several hundred points of light get projected onto the map and scatter across the city. Nearly half of them are concentrated in the Founders District closest to the mainland. Another big clump forms in the Smith Heights area, next to the ocean but elevated enough to be floodproof.

"Each point of light represents a customer," Lake says.

"You have this many?"

"I pay other holo workers to track their clients," he replies.

"The largest number of points are in the areas of NeoCity with the highest concentrations of wealth, even though residential allotments are supposed to be evenly distributed based on income. Eventually, rich and poor neighborhoods will form, followed by inequality in public services like they have on the mainland. There's only so much conscious planning you can do before human nature takes over."

"So how would you address the problem?" Inesz asks.

"My job as an artist is to provoke questions, not provide answers."

Inesz lingers on the piece for a while, as the points of light move around and trace the boundaries of the districts they belong to. Eventually, Lake asks Inesz what she's thinking.

"I'm wondering about human nature," she replies. "So I guess you've done your job."

Lake walks her through other parts of the show: a graph of holo workers' average incomes compared to their customers; a visualization of how much money he's raised for climate refugees by selling his used underwear. As the two of them reach the back of the gallery, he pushes a button. A hidden door in the wall slides open. Inesz finds herself in front of a queen bed with white sheets and a headboard made of brushed metal.

"Go sit," Lake says, and when Inesz narrows her eyes: "It's how you activate the piece." She walks over to the bed and lowers herself onto it. A holo version of Lake without a shirt on appears and asks her what she wants.

"I'm not sure—"

"Just tell him you want to be entertained," says Lake.

Inesz does as she's told. Some jazzy music comes on and holo Lake begins a silly dance, pursing his lips and stripping off his jeans with jerky, awkward movements. Inesz shields her eyes as she giggles.

"I fed my encounters into a neural network that produces novel behaviors based on my experiences," Lake says, moving next to her at the edge of the bed. "This piece is the distillation of my life as a holo boy."

"And you're showing this in public?" Lake nods. "I assume the hologram would be willing to take off more than his jeans?"

"Is that so bad?"

"Aren't you worried about what people would think?"

Lake turns off the holo. "That's kind of what I want. Social privilege needs to be examined as much as material privilege," he intones, as if he's reciting from his artist statement. "Being a straight, cisgender, white, able-bodied man who comes from wealth, the most effective way for me to let go of my social privilege without doing something immoral is to do something that's socially stigmatized, like becoming a holo boy."

Inesz angles her head. "Straight?"

"Yes. A lot of holo boys are." He grins, and she can't keep herself from smiling back. Her eye catches a shallow curve where Lake's hair meets the top of his neck, and she wonders what he smells like there. Before she can stop it, her body is rising, her nose seeking the spot, which Lake takes as his cue to lean down and kiss her. Inesz's senses heighten when their lips touch, and she smells his sweat from having worked all day. She feels like a magnet on the verge of repolarizing, so attached to Lake that she wants to get as far away from him as she can. The invisible rope of his scent tethers her to him, gripping her tighter when he unzips his coveralls and shucks his underwear at the same time. His naked body is immediate and thrilling in its stark, physical reality. Inesz isn't as practiced at undressing quickly, so it's Lake who pulls her jeans down. Once she's naked, she rests her hand on his flank and tips her momentum back so she lies back on the bed with him on top of her. She pulls him closer and inhales his hair, his neck, under his arms. She guides him inside her and nuzzles against the smattering of hair on his chest, breathes the sweat on his neck and tastes its salt.

She sniffs at his mouth when he starts to breathe heavily, and even this—the combination of synthetic food and his own saliva—pleasures her, making her wonder if he produces any odor she would find unappealing. He rests his entire weight on her as his cock plunges deeper inside her. It feels just as power-ful as she imagined, and she breathes him in with each thrust.

"Raise your arms," she says when she's close, pleased when she licks under them that she smells only him. This is the only place her nose, her tongue, and her body want to be as smell, taste, and desire collide, over and over again in a long series of eruptions. Even after they dissipate, they continue to send little shocks to her senses, like a fine brandy's lingering aftertaste.

"Maybe you can be my date for the opening," Lake says afterward as he pets her hair.

"Are you sure? You don't really know me."

"I can tell you're interesting," he replies with a grin. "Also, I wanna show you my crop and mallet for real."

Inesz removes his hand from her hair and sits up. "You knew I wasn't really a messenger?"

"I hate to inform you, but you're not the first woman to pre-tend she's a man for holosex."

Inesz blinks. "Wait, you've followed other women before? Is this some kind of game to you?"

"That's not what I mean. I don't—"

"Stop talking."

Inesz hops out of bed and slips into her underwear and jeans. She puts on her blouse, but doesn't bother to button it before she throws her jacket on and zips it up.

"Wait, I'll walk you out," he says. "I can explain."

Inesz ignores him, striding through the gallery to the exit, not noticing that she's been holding her breath until she's outside. She hails a passing Dryve and gets to her penthouse in less than ten minutes. She sheds her clothes and takes a quick shower. Seven minutes later, she's back at her workbench, ready to lose herself in the one thing she has control over.

Inesz takes a titration flask and sets it on a ring stand. Clamps a stoppered funnel over it. Fills the funnel with two hundred milliliters of alcohol. Puts rubber gloves on, removes the organic specimen from its sealed bag, and immerses it in the liquid.

After she finishes, Inesz ambles back into her bedroom, takes off her robe, and lies naked under the covers. She'll leave the briefs soaking overnight. Tomorrow morning, she'll take Lake's distilled axillary extracts to work. There, she'll run the solution through an analyzer to determine its exact chemical composition in precise ratios. She'll synthesize those compounds to end up with a faithful re-creation of Lake's odor, which she'll turn into cologne with some bergamot, and maybe vetiver. Her nose will never rule her choice in a man again.

Her partner, Rufus Lee, will be in the office tomorrow. She'll take him out for a drink after work, and eventually, when they start sleeping together, ask him to wear her favorite scent.

Rufus with his languid eyes, who prioritizes her, and whose motives she'll never have reason to doubt.

The Great Artist

C ome to the studio. *I will* have my mulatto there," the Great Artist promised. "She is both dancer and horse."

I arrived at half past two. The light was best at that hour, the Great Artist—or E., as I shall call him—claimed. He sat by the window twiddling a small ceramic doll as if studying its shadows. He acknowledged me with a flick of his hand and I sat in my usual chair.

I couldn't get enough of these sessions, though he rarely invited me. I was what he called "the commerce man," who should focus on making him money from his art.

When I'd last visited the studio, he'd had two young dancers posing for him. For the better part of three hours, he had them stand in what must have been the most excruciating, but also alluring, positions. As night crept in, he turned up the volume of his favorite Italian opera and asked the girls to perform. In short measure, he was on his feet, too. He tossed off his painter's smock, shed his pants, and danced around the studio with them, naked but for a pair of slippers, as he sang along with the music. His sex swung limply before the girls as he spun them around.

E. never appeared aroused, but I knew he was. His desire,

he told me, was the center of his art, so he didn't dare ejaculate with anyone present. He kept the climax to himself, believing it held his creative genius.

That night, I followed the girls as they left the studio. At the alleyway, they seemed to spot me, but instead of hurrying on, they stopped as if to give me a chance to catch up.

You could see they had been strangely excited by the Great Artist. Their cheeks were flushed and redness had risen into the tips of their noses as if they had been drinking. They both had a curious rhythm to their breath.

"You make quite the muses," I said. They tittered.

"I haven't seen E. in such a gay mood in some time," I continued. "Do let me invite you for a drink and a hot meal. I know he doesn't pay you much for your modeling. And it's the least I could do as a thank-you for keeping him inspired and my gallery walls filled with his art."

As they lounged after dinner, they laughed about how he had stoked his own appetite for them by watching them wriggle through uncomfortable poses. They knew their power over him and took delight in it. Their giddiness stirred my desire for them, which they also recognized. I made no commands, but that night, whatever creativity I had in me I poured into the larger one, while the smaller one sat on my face and I drank her in.

The next day, E. delivered the finished portrait of the dancers. I never told him what had happened. But I never put it on the gallery wall to sell.

As we waited for the mulatto to appear, E. bellowed, "I hear you're showing Toulouse next month." His voice was all gravel, and his eyes were half shut.

We'd gone out last night after attending the mulatto's performance at the Cirque Fernando. The generous pours of absinthe and claret had kept us at the Cafe de la Nouvelle Atheneés well into the night. I woke up with one of the waitresses in my bed and a pounding in my head that I cured with a healthy portion of cognac in my morning coffee.

"Yes," I said. "But not solo, of course."

"I saw him at the Fernando the other night," E. said, pointing at me with one of the small wooden horses that adorned his windowsill. "He was watching my mulatto. That cretinous fuck."

E. disdained would-be acolytes, but he was also a jealous, irascible man who had only grown more bitter as his eyesight continued to fail. The deterioration had begun the year he spent in New Orleans, near the beginning of his career.

"Not to worry," I said. "He's not interested in her. She's German. You know how he feels about the Germans, even a dark-skinned one. Toulouse has focused his work on the clowns."

E. grunted and turned to look out the window again. I knew he could not create great art when he was agitated. But if he was drunk? Well, that was a different matter. His imagination could soar.

"Here," I said handing him my flask. "Drink up."

Fifteen minutes passed. E. was stroking his beard as if deep in concentration, with the flask now nearly empty in his hand. I felt myself growing more eager to see the mulatto. She was to wear her usual performance outfit: a ruffled leotard, lacy white knickers, tights, and high white boots. And she was to bring along her trapeze partner, a Circassian beauty herself.

For the afternoon, E. had borrowed a number of props from the summer circus, which was closed for the season: a bullwhip, a thick rope, a cage, a barbell, and a mule saddle. The mulatto used none of these in her performances, and E. knew this. Perhaps he thought she had more tricks to share.

I confess I had my own hopes for the afternoon. Each night at the Fernando, I fell more under the mulatto's spell. With her head thrown back and her spine arched, she twirled at the end of a cable at a dizzying speed as she was hoisted to the circus top. She was in a perfect position of surrender. I imagined her in my bed yielding to me in the same pose later that night. I would ravish the tawny Venus: fill my mouth with her small taut breasts, bite her sinewy biceps and shoulders and neck, and lick slowly and rhythmically between her legs. Only once I felt her spasm against my tongue would I finally penetrate her, hammering my sex into her until we were both spent.

That never happened. But still, you will now have imagined your lips on my breasts and feasted on the image of my firm brown ass in the cradle of your hands. Perhaps you have pictured thrusting inside me, my sepia skin sending you into a tropical frenzy. The "Great" Art Dealer tells a sexy tale.

What he can't articulate is that his fanciful longings came from the sense of wonder he experienced watching me perform. Men always substitute sex for the sublime. This did not seem true of the Great Artist. In his simple sketches, he captured my strength as I ascended to the rafters, hanging by bent knees backward on the trapeze bar, hoisting a full-grown man by each hand. He sketched an artist in motion. Me.

I went to pose for him that day because his plea was very simple: "I've seen you both gallop and dance through the air. Now I would like to see your eyes."

When the housemaid escorted the mulatto and her partner into the studio, E. stood to greet the pair.

"Play the Verdi," he yelled, and I sprang from my seat at his command.

He crossed the studio, unsteady on his feet. He nearly tripped over the barbell as he rushed over to help the mulatto remove her winter coat.

"Today you must show me how you dance in midair," he said. His words were deeply slurred, and he swayed a little on his feet. He often became almost silly when he found a subject particularly bewitching, but I had never seen him like this, on the edge of being undone from a few drinks.

As he hung her coat, I heard him say loudly and breathlessly: "Brugmansia." It was as if something came loose in his voice. I thought it might be a German word he had learned to put the mulatto at ease, but she and her partner looked equally as confused as I.

As he turned toward her again, you could clearly see the enormous bulge in the front of his pants.

All that happened next happened very quickly: E. pulled the mulatto into his arms and pressed his hard sex against her. "My walking silhouette," he said into her neck as he held her buttocks and rubbed against her. "You've found me again."

She could certainly have freed herself from his grip, but she was frozen, so shocked was she. The next thing I heard was a loud crack like lightning had struck the studio. It was the mulatto's partner, who had slammed the bullwhip just shy of E.'s feet.

Startled, she broke away from him. Only then did she see that he had satisfied himself against her, and that the foul wet front of his pants had soiled her costume, too.

It was only later that I would learn from a mutual friend what happened that day. In short, E. had gone into an alcohol-induced psychosis in which his past and the present became a jumble. He thought he smelled on the mulatto's coat the scent of the yellow flower, brugmansia or angel's trumpet, that grew in his uncle's New Orleans garden, where he'd used to make love each night with the family's Creole cook.

That was the last day I ever saw him. I don't know whether he continued to paint. Perhaps the theory of his creativity had proven true, because he certainly never exhibited his work again. Just a year later he lost his eyesight completely and then, shortly thereafter, his life.

The next time I attended the show at the Fernando the mulatto was no longer there. She and her partner had departed to headline at London's Royal Aquarium for an extended run.

The Great Artist seemed as stunned as I was by what happened that day. He grabbed a painter's smock that hung from the wall and wrapped it around his pants. As much as I felt disgusted by what he had done, I felt a measure of sadness, too. You could see on his face his own horror, but most clearly you could see his fear. I recognized that look in performers who lose their grip on the trapeze and fall heavily to the ground, and voltigeurs who miss a jump and tumble from the saddle. It was as if the daring had completely drained out of the man.

I learned of his death many years later. My former agent, Rosinsky, sent me a newspaper clipping with the headline: "Sketches by Master Painter Fetch Record Price." The sketches, it turned out, were of me.

Two photos accompanied the article. I recognized a man in one of them as the art dealer. "I don't think collectors care much what he sketched," he was quoted as saying. "But these are the last known sketches of the greatest artist of our era. The girl was simply some circus act."

The second photo showed the sketches. There was only one I had not seen before, a pastel. Arching oak and orange trees fill almost the entire page, but if you look closely you see two figures—a man and a woman—standing near a white gate, bathed in a strange golden light that could be sunrise or sunset. His arms are around her waist. His face is nuzzled into her hair, where she has a yellow flower tucked behind her ear. She holds his hands on her stomach with her head slightly bent. You cannot see her eyes.

I often wonder about that afternoon in his studio, and what would have happened if the Great Artist had immortalized me in a painting? If my portrait had been exhibited and revered as one of his greatest works? Perhaps then you'd know something more about me than a little man's salacious tales. Perhaps then you'd know my name.

Posseeblay

Will Gall *swiveled in his chair,* away from the freelance piece he was writing about people who eat their own hair, and turned to his wife, Erin, who was typing away on an article of her own about ghost nets floating in the seas of the North Atlantic.

"Louisa just emailed," Will said. "She wants to know if Sadie will ever write for her again." When Erin didn't answer, he added, "Björn likes the idea."

Björn Borg was their shared tennis hero and Will's occasional imaginary life coach. On the wall above their side-by-side black IKEA desks, Will and Erin had each affixed their favorite photo of the charismatic Swede.

His showed Borg's triumphant 1980 Wimbledon Gentlemen's Final win against John McEnroe. Will often turned to this image for guidance during particularly deflating writing periods, and Borg would come to life and share a series of hard-earned wisdom: "Tough times don't last, Will; tough people do." "Stop trying to write like fucking Jonathan Franzen, Will." Some days Björn simply reminded Will to slip on his lucky

Adidas headband and shut up and serve the fucking ball: "Just write, Will, write!"

Erin's shot of Borg was from the 1976 US Open in which Jimmy Connors had defeated him in the men's singles final. It reminded her that even perfection gets beaten sometimes, so why should she agonize about being beaten up by her editor over a story nobody was going to read anyway? Nobody, that is, aside from her family and Elaine, the aging and opinionated newsagent on Chatswood Road, who would no doubt tell Erin how she battled through, reluctantly, to the end of the piece that Erin put every part of herself into—every vein, every blood cell, every swallowed self-doubt—and then say, as she always did, "You do love your commas, don't you?"

"Tell Louisa and Björn, Sadie's dead," Erin said, not looking up from her computer. "I'm afraid she's blown her last beef whistle."

Will smiled. Louisa Lee was an old friend from their graduate school days and the commissioning editor of the erotic journal *Kinky Ink*, where their Sexy Sadie stories had been published. Once, after drinking five pints of Guinness, she'd boisterously shouted her top-five slang terms for the male genital appendage across a crowded bar. "Heat-seeking moisture missile!" she hollered, pint raised in her right hand. "Sexcalibur! Tallywacker! Quiver bone! And the crowned king of cock slang"—Louisa swayed, dropped her head, then raised it back triumphantly—"*beef whistle!*"

Several minutes passed in silence. Not a single word from Erin or Björn. "It's called Rapunzel syndrome," Will said.

"What's that, hon?" said Erin, biting a thumbnail, lost in her work.

"People who eat their own hair. The official name for it is

trichophagia. It can be incredibly dangerous, because if you eat too much, a hair ball starts to grow inside your stomach and eventually it forms a kind of rat's tail that slips into your intestine."

"I don't see how it's even possible for a hair ball that big to form inside a human stomach," Erin scoffed.

"Oh, it's possible!" Will said, affronted. "One hundred percent *posseeblay!*"

"I love it when you try to talk French, but that's not how you pronounce it."

"Mmmm, is that so, *mon cher*?" Will said, left eyebrow raised, adopting his French voice, a hammy cross between Serge Gainsbourg and a treasure-lusting Tintin villain, that Will had used before and after intercourse for the past nine years—one year longer than their eldest child, Ollie, had been alive.

"It's actually *ma chérie*. You just called me a man," Erin said.

Will glanced down at his wife's right leg. Erin was still in her morning gym leggings and running shoes. "You torture me, *ma chérie*, with that half-exposed calf *musceel*," he whispered seductively. He leaned down and ran his right forefinger along his wife's calf as reverently as if it were a da Vinci oil painting. "This leg belongs in a museum," he purred. "This calf *musceel* belongs in a sacred box under mood lighting in the *Loovera*."

"*Tu parles français comme une vache espagnole,*" Erin said, not taking her eyes from her work.

"What did you just say to me?"

"You speak French like a Spanish cow."

"Oh, how you hurt me," Will said, his fingers walking slowly up Erin's right thigh toward the space between her legs. "But how I yearn to caress your *petite pomme*."

"Now you just called my vagina an apple."

"So sweet. So delicious."

"Buzz off," Erin said, slapping his wandering fingers.

"Skyrockets in flight?" Will whispered, waggling his eyebrows.

Erin shot a glance at her desk clock, the hands turning in the center of an image of the Beatles making their brief and fabulous journey across Abbey Road.

"Can't," Erin said. "School pickup."

"Not for another hour. One hour is a lifetime for Sexy Sadie."

"I told you, Sadie's dead."

Sadie had died some years ago, killed by time and circumstance, parenthood and afternoon school pickup. Or was it, Erin wondered, just the part of herself that helped bring Sexy Sadie to life that had died?

It had always felt absurd to her that Sexy Sadie developed such a large following among the readers of *Kinky Ink* in the first place. She was just a dumb lark, a frivolous experiment born under the influence of one of Will's signature whisky sours.

They'd been listening to the *White Album* and bitching about the big-effort/small-reward reality of producing a three-thousand-word cowrite exposé for the *Telegraph*. They hoped the nationally significant piece would find its rightful place on page one, but knew, deep down, it would be pushed to the back of the newspaper somewhere between the form guide and a story about a sheepdog that miraculously dragged its paw across the week's winning lottery numbers.

"You remember Louisa Lee?" Erin said.

Will closed his eyes, trying to jog a memory clouded by too much Glenfiddich. "Underground poet from second year?"

"Yeah. Guess where she's working now?"

"Please say MI5."

"She's commissioning editor at *Kinky Ink*."

"Stick mags?"

"More like dick lit. Words, not pictures," Erin said. "What would you say if I told you that *Kinky Ink* pays double the word rate of the *Tele*?"

By side three, track four, of the *White Album*—"Everybody's Got Something to Hide Except Me and My Monkey"—Erin had all but sold Will on the idea of cowriting an erotic fiction piece for Louisa Lee.

"But what do we know about writing erotic stories?" Will said.

"How hard could it be? A, elaborately described vagina, plus B, elaborately described bell-end, equals one big C, a mind-blowing and uncommonly wet climax."

Will laughed and enthusiastically slammed the last of the whisky. "So where do we start?"

John Lennon's singing voice echoed through the kitchen. Side three, track five. A song about a woman who broke the rules. A woman who laid it down for all to see. The greatest of them all.

"Sexy Sadie." Erin smiled.

Will removed his fingers from his wife's right thigh and turned back to his work, flipping unenthusiastically through thirty-five pages of harrowing interviews of men and women who once regularly ate or were still eating their own hair. He didn't know where to start. He didn't want to start. He turned to Björn for advice.

"Sexy Sadie and the Little Deaths," Borg said. "That could be the next one."

"Nice title," Will thought. "I miss her, Björn."

"Who doesn't miss Sadie?" Borg said. Will laughed out loud.

"What's so funny?" Erin said.

"I'm thinking about that first Sadie story we wrote for Louisa: 'Sexy Sadie and the Cleopatra Buzz.'"

Erin chuckled. "Ridiculous."

"It was a masterpiece of erotic adventure," Will said.

"Sexy Sadie and the Cleopatra Buzz" introduced Sadie as a globe-trotting reporter with a PhD in anthropology, specializing in the physiology of ancient sexual behaviors, who detailed her thrilling quests to uncover lost treasures centering on the secret sexual proclivities of prominent historical figures.

Each piece, cowritten by Erin and Will under the nom de plume Sexy Sadie, climaxed with Sadie having some wild, kinky form of intercourse after discovering some long-lost, priceless sexual artifact.

"Sexy Sadie and the Emperor's Skin," for example, saw Sadie travel through Rome in search of the tiger skin that the famously filthy Emperor Nero wore during intercourse.

In "Sexy Sadie and the Eagle's Nest," Sadie journeyed to the Bavarian Alps in search of a rumored chalet sex dungeon once frequented by Nazi officers of the SS. There, she stumbled upon the find of her career: Adolf Hitler's butt plug.

"Sexy Sadie and the Cleopatra Buzz" found Sadie in Egypt on a deadly mission to uncover proof that Cleopatra invented the world's first vibrator: a hollow gourd that she filled with angry bees.

Erin shook her head. "I'm not sure what was more impossible, Sadie finding Cleopatra's dildo or the ridiculous levels of pleasure she got from using it."

"All totally possible." Will smiled. "One hundred percent *posseeblay.*"

Erin's laughter faded as she read the sudden melancholy in her husband's face: the straight line of his closed lips, the resignation in his breathing. She knew what was coming.

"Did we stop shagging when Sadie died?" he asked.

"We stopped *having sex* because the kids stopped going to bed at six p.m."

"Why did she have to die?"

"Sadie died because I could no longer stomach your stupid narratives," Erin said. "The outlandish positions, the toys, the fucking climaxes within climaxes. It was all getting more and more preposterous."

"Well, I was just about to tell you another one of those stupid narratives," Will said, turning back to his computer. "But I guess I'll save you the stomachache."

They worked in silence for two full minutes. Erin did a Google search for migration patterns of harp seals. Will conferred with Björn Borg.

"Just tell her the idea," Borg said.

"She's going to hate it."

"She'll love it," Borg said. "It will write itself. Just tell her."

Will turned his chair to face Erin. "Sexy Sadie and the Little Deaths," he said. "Sadie's editor instructs her to track down an old man from Nashville, Tennessee, who, from 1965 to 1987, accidentally killed several women through his unparalleled ability to stimulate the female genitals. The way this old man yodeled in the canyon literally slayed them with pleasure. Sadie finds him in a remote Moroccan kasbah, where he tells the painful tale of how each woman's life was in his hands—or in his mouth, rather—and how each ultimately chose passion over existence. Sadie decides there's only one sure way to test the veracity of the old man's story: to be pleasured by the cunnilingus killer himself."

Erin said nothing. Will pressed on. "But there's a tender heart to this particular Sexy Sadie yarn. A deeper layer we're not expecting. Through a dazzling and kaleidoscopic series of dangerous cunnilingus methods, the old man brings Sadie to the edge of a euphoric death. It is a pleasure so addictive, she decides that every moment of life she will miss will be compensated by every star-bursting second she spends inside that climax.

"But she does not die," Will said, smiling. "In the afterglow of their intimacy, the old man reveals the missing secret ingredient that he gave each of those women, that he cannot give to Sadie. 'True love,' he says. 'I loved all three of them with all of my heart.' And that, Sadie realizes, is what is needed to experience the greatest pleasure of all."

"I hate it," Erin said, turning back to her computer.

"What's wrong with it?"

"Three women, all so thrilled by a bit of fanny fiddling that they pop their clogs? What do they actually die of?"

"Heart attack."

"For fuck's sake, Will, it's an orgasm, not an electric shock treatment. Yet again, you're revealing your misguided faith in the all-conquering power of a man pleasuring a woman. I mean, seriously, I don't mind you going down to funky town occasionally, but I'm not going to die for it. Not. Fucking. *Posseeblay.*"

"Well, I just thought it might be a bit of fun," Will said softly.

He turned back to his computer, acting defeated, and tapped haphazardly on his keyboard. "Forget about it. Sadie's dead."

Erin sighed. Deep breath and a long exhale. "Look, grumpy pants, if it makes you feel better, I did have an idea for a new series we could offer Louisa."

Will snapped instantly out of his overegged melancholy and turned back to his wife. "I'm all ears."

Erin rolled her eyes. "It's probably a dumb idea."

"No such thing."

Erin took a breath, held her palms out in the air. "We come clean."

"What do you mean?"

"We write the truth. The real sex life of the writers behind Sexy Sadie. Ordinary couple, parents to two kids, trying to squeeze sex in between breakfast, school drop-off, work, school pickup, trumpet lessons, dance lessons, choir practice, football practice, dentist appointments, *walking the fucking dog*... homework, dinner, relentless bedtime nagging, and the slim fucking possibility of a half-decent night's sleep."

"Real husband, real wife, real sex," Will said. "You're fired up. I love it."

"Nobody ever writes real sex. Nobody ever captures the way it can be so boring and awkward and mundane and disappointing..."

"Well, it's not always—"

"—but beautiful as well," Erin said, cutting her husband off while resting a gentle hand on his thigh. "And deeply intimate in the most honest way, and connecting, and filled with history and fun and feeling. True love isn't always lust and near-fatal orgasms. True love is embarrassed giggles and sweat between rolls of fat and bad breath from last night's Indian."

Will laughed, eyes alight. "Real married sex, microscopically reported. A hundred tiny details across one fifteen-minute bedroom romp squeezed between homemade pizzas and parent-teacher conferences. It's brilliant."

His left hand grabbed his iPhone on his writing desk, and his right hand swiftly reached for his wife's left wrist. "Come upstairs with me," he said.

"What for?" Erin said.

Will's thumb swiped through his iPhone screen to his voice recorder app. He tapped the red record button on the voice recorder and put his lips to the phone's speaker. "The truth," he said.

Will slipped his trousers down his legs as he noted the details of the bedroom.

"Picasso print on the wall facing the bed, black frame," he said. "*Guernica*. Shutters closed the way Erin likes it. Jackhammering down the street. Bedside table to my right. Phone resting on a copy of *Mrs. Dalloway*, which itself rests on a copy of *The Oxford Book of Aphorisms*. Time: 2:37 p.m. We need to be done here by 2:55 p.m. at the latest to make school pickup. Pressure is on, but we've made do with less. Struggling to pull my right foot from my khaki chinos because I'm fatter than I was the last time Erin and I made love."

Will was wearing green boxers that were moth-eaten at the crotch. They slipped down his thighs with ease as he made more notes. "Penis flaccid and ugly, as per usual. I'm feeling instantly self-conscious at the sight of my exposed scrotum carrying one oversized left nut and one undersized right nut."

"There's nothing wrong with your deformed balls," Erin

said, patting Will's arm the same way she'd patted Ollie's a week ago when he came in last in a swimming race.

"You feeling self-conscious about anything?" Will asked for the record.

"Oh, no, I'm perfectly fine, *perrrfectly fine*, with the way my body bounced back after carrying two ten-pound heffalumps and expunging them through a birth passage that was once as narrow as the Huddersfield Canal but now feels like the bloomin' English Channel. No, really, I'm all good, allllll good," she said, theatrically tilting her head and widening her eyes.

Will cast his gaze farther across the bedroom.

"Dirty clothes pile on the chair by the king-size bed. Marimekko design on the duvet cover. Matisse print on left-side bedroom wall: *Blue Nude II*. Erin smiling to my left on the bed in her black sports bra and black nylon underpants. Erin soon to be on the receiving end of a potentially fatal dose of top-shelf quim quivering, just as soon as I pull my leg free of these trousers."

"You're a goose," Erin said, chuckling. "I don't think you need to document every single detail. A few key points will suffice."

"Such as?"

Erin rested on her elbows and drank in her surroundings.

"It's too hot to really be in the moment with this, but we'll push through," she said. "I just remembered I need to phone Mum and tell her I can do my custard sponge cake for Jenna's christening party. I can smell the pickles you had with lunch on your breath. I can tell you are already settling in for third base and then, most likely, home, and yet, like always, you've devoted about a minute and a half to any form of foreplay. Despite all these setbacks, I'm still vaguely intrigued by your promised attempts to kill me with your enthusiastic pleasuring."

"Any last words before you depart this world in an explosion of ecstasy and gratitude?"

"You talk a big game, Romeo. Just don't go too fast."

"I never go too fast."

"Don't go too slow."

"Never."

"Sometimes you do that weird clicking thing."

"I thought you loved the weird clicking thing. That's my signature move."

"You might want to work on that one. Anyway, maybe we have enough notes for now. I'm starting to feel like I'm listening to a David Attenborough documentary."

It was then that Will rolled Erin's underwear gently down along her thighs and over her bent knees.

"Here we go," Will said, rubbing his hands together theatrically. His wife rolled her eyes. "Time: 2:41 p.m.," he added, loud enough for the iPhone recorder. "Have identified point of stimulation. It promises more wonders than those that were ever contained in the mighty Indus River. Illusive. Intoxicating. Illuminating."

"Jesus, Will, just get on with it."

"Commencing descent. Touchdown in ten, nine, eight, seven . . ." He moved closer to her. "About to make contact," Will said. "And now the eagle has landed. Commencing maneuvers."

Will wasn't too fast and Will wasn't too slow, and for two straight minutes he gently and methodically set about bringing his wife to what he hoped would be a glorious and profound sexual rapture, all while the relentless clock of life ticked ever closer toward their woefully mundane school-day deadline.

Erin released a long sigh of apparent satisfaction. Will glanced briefly up at her face. "Erin's eyes are closed," he noted. "Distinct physical arousal."

"Uh-huh," Erin confirmed.

"What are you thinking about right now?"

Erin was silent. The only noise Will could hear was her strong, slow breathing. He returned to his gentle labor for another thirty seconds, pausing intermittently to continue their one-sided conversation.

"I'm thinking about you as Sexy Sadie," Will said.

"Uh-hum," Erin said, eyes closed, her back sliding slowly toward the headboard as her inner thighs pressed closer, harder, deeper against his rhythmic pleasuring.

"I've always thought of you as Sexy Sadie," he said. "It was always you I pictured going through those silly adventures."

"That's great. Don't stop."

"You'll be the hero in every story I ever write." He picked up the tempo.

"Yep," Erin said.

Quicker now.

"Yep," Erin said.

"What are you thinking about right now?" Will asked.

"Hon, you're really killing the mood," Erin said. "I'll tell you later."

"Of course. Sorry."

And with that, Will Gall tripled his efforts and remembered the key ingredient to the mastery of that fictional cunnilingus killer from Nashville, Tennessee: true love.

Erin's heart raced and her breathing raced with it. Her arms pushed down into the mattress, hands clenching the sheets. Tremors shuddered beneath the silken landscape of her body. Her breathing became deeper and faster and harder and more necessary, and she turned her head and bit her lip, trying to muffle a final wail of ecstasy.

Then silence.

Will pulled away. He took a long, deep breath as he rolled to the side and worked a kink out of his neck with his right hand. He lay down beside his wife, kissing her exposed left shoulder. "You still alive?"

"Can't talk," Erin said. "I'm dead. Another hapless victim of the cunnilingus killer. I tried to resist him. But he made me feel so good." She let out a snort as they both laughed. He rested a hand on his wife's shoulder, and they lay in that position for a full minute.

Will broke the silence to continue his bedroom documentation. "Time: 2:53 p.m. Jackhammer seems to have stopped. I've had "Bohemian Rhapsody" in my head for the past fifteen minutes. It's hot. Pictures from our wedding on the bookshelf by the window. Pictures of the kids when they were just born. Love those pictures so much. Love how far they've come. Love how far we've all come. There's that picture of Mum and Dad from when they were still together. I wonder if that's how I was born, moments of passion squeezed between day jobs and dinner. A blue and black bird just flew by our window. Erin's head remains on the pillow, eyes closed. She's still the most beautiful creature I've ever seen in my life."

Erin gave a half smile.

"I still want to know what you were thinking about back then," Will said.

Erin looked at him. "It's ridiculous."

"But I genuinely want to document every thought flowing through your head."

"The truth?"

"Truth. Real husbands and wives. Real married sex."

"The truth is I was pretending you were Björn Borg and you'd just won the 1976 Wimbledon final and we were celebrating inside a snow-trapped Swedish mountain chalet."

Will laughed. Erin laughed with him.

"Actually, that's bullshit." She moved closer to look into Will's eyes and cupped her hands around his face. "I never see anyone in my head but you."

She kissed the top of Will's cheek, then his shoulder, then his chest, then reached for his phone to check the time. "Pickup's in five," Erin said. "I hate to leave you dissatisfied, but can Sexy Sadie arrange a date with her oddball Casanova later?"

"Can't wait," Will said.

"I'll go get the kids," Erin said.

"No, I'm on it," Will said, but still not moving.

Erin pressed her right ear to her husband's chest.

"Did I ever tell you I love you?"

"Did I ever tell you I love you more?" Will said.

Erin could feel the pulse of his heartbeat. *Thump. Thump. Thump.*

"Not possible," Erin said.

"Possible!" Will said. "One hundred percent *posseeblay.*"

Thump. Thump. Thump.

"You think we got enough details for a piece?" Erin asked.

"I think we can make it work," Will said. "Not the most arousing sex yarn ever written, but at least it'll be true."

Spectacular

There was nothing spectacular about him, but I wasn't looking for anything like that. It was the way he looked at me that I wanted.

He was intelligent. A scholar from a country I hadn't been to. He was the type of person who thought good things never happen to him. He hadn't been in love, though he did not say that. Just two girls in college, he said. He was so honest. Someone else would have at least lied about the number, or been more vague. I don't know why he told me the truth. So bare and clean.

I didn't like his leather jacket and his cologne, but that could be improved. He washed his hair and put gel in it to smooth it down, but he'd be so beautiful if he let the dark curls loose and wild around his face. Someone hadn't ever taken the time with him, I thought.

When I looked at his eyes, and then into them, he blinked quickly and forgot what he was saying. It was like no one had ever looked at him there before.

I told him I had been married for a long time. Wasn't looking for anything serious or heavy. Just someone to come over a few times a week, for dinner, and to touch.

He asked if it was okay to ask why things hadn't worked out. I told him.

He didn't say anything. He hadn't any life experience. What could he possibly know with just his two times.

I invited him over to my place. Ordered sushi, delivered. I gave him the buzzer code and the apartment number. I thought of myself at that age, twenty-seven. It was such a long time ago.

He sat in front of me. I reached over to fix his hair, the way I wanted it. I ran my fingers to the left and then to the right, and from behind I pushed up a palmful.

He let me.

He lifted his hands to touch my hair but didn't have the courage to come so close. I inched closer to him. He removed his glasses. I could feel his warm breath and brought mine close and waited for him. He was there, all he had to do was move a bit closer. He did. After each kiss, he pulled back a little. Surprised, maybe, that I was still there, and that he could do it again. After three times, he opened his mouth wider and I went in.

"Is this okay?" I asked. He nodded.

"Let's only do what makes you feel good," I told him.

"I haven't done this in a long time. You have to be gentle," I said.

I told him that I had a few gray hairs, but not on my head. He smiled, amused. I unzipped his pants. I knew what he felt and wanted then. How grateful he seemed. I hadn't even done anything yet and he was panting, breathless.

At the start, he gasped. And when I lowered myself onto him each time, his gasps became louder. He felt harder, and hotter.

"Oh my God!" he kept saying.

There was nothing cool about him. He behaved like a

woman. All the moans and noises, the encouragements, the expressions of pleasure—they all came from him. "Yes, oh yes," he kept saying. I could feel his pleasure and joy, because he made it so known to me.

After it was over, he asked if he could spend the night. He wanted to be held. He snuggled. His sleep was so peaceful and quiet. His black hair spread out around him like the mane of a lion. I wondered if he'd come back, or if this was the last time I would see him. There were no promises made. No courtship. No meeting of friends and family.

A few days passed, and he was still there.

I asked him what it was like to be inside me. Something I can't ever know. He told me, and I believed him.

He watched me put red lipstick on. The upper lip, then the lower lip. Eyeliner. Mascara. Then the eyelash curler. Brush dipped in pink blush. He was captivated, watching. He then asked me to do the same to him. I took a brush, swept a brown color across the lower lid, to outline his eye. Mascara. Silver sparkle on the lids. Peach lip gloss. He looked at himself in the mirror, surprised by his own face.

I told him how he was not like the others, and what the others were like. I wasn't allowed to be enthusiastic or use the word "love." There are other women always available, more willing to want less, to be more cool, and they were all around the corner. When I could feel what I needed, I tried not to need. I readjusted to not need.

Something was always wrong with me.

His eyes watered, and he asked me, "Why do you accept so little for yourself?"

I didn't answer, thinking how he had no idea a man can give so little. I never thought it was little, actually. I thought that's how it was with them. No one had been promised to me. No one was waiting for me. No one gave me their future. That's the thing about choosing for yourself. The one you chose had to choose you, too. And the problem then was happiness. How dare I ask what about being happy. What that might feel like. That I can feel the question, that I can form it, that I can hurl it out of my mouth.

Vis-à-Vis 1953

A   *udrey was sitting on the train* from Chicago to Kansas, reading *Sexual Behavior in the Human Female,* when a deep voice said, "Is this seat taken?"

She looked up and saw a man who resembled that actor—what's his name, the one who played Stanley in *A Streetcar Named Desire*—standing there. He tilted his head to the red-velvet banquette directly across from her. "Do you mind?"

"Not at all," she said, trying to be demure while stealing glances at him; taking in the dark plaid sport coat over a tight black turtleneck, his messy quiff of brown hair, his face with a day's worth of stubble that seemed to say, *I don't care what anyone else thinks.* The cavalier way he lit a cigarette, then another, and handed it to her without asking if she'd like one.

Audrey thanked him, then put it to her lips and took a long drag, blowing smoke from her nostrils the way the girls in her dorm had practiced, doing their best imitation of Veronica Lake. She sat back, admiring the strawberry lipstick stain on the rolling paper, feeling the warmth of the cigarette fill her up inside. She watched the man open a book he'd been carrying under his arm, a hardback with no discernible title. He lingered on the pages, engrossed. She liked the way he stroked his chin as he read, and how he didn't have a wedding band.

"What are you reading?" she asked, her fingertip absently tracing the line of her décolletage. "Whatever it is it must be good."

He licked his lips then looked up at her. "It's my journal."

Really, Audrey thought, hoping he wasn't boring or hopelessly conceited. You'd almost have to be, to not only put your life on paper, but reread it for entertainment.

He regarded her with warm hazel eyes. "And what is it that you're reading?"

Audrey hesitated, then said, "The book that got me kicked out of college."

Until last week, she'd been a sophomore at the University of Illinois. Then the resident director of Busey Hall (all-male) had caught her reading the latest Kinsey book while sunbathing on the lawn between it and Evans (all-female) in her polka-dot bikini, and that was that. Audrey's predicament had only worsened when her mother showed up to bring her home and discovered newspaper clippings of the actress Frances Farmer on the wall above her bed. Her mother threw all of it in the trash, except one photo that Audrey managed to save, of Farmer after she'd been arrested a few years ago for punching her hairdresser in Los Angeles. When the booking officer had asked what her occupation was, Farmer smiled and said, "Cocksucker." To Audrey, the actress looked like Aphrodite, if she snarled when she smiled and smoked Lucky Strikes.

Now she was heading to Kansas because her parents said they would only keep paying for her education if she transferred to Wichita State, ostensibly so her mother's best friend, Edith, could keep an eye on her. *Edith*, Audrey thought. *That'd be a*

good name for a nun. A sweet woman of devotion whose uterus be-
longs to Jesus and whose vagina could use a good dusting.

Audrey's own vagina was sadly neglected. The boys at college had touched her like they were shoving their fingers into
a baseball mitt and then filled her mouth with their bliss after
less than a minute—which might have been tolerable if they'd
returned the favor, but they were too busy apologizing and zip-
ping up their pants.

She'd always been sexually precocious. In high school the
boys called her easy while privately begging her for dates, and
the girls treated her like she was part Joan of Arc, part Lady
Godiva; especially after the incident in English class, during
the group discussion of *Romeo and Juliet.* "Don't you think it's
a little ironic," Audrey had said, "that we're considered delin-
quents and deviants if we have sex in high school, when all the
great lovers of history were our age?" Before her teacher, Mr.
Hausner, could stop her, Audrey said, "Daphnis was fifteen and
Chloe was thirteen, Tristan was nineteen when he met Isolde,
and Juliet was fourteen when she, you know, let Romeo climb
her balcony."

The school called her mother, who'd lectured Audrey
on chastity all the way home and said not to tell her father.
After that, Mr. Hausner could never look at her again without
blushing.

Now Audrey hesitated, then raised the book so the handsome
stranger could read the title.

"Ah, that's an excellent book," he said. "I read it cover to
cover. It's not surprising that *Time* put Kinsey on the front of
the magazine this summer."

Audrey opened her mouth, but for once didn't know what to say. She stared at him curiously, appraising everything about him, from the thick, dark veins on the back of his hands to the shine of his leather oxfords to the way his eyes sparkled.

He crossed his legs. "What do *you* think of it, if I may ask?"

"You may," she said, taking another drag on her cigarette, hoping he wouldn't see that her hand was trembling. "I find it refreshing. But also a bit tragic, you know?"

He tilted his head, listening.

"While it's heartening that girls don't get sent to the asylum anymore for wanting to have an orgasm," she said, "it's sad that so many women don't even know where to begin." Audrey expected a reaction to her proclamation. He merely nodded. She held up the book. "And that their husbands, statistically, are of so little help."

"I agree." He looked amused. "I'm Jens. Where are you off to?"

Audrey introduced herself and gave him a brief account of her recent history. She was careful not to offer her last name or divulge where she would be staying. She'd learned to cherish the power of anonymity.

"How about you? What do you do?" A zoetrope of occupations flickered through her mind: salesman, dentist, engineer. None of them seemed to fit. Musician, poet, or wealthy bon vivant seemed more appropriate.

"I took a new job in Kansas." Apparently, Jens enjoyed his anonymity as well, because he didn't elaborate. "And I do whatever is desired of me, whatever is asked, without judgment, and without restraint."

He smiled at her the way Audrey used to smile at boys at parties: *You don't know it now, but I'm going to fuck you later.* She felt herself getting warm. He was almost twice the age of the boys she'd deflowered, and she couldn't help but wonder if he was also twice as . . . durable.

"What's in your journal?" she asked, her pulse racing as though she were thirteen again and she'd discovered a box of French postcards while babysitting for her neighbors. After weeks of studying the images of curvaceously nude women, their luxuriant bodies at the mercy of men—and women— Audrey had found the courage to sit in front of a mirror, her skirt pulled up, her legs spread, and pleasure herself the way those French women did in those old photos.

"It's actually not *my* journal, per se," he said, running his fingers along the leather binding. "It belongs to friends. Past acquaintances—their words, not mine. I'm just the facilitator. They write what they'd like me to do for them. Then I obey."

Audrey chewed her lip in the darkness as they passed through a tunnel. She had no idea who this man was, and for now, it didn't matter. "Would you show it to me?"

"I'm going to be honest with you, Audrey," he said. "This book is not for everyone. You're so young . . ."

"And impressionable?" she said with a laugh. "I've heard that before."

"I was going to say . . . exquisitely beautiful."

"Really?"

"Yes. Look at you, sitting there. You're a Cleopatra, the kind of charismatic young woman who makes Roman men neglect their duties."

"Well," Audrey beamed. "She *was* only eighteen when she ruled Egypt."

"And if I were Mark Antony, I'd fall happily fall on my sword for someone like you. Or was it Cleo who was impaled by Mark Antony's sword? I forget."

"Oh my God, you're such a tease." *And a well-read one at that.*

"I prefer the term 'libertine.'" He smiled. "Everything sounds better in Latin."

"Okay, Lord Byron," Audrey said. "Just tell me what's in the book."

"See for yourself." Jens handed her the book. "But don't say I didn't warn you."

"Good evening." A man in a bow tie and apron appeared, asking, "Can I bring either of you a drink or an appetizer, or would you like a dinner menu?"

As Jens listened to the waiter recite tonight's specials, Audrey opened the journal. On the first page was the name Nancy followed by a narrative—a wish list—describing something simple, romantic, and plainly sexual, all of it written in a woman's neat cursive script. As she flipped through the journal, Audrey saw there were dozens of other names, each woman's fantasy described in her individual handwriting. There was Beth, who desired to make love at night on a fire escape overlooking the city. Another, Maria, asked to be ravished by a stranger as her husband watched. Linda wanted to have sex in the shower while menstruating. Karen wanted to be on her knees, hands tied behind her back, blindfolded, and be used like a whore. Moira, sadly, just said, "Dear God, I just want someone to finally fuck me properly. Is that too much to ask?"

Audrey glanced up at Jens, who said, "What would you like?"

She imagined Jens between her thighs, her fingers gripping a fistful of his hair, his tongue spreading her wet, swollen lips, his fingers inside of her. Or being facedown, pressed into sheets that smelled like him, his hands on her hips, driving her closer to the edge.

"From the menu?" Jens prodded.

She blinked, remembering the waiter.

"Why don't you just bring us two club sodas with lime," Jens said to the man. "And something sweet. I have a feeling we'll eat dinner much later."

"I'll be right back with the dessert menu—"

"That's not necessary," Jens cut him off. "Just bring us one of everything."

As the waiter disappeared into the next car, Audrey delved back into the journal. Each page was a confession, a testament, and a validation of a woman's needs—needs she had shamelessly, unapologetically asked to be met. And these secret desires—if she was to believe Jens—had all been righteously fulfilled.

Jens cleared his throat. "Well, what do you think?"

Trying to regain her composure, Audrey looked around the crowded club car. She felt as though everyone must know what she was thinking, what she was feeling, the tingling sensation between her legs, how the tip of her nose itched whenever she began to get wet.

As Jens watched her, she thought of something else, something she'd never allowed herself to explore. She caught her breath and looked back at him. "Do you have a pen?"

Audrey was done writing by the time the waiter returned. She felt deliciously vulnerable watching Jens read what she'd written as she licked chocolate mousse from a long silver spoon. This wasn't going to be like all the times when a nervous college boy erupted in her hand before they even got started and then left her to get herself off. This time, she wouldn't be settling.

Jens's brow furrowed and she worried she'd been too candid.

"Well?" she asked.

He gently closed the book, then stood up and straightened the cuffs of his jacket. "Okay," he said. Then he offered his hand and led her to a sleeper car.

Jens's stateroom was small but cozy, with a plush daybed on one side and a cushioned bench on the other. In the middle was a tiny folding table in the down position. The decor was gaudy, with floral carpeting and the kind of old velvet wallpaper that Audrey imagined would be more suitable in a brothel. *This will do*, she thought. She smiled as she opened the curtains and saw rolling hills, a blur of trees rushing past. Everything felt bigger—the landscape, the sunset.

Audrey grinned in anticipation as he removed his jacket and tossed it onto the bed, next to his journal. She pointed at the book. "Do you need a reminder?"

"I'll follow your lead."

"Then sit there." She pointed to the soft bench. "Don't speak unless you're spoken to."

He nodded and did as he was told.

"Good boy." She stood in front of him, unbuttoning her blouse and easing it from her shoulders. Then she slowly unzipped the back of her tulip skirt and shimmied her hips so it dropped to the floor. She held on to a metal railing to steady herself as she stepped out of her leather pumps. She looked at him as the train rocked back and forth, enjoying his quiet confidence, the way his eyes caressed her body, wandering down over her breasts, to her navel, then finally resting his gaze where a mound of soft dark curls awaited him behind a layer of silk, framed by garters and white stockings. She touched her stomach, then let her fingertips linger on the tiny flower on the front of her waistband. She circled it with two fingers, the way she liked another rosebud to be touched.

Audrey put a finger to his lips to remind him that he was to be silent. Then she straddled him, pleased with the warmth of his hands on her ass and the rigidity she found rubbing against her wetness. As he looked up at her, she thought of all the women he'd been with—the women he'd been *allowed* to be with. Then she remembered Shakespeare's plays, how women had been called whores, harlots, strumpets, and tarts. How she'd been called the modern variations of those names: slut, tramp, hussy, jezebel, party girl, fuck bunny.

At first those insults had stung. But when she saw the jealousy in the eyes of her many accusers, she dried her tears and wore those insults as badges of honor. They all wanted what she had: freedom.

She reached down and pulled Jens's turtleneck sweater over his head, tossing it aside. "I'm going to use you," she said, "because I can."

She kissed him, and as his lips parted she felt the delicious probing swirl of his tongue. She tasted him, inhaled the essence of him. She bit his upper lip, then reached up and retrieved a green silk tie that was hanging from a coat hook. She took his arms, enjoying the feeling of his thick ropes of muscle as she bound his wrists together. She cinched the knot as tight as she could and asked, "Tell me. Does this hurt?"

"A little."

"Good." She smiled, then reached up and tied the other end around a handrail, pressing her supple cleavage to his face. She enjoyed the feel of his warm lips on her breasts, the scratch of his unshaved chin. She traced her fingers down his raised arms to his shoulders, then down his chest. It was firm, though not as hard as the gift that remained inches below. She spread her thighs and settled onto it, pushing her hips forward and rocking against his cock.

"How do you like this?" she asked.

He looked up at her, trying to remain calm, but by the way he was thrusting upward, raising up off the bench, she knew he was suspended in that exquisite place between wanting and having. He opened his eyes wide, as though asking a question.

"You can answer me," she whispered.

He swallowed, closed his eyes, and softly groaned, "I'm here for your pleasure."

She gripped his shoulders, dug in her nails, and kissed him again, their tongues melting together as she rubbed herself against him. When his breathing quickened and his chuffing became moaning, she eased herself off him.

"Call me a slut," she said. "Do it or I'll leave you like this all night."

"You're a sl—"

Before he could get the word out, she slapped him hard across his face.

"What am I?"

"You're a—"

Another slap.

His hazel eyes were searching, pleading, hoping. "I know exactly what I am," she cooed. She pushed his legs apart, kneeling on the carpeted floor. She unfastened his belt, unbuttoned his pants, and looked up at him as she lowered his zipper. She watched him lick his lips, a frantic, begging look in his eyes as she lifted the fabric of his briefs to grasp the length of his shaft. She removed his clothing and felt the warmth of his body as she wrapped her fingers around him, rubbing her thumb across the wet, sticky tip. "It pleases me to hear you beg," she said.

She brushed her hair to one side as she slowly rubbed the tip of his cock against her lips, then she parted them, flattening her tongue and easing the length of his shaft into her mouth. She sucked the head, tasting the sweet saltiness, before taking the purpling length of him to the back of her throat. Then she withdrew him from her mouth and slowly stroked him, impressed not only by his physique, but his ability to stay in the moment. This was no boy who would spill his promise early.

"I don't hear any begging," she said.

He moaned, stammering, "Please, I'll do anything you want."

"Close your eyes," she ordered, and he complied.

She stood up, unfastened her garters, and slipped off her underwear, taking her time as she set them on the bench. Then she climbed back on top of him, using her fingertips to rub the tip of him against her wetness. "Open your eyes."

He opened them.

"Keep them open," she said, relishing the aching sensation of wanting him so badly and the pinch of fear that it would hurt as she felt his thickness spreading her apart. She stared into his eyes, slowly welcoming him inside. She smiled when his stoic facade cracked and his lower lip began to quiver. He looked into her eyes, unblinking, until he was deep inside her.

"You're doing so good," she said, wondering how long he would last, raising her hopes along with her hips before plunging back down, letting him fill her up.

She reached behind with one hand and unclasped her bra,

then pulled it from her shoulders, letting it drop to the floor. She arched her back, resting her hands on his knees as she slowly, deliciously fucked him, her pert nipples pointing to the ceiling.

He let out a soft moan, "Fuuuuuuck..."

She sat back up, took her underwear, and shoved it into his mouth, pushing so hard he gagged and his eyes watered. "No talking unless I say so."

She rode him until she got close, then eased herself off him. From her past experiences with men, she doubted his ability to please her would increase if he came first. She leaned in, her face next to his. "What am I?" she asked, but he could only mumble. She pulled the ball of wet silk from his mouth.

"You're my goddess," he said.

"Then get on your knees and worship me." She untied him and sat on the bed. She leaned back, admiring the sunset through the window as she spread her stockinged legs.

She threw her head back and felt his hands cupping her ass, his stubble on the inside of her thighs, felt his breath, and then his lips brushing against her wetness. She embraced the vibration of the train as he slipped fingers inside of her, curling them up and back toward him as he offered his tongue upon her wet, pink altar. She gripped the mattress with both hands, pressing against him as her legs went numb. Her body tightened like a fist and her moans and cries became insatiable songs of gluttony and rapture.

She floated weightless as her pleasure receded. She opened her eyes and saw him on his knees, panting, her wetness lustrous upon his smiling lips. His eyes sought her approval, but the rest of his body was pleading for release.

"I suppose you want something now?" she said.

"If it pleases you."

She told him to sit back on the bench, and he gratefully complied. Then she knelt again, stroking him with her mouth until she felt his body begin to shake. As he let out a groan she released him from her grip, from her mouth. She looked into his eyes and then at his bobbing cock. A rivulet of clear fluid ran down the shaft like a tear. She flicked him with her finger, hard, just beneath the head, and he erupted in pulsating ribbons. He didn't use words, but his body was craving her heat, and with the benevolence of a goddess, she squeezed the sticky length of him and eased him back inside her mouth, sliding down to the base of his softening manhood and then back up again, her lips and chin wet and sticky. He bucked, and a single word escaped his lips: "Mercy."

The sun was shining in a bluebird sky, even though it was near freezing when Audrey stepped off the train at Wichita's Union Station. It looked like an acorn compared to the mighty oak that was Chicago's Union Station. Amid metallic whistles and porters calling out names of passengers, she headed toward the exit.

As she departed, she didn't look for Jens. Her notations in his journal and their shared memories were all she was willing to give, and by her reckoning, that was more than enough. He had been content with their night together and hadn't asked for more, not even her mailing address or her last name. It left her a bit disappointed, but also freed her from entanglement. She was young, after all, and had her whole erotic life ahead of her—even if its next chapter would be written on the exceedingly blank pages of Kansas. Though as she walked through the terminal, she was heartened to see a large rack of Little Blue Books. Then she remembered that they were published here, by a mail-order company that sold millions of books for the price of a dollar and a postage stamp.

O brave new world, Audrey thought, quoting Ariel from Shakespeare's *The Tempest.* Audrey's own mother had a small collection of Little Blue Books, mostly on sewing and gardening. But what Audrey remembered were the notorious ones that had been passed around in junior high, like *Illicit Love, and Other Stories, Twenty-Six Men and a Girl,* and *The Evolution of Sex.* Maybe there was more to Wichita than met the wandering eye.

A few days later, she found her way to her first class—Art History—and took a seat near the back, wondering how long it would take before someone turned her in for the heinous crime of wearing pants, which was against the dress code for women.

That's when a familiar face breezed into the room, wearing a dark plaid sport coat and a green silk tie. "Good afternoon, my brash young bohemians," he said.

He was handsome enough to draw the attention of the young women and forceful enough to command the respect of the boys. He snapped his fingers and asked a student in the front row to erase the blackboard. Then he stood at the lectern, chalk in hand, and said, "Ladies and gentlemen, I'm new here so be patient with me. I'm Professor Ackerman, but you can call me Jensen. For your first assignment, we'll be studying Tiziano Vecellio, otherwise known as the Renaissance painter Titian. His paintings inspired another notable man named Leopold von Sacher-Masoch, who wrote the novella *Venus in Furs,* about a man enslaved to a woman."

A giggle swept through the classroom.

"Yes, in case you're wondering, the term 'masochism' is derived from his last name and yes, he famously derived pleasure from pain and humiliation. Speaking of pain, why don't we start off with a pop quiz on the materials from last semester . . ."

The students' laughter turned to groans. Audrey stared at him, waiting for him to notice her. When he finally saw her, she smiled and raised an eyebrow. There would be much to learn in this small city, she thought, and even more to teach.

Interruptus

"Sure, *it's the Chinese Romeo and Juliet,* but could one reasonably argue that the *Butterfly Lovers* violin concerto is, actually, a decent work of art? I mean, it's so unabashedly earnest."

In the creamy candlelight, as her words landed, Geraldine saw a flicker, that almost imperceptible twitch in Andrew's cheek that she'd seen flash at times as he pondered the moo shu pork or the "beef with orange flavor," The Cottage delivery menu in hand.

"Good art can be earnest," Andrew said, shaking his head. "And why should one be ashamed of being emotional and forthright and boldly naked when it comes to art?"

Geraldine felt her left eyebrow rise as she shifted an inch back, propping herself up on an elbow as she turned to look—really look—at Andrew.

"What?" Andrew asked.

If his hands had been free for the tossing, Geraldine knew him just well enough by now to know that they would have been flung. She laughed, suddenly wanting to reach out to touch his cheek. Instead, she kept her hand where it was, her vermilion nails circled around his turgid cock, her fingers firmly kneading its slow throb as she rhythmically pumped.

Andrew glanced down, taking his hand off her stiff nipple so he could trace an index finger down hers, following the curve of it as it wound around himself. "You have the fingers of a violinist," he said, gently now.

Geraldine reached her head up, darting out her tongue to give his ear a quick lick before whispering into the crevice, "I bet you say that to all the girls who dare to have stroppy opinions about Chinese Communist-era concerti while stroking your dick."

"Hey! . . . What's going on up there?"

Geraldine and Andrew disengaged. Andrew cleared his throat; Geraldine rolled her eyes. She took her hand off Andrew's cock and reached down to ruffle the top of Ian's head.

"Baby, you feel so good down there," she said. Ian looked up, beaming, his upper lip glistening. "Oh, I'm so glad, Gerry-girl," he said. "I want this to be so amazing for you."

Geraldine looked back up at Andrew and shrugged. They stared at each other, unblinking, as she felt his fingers reach up, brush her fringe aside, and then pull her face close so he could cover her lips with his.

Geraldine had wondered what this first kiss might be like from the moment they had met.

It had been with no small amount of reluctance that she'd finally gone home with Ian. But she knew it might as well be done at some point, and the Saturday night after the third fuck seemed as good a time as any. *Fourth time may be the charm,* she'd thought as she trudged up the narrow blackened stairs behind Ian. Ambivalence had troubled Geraldine throughout the well-meaning dinner at the fashionable Mexican restaurant she had confessed a fondness for, but now she felt her mouth moisten as she watched his taut behind ascend. The first time had been drunk-fantastic, the second, a more sober and sobering affair, but Ian had rallied magnificently for the third and surprised Geraldine by soaring above the mediocrity she had anticipated after Time Two. So now, here, yet again, was that splendid clutch of muscles before her. *My kingdom for a beautiful bottom. There are worse things.*

"Just three more flights!" Ian said brightly as they rounded the second landing.

Fifth floor. Walk-up. *What are we, undergrads?*

"Lovely," Geraldine said, squeezing out a smile. "That must be how you're so toned."

Ian turned around, winked, then sprinted up the last few flights. By the time Geraldine reached 5N, the door was open and she could hear Ian saying, "Oh, hey, I didn't think you'd be at home . . . No, no, stay. This is great. You can meet my new girl, Gerry."

A pair of glasses, dark tortoiseshell, rectangular, came into view. Eyes, glimmers of mahogany, framed by the unruliest eyebrows Geraldine had ever seen. The nose, sculpted up top, the tip of it hovering on the border of bulbous, and lips, thin, firm, determined. Geraldine actually heard her breath catch. She could feel her plan to end things with Ian that night—after, that is—receding.

Through the haar that suddenly seemed to swaddle Geraldine and this man came a foghorn. "Gerry! My roommate, Andy!" Ian said. "I told him all about you. I love this—you two are going to LOVE each other." Ian was that way, Geraldine had realized in Times One through Three. He spoke in all caps. Frequently.

Andrew stretched out his hand. By the time Geraldine had shaken it, her panties were soaked.

Geraldine was on her back now, freshly shorn legs dangling off the edge of Ian's bed. "Go slow, baby," she said, watching Ian nod as he grasped his penis, gave it a few rough pumps, and gingerly began his poke-prod into her. Ian liked to please, so she knew that since she'd asked, he would be gentle. She had been waiting all week for this moment and wanted to savor it without barnyard jiggling. Once Ian seemed comfortably situated and sufficiently occupied, she turned to Andrew, reaching up to cup his face.

"This is mad," he mouthed.

"Kiss me again," she mouthed back.

Geraldine had thought Andrew, with his barely there lips, might be one of those hard kissers, all bone and not much pillow. But as he leaned into her once more, he extended his lips in an exaggerated pucker. An image of that sexually harassing Warner Brothers skunk flitted into Geraldine's head and she giggled.

"What?" Andrew asked.

"Yeah, what, Gerry-girl?" Ian said, pausing midstroke.

"Oh, nothing—nothing," she said, waving her hand at Ian. "Just—just keep going."

"Oh my God, Gerry-girl, you feel so good," Ian said, quickening now.

Tempo was Ian's genius. The man might not know the difference between Schumann and Schubert, but he did understand the ebbs and flows of fucking—when an adagio was called for, when to shift into an allegro, when to presto, presto, presto, when to finally flourish, and when to lay down the bow.

In these weeks, Geraldine had come to appreciate the wordless moments between them and often found herself wishing there were more. Though she'd learned that simply placing her hand on Ian's cock managed to stem the chatter about whatever latest paper he was researching on whatever blah-blah history topic he had dreamed up. *American* history. It wasn't even the good, meaty, colorful history packed with true heroes and glorious art; merely the recountings of the once conquered, the predictably pedestrian, and the constantly bickering.

A river of Sancerre had been the lubricant the night they met. Ian, just slightly in his cups, had stepped up to Geraldine, quite a bit further in her cups, at the French bar across from the library, casually placing his arm around the back of her chair as he leaned in to say, "Hey, how you DOO-ing?" Geraldine's first instinct had been to swat this *Friends*-quoting tool away, but his tree-trunk arms, sunny smile, and voluminous floppy fringe, so not of these times, intrigued. So instead, she'd said, "Wasn't it Ross, not Joey, who shagged the English girl?" Ian had laughed and pulled up the stool next to hers. The river continued to flow.

Andrew leaned in again, his puffed-up lips mashing into hers, his thick tongue snaking in. Geraldine closed her eyes and sucked on it, massaging her own lips up and down, stripping down the flavors: a hint of tarragon; the beautifully charred chicken Andrew had roasted; then, layered on top, the sweetness of those sliced Honeycrisp apples dipped in Trader Joe's almond butter that she had come to know as his favorite sort of pudding. Ian had splurged for the occasion, had walked the twenty-five blocks down to the Magnolia Bakery on Columbus, had returned brandishing a box of frosted abominations. Nine of the dozen now languished in said box by the bed. Geraldine had thought of stopping Ian when he, wounded by the resounding disinterest, had made a show of eating a second, then reaching for a third, but she quickly realized the prudence of refraining. *Surely, three mounds of cloying buttercream will have some gastric impact.*

That morning, while Ian was on his cupcake expedition, Geraldine had suggested a visit to the 79th Street Greenmarket to pick up some apples. Andrew had been silent in the short walk over. Geraldine, worried, had contrived to reach for the same Honeycrisp, fingers touching fingers, their first physical contact since the handshake. When Andrew didn't recoil, she turned to look at him.

"You all right with this?"

"Yes."

"You want this?"

"Yes."

"No, I mean really want it."

"Yes!"

"Because if you don't . . ."

"Oh, Geraldine, you have no idea."

"Good," she said, picking up five Honeycrisps without even looking and stuffing them into a paper bag. "It's sorted, then."

Ian was really going now. From his grunts, Geraldine could tell he was on the brink of disregarding her earlier request. Breaking off the kiss with Andrew, she asked, "Where . . . did you . . . grow up?"

"What?"

"You know. Where? You've never said."

Andrew tossed his head back, smiled, then trailed the back

of his index finger down the side of her cheek and nipped her chin with his fingers. "Somewhere very unsexy," he said, picking up a tendril of her caramel hair and twirling it around his fingers. "Schaumburg, Illinois, where everyone in the Chicago metropolitan area bought their first car."

"Well, that's terribly exotic to us yokels from Oxford, I can assure you."

Andrew laughed and leaned in for another kiss. Tarragon, chicken, apples, almond butter. Geraldine was hungry again.

"Gerry-girl, am I giving it to you good?"

"Mmm-hmm."

"Yeah? Do you want me to come for you?"

"Mmm-hmm."

Ian resumed his grunting.

Geraldine turned back to Andrew. "Siblings? Parents? Are they in music, too?"

Andrew was stroking her arm now; Geraldine watched the callused tips of his fingers rake the freckled ivory. "One sister, a banker; parents in finance. I'm the only misfit. *Et tu?*"

"Only child; only one in this mad world, too."

Geraldine felt the fingers leap and *attraversano*, landing on her belly, where Andrew spread his full palm out, circling, gliding.

"What's your favorite piece to perform?" she asked.

"Mozart's Piano Concerto, 22."

"But . . . "

"Yes, I'm not a pianist. There's such majesty in that piece— it's sublime just to be there, to be a part of it."

Geraldine felt her heart begin to truly pound.

"Oh, baby," Ian said, loud and ragged now.

"Keep going, keep going—you're almost there," Geraldine

called down as she pulled Andrew's head to her, settling his ear close to her mouth.

"In this world
love has no color—
yet how deeply
my body
is stained by yours," Geraldine said softly.

"Now please," she added, "put your cock in my mouth."

Andrew rose now, looking back at Ian, standing, pumping; he took care not to swipe Ian's torso as he swung his leg across Geraldine, shimmying up so his balls rested on her chin. Geraldine opened her mouth.

The ache for Andrew had begun almost instantly. That first next morning, as Geraldine lay in bed, the soft rumble of Ian's snoring beside her, she had heard the starting notes through the wall. In her morning bleariness, she had thought, *Erhu*, and opened her eyes. As the fluttering trills wafted in, Geraldine sat up. No. It was violin masquerading as erhu— perfectly. "*Butterfly Lovers*," she whispered, closing her eyes as she listened to the violin solo rise and fall in silken waves, the highest of notes pregnant with yearning, love, desire. Feeling her eyes moisten as Zhu and Liang confessed their love to each other, the ask-and-answer of the violin and the imagined, absent cello, Geraldine placed her palm on the wall that separated.

Ian was rounding the corner at full gallop now; the jostle was real. Above him, Geraldine picked up her pace, keeping her eyes on Andrew as she sucked, his mouth now firmly shut, his chest heaving.

Finally, the southerly yawp. "GERRY BAY-BEEEEEE!" Ian erupted before collapsing on Geraldine's belly, missing Andrew's ass by an inch. Andrew softened. Geraldine blinked and removed her mouth, gently nudging Andrew off her.

"Ian," she said, "why don't you take a shower?"

"Okay!" he said, jumping up and climbing toward Geraldine for a kiss. She offered him her cheek, then watched him bound off.

Geraldine had not been surprised that Ian had agreed so readily when she first suggested it. But Ian was agreeable. A yesman. Up for anything—TOTALLY. No, Geraldine had known that Andrew would have been the tougher sell, even after their now-regular lingerings over the kettle and the weekly tug-of-war over the *New Yorker* when it arrived. So she was surprised when Andrew's only response was, "When?"

When Ian had shut the door behind him, Andrew leaned down, softly smoothing Geraldine's hair around her face, then nipping her chin with his fingers again.

The words weren't necessary, as Geraldine could already feel the decisive shift in Andrew's body over hers, but she said them anyway: "Fuck me."

The entrance was a crash of cymbals, followed by the steady thumping rolls of timpani, layered with the howl of a thunder sheet. Geraldine had closed her eyes at first, but now she wanted to see Andrew, she wanted to see all of it. His eyes seemed darker, his skin was aglow.

"I'm breaking up with Ian," Geraldine said suddenly, hoisting her thighs up to grasp Andrew's sides. She wanted him, deeper, faster, all, every day, more.

"You sure? My God, Geraldine . . . you're so . . . alive," Andrew said, breathing harder as he started a rhythmic jackhammer.

"I have to," Geraldine said, her fingers reaching for Andrew's back, pulling him toward her.

"But he's going to be devastated," Andrew said, really huffing now. "You sure? How can we?"

"He'll understand! He must!" Geraldine said, clawing at Andrew's back. "God, Andrew, I'm so close."

"He's my best friend! Oh God, oh God . . . oh my God, it'll be awful."

"Think of Zhu and Liang," Geraldine said, gasping. "True love, true connection . . . it just . . . has to win."

Geraldine felt Andrew slowing. "It has to, Andrew. It has to."

"*Butterfly Lovers* ends tragically, Geraldine. Zhu flings herself into Liang's grave so she can die and be with him!"

"No grave flinging here, Andrew. It doesn't have to be tragic. We have a choice."

Andrew plopped out, rolling off onto his back. Geraldine reached her hand down, her fingers encircling a slimy softness.

Andrew sighed, raising his arm to rest the back of his hand on his forehead. "That's allegory, Geraldine. This is life."

Geraldine looked at Andrew's face, squinched.

"Artists choose love, Andrew."

"Artists also choose discipline, Geraldine."

Andrew turned onto his side to face Geraldine, reaching up to trail his fingers down her cheek.

"*Das ewig-weibliche*," Andrew said gently. "'*The eternal feminine.*'"

Geraldine turned her face to kiss his fingers. The lovers leaned forward, mouths open, words poised.

Just then, footsteps, the creak of a door. And through it, a fresh burst: "CUPCAKES?"

Partita

She sits on the bare floor, against a pile of boxes. It is summer, hot; the evening sun is fading through the windows, and she wears a linen dress as light and loose as a puff of air. The neighbor's dog barks tirelessly at nothing. No matter. Tomorrow the boxes will be loaded in a truck and whisked away, and afterward they'll close the door behind them and be done. No more lawn to tend, no more garden, no more barking dog. Goodbye thirty years spent growing gray, raising children, watching fireflies from the porch. Goodbye creaky stairs, goodbye honeysuckle, goodbye ceiling stain we never fixed. Goodbye crayon marks on the wall, goodbye old plank floor, goodbye, goodbye, goodbye.

Her husband comes in humming from the kitchen, paper plates and plastic cups balanced atop a box of pizza, two beers tucked into his pockets, and for a flicker of a moment, the bareness of the room renders her husband strange to her, transports her to her college years. She reaches up and pulls the beers from his pockets. In college, would this have been flirtation? At his retirement party, surrounded by his old friends, they'd looked so small and stooped together that a pang shot through her chest. She'd sat down, fighting tears. Let this not be the end, she thought, let us still have years and years.

Her husband lowers himself carefully down with a grunt, joints crackling. They'd made a joke out of such noises in their thirties, laughing at how old their bodies were becoming, at the aches and pains that came and went—so young they didn't know those aches and pains would one day come back to roost.

The dog finally shuts up. They eat. They wipe their greasy fingers on their clothes like children. They drink their sweating beers. Remember, he says, when we first moved in here? He strokes her leg, the lightest touch—and she knows he's not thinking of the broken furnace or the doorknobs that twisted off into their hands. He's remembering when the house was still bare of furniture but full of boxes just like now, and how every single thing they did was somehow an invitation. She'd come in with a pile of mail and he'd fling it onto a box and take her on the floor. Or he'd be opening that box as she walked by, and she'd press herself against him, front to back. When he turned around she'd fall to her knees and strip his pants down to his ankles, and there he'd be, already hard—it took only an instant then—and she'd watch him as she took him in her mouth, locking eyes, tracking how his expressions changed with each thing she did.

She says, Our curtains were delayed for weeks.

He tilts his head at her, a question—he is almost completely deaf in that ear these days (this ear she used to whisper into! sweet nothings, dirty invitations)—so she says more loudly, We didn't have curtains for weeks! He leans back laughing, remembering, as she meant him to, how the light streamed in those days, and how she could see clear to the road before they planted the trees, and anyone driving by could glance right in and see them making love. She'd made him be on top so it'd be his bare ass not hers, waving in the air, for anyone and every-one to see.

There was a day he carried her from room to room, her legs wrapped around his waist and him inside her, like she was noth-ing in his arms, just a shape, an emptiness, a heat to embrace his matching heat. He carried her up the stairs, a bounce and a jostle on each step, and just as they got to the top, she came. It felt both beyond her and of her, how the core of her clenched him tightly—and then he came, too, stumbling to his knees on the landing, crying out and laughing, cushioning her fall with his arms.

And now he leans forward to kiss her, everything both fa-miliar and unfamiliar, remembered and unremembered: the scratch of his scruff, the clove-woods-musk of his soap, his skin rough and loose against the soft looseness of her own—a shock after the memory of younger days, though her skin has been this way for years. Hello, old friend, she thinks. Nowadays the sex they have is scheduled, careful. They choose positions based on what angles, what weight, what pressure their joints can take. She can feel the fragility of their bodies. We're like paper dolls, she thinks, too easily torn, already tearing. But then she feels the strength and tenderness in his hands, and they call forth the same in her, undiminished, ageless, as she presses her own body into his.

9

Her husband has a running list: he likes her to describe them while he masturbates. That time on your office floor, he'll say. The blow job in the garden. Wear that green dress again from that party where I fucked you in the closet. He likes dirty talk and she complies, narrates their memories as he gets off.

She knows that he assumes her list is identical to his, but the truth is that it's very different. At the top—the day they dropped their oldest off at college. For weeks before she'd been dissolving into tears, and he'd tried to comfort her. Just two more and we'll be free at last of the little terrorists! He'd been so cheerful.

But on the actual day, as their daughter laughed and hugged them from the threshold of her dorm room and sent them on their way, he was the one sobbing, on and off all the long way home. In the rental to the airport, as their flight took off, standing in the taxi line—the tears would overtake him.

Here's a secret: it has always turned her on to see him cry. A frenzied tenderness comes upon her, a pressing hunger.

That afternoon they walked into an empty house, their other two still at school. She turned to him. His face was damp under her lips, his own lips soft and open, as if still on the verge of tears. She took his hand and led him to the sofa, pushed him down, and climbed on top of him. He looked up at her, open, fragile, as if all the crying of the day had washed him clear, transparent, and she could see right to the very core of him.

It made her want to be so gentle, like the softest breeze. She touched him lightly with her fingers. When she kissed him, he did not kiss back. Had he ever been this passive? She felt the burn of her desire against his stillness. In silence, she pulled off his shirt, then hers, dragging down his pants. In the beginning he was soft, his hands limp by his sides. She slid herself against him lightly, coaxing him, teasing him, patient but insistent, and when a moan escaped him and she finally felt him, hard against her leg, she laughed, triumphant.

I love you, she mouthed against his palm. And how she loved him, this man with whom she had made children—life itself! An aching built and built between them, for all they'd made and would make and would let go. They passed it back and forth until it was all there was.

<h1 style="text-align:center">8</h1>

Never again, she says. I will never fuck you again. Her arms are full of laundry, and her husband's trying to take her in his arms.

Now, honey, look, calm down. I'm sorry I didn't get to it, I was going to do it. Don't be mad. He reaches for her again, smiling in a way she knows and hates, the smile he wears to show how reasonable he can be in the face of her unreason, the smile that says your anger doesn't matter, we're married, and we're stuck, and aren't I charming, and let's skip this part and just say I love you, and then let's have sex, too.

Don't touch me, she says, elbows out, fending him off, shedding underwear and socks. She knows she looks ridiculous, and it only makes her madder. I do not want your touch, she says, I want your help.

Just tell me what to do, he says.

I did weeks ago, she says, now get out of my way. But he has planted himself in front of her, this man, her husband, her life partner, who says he wants to help but never does, who asks for instructions for every single thing and then resents them or ignores them, who wakes when she's been up all night with the baby and tries to grab her breast as if what she needs in her life is another hand to paw at her. You can pick up the laundry is what you can do, she says, and he bends over, picks up everything that's fallen, puts it at the top of the basket she carries in her arms.

You hurt my feelings, he says. I always forgive you when you're sorry.

She wants to shriek in his face, to kick him, but she swallows it. Instead, she stomps around him, icy in her silence; she is an asshole and she knows it.

How has she landed in this life? A life she should be grateful for, though right now she does not feel grateful. Oh, but she is a mother now, and a mother must never forget how much she has to be happy for. She is more symbol than person: home, caretaker, constantly shaving off her edges.

How else could she bear the never-ending laundry, the crumbs in the bed, the sticky stains, the scraps of toilet paper everywhere. The children always touching her, though she'd die for their dear touches, is undone by them. The mayhem can be ecstasy, their plump naked butts she wants to bite, the sweet abandon in their voices, the way they need her, the way they love her, always hungry for her, the way she melts into them and dissolves. How else can she be tame for them. How else can she be safe.

But all the edges she must swallow don't go down gently, they collect instead, an undigested spiky knot. When she sits at the kitchen table after everyone is tucked in and read to, soothed and lulled, when all she wants to do is sink into a dark, dark sea, and she must instead get up and wipe that table, tidy what the day has wrecked—dishes, counters, toys, floors, all that grubby hands have touched and will touch again—that's when her husband comes and tries to pull her away from what she's doing, expecting his desire to spark hers.

How does he not see the constant effort it requires to hold herself together, that a single spark could set her off?

7

I want to take it slow, she said when they first met. And then that slowness became its own exquisite torture. Weeks after weeks of almost touching replaced by days in which they exchange only the lightest, briefest touches.

She is so hot for him she cannot stand it. They spend whole evenings talking lips to lips, but do not kiss. They sleep side by side, the full length of her right arm against the full length of his left. One night she dreams of the slow, slow slowness of glaciers. Their imperceptible movement, ripping up lakes and rivers. When they finally meet, shelves of ice explode in the collision.

When she awakes their legs and arms and breath are entwined, and she knows the period of waiting has now ended, that this is how it is and will always be from now: the two of them entangled, the very earth re-formed and changed.

6

If everyone had to teach just one class on sex, this would be hers:

Materials:
1. A pair of ben wa balls, the kind with a string that hangs down from the bottom.
2. A good vibrator, the kind that you plug in, that's maybe even too fast, the kind that can get you to climax in a minute.

Activity:
Insert the balls in your vagina, string side down. Walk around, feel how they bounce with every motion, how the walls of your vagina shake and flex. Did you know that this was

possible, that you didn't need another person to feel this way?
That tickling, quivering feeling inside demands your whole attention.

Lock the door.

Lie on your back. Pull at the string between your thighs until
the lower ball slides partly out. Now lift the string up, toward
your belly button, so the lower ball presses against your clit.

Turn on your vibrator. The positioning is slightly awkward,
more technical than hot, but here is where the fun begins. Touch
the vibrator to the string as you hold it taut. The vibration will
run up the string and activate the inner beads, which will go
crazy, spinning and clanging against the outer beads, against
your clit, beneath your clit, a tiny cyclone inside you.

You may feel your pussy clench, you might resist the gathering wave. It might feel like it's too much. Do not be alarmed.
The beads will spin, the cyclone will build, and despite your ap-
prehension, you will ride the storm as it squeezes and releases
you, as you squeeze and release within it, and when you come—
harder than you knew was possible—the storm will overpower
you, obliterate you, leave you flattened and scoured bare.

Afterward, the ben wa balls will be sucked so deep that
you'll have to hunt inside yourself for the lost string, and when
you tug it down, you'll hit resistance, discover that you've
closed around the balls, tight as a trap. Relax, don't rush, your
body will release them—its last reminder that it, too, has power.

5

A man is meant to hurt a woman, that's why we fuck you where
you bleed from, that's how I came to be, was *born*, tearing a cunt
open just to breathe. That's what this guy says before walking
out the door.

Weeks ago, when she'd shown her friend his picture, her friend had said, Oh, he's very hot, but he looks like he'd punch you in the face.

She'd cackled: Isn't that what sexy is?

You are so fucked up, her friend had said. But so am I.

They loved to talk about bad men, the men of honest violence. No lies, no false tenderness. The men who'd fuck you in an alley, the men who'd punch you in the face. The men who'd break everything around you, shear loose whatever they could reach.

She and her friend were fools.

I want you to choke me, she'd said to the man, a dare. Would he hurt her? Was she right? Whatever he can do to her, she has already done far worse. Because she's the one who asked for it. She's the one in charge.

Do whatever you want, do everything: don't stop until you make me scream. And for a moment, she saw him falter, saw him hesitate, watched him go helpless with desire. Look at what I can do to you, she'd thought.

She might have known she would not enjoy the hand around her throat when it squeezed closed, or the slap of his palm across her face. What she had not expected was how she'd shriek when he twisted her arm behind her, sob blood and snot and tears across the sheets, but fall silent when he bent her over and pushed himself into her ass.

Why had she thought that asking for it would give her power, somehow break her free?

Still, now she knows. Another triumph: she did not scream, even when she feared that she might die. She feels contempt for him, for the marks he left, the leaking ruin, proof of what she made him do, what was in him, what he wanted all along.

4

College in the city: books and thoughts and conversations that light her mind on fire. Drinking in the bars and dancing in the streets. Late-night walks and taxi rides and falling in love and out again. All this freedom! She feels alive.

Of course there are indignities. Strangers on the street expose themselves to her, homeless men masturbate next to her on trains. Men rub up against her in crowded places; once on the subway she feels a bare penis press into her palm. Once a man chases her as she walks home alone.

One man burns her thigh with his cigarette. Another proposes to her after a long and tender courtship, and she accepts before discovering he has a wife. More than one holds her down in her own bed—always joking!—just to show her or themselves that they can, what they could do if they had the nerve, if they chose to.

But no matter, no big deal. It could always be much worse. She prefers instead to notice how lucky she is, doing what she wants, surviving on her own, creating her own life. See here the gentle lover who builds a row of bookshelves along her wall, see here the other who paints a tree above her bed. See the lifelong friends she makes, men and women. Hear how they read lines of poetry to each other, voices wavering with emotion. How they bring each other dinner, how they gather, how they sing. This is her life, these are her people. Once, after a snowstorm, she and a friend wake early in the morning and walk hand in hand in the glittering hush of the strange, snow-muffled streets.

3

Once upon a time there was a girl. And like most girls, she believed a story: she must be beautiful to be loved, loved to be protected, protected to be safe. So she spent much of her childhood trying to be beautiful, so that one day she might deserve the gifts of love and safety. She waited for the boy who might bestow them.

Beware the story that teaches you that you are weak: beware the story that teaches you to pour yourself into another's hands. It will not lead you anywhere you wish to go.

The girl will survive this story, but the story itself will splinter, its enchantment broken. One day, she will come to understand that it was always broken.

2

Bunk beds and whispered secrets, the smell of smoke, of pine, and cherry lip balm shared. The lake. The horses. Campfires and songs. Fireflies blinking across the evening field. The way rain lingers in the air.

A boy. Light on his feet, easy to smile, quick to throw an arm around the shoulders of his friends. They horse around all day, the boys, jumping over each other, tussling, whooping with their fists up in the air.

One night he runs across the dark with a sparkler in his hand. One early morning she catches a glimpse of him from her window as he walks back to his cabin from his shower, shirtless and shining in the dappled light. She leans her head against the cool glass and she stares. The dark tan of his arms, the lean tuck of his waist. He looks up and sees her watching him, meets her eyes: a shock sparks through her entire body. He smiles. They are thirteen.

That summer the bees are drunk with longing. The birds are frantic with lust. How does anyone survive intact with all this yearning? What is to be done with it? Within her something tense and coiled, like a seed getting ready to burst open, to unfurl its stalk and sticky leaves beneath the sun.

1

The phone rings three times. Her parents are not yet home. She picks up.

What's your name? a man's voice says.

She's been taught to say her parents are busy, and ask to take a message. She's not supposed to talk.

I'm doing a survey for your school, and I have a few questions to ask. Can you help me?

Okay, she says.

Wonderful. His voice is delighted, friendly. Thank you. Shall we get started?

He asks her name. She tells him.

He asks her age. She tells him.

He asks what grade she's in, who her teacher is. She tells him.

Now, he says, this survey is anonymous, do you know what that word means?

She says she doesn't. It means, he says, that everything you say is secret between just you and me. Do you understand?

She says she does.

What's your favorite television show? he asks. What number can you count to? How many books do you read a week? She tells him, she tells him, she tells him.

You're doing great, he says. You're doing fine.

Now, he says, social behavioral questions: Have you ever had a crush? Yes or no, he says. You don't have to say their name.

Yes, she says.

And what do you feel when you see him?

Silence.

Don't be afraid. Do you not want to answer? It's okay if you don't want to answer.

I don't know, she says politely, not wanting to displease him. I just want to smile at him and him to smile at me.

Have you ever touched him? Has he touched you?

No, she says.

Do you touch yourself?

What do you mean?

Do you get wet?

I don't know what you're asking, she says carefully. She doesn't want to hurt his feelings.

Do you ever put your hand where your privates are? He sounds apologetic, a little breathless, as if he's sorry to be asking her, or worried she won't like the question. Do you let anyone else touch you there?

She laughs, No!

Do you want to? His voice is pained. It sounds like he's going to cry.

Did she upset him when she laughed? she worries. Is she going to get in trouble?

No, she says, uncertain.

Well, thank you very much, young lady, his voice suddenly brisk.

Wait, she wants to say. I'm sorry! But he has already hung up. She sits there holding the receiver until the dial tone comes on.

0

They are lying on their stomachs in the grass, daisies in their hair. They have caught a green striped caterpillar, have named it Gus, and made a house for him with sticks and leaves.

What's your favorite animal? she asks.

Unicorns, says her friend.

Boys can't like unicorns, she says.

Says who?

I like horses, she says, no dogs. No dolphins. The grass tickles the backs of her bare legs. Wait, wolves, she says. Or geese.

You're supposed to pick just one.

Says who? They're all my favorite.

Okay, he agrees. They can all be your favorite.

Everywhere it smells of sunshine and mowed grass and flowers.

They lose Gus. They catch a frog. They see a falcon overhead. No that's an owl, she says, or maybe he does, no an eagle. No a hawk. But an eagle is a hawk. No way.

They have lemonade. They swing on swings. They twirl themselves dizzy. They've lost the frog.

They sneak underneath the branches of a pine tree and lie down on a bed of needles. It comes to pass they're holding hands: who knows who reached for whom. It doesn't matter. They lie there for a long time talking, until the day grows cool and the sun begins to set, until the mosquitos start to hum around them, and the streetlights flick awake. They hear their mothers calling, but they stay a little longer before they scramble home.

Contributor Bios

Hillary Jordan is the bestselling author of the novels *When She Woke* and *Mudbound*, which won the PEN/Bellwether Prize for Socially Engaged Fiction and an Alex Award from the American Library Association, among other honors. *Mudbound* was adapted into a critically acclaimed film that premiered at Sundance and went on to earn four Academy Award nominations. *When She Woke* was a Lambda Award finalist. Both novels were longlisted for the International IMPAC Dublin Literary Award. They have been translated into sixteen languages.

Hillary is also a screenwriter and occasional essayist and poet whose work has been published in the *New York Times*, *McSweeney's*, and *Outside* magazine, among others. She has a BA from Wellesley College and an MFA in creative writing from Columbia University. She lives in Brooklyn, New York, along with half the writers in America.

Cheryl Lu-Lien Tan is the author of the international bestsellers *Sarong Party Girls* and *A Tiger in the Kitchen: A Memoir of Food and Family*, which *New York* magazine named one of the "Top 25 Must-Read Food Memoirs of All Time." She is also the editor of the fiction anthology *Singapore Noir*. Cheryl was a staff writer at the *Wall Street Journal*, *InStyle* magazine, and the *Baltimore Sun*, and her stories and reviews have also appeared in the *New York Times*, *Times Literary Supplement*, the *Paris Review*, the *Washington Post*, and *Bon Appétit*, among others. She has been awarded multiple grants from the National Arts Council of Singapore in support of her work.

Born and raised in Singapore, she crossed the ocean at age eighteen to go to Northwestern University, from which she has a BS in journalism. She lives in New York City, though her heart and writing are never far from Singapore.

Robert Olen Butler has published eighteen novels and six volumes of short stories, one of which, *A Good Scent from a Strange Mountain*, won the Pulitzer Prize in Fiction. He has also published a widely influential volume of his lectures on the creative process, *From Where You Dream*. His latest novel, *Late City*, takes place in the nanosecond of the death of the last living World War I veteran. In 2013, he was the sixteenth annual recipient of the career-spanning F. Scott Fitzgerald Award for Outstanding Achievement in American Literature. He teaches creative writing at Florida State University.

Catherine Chung is the author of *The Tenth Muse* and *Forgotten Country*, for which she won an Honorable Mention for the PEN/Hemingway Award. She has been a National Endowment for the Arts Fellow, a *Granta* New Voice, a Director's Visitor at the Institute for Advanced Study in Princeton, and the recipient of a Dorothy Sargent Rosenberg Prize in poetry. She has a degree in mathematics from the University of Chicago and worked at a think tank before receiving her MFA from Cornell University. She has published work in the *New York Times*, the *Guardian*, and *Granta*, among others.

Trent Dalton's debut novel, *Boy Swallows Universe*, was published across thirty-four English-language and translation territories. It won a record four 2019 Australian Book Industry Awards, including the prestigious Book of the Year Award. His second novel, *All Our Shimmering Skies*, was shortlisted for a 2021 Indie Book Award, a 2021 ABIA Award, and the Booksellers' Choice Fiction Book of the Year. Trent has been a journalist for more than twenty years and is a two-time winner of the Walkley Award and a five-time winner of the Kennedy Award for excellence in Australian journalism. His new work of nonfiction, *Love Stories*, will be published in Australia in October 2021.

Heidi W. Durrow is the *New York Times* bestselling author of *The Girl Who Fell from the Sky*, which received the PEN/Bellwether Prize for Socially Engaged Fiction, was hailed as one of the Best Novels of 2010 by the *Washington Post*, and was an NAACP Image Award nominee for Outstanding Literary Debut. She heads the Mixed Remixed Festival, a free public event that celebrates stories of the mixed-race and multiracial experience, and has been featured as a leading expert on multiracial and multicultural issues and identity by *NBC Nightly News*, the *New York Times*, CNN, National Public Radio, the BBC, *Ebony*, and the *San Francisco Chronicle*. Heidi's writing has appeared in the *New York Times*, *Essence*, *Callaloo*, and the *Literary Review*, among other publications.

Tony Eprile's novel, *The Persistence of Memory*, was a *New York Times* Notable Book of the Year, nominated for the International

IMPAC Dublin Literary Award and Sunday Times Fiction Prize (South Africa), and the winner of the Koret Jewish Book Award for fiction. His short story collection—*Temporary Sojourner*—was also a *New York Times* Notable Book, and his stories have appeared in *Ploughshares*, *Agni*, *StoryQuarterly*, *GlimmerTrain*, *Post Road*, and elsewhere. He grew up in South Africa, where his father was the editor of the first mass-circulation multiracial newspaper, the *Golden City Post*. Tony is on the fiction faculty of Lesley University's low-residency MFA in creative writing program.

Louise Erdrich is the author of fifteen novels as well as volumes of poetry, children's books, short stories, and a memoir of early motherhood. Her novel *The Night Watchman* won the 2021 Pulitzer Prize for Fiction; her novel *The Round House* won the 2012 National Book Award for Fiction. Her new novel, *The Sentence*, was published in November 2021. She lives in Minnesota with her daughters and is the owner of Birchbark Books, a small independent bookstore.

Jamie Ford is the great-grandson of Nevada mining pioneer Min Chung, who emigrated from Hoiping, China, to San Francisco in 1865, where he adopted the Western name "Ford," thus confusing countless generations. Jamie's debut novel, *Hotel on the Corner of Bitter and Sweet*, spent two and a half years on the *New York Times* bestseller list and went on to win the Asian/Pacific American Award for Literature. His second book, *Songs of Willow Frost*, was also a national bestseller. His latest novel is *Love and Other Consolation Prizes*. His work has been translated into thirty-five languages.

Julia Glass is the author of a story collection and five novels, including *A House Among the Trees* and the National Book

Award–winning *Three Junes*. She has also won fellowships from the NEA, the New York Foundation for the Arts, and the Radcliffe Institute for Advanced Study. A Massachusetts resident, Julia is a Senior Distinguished Writer in Residence at Emerson College and a cofounder of Twenty Summers, a nonprofit arts and culture festival in Provincetown.

Peter Godwin was born and raised in Zimbabwe. He is an award-winning foreign correspondent, documentary maker, screenwriter, and author of six nonfiction books, including *Wild at Heart: Man and Beast in Southern Africa* (with a foreword by Nelson Mandela); *Mukiwa*, which received the George Orwell Prize and the Esquire/Apple/Waterstones Non-Fiction Award; and *When a Crocodile Eats the Sun: A Memoir of Africa*, which won the Borders Original Voices Award. His book *The Fear: Robert Mugabe and the Martyrdom of Zimbabwe* was selected by the *New Yorker* as a best book of the year. He currently teaches writing at Columbia and Wesleyan Universities.

Rebecca Makkai's latest novel, *The Great Believers*, was a finalist for both the Pulitzer Prize and the National Book Award; it was the winner of the ALA Carnegie Medal, the Stonewall Book Award, and the Los Angeles Times Book Prize; and it was one of the *New York Times*' Ten Best Books of 2018. Her other books are the novels *The Borrower* and *The Hundred-Year House*, and the collection *Music for Wartime*—four stories from which appeared in *The Best American Short Stories*. Rebecca is on the MFA faculties of Sierra Nevada College and Northwestern University. She is artistic director of StoryStudio Chicago.

Valerie Martin is the author of twelve novels, including *Trespass*, *Mary Reilly*, and *Property*; four short story collections, including *Sea Lovers* (2015), a volume of new and selected short fiction; and a biography of St. Francis of Assisi. She has been awarded a grant from the National Endowment for the Arts and a John Simon Guggenheim Foundation Fellowship, as well as the Kafka Prize (for *Mary Reilly*) and Britain's Women's Prize (for *Property*). Her most recent novel, *I Give It to You*, was published by Nan A. Talese/Random House in 2020. She resides in Madison, Connecticut.

Dina Nayeri is the author of *The Ungrateful Refugee*, winner of the Geschwister Scholl Preis, finalist for the Los Angeles Times Book Prize, Kirkus Prize, and Grand Prix des Lectrices de Elle. Dina is a fellow at the Columbia Institute for Ideas and Imagination in Paris and winner of a National Endowment for the Arts grant. Her short stories have been published in *The O. Henry Prize Stories*, *The Best American Short Stories*, *New York Times Magazine*'s "The Decameron Project" (twenty-nine American short story writers on the pandemic), and many other publications. She is a graduate of the Iowa Writers' Workshop.

Chigozie Obioma was born in Akure, Nigeria. His first two novels, *The Fishermen* (2015) and *An Orchestra of Minorities* (2019), were both finalists for the Booker Prize, one of only two writers in Booker Prize history to achieve this. His novels have been translated into more than twenty-eight languages and won the inaugural FT/OppenheimerFunds Emerging Voices Award for fiction, an NAACP Image Award, the Los Angeles Times Book Prize, the Internationaler Literaturpreis, a Nebraska Book Award, and were nominated for many other awards. He was named one of *Foreign Policy*'s 100 Leading

Global Thinkers of 2015. He is an associate professor of creative writing at the University of Nebraska, Lincoln, and divides his time between the United States and Nigeria.

Téa Obreht was born in Belgrade, in the former Yugoslavia, and grew up in Cyprus and Egypt before eventually emigrating to the United States. Her debut novel, *The Tiger's Wife*, won the 2011 Orange Prize for Fiction, and was a 2011 National Book Award finalist and an international bestseller. Her work has been anthologized in the *Best American* series, and has appeared in the *New Yorker*, the *Atlantic, Harper's, Vogue, Esquire,* and *Zoetrope: All-Story.* Her second book, *Inland,* was an instant bestseller and a finalist for the 2020 Dylan Thomas Prize. She serves as Endowed Chair of Creative Writing at Texas State University in San Marcos.

Helen Oyeyemi is the author of nine books, including *Mr. Fox,* which won a 2012 Hurston/Wright Legacy Award, and the short story collection *What Is Not Yours Is Not Yours,* which won the 2017 PEN Open Book Award. She was named one of *Granta's* Best Young British Novelists in 2013, and is a fellow of the Royal Society of Literature. Her most recent novel, *Peaces,* was published in April 2021.

Mary-Louise Parker is an Obie, Tony, Golden Globe, and Emmy Award–winning actress and writer. Her *New York Times* bestselling book *Dear Mr. You,* published by Scribner, was translated into multiple languages and included on the *San Francisco Chronicle's* list of the Ten Best Books of 2015. Parker was an on-staff writer for *Esquire* for more than a decade. Her writing has appeared in the *Atlantic,* the *New York Times,* the *Riveter, Bust,*

O, Bullett, InStyle, Bomb, the *Chronicles of Now, Hemispheres,* and other publications, and her poetry has appeared in *3 Views on Theater.* She lives in Brooklyn with her children.

Victoria Redel is the author of three books of poetry and five books of fiction, most recently the novel *Before Everything.* Her new collection of poems, *Paradise,* is forthcoming in 2022. Victoria's work has been widely anthologized, awarded, and translated. Her debut novel, *Loverboy* (2001), was adapted for feature film. Redel's short stories, poetry, and essays have appeared in *Granta,* the *New York Times,* the *Los Angeles Times, Bomb, One Story, Salmagundi, O,* and *NOON,* among other publications. She has received fellowships from the John Simon Guggenheim Foundation, the National Endowment for the Arts, and the Fine Arts Work Center. Victoria is on the faculty of Sarah Lawrence College and lives in New York City.

Jason Reynolds is the *New York Times* bestselling author of *All American Boys,* the Track series, *For Everyone,* and *Miles Morales: Spider-Man.* He writes novels and poetry for young adult and middle-grade audiences. His story collection, *Look Both Ways,* won the 2021 British Carnegie Medal; his first novel, *When I Was the Greatest,* won the Coretta Scott King/John Steptoe Award for New Talent; and his novel *Ghost* was a National Book Award finalist. His other novels include *Patina, Sunny,* and *As Brave As You,* winner of the 2016 Kirkus Prize, the 2017 NAACP Image Award for Outstanding Literary Work for Youth/Teen, and the 2017 Schneider Family Book Award. Reynolds returned to poetry with *Long Way Down* (2017), a novel in verse that was named a Newbery Honor book, a Printz Honor Book, and won the Edgar Award for Best Young Adult Work from the Mystery Writers of America.

S. J. Rozan is the author of eighteen novels and more than seventy short stories and the editor of two anthologies. She has won multiple awards, including the Edgar, Shamus, Anthony, Nero, Macavity; the Japanese Maltese Falcon; and the Private Eye Writers of America Life Achievement awards. S.J. lectures and teaches widely. She has been a workshop leader at Art Workshop International in Assisi, Italy; master artist at the Atlantic Center for the Arts in Florida; and writer in residence at Singapore Management University. Her latest novel, *Family Business*, was published in December 2021. Her website is www.sjrozan.net.

Meredith Talusan is the author of the critically acclaimed memoir *Fairest* from Viking/Penguin Random House. She is also an award-winning journalist who has written for the *Guardian*, the *New York Times*, the *Atlantic*, the *Nation*, *WIRED*, *SELF*, and *Condé Nast Traveler*, among many other publications, and has contributed to several essay collections. She has received awards from GLAAD, the Society of Professional Journalists, and the National Lesbian and Gay Journalists Association. She is also the founding executive editor of *them*, Condé Nast's LGBTQ+ digital platform, where she is currently contributing editor.

Souvankham Thammavongsa is the author of four poetry books and the short story collection *How to Pronounce Knife*, winner of the 2020 Scotiabank Giller Prize. Her stories have won an O. Henry Award and have appeared in the *New Yorker*, the *Paris Review*, the *Atlantic*, *Granta*, and *NOON*. She was born in the Lao refugee camp in Nong Khai, Thailand, and was raised and educated in Toronto.

Jeet Thayil was born into a Syrian Christian family in 1959. He worked as a journalist for twenty-one years in Bombay, Bangalore, Hong Kong, and New York. In 2005, he began to write fiction. His first novel, the bestseller *Narcopolis*, was awarded the DSC Prize for South Asian Literature and was shortlisted for the Booker Prize. His five poetry collections include *These Errors Are Correct*, which won the Sahitya Akademi Award (India's National Academy of Letters), and *English*, winner of a New York Foundation for the Arts award. He wrote the libretto for the opera *Babur in London*. His most recent novel is *Names of the Women*.

Paul Theroux is the author of *The Great Railway Bazaar* (1975), *The Mosquito Coast* (1981), and *Riding the Iron Rooster* (1983), among other acclaimed works. His most recent work is *Under the Wave at Waimea* (2021). Paul's numerous awards include a Royal Medal from the Royal Geographical Society, the American Academy of Arts and Letters Award for literature, the Whitbread Prize for his novel *Picture Palace*, and the James Tait Black Award for *The Mosquito Coast*. His novels *Saint Jack*, *The Mosquito Coast*, *Doctor Slaughter*, and *Half Moon Street* have been made into films, and his short story collection *London Embassy* was adapted for a British miniseries in 1987.

Luis Alberto Urrea is a 2019 Guggenheim Fellow, a Pulitzer Prize finalist for nonfiction, and the bestselling author of eighteen books of fiction, nonfiction, and poetry. He's been honored with a 2019 Pushcart Prize, an American Academy of Arts and Letters Award, and an Edgar Award. His most recent book, *The House of Broken Angels*, was a *New York Times* Notable Book of the Year, a finalist for the National Book Critics Circle Award, and was recently acquired by Hulu for adaptation as a series. His novel *Into the Beautiful North* is a selection of the NEA Big Reads program. He is a Distinguished Professor of Creative Writing at the University of Illinois, Chicago.

Edmund White is the author of many novels, including *A Boy's Own Story*, *The Beautiful Room Is Empty*, *The Farewell Symphony*, and *Our Young Man*. His nonfiction includes *City Boy*, *Inside a Pearl*, and other memoirs; *The Flâneur*, about Paris; and literary biographies and essays. He was named the winner of the 2018 PEN/Saul Bellow Award for Achievement in American Fiction and is the recipient of the honorary National Book Award for 2019. His most recent novels are *A Saint from Texas* (2020) and *A Previous Life* (2022).

Acknowledgments

Deepest and first thanks to our contributors for the gift of your trust and for taking this leap with us; and especially to Julia Glass, whose instant and early belief in this project meant the world to us—as have your love and friendship all these years.

Huge gratitude to our indefatigable agents and champions, Jin Auh at the Wylie Agency and Chris Parris-Lamb at the Gernert Company, for your faith, patience, and guidance; and to Andrew Wylie, Sarah Bolling, Rebecca Gardner, Elizabeth Pratt, and Caspian Dennis. Thanks to our editor, Kara Watson, and the fantastic Scribner crew—Nan Graham, Emily Polson, Clare Maurer, Zoey Cole, Katie Rizzo, and Faren Bachelis; to Suzie Dooré, Emily Goulding, and the whole team at Borough Press; to Malika Favre, for her gorgeous UK cover illustration; and to all the friends and colleagues who helped us in countless ways on this journey—Peter Blackstock, Kirsty Doole, Clare Drysdale, Jamie Ford, Peter Godwin, Jeff Gordinier, Nan Klingener, Hamish Robinson, and Michael Taeckens.

From Cheryl: Thanks, as always, to my family: Tan Soo Liap, Cynthia Wong, Daphne Tan, the Tans, the Wongs, the Lees, the Chans, and the Chetrets—your love and unconditional support buoy me every day. For the best friendships anyone could hope for: Jeanette Lai, Kevin Cheng, Regina Jaslow, Hamish Robinson, Willin Low, Carter Brey, Charles Christopher Chiang, Michael Rezendes, Drew Larimore, Guy and Jan Klucevsek, Francis Goh, Jeremy Tan, S. J. Rozan, Tony Eprile, Rachel Cantor, Magnus Linklater, Michael Yeo, Elizabeth Yuan, Bobby Caina Calvan, Zvonko Nikolich, Beth Heidere, William Chang, Jessalyn Peters, Georgina Murray, Joanne Balaraj Milford, and Chew-Mee Foo Kirtland. I have the Cafe Luxembourg crew to thank for my restored soul and sanity at the end of many long writing days: Bud Burridge, Stephen Cirona, Ryan Carey, Rachel Bender, Wendy Sachs, Peter Soboroff, Caleb Charles, Krystel Lucas, James Tomaszewski, Nick Minas, and Jimmy Bain. And also my Manny's Bistro family, who care for me so well: Abad, William, Tony, Nadine, Sebastian, Carmen, Mark, and Rodrigo. I am beyond grateful for my tireless reader Gordon Dahlquist, who inspires me endlessly, as well as my dear friend and anthology partner, Hillary Jordan. (We did it!) And for *mi amor*, Manny.

From Hillary: There's the family you're born with and the one you choose, and I'm uncommonly blessed in both. My thanks to my mom and dad, my aunt Gay, Michael, Jared, Sarah, Erik, Jill, and all you lovely Prices, Coffmans, Fishers, Lewises, Hugheses, Colberts, Rays, and Washingtons, for your love and belief in me. To Denise Benou Stires, for thirty-nine beautiful years of best friendship. To Laura Brown, Pam Cunningham, Charlotte Dixon, Heidi Durrow, Jenn Epstein, Victoria Redel, and Kathryn Windley, soul sisters who are also thoughtful readers of my work; and the other true-blue friends who've kept me afloat: Julie Curtis, Carl Effenson, Sally Jo Effenson, Mark Erwin, Karen Flusche, Doug Irving, Guy and Jan Klucevsek,

Leslie McCall, Lizzy Molsen, Marc Pavlopolous, Katy Rees, Anna Rudowski and Ben Jackson, Ethan Seidel and Emily Baldwin, Zachary Washington, Virgil Williams, and Alice Yurke and Rob Davis. To the WGAE Women's Comedy Writing Group, for the weekly injections of sanity and laughter. And finally, to my friend and co-conspirator, Cheryl Tan. Hell yeah, we did!